a brooding bodyguard

ANGELA CASELLA

Highland Hills

(co-written with Denise Grover Swank)

Matchmaking a Billionaire

Matchmaking a Single Dad

Matchmaking a Grump

Matchmaking a Roommate

Bad Luck Club

(co-written with Denise Grover Swank)

Love at First Hate

Jingle Bell Hell

Fraudulently Ever After

Matchmaking Mischief

Asheville Brewing

(co-written with Denise Grover Swank)

Any Luck at All

Better Luck Next Time

Getting Lucky

Bad Luck Club

Luck of the Draw (novella)

All the Luck You Need (prequel novella) by Angela Casella

To my mom, for being nothing like the mothers in this book.

SINCLAIR

EDGAR HANDS me a rock across the crisp white tablecloth of our table for two at Steak Haus. Since he obviously intends for me to take it, I do, but I'm not sure what I'm supposed to do with it. Under the weight of his intense, expectant gaze, I make a sound of appreciation in my throat as I lift the smooth stone to study it under the low lighting of the restaurant. It looks like...well, a rock. It's gray, hard, and cold to the touch. Presumably there's something special about it, though, so I beam at him and say, "It's *beautiful*. Thank you so much. Is it a precious stone?"

There's a snort from the two-top directly next to us, and I grit my teeth, very pointedly not looking at him. *Him* being Rafe, my discount bodyguard.

I don't like bringing Rafe to things. In fact, there's a lot I'd do to avoid it, but my friends insist that I bring him along on any outings where there's likely to be press.

There will *definitely* be press tonight, because the brand manager both Edgar and I work with, Enoch Laskin, called them and informed them of where we'd be dining and when, approximately, we would be leaving. That's why I'm in this fake relationship with Edgar, after all, so we can both reap the benefits of the publicity.

Edgar James is a very handsome man, with a flinty appearance and the kind of body you get from spending time outdoors rather than in a gym. There's something exciting about that, or at least there was when I first agreed to this arrangement. We've been spending time together publicly for weeks, and if he were interested in making things official, I'm guessing he would have done something about it by now. We haven't even kissed for the cameras, although I'm sure that's coming. He's a famous outdoorsman who's about to be on a new reality TV show—a follow-up to his previous hit show, *Extreme Camping*—and I'll be putting in a few guest appearances on *Camping to the Max* as his "girlfriend."

I'm not even sure I want Edgar to make a move anymore, to be honest. Because this is how most of our conversations go—he hands me a rock or makes a cryptic comment about the ecosystem or how the beauty of the sunset being caused by pollution, and I'm left scrambling to make a conversation out of it. I guess some people wouldn't feel compelled to fill the silence, but that's what I was raised to do—to entertain. To dazzle. Maybe that's the problem: Edgar James isn't the kind of man who wants to be entertained, at least not by me.

He wants to *live*.

I do too, but if there's one thing I've realized since I quit my Netflix show, *Sisters of Sin*, earlier this year, it's that I'm not quite sure how to manage it. I've *tried* since coming to Asheville. I've taken up gardening, painting, molding clay, and making amuses-bouches. I've sat through one and half guitar lessons, and I even went on a hike with Edgar that left me panting and dirty and dissatisfied.

None of those things have brought me the kind of high I saw in Edgar's eyes when he took in the mountain peaks around us from the top of said dirty hike. I've only felt the dissatisfaction of having tried and failed, of not being good at something. Of not having enjoyed something the way I should have.

Of being a woman of thirty-two who doesn't know what she likes.

I guess that's what happens when the only focus you've been given from childhood, from when you were an infant videotaped for commercials for packaged spinach paste, is to be famous.

Maybe I'm broken, because to me, that rock Edgar just handed me is nothing more than a cold stone.

I run my fingers across its surface, finding nothing much to recommend it other than that it's tolerably smooth.

"It's just a rock," Edgar says.

I'm pretty sure I hear laughter from the adjoining table, and this time I *do* give Rafe a withering look.

He has his sunglasses on, even though we're indoors, and his button-up shirt shows off a sliver of his chest tattoo, the fabric straining from the job of holding in his massive arms. Have I wondered about the appearance of the rest of that tattoo?

Obviously.

Rafe looks like a Viking warrior who got lost on the way to Valhalla, all muscles and intense dark eyes, the irises nearly matching the pupils. His hair is dark and short, like he doesn't want to be bothered with taking care of it. The only thing missing from the Viking picture is a beard. He's attractive in an annoying way that makes me want to throw things at him.

Literally.

The first time we met, before he interviewed to be my bodyguard, was when I threw a clay banana at his back after a Play with Clay class gone wrong. More accurately, I threw it at the trashcan next to where he was walking, but it was a bad toss. Hitting him was an accident, sure, but if I'd known him, I would have done it on purpose.

He claimed it was a dildo.

Which brings me to my point: Rafe is a jackass, always watching and making snide comments. Always lingering in the background on my public-facing outings.

When I complained to my sister, Marnie, about that the other day, she sighed and said, "That's his job, Clair. That's why we hired him. He's supposed to keep you safe."

"I never had a bodyguard in California," I retorted. "Isn't my whole purpose for being here that I can live a normal life?"

That was the point in the conversation where Marnie reminded me that I have a stalker—one who doesn't much like that I'm in this fake relationship with Edgar James. I've made the argument that the stalker can't be very intelligent or observant if he thinks that I'm in an *actual* relationship with Edgar, to which she replied, "He doesn't have to be intelligent to kill you. Plenty of unintelligent people kill other people every day."

I guess she had a point, although my superfan has only sent me one threatening message since I acquired Rafe's services several weeks ago. Before that, there was a bouquet of dead flowers, delivered after word got out about my supposed relationship with Edgar.

The private detectives who signed on to help me look for him seem bored by their task. There's nothing for them to do but study the note and those flowers. The flower trail goes to the courier service used to bring them to my door and no further. There have been no fingerprints, no telltale trails, and although there *was* camera footage of his in-person "visit" to deliver said threatening note, he wore a mask in the likeness of Justin Bieber that completely concealed his face. Either that, or I inadvertently did something to piss off Justin Bieber when I saw him at the MTV Movie & TV Awards last year.

Rafe smirks at me. I give him a look that would make a plant shrivel and die.

Edgar clears his throat.

Shifting my attention back to him, I lift my eyebrows and shape my mouth into a little "oh" of surprise. I'm aware this expression serves my features well because my mother once had me practice it in front of a mirror for half an hour. "Where's this just-a-rock from?"

If it's not valuable because of what's inside of it, it must be valuable for another reason.

"It's from the first site where we'll be filming the show," he says. Most men would smile here or offer some sort of expression to telegraph what they're thinking, but Edgar never gives any cues. It's disarming, because cues have always helped me craft my own reactions.

There you go again, not knowing to how to react naturally.

I hug the rock to my chest, and an unexpected sharp edge nips at my skin. I smile through it. "I'll treasure it, Edgar. I'll miss you when you're gone. I can't believe they were able to get everything sorted so quickly." Filming starts next week. It would have taken months longer, but the network had all of the arrangements made for another show that got cancelled because the star was arrested for taking videos of women using the restroom without their permission.

"You won't need to miss me," he says, literal as always. "You'll be visiting me on set. Sooner rather than later, hopefully."

The thought of extreme camping doesn't thrill me, to say the least, but Enoch is adamant that if I don't want to go straight from being cast as a teenager to being the teenager's mother, I need to change my image. Hence the whole Edgar thing. Fake dating him is supposed to make me look edgier, like the kind of woman who wouldn't cringe if she broke a nail. I would, obviously, but if people think I wouldn't, then maybe they'll ask me to be in adventure movies. Or films or shows that are actually good.

I think I want that...although part of me wonders if that's just because I don't know what else to want.

"Yes," I say with a smile that I know is convincing. "I can't wait."

Another laugh-cough issues from Rafe, who doesn't even have

the decency to pretend he's not listening. I avoid the itch to look at him. Scratching that itch will lead nowhere good.

"Will you keep it for luck?" Edgar asks, nodding to the rock.

It's too big for my clutch bag, so I'll have to walk around with a rock in my fist like a kid who's up to no good, but I widen my smile. "I'd be honored."

Our food comes, and we continue to pretend to have a conversation. Or at least *I'm* pretending. Edgar seems quite content with silence as he eats a steak that looks so good my mouth is salivating. I have a salad, dressing on the side. I almost always have a salad, dressing on the side.

Food always goes to your hips, my mother would say, clucking her tongue. *No one's going to give a hippy girl a place on TV. You know the camera adds ten pounds.*

Except...fuck my mother. *Fuck* her. I may have let her control my life for the better part of thirty-two years, but that's over now.

I flag a server down. "Can I get a steak, medium rare? And... french fries. A lot of french fries."

I think the last time I had a french fry was when my father brought us kids to McDonald's after school one day when I was twelve. I said I wasn't going to order anything, but Marnie gave me a look and in a small voice said, "No one will know, Clair. We won't tell."

If my father heard her, he didn't say. And if he knew my mother was already talking to me about hips and extra pounds, he didn't say anything about that either.

Still, I got those fries, and I ate every last one. Marnie was right. No one told.

Twenty years ago. That's twenty years too long to have gone without a french fry.

I feel like a kid doing something naughty, but Edgar nods in approval. "Lots of iron in steak. Don't want to get anemic."

Shit. While I'd gnaw off my own arm for that steak and those fries, there'll be a price to pay. I inadvertently made this silent dinner even longer.

If we're going to be sitting here much longer, I need him to talk. I physically require it, so I say, "So, Edgar, tell me about your family. I don't think I've asked you before...do you have any brothers or sisters?"

"One sister, Denise. She's a stained-glass artist. Lives in a small town a few hours away."

She sounds like more fun than him, but it's shitty of me to think so. "That's wonderful, being so close to family. I have a sister and brother here in Asheville."

"I know," he says flatly. Which is fair enough. My sister does freelance graphic design work for him.

"It's one of the reasons I decided to move back here."

"You have an aunt too," he points out.

"Yes, I do," I agree enthusiastically.

He gives a nod and takes a bite of steak, and I realize with horror that the conversation has again dried up, and he has no interest in doing anything about it.

"My aunt's a swinger," I blurt out, and Edgar chokes on the bite of steak. There's an instant when I'm worried he's actually choking —will I have to do something about it, or will Rafe leap into action? —but the sound suddenly stops, and he places a hand on the table.

"Excuse me," he says, then promptly gets up and heads to the restroom in the back of the restaurant.

I can feel Rafe staring at me. Frowning, I glance at him. Sure enough, his eyes are on me, and there's that little quirk to his mouth that says I've amused him again. "What?" I say, putting plenty of wither into my voice. "You obviously have something to say."

"You can't bully him into talking, Clay."

"I'm not bullying him into anything," I say with a scowl. "And most people wouldn't consider it a hardship to talk to me."

He lifts his hands in a warding-off gesture that only pisses me off more, because he's acting like I'm irrational and possibly dangerous —the sort of person he'd wave off if they tried to approach me.

"Well, they wouldn't," I mumble.

Our server comes by with my plate, the steak glistening, the fries a golden masterpiece more beautiful than any painting in the LACMA in Los Angeles or MoMA in New York. My mouth waters, and everything in me lifts in expectation. When the plate is set down in front of me, I thank the man, and he walks away.

"Try looking at Edgar the way you're checking out that steak," Rafe says as the server retreats, "and maybe he'll stop handing you hunks of rock and grunting."

I bite back the response that wants to come out—*Oh, screw you* —and pick up one of the fries. When I bite into it, the crunchy exterior giving way to a pillowy interior, a moan escapes my lips.

"Or make that sound," Rafe says conversationally. "That'd do it."

"Yeah, right," I scoff. "He'd probably tell me it's the sound a raccoon makes when it's in heat."

Rafe shocks me by laughing.

It's a nice moment, so I'm not sure why I snap, "Hasn't anyone ever told you that bodyguards are supposed to be seen but not heard?"

"You have—several times," he says, leaning back in his chair. "But Enoch gave me permission to make a nuisance of myself. He says the more people who notice me, the better. Less likely anyone will mess with you if there's a big guy following you around."

I purse my lips. "You don't have to wear sunglasses indoors, you know. It makes you look like an idiot."

I'm being foul to him, and I'm not sure why. It's just...I'm *mad* at him. He's right—he's doing what Enoch told him to—but I hate feeling like I'm being watched and followed, maybe because it's a reminder that someone *else* is watching and following. Besides, I really did come to Asheville because I wanted to feel normal. That's not something I know how to do anymore, though, and with a bodyguard and a fake boyfriend who climbs mountains on television for a living, it's unlikely to happen anytime soon.

"Good," Rafe says lazily, not even lifting a hand to the side of his sunglasses. "I thrive on being underestimated."

I eat another fry, then another, suddenly starving. By the time Edgar returns, I've plowed through half of them and taken several bites of steak.

"Ah, a healthy appetite," Edgar says, and I instantly feel a wash of shame. He didn't mean it in a bad way, but it triggers memories nonetheless. I set down my fork.

"Did I offend you earlier?" I ask.

He gives me an inscrutable look. "What could have offended me?"

"The thing about my aunt. You know, you'd probably like her, actually. She's a pacifist, and she has this thing about coexisting peacefully with bugs."

His brow furrows. "We all coexist with bugs."

"What I mean is that she won't, like, smash a spider or try to rehome it outside. She'll let it stick around."

"That's wise," he says with a decisive nod. "Spiders kill other bugs."

Another snort.

Goddammit, does Rafe have to listen to every word we say?

The conversation carries on in this way—me trying too hard, Edgar stone-walling me—until it's finally time for the big show. Edgar pays the bill, and we receive Enoch's confirmation that the press is outside and waiting. Before we leave, I head into the bathroom to make sure my appearance is immaculate. My dress is silky and pinkish purple, a shade I've been told brings out the gold flecks in my eyes. I've never much liked it. I feel numb as I smooth down a couple of flyaway hairs and smile for the mirror. I feel...

Broken.

But acting is what I do. It's what I know. So I step out of the bathroom with a big smile on my face, and Edgar nods to me as he gets to his feet. "You look radiant. Are you ready?"

"I am," I say, sounding happy about it. But for some reason I glance at Rafe, and he's not smiling back. If I didn't know better, I'd say he looks...concerned.

"Don't forget the rock," Edgar says just as I shrug on my light coat. It's spring, but spring feels different in Asheville, the nights and mornings usually crisp. I'm about to step away from the table, and I barely manage to hold in a sigh as I pick it up. I doubt he'd notice anyway, since he's pulling on his windbreaker.

Rafe leaves first, presumably to make sure there are no maniacs waiting for us other than the ones Enoch's summoned to take photos.

Then Edgar takes my hand, the first time he's touched me all evening, and we walk out together. We look good, and I know it. That used to matter to me, but now I'm more aware of the kernel of emptiness inside of me, radiating outward—the realization that looking good means nothing if you don't *feel* good.

I touch the rock to my chest in feigned surprise when the reporters approach us with cameras in tow. "It looks like we've been found out," I tell Edgar warmly.

"I don't mind," he says. "*Anyone* would be proud to be seen with you."

It's hard to know whether he means it. I'm guessing he's acting too, but he's always seemed to appreciate my appearance. He's almost protective of it.

"Will you pose for a few photos?" one of the reporters asks.

"What do you think, EJ?" I ask, using the nickname I picked out for him.

"If it'll please you, I'll do it happily," Edgar announces with a smile.

Where was *this* guy twenty minutes ago? Then again, maybe he's wondering where this version of Sinclair was at the restaurant while

I was hoovering up steak and fries and throwing out irrelevant information about my weird aunt.

We've posed for several photos when suddenly a tomato hurtles toward us and smashes against Edgar's Patagonia windbreaker.

He looks down at it in shock, and I'm looking at it too, my lips parted, as Rafe shoves his way in front of me. He's so big, he partially covers Edgar too, and he shouts, "Get down!" as another tomato pelts him. I'm no idiot—I listen, but not before I get a glimpse of a broad masked figure racing past on a bike. I'm almost certain it's a man, although his entire face is covered by the same Justin Bieber mask as in the video. It's impulsive, but I hurl the small rock Edgar gave me at the masked figure—just before he or she hurls something at us. The rock hits; our attacker's aim fails. The projectile lands at Rafe's feet.

A brick.

Horror licks through me because *it could have hit him.* If it had hit him in the head, it might have seriously injured him.

Then it occurs to me that my worry should be that it could have hit *me.* Because it was obviously meant to.

two

SINCLAIR

"SOMEONE ELSE FOUND out you were going to be here," Officer Nutman says, chewing his gum like he's afraid someone's going to take it away from him. He's a tall man with a gut that looks like it belongs on a different body from his spindly arms and legs and a head of sparse but wavy blond hair that looks surprisingly well conditioned.

I resist the urge to tell the officer that what he's saying is obvious—and also the urge to ask him if Nutman is really his last name. It sounds like the kind of thing my screenwriter ex-boyfriend would have come up with because it made him—and no one else—laugh.

"Yes," Rafe says, watching as another officer wraps the brick up in a plastic bag. He saw the note attached to it, just like I did—*Remember, if he gives you a rock, I'll give you a bigger one.* "We'd worked that much out." He looks pissed as hell, but maybe he really liked the jacket that got covered with tomato pulp. That'd be enough to ruin anyone's day.

Officer Nutman shoots him a look of dislike. "Don't think I don't remember *you*, son," he says, hitching up his belt. Despite having called Rafe "son," he can't be much older than us—late thirties at most.

"No charges were filed," Rafe tells him with a shit-eating grin, "and don't think I don't remember *you*."

My gaze snaps back and forth between them. "What's the meaning of this?"

Neither of them answers me, and Edgar, who's standing just behind me, fidgets on his feet as if he's bored.

The reporters Enoch called in are still present, and they've been documenting everything, from Rafe's heroic save of my dress and coat to my impeccable aim with the just-a-rock Edgar gave me. I have no doubt it'll be all over the news tomorrow.

"Anyway, as I was saying," Nutman says, looking back at me and Edgar, who's standing just behind me. A third officer has moved the press off to the side, although people keep snapping photos over his shoulder, so I can't say he's doing his job. The restaurant has continued operating, leaving a little pocket of space for us to talk to the officers on the sidewalk. Asheville's a tourist town, so there are plenty of people walking past, most of them ignoring us, although I know we've been recognized by a few.

"Someone found out you'd be here," Nutman continues. "That's the risk you run when you want to put on a little show. Far as I can tell, you got yourself a big one." His gaze drills into me, and I see a familiar look in his pale blue eyes, a toxic blend of desire and dislike. Men have looked at me this way for years, ever since I was the winner of the *Little Miss Star* competition when I was sixteen. "You'll want to be more careful if you really do think you have a stalker following you around, Miss Jones."

From the way he says it, it's obvious he thinks the stalker is either a product of my imagination or someone I paid.

"Are you implying I made this up?" I ask, my fury breaking through. "What, you think we hired that guy to run around in a Justin Bieber mask and throw tomatoes and bricks at us?"

Nutman lifts a hand. "Now, real life isn't an episode of your show, Miss Jones. No one's suggesting anything as wild as that." He smacks his gum. "Probably just a little practical joke gone wrong, is all." He lifts his eyebrows. "But you *did* call the press, and it seems mighty convenient that they got to see a spectacle like that, wouldn't you say?"

"So you *do* think we hired that guy," I say, giving him a hard look. "Why would I ask someone to throw a brick at me? What could possibly make that worthwhile for me?"

He shakes his head slowly, as if he can't bear to listen to any more of my rational thoughts.

"I assume your department is going to look into this incident further," Edgar states, his tone firm, and I'm annoyed by the way Nutman instantly transforms for him, standing to attention like Edgar's an authority figure whose approval he wants.

"Of course, sir," he says, and Rafe doesn't attempt to mask his laughter. Nutman slips into a scowl but keeps his gaze on Edgar. "To be on the safe side, we'll be running the brick and note for prints."

"What about the just-a-rock?" I ask.

"*Excuse* me?" Nutman asks.

Damn. I hadn't meant to say it like that out loud. "The rock I threw," I say. "The one that hit him. What if there's, like, DNA evidence on it? Will you be checking that?"

Nutman makes a huffing sound and hitches his belt again, as if it's really digging into him. "What do you think this is, *CSI: Asheville*?"

"If it's not going to be used for evidence, can she have it back?" Edgar asks, and I can't help but do a double take. He thinks I want it now? He puts a hand on my shoulder. I don't really like the way it feels, but I don't try to shove him off. "It has special significance to us."

I don't want a rock that might have my stalker's DNA on it sitting around in my loft. Where am I supposed to put it? On a display shelf? Does he want me to dip it in gold? But I don't have to say so, because Nutman does another belt hitch and purses his lips.

"No can do, boss. We should collect it just in case. Presuming we can find it."

I'm not sure what he intends to do with it, but I'm happy to let him have it. Nutman passes on his directives to the guy who just bagged the brick, and off he goes to look for the just-a-rock.

"Don't you love the feeling of law and order being restored?" Rafe says. I'm not sure whether he's talking to me, but a laugh almost rips out of me. Then he looks up at the dark sky in his sunglasses, and the laughter I'm holding back dries up. He's obviously only still wearing them to mess with me. It has to mess up his vision to wear dark glasses on such a dreary night.

"You're trouble, O'Dooley," Nutman tells him, then spits out the gum he's been chewing onto the ground.

My mouth falls open, and I can feel Edgar straighten behind me. He's not the kind of man who'd care for littering.

"Littering's against the law," Rafe comments lazily.

"Who're you going to call? The Ghostbusters?" Nutman asks with a laugh.

"Doesn't seem like an appropriate occasion for humor, Officer Nutman," Edgar says. He sounds pissed, and I'm strangely grateful for it. I've never been able to suck any emotion from him up until now, and it's nice to know that he feels them. I don't want to be the only one who's a mess behind my makeup and nice clothes.

Nutman straightens as abruptly as if someone just pinched his ass. "Sorry, sir, gallows humor. I take the situation seriously, of course." He nods to Edgar, then to me, although it might as well have just been a second nod to Edgar. His scowl slips back into place. "Still, I feel I should warn you about this menace." He gestures to Rafe. "He's not someone you want your woman around, sir. I don't know how he wound up getting hired to be a bodyguard, of all things, but he's as likely to get her into trouble as he is to do anything useful."

To my surprise, Rafe doesn't say anything. He just stands where he's been, his face slightly inclined toward the sky, like he's hoping a meteor will plummet down and wipe Nutman off the face of the earth.

I expect Edgar to tell the officer he'll take it into consideration, but he surprises me by saying, "Seems to me that he acted just the way a bodyguard should, Officer. If our assaulter had started with the bricks, I assume we'd be having a very different conversation right now."

Go, Edgar. I like this hard line he's taking with Nutman. Do I think it will have any impact on this investigation or the police's lack of concern about my stalker? No, absolutely not, but at least he's not coasting through this encounter. Maybe he *is* interested in me.

A voice in my head quietly asks, *Yes, but are you interested in him?*

That's exactly the kind of question I'm bad at answering. If I were good at knowing what I liked, I wouldn't be in my present situation. I wouldn't have blown through fifteen thousand dollars on hobbies that I don't really like over the past months, producing pieces of "art" that look like they were pity-bought from a yard sale.

Nutman nods five times in quick succession. "Sure, sure. He did take those tomatoes bravely." He spurts a nervous laugh.

The other officer, the one who went off looking for the just-a-rock, returns and lifts an evidence bag in victory. Sure enough, it's still a rock. "I found it."

"Yes, well, be sure to give it back to us once you've gotten what you need," Edgar says, his tone suggesting he knows as well as I do that it's going to molder in an evidence box until the end of time.

"We will," Nutman says, rocking on his feet. "Now, we have all your information."

"Don't you want to know about the bike he was riding?" I blurt.

"Oh, did you notice the make and model?" he asks, not taking out a notebook or a phone or anything.

"No," I admit, "but I'm guessing someone did."

"We'll ask around," he says unconvincingly. "And we'll let you know if we need anything else."

"Don't you need to officially take our statements?" Edgar asks, not budging.

"We'll let you know if we have any questions, sir," Nutman demurs.

"You're not planning on doing anything," Rafe comments. I have to say I agree with him. He finally takes off his sunglasses, sticking them into his coat pocket.

"Oh, decided you want to see, huh?" I comment without thinking.

"Sinclair, he saved your life," Edgar says in a tight voice. Which is pretty rich, since I'm the one who might have saved *Rafe's* life. "He got there before I could."

"She's the one who threw the rock," Rafe says, surprising me. "If she hadn't, I'd have one hell of a bruise right now, but no one's life was seriously in danger tonight." I squawk, my mouth opening to argue with him, but he cuts me off. "Which isn't to say this asshole isn't dangerous. He's escalating, Nutman. Do you even know what that means?"

"Why, you insolent little—"

The other officer grabs Nutman's arm and gives it a tug, and he pales, his gaze darting over my shoulder to Edgar. He instantly shuts his mouth.

"This guy started off by sending her notes," Rafe continues. "Dead flowers. He had them delivered to her apartment that no one's supposed to know about. Then, tonight, he must have been in the restaurant at some point. He was close enough to see that"—he waves at the rock in the evidence bag—"thing Edgar gave Sinclair. And he threw a brick at her. Isn't that enough to tell you she needs protection?"

"We don't have the resources to send a squad car around to follow a celebrity," Nutman says, rocking on his feet. "Haven't you seen the headlines in the papers? We're down to a bare-bones staff."

"I'd follow her in a heartbeat," said the other officer, grinning at me. He looks like he's in his late teens or early twenties, just like I've been pretending to be on TV for years.

"She's already got a stalker," Rafe quips.

"Can it, Williams," Nutman tells the younger officer. "The thing is, Rafe, she doesn't need protection from us." He grins, but it's not a particularly friendly expression, and I definitely don't like it. "She's got *you*."

three

RAFE

OF COURSE they called Nutman in. The guy was an asshole after the incident at the gym where I used to work, and he's even more of a sore on humanity's taint now. I mean, sure, I *did* punch a customer when I was a trainer there, and yes, that's definitely not the kind of thing we were supposed to do. But if you're the kind of man who thinks it's funny to try to bench-press a woman who's told you no several times and you keep at it, in front of a room full of people who are asking you to stop, then you deserve a punch. Take it like a man.

The kid's friends called the cops, and Nutman was the officer who showed. By then, my friend Shauna, the woman who'd been bench-pressed, had persuaded the kid to stand down by threatening to press charges of her own, using the footage several people had filmed of the incident as evidence.

No charges were filed, but the kid's nose was broken.

Nutman was pissed that he didn't get to take me in. It probably soothed him at least a little when I was fired on the spot.

Later that night, I walked over to a bar to meet Shauna, who said she owed me a stiff drink and wing-woman duties for being her champion, and I was on my way there when a woman threw a clay dick at my back.

Sinclair claims to this day that it was supposed to be a banana, but if so, she's worse at modeling clay than she is at any of her other twenty thousand hobbies. The story goes like this—she went to a Play with Clay class with her sister and a couple of their friends, and they decided to ditch the evidence in a trash can. I got in the way. I objected to serving as target practice, we got into an argument, and then we went our separate ways.

A couple of weeks later, my father, who'd turned back up in Asheville a couple of years back like a jacked-up seashell the ocean had spat back onto sand, told me he had a job for me. I was skeptical, and when he said it was as paid protection for a celebrity, I straight up didn't believe him. For once the old coot wasn't lying.

When I figured out who I'd be working for, I wanted to tell Sinclair that she could pelt someone else with clay dicks, because I didn't want her thankless job. But her friends had told me about her stalker, and the sentimental side of me had wondered if maybe this was the universe's screwed-up way of offering me a kind of second chance.

So I gave her a nickname and took the job.

It's not steady work. It's an every-now-and-then kind of job. Clay has only agreed for me to come to public-facing outings—ones where word could get out, like it did tonight. But a couple of the people I trained at the gym are paying me to train them at home instead, and I'm making enough to get by.

Clay doesn't want me around; I don't particularly want to be around her either. She can't walk past a reflective surface without checking herself out. I told that to Shauna, and she laughed and said, "If I had tits like that, I'd be checking myself out in every reflective surface too." Fair.

Still, Clay's the kind of woman who takes two hours to get ready for a hiking date with a man she doesn't even *like*. I've sat in on every last one of her "dates" with Edgar James, and there's not enough electricity between them to power a nightlight. It pisses me off that she wants him to want her anyway. He's not a bad guy, I guess, if you like being put to sleep by PBS documentaries, but he's like flat soda. You might drink it if you're thirsty and need a caffeine fix, but you won't enjoy it.

That's their business, I guess—hers and his and Enoch Laskin's. All I have to worry about is her stalker and my paycheck. Up until tonight, he's been MIA and the paychecks have been both good and on time. It's saving me from taking another full-time training job at a shittier gym. But now...things are changing, and they're not good changes.

Nutman is leering at me, which is both annoying and amusing, and his buddy is leering at Sinclair, which makes me strangely itchy to punch him.

"I'm dissatisfied with the response to this incident," Edgar says flatly, and Nutman shifts his gaze to the outdoorsman, looking like a punched puppy. Edgar nods to the bagged rock, which seems a lot less stupid now that it saved me from a serious bruise. "You be careful with that. It's important to my lady."

I almost snort, but I manage to keep this one in. It sounds like we're leaving after all, which is what I want. I don't like that Clay's still here, out in the open, after what happened. It's irrational, since Justin Bieber's not going to roll back in on his bicycle and risk the wrath of Nutman, but there you go.

Edgar takes Clay's hand and starts walking away from the scene. As soon as we're out of Nutman's periphery, the press start to bob toward us. I scowl threateningly at them. Edgar lifts a hand and says, "Thanks for your concern, friends, but I need to get Sinclair home. You understand."

She doesn't say anything, which has to be a first. My glower deepens. They shout questions but give us space. I have that effect on people, and I don't regret it one bit.

Edgar leads us back to Clay's car, a dark gray Range Rover that I've been chauffeuring her around in for her public-facing events, and steps aside. I unlock it, and Edgar nods to me. "Can you give us a minute, Rafe?"

"Of course, boss," I say as a reminder that he is not, in fact, my boss. Like I said, an okay guy, Edgar James, but something about him rubs me the wrong way. Clay shoots me a panicked look, like she thinks I'm going to drive off in her expensive ride.

Or maybe she's worried you're going to leave her with the Bieber wannabe, you jackass.

"I'm not going anywhere," I tell her.

"Your...jacket," she says, which is when I realize it's still dripping tomato juice.

Ah, it's her seats she's worried about.

Swallowing the temptation to sweep into a bow like the peasant she takes me for, I take off the jacket and roll it into a ball. Then I get into the driver's seat and close the door behind me. It's an expensive enough car that the soundproofing is pretty damn good, so I can't hear what they're saying. But I can tell she doesn't like it. There are never any of the usual tells with Clay—no furrow in her brow, no crossed arms. It's just...I've gotten good at reading her. That's what happens when you spend a lot of time with someone, watching and listening.

My mind jumps back to the restaurant. Someone was in there, *watching and listening*, and I fucking missed it. I don't like that one bit.

They've stopped talking, and I watch as she makes a phone call, Edgar observing her without any expression on his face, as if it could be boring to look at a woman like her. Idiot.

When she hangs up the phone, he leads her around to the back of the car and opens the door for her. She slides in, her cheeks pink from the cold. He doesn't slide in after her.

"You'll let me know after you talk to him?" he asks.

"I will," she confirms.

"See you around, Rafe," Edgar says, giving me a little salute.

It's a factual statement, so I nod. I can't help but judge him for not coming with us. Doesn't he feel some responsibility for Clay's safety? Maybe he's like Nutman, happy to pass the buck along to someone else.

"Where to, Clay?" I ask. I can see her looking at me in the rearview mirror, her hazel eyes like burnished gold. I think of Shauna again, saying if she had tits like that she'd look in every reflective surface too. It's not just Clay's tits either—it's her everything. I'd prefer not to notice, but I have eyes and a dick; *they've* noticed.

"You slid in front of me earlier," she says.

"Yes, I saved you a dry-cleaning bill. Let's not make a big deal out of it. I didn't like the jacket anyway, and you're wearing a nice dress."

"I hate this shade of purple," she blurts.

I raise my eyebrows. "So why the hell are you always wearing it?" Seriously, this woman must have two dozen outfits in that exact shade. Each time I come to pick her up, I find myself wondering which purple thing she'll come out in next.

"Because it's a good color on me." She looks away. "Other people have told me so. And—and that doesn't matter. We both know that brick could have hit you. Or me."

A side of my mouth hitches up. "At least it wasn't a bullet."

"You don't have a gun...and you wouldn't have been able to shoot him to defend us anyway," she says with tremble in her voice.

"Don't like guns," I say, something I was upfront with her and her team about from the beginning. Given that the law is particular about people using deadly force, I was told it wasn't a problem. "But I know how to disarm someone. I've taught classes on it."

Of course, that wouldn't do any of us any good if this asshole took a shot at us from the shadows, but she's already frightened. I don't want to terrify her. "Anyway, it's a good thing you have a Little League past you've been hiding from everyone. Who would have thought you had a pitcher's arm?"

She smiles tightly. "Anyone who's watched the show, I guess. They made it a plot point on *Sisters of Sin*."

She sounds a bit sad about it, as if they took something away from her by doing that. I almost ask her about it, but I don't want to make her feel any worse.

She's the one who breaks the silence. "What was that guy talking about? Nutman?"

I grip the wheel, wishing she'd tell me where the hell we're going so I could take off. "He's a jackass. He's the guy they called in after I hit that guy in the gym." She knows the story—it's part of the reason I got hired, I think. They certainly didn't want me for my resume. I'm a personal trainer who's worked as a bouncer, nothing fancier than that. But I do have the distinction of being willing to get physical with people who cause trouble, without ever starting said trouble myself.

"They called the police on you?" she asks, shocked, as if she thinks police are just called out for murders or drug busts. She's innocent in some ways, Clay, as if a soft gauze has been covering her for years and she doesn't recognize the world without it.

"Sure," I say. "Would've gotten arrested too, but my friend said she'd go scorched earth about being treated like a dumbbell if he tried to press charges for me taking a swing at him."

"It was good of you to stand up for her," she says, then falls silent for a moment. "I need to talk to Enoch."

"Just tell me where to park the chariot," I say, wondering again why Edgar James had to peace out on this conversation. Isn't this both important and relevant to him?

"The bar," she says. We both know which one she means. Her friends always hang out at Summer Nights, the bar run by her sister's boyfriend. The bar my father has, coincidentally, decided is his second home, the first being the couch in my apartment. He's only been staying with me for a few weeks. Color me unsurprised when it turned out he expected payback for the "good word" he'd put in for me with Enoch Laskin and Sinclair's other friends. He's a good guy in a lot of ways, my dad, but he's not above pulling a tit for tat.

"Might not be smart," I say. "It's not likely to be crowded on a Monday night, but you don't need more attention right now."

"I don't *want* more," she snaps.

I lift my hands from the wheel. "Never said you did."

Despite her tone, she's not pissed. She looks brittle, on the verge of breaking. There's nothing polished about her now. I'm surprised by how much I wish there were—not for my sake, but for hers. Then again, I could see some stress fractures beneath her lacquer earlier, before they left the restaurant.

"They're closing early for the night," she says in a small voice. "No strangers will be there."

"It's going to be okay, Clay," I tell her. I'm not sure why I said it. It's just…maybe she needs to hear it. And I decide then and there that I'm going to do my damnedest to make it true.

"We need you to go full time, Rafe," Enoch says.

My gaze shoots to Sinclair, whose mouth is pressed into a line that does nothing to hide the plumpness of her lips. We've just arrived at the bar, which is, as advertised, mostly empty. The exceptions are Enoch, the bartender, and Damien and Nicole, the private-detective couple who've signed up to help Sinclair find her stalker. They call themselves the Fairy Godmother Agency. The woman has short, pink hair that seems like a shit idea for someone who needs to remain anonymous, and the guy is a big guy with the pretty-boy looks of an actor on one of the soaps my father watches in between bouts of classic movies.

I'm pissed at them. Unless the little shit who's stalking her really is Justin Bieber, they haven't done a good job so far.

My father's not present, so he's presumably at my apartment, eating all of the cold cuts and cheese in my fridge and breaking things under the pretense of fixing them.

"You agree with him, then," Sinclair tells Enoch.

So *this* is what she and Edgar were arguing about outside the car earlier. Figures.

"I do," he says, straightening his tie. From what I can tell, Enoch's a guy who sleeps in his suits. It's no surprise he's wearing one tonight, on a weekday evening. "You shouldn't leave the apartment by yourself until this is resolved."

Her gaze shoots to me, then back to him. "But that means…"

Laughter tears out of me. "You want me to move into that building?" It's the kind of place that has heated floors and bidets, and smart refrigerators that can probably fix you a damn meal.

Enoch frowns and taps his fingers on the bar. Other than Nicole, who's lounging on her barstool and popping pretzels from a bowl the bartender set out for her, we're all standing. "I made an inquiry, but there aren't any units available. We'll have to make do." He gives Sinclair a significant look. She risks frown lines, something I know she'd go to great lengths to avoid, to scowl at him.

"Wait," I say, the pieces clicking together. "You want me to *move in* with her?" Turning to Sinclair, I say, "No offense, but I've never lived with a woman, and I figured it would play out differently when I finally gave in."

Nicole laughs, nearly spitting out her drink. "Are they lined up outside your door, Rafe? Have you given them numbers?"

I scowl at her. She clearly doesn't give a shit, because she continues to laugh.

"My home is private," Sinclair tells Enoch. "It's my *sanctuary*. I want to keep it that way."

"I get that," he starts, "but—"

"Are you afraid he's going to find your vibrator collection?" Nicole interrupts. "Because you should keep that tucked away anyway." She smirks. "Ask your sister."

I don't know what the hell she's talking about. The look on Sinclair's face suggests she does, but she doesn't offer an explanation, and I don't ask.

"Never mind that," I say to Nicole and her husband. "Isn't it your job to find this asshole? He was there at the restaurant tonight, watching. He's smart enough to use gloves and a mask that covers his whole head. What are you doing to find him? Because I'm pretty damn sure Officer Nutsack doesn't give a shit."

"Nutsack?" Sinclair asks, shocking me by bursting into spontaneous laughter. I've seen glints of her sense of humor, but it's something she usually keeps under lock and key. Like her apartment, I guess.

I find myself smiling along with her. "Doesn't he look like one?"

"He does," she says through gusts of laughter.

Nicole's watching us closely, an inscrutable look on her face, then she claps her hands and pops up off her stool. "Let's sit down and talk." She nods to a booth across from the bar. "Griffin will bring us some drinks."

I've been distantly aware of Griffin watching us from behind the counter, because that's what I'm supposed to do here—keep tabs on people. No doubt he's soaking it all in so he can recount our conversation for Clay's sister later. He leans his elbows on the bar. "Oh, I will, will I?" he asks good-naturedly.

"Strong ones, please," Sinclair says.

"I won't be drinking," I tell him. "Obviously."

"You're always on the clock, aren't you, you big slab of muscle?" Nicole says, stepping forward and nudging my arm with hers. I don't budge. "You're probably one of those guys who has thirty chickens in your refrigerator and nothing else. You know, I'm going to call you Beefcake."

"By your logic, wouldn't Chicken be more appropriate?" Enoch asks wryly as he re-adjusts his perfectly aligned tie.

"Yes, but he's no chicken," Nicole says. "He took that tomato like a champ."

Enoch makes a move on the table, but Nicole tsks and waves a finger at him. "Nope. No can do. You can't join us. Fairy Godmother–client privilege."

"That's not a thing," he says, quite rightly.

"It is now." She hitches a thumb at me. "Beefcake here can come, but only because he was there."

"You can't call me Beefcake," I object.

"She wasn't asking," Damien says with a wry smile.

"I'm all for it," Clay says loftily. "You're not the only one who gets to give people nicknames without their permission."

Hell, if it makes her feel better, I'll allow it. For tonight.

"Beefcake, reporting for duty," I say with a salute.

SINCLAIR

"OKAY, BEEFCAKE," Nicole says as we settle into the booth. Rafe is sitting next to me on the bench, and he's so big—*there's so much of him*—it's a little unsettling. In an unpleasant way, obviously. "Tell us your side of the story."

"It started with a rock," he says, glancing at me. There's amusement in that look but also a glint of appreciation, like he remembers that I helped him and appreciates it. Like I surprised him for maybe the first time since we met.

He talks Nicole and Damien through the dinner, and the experience is just as unpleasant a second time, recounted by another person. He didn't notice anyone, *I* didn't notice anyone, but as he describes the layout of the restaurant, I realize someone definitely could have been there. They could have snuck in from the back and watched us from the hallway leading to the restrooms. Hell, they could have sat at an adjoining table, and if it's someone I don't know, a stranger, then I'd be none the wiser.

When I think of my stalker watching us, listening, waiting, it feels as if spiders are dancing on my skin. I'm used to people watching, of course, without me knowing a thing about it, but those are public moments. This is different. Whoever's doing this is stealing the slices of my life I've reserved for myself.

It's a relief when Griffin comes by with a tray of drinks.

When Rafe's finished, I tell them what I remember, which isn't much beyond Rafe being annoying, the food being delicious, and Edgar James being monosyllabic when he wasn't talking about the show or the location where it's being filmed.

"They might have a security camera on the front door and back," Damien says. "I'll ask for footage. And we'll talk to the press to see if anyone noticed the make of the bicycle."

"We should talk to the servers too," Nicole says. "If this guy knew about the dinner in advance, he could have taken a temporary job there just to get to her." She shrugs. "That's what I would have done."

"You *have* done that," Damien says with amusement. Then, turning to us, he adds, "I've got a friend on the force. He can work Nutman, see if he's figured anything out."

"But despite what Beefcake here thinks," Nicole says, shooting Rafe a dark look, "we haven't been sitting around with our thumbs up our asses."

"Well?" Rafe prods. "What have you got for us?"

I take a long sip of my vodka tonic, which gives me a deeper appreciation for my sister's boyfriend. He's made it good and strong, as requested. Griffin's much better to me than I've given him any reason to be.

"We have a few prime suspects," Nicole says, her eyes gleaming. Like Enoch, who at least has the grace to pretend otherwise, she is clearly way too pleased by this turn of events. It's like my life has become a real-life version of a show they're watching—the pain someone else's, the risk someone else's.

Maybe that's unfair since Rafe, at least, is risking his safety for mine, and Nicole and Damien might be putting themselves in harm's way too, but that's the way it feels.

"No need to drum up suspense," I say. "Go ahead and tell me already." It would sound more authoritative if my voice weren't quivering.

"Aw, come on Sin," Nicole says, tilting her head to study me. "You of all people should understand why we enjoy taking a little dramatic license."

Damien must've decided to rip the Band-Aid off, because he says, "Your mother's suspect number one."

"But she hates Justin Bieber," I say inanely. That's not totally accurate. She likes Bieber just fine; it's his mother she resents. She's always seen any other successful momagers as competition, and his mother launched his early career, just like my mother launched mine.

"I doubt she's the one running around in a mask," Nicole says, then shrugs. "Although that *would* be pretty funny. But she has a good chunk of your money. She could afford to pay someone. Pretty good alibi for her. She's in one state and the stalker's in another."

The thought cracks my head open like an egg. My mother is a terrible person. I know that's a word people throw around a lot, but in her case it's accurate. When she found out my sister's ex-fiancé was planning to call off the wedding, she convinced him to do it at the altar—and then circulated footage of Marnie running from the wedding-that-wasn't. She did it for me, she said, to deflect attention from my disagreements with the director of my old show. But that only made it worse. I fired her the instant I found out, and then she went nuclear on *me*, spreading shitty rumors. Still, it's a long walk from doing that to *paying someone to stalk and terrorize your own daughter.*

"She's probably going to reach out to you after news of this gets out," Damien says, and I get the sense he's the good cop to Nicole's bad.

"You're gonna want to tell her to fuck off," Nicole says. "But you can't. Not yet."

"Why not?" I ask, instantly annoyed. "You just told me you think there's a chance she's paying someone to stalk me."

"Because if she *is* doing that, the best way to find out is to get her talking."

I laugh bitterly. "She's not just going to *tell* me. She only shares what she wants to."

"So we'll make her think she wants to," Nicole says with a sharp-toothed smile. "We're good at convincing people to do things against their personal interest."

I can't help but wonder if I'm one more person who will regret the things I've told them, but it's a little late to worry about that. Besides, she's right. If my mother's involved with this, I'm going to need help dealing with her. She's always had a certain power over me.

"Fine," I say through tight lips. "And the others?"

"Tell us about your ex-boyfriend," Damien says.

"Which one?" I ask suspiciously.

"Penn," Damien answers.

Rafe, of course, laughs. It's disconcerting, because I'd almost forgotten he was there. He should be too big to go unnoticed, but he's a good listener. A good *observer*. I'm glad for that, because he'll be using those abilities to protect me. Still, I poke him, and it's a definite mistake. His body is as hard and toned as it looks. I scowl at him for being...hot, I guess. That's definitely his fault. It's a distraction I don't want or need.

"Who's Penn?" he asks.

"Penn Reed," I tell him.

Merriment lightens his dark eyes and almost makes them dance. The edge of that infernal tattoo catches my eye again from beneath the buttons of his shirt, and I squirm in my seat, inching away from him. "That's not a real name."

"It is," I say. "It's literally his name."

"It sounds like a porn star name for an author. He made it up."

I scowl at him. I'm about to say, *Did not*, when I realize a couple of things—one, we're having a second-grade argument, and two, he might be right. For all I know, Penn *did* make up his name because he thought it would make him sound like a literary genius. It's the kind of dumb thing he'd do.

"Anyway," I continue, "*as I was trying to say*, Penn was a writer on my show for a while."

"And he got fired after you broke up with him," Nicole says. She clucks her tongue. "Cold. I like your style."

"I didn't get him fired," I snap. For some godforsaken reason, I glance at Rafe, whose expression suggests he doesn't believe me. "I *didn't*. It was pretty amicable. He was just..." I wave a hand through the air, hoping an "amicable" word comes to mind.

Boring.

Nope, not that.

Conceited.

Try harder.

Obsessed with me.

That'll make you sound conceited.

"A little overenthusiastic."

"Like the kind of asshat who'd follow a woman around and throw bricks at her for playing make-believe with other boys?" Nicole asks, lifting her eyebrows. "Because that seems awfully *enthusiastic* to me, if you're picking up what I'm putting down."

The corners of Damien's mouth twitch. He puts an arm around Nicole, sliding her closer, and their ease with each other makes me feel a twinge of...annoyance? Jealousy? Maybe both. I've never felt that natural with anyone, even myself. They're not nice emotions, though, so I bury them.

"You may not have gotten him fired personally," Damien says, "but I've made a few calls. A lot of people think your mother did."

"Goddammit," I say, fisting my hands. It's been months since I've seen her in person, but it feels like she's still lurking behind me in the shadows, pulling my strings like she had since I was small. For as long as I can remember, I've felt like I'm in a game someone else is playing, and nine times out of ten, that someone is her. I was blind to it for so long, but now it's all I can see.

"So, this Penn guy might be pissed," Damien continues. "How'd he take it when you broke up with him?"

An image flashes through my head: a crystal vase full of blackened stems and rotting buds. I dropped it and the vase broke, and for weeks I was stepping on pieces of it in my trailer. Each time I did, it felt like a reminder that nothing could be normal for me. That I wasn't the kind of person who could date a random guy just because I wanted to get to know him—unless I was prepared to deal with the fallout.

"You just thought of something," Nicole says, practically thrumming with excitement. "What?"

I can feel Rafe staring at me as I say, "Penn dropped some dead flowers off at my trailer before he left set the last time. I didn't think of it until just now, but..."

"Your stalker sent you some after you were first seen with Edgar James," Rafe says, his voice gruff.

"Interesting, *very* interesting," Nicole says, propping her elbow on the table, her head in her hand. "Want to hear something even more interesting? Your dumpster dive of an ex is from Hendersonville, just a hop, skip, and a forty-five-minute drive away."

Damien nods, a smile playing on his mouth. "That's practically next door for someone who's used to LA traffic."

"We'll be paying him a visit, obviously," Nicole says. "The flower tip will be helpful."

"Anyone else?" Rafe asks her.

"Our third prime suspect was none other than Brock Tilton."

A gasp escapes me, because Brock Tilton is my sister's dirtbag ex-fiancé. "But why?" Then her wording hits me. "Was?"

"Sounds like he had a bit of a fixation on you," Nicole says, her head still cradled in her hand. "But Damien and I already went to talk to him, and he nearly shit his pants. It was very satisfying. He also has an alibi for tonight."

"How'd you already find out?" I ask, impressed.

"We hid a camera in his house," she says offhandedly. "He's been in his living room all night, drinking wine coolers and watching old episodes of Edgar James's camping show. I'm guessing that's still a sore spot."

Brock, who owned an outdoor expedition company, was an Edgar James fanboy, or at least he had been. The two of them had formed a collaboration, but the whole thing was predicated on a lie. Edgar was having a hard time recovering after a near drowning, so Brock had struck up a friendship with him by pretending he'd had a similar experience. Which he hadn't. Nicole and Damien revealed his lie and killed the deal.

"*So*, we haven't ruled him out, exactly, but he's not high on our list." She pauses, taking a sip of her drink. "You know, there's always the chance the stalker is just your garden-variety psychopath—some guy you smiled at when you bought flowers at the store one day, a busker you gave a few bucks to."

"So you're saying the problem is that I'm too nice," I say slowly.

"I don't think anyone would accuse you of that, Clay." Rafe gives me a sidelong look, and I take a sip of my drink so I have something to do with my hands. "What they're saying is that it could still be a random person. Someone you don't actually know personally... although they might have convinced themselves otherwise. Still, whoever it is knows enough to have found out about the restaurant tonight and hunted down the address of your apartment. If it's a rando, it's a dedicated rando."

"Lucky me," I say, rubbing the base of my neck. It feels raw suddenly, exposed. I take another sip of the drink.

"You *are* lucky," Nicole says, winking at me, her pink hair practically glowing under the bar lights. "You've got us. We're going to find this stalker and make Officer Nutsack wish his testicles hadn't descended."

Rafe's grin is like a wolf's. "Is that a promise?"

RAFE

MY MONEY'S on the little shit with the porn name. Penn Reed. I'd like to be there when they question him. I'll suggest it to Nicole later, though I suppose I won't have much room on my dance card if I'm on Sinclair duty full time.

The four of us head back to the bar, where Enoch is chatting idly with Griffin. Something to do with romance novels and cheese. Maybe they're planning a book club meeting for their ladies.

If Enoch's pissed to have been cut out from our discussion of the stalker, it doesn't show. "Had a nice chat?" he asks, lifting his brows.

"Very enlightening," Sinclair says. I glance at her. There's a little furrow in her brow that would probably give her a minor heart attack if there were a reflective surface nearby. It showed up the second they mentioned her mother.

There's a rattling at the door. Without thinking about it, I step in front of Clay. The door swings open an instant later, revealing a short brunette woman who resembles Clay and a tall, lanky man with messy brown hair and brown eyes. Marnie and Drew, Clay's sister and brother.

Makes sense. Marnie's with the bartender, so she would have a key to this place.

"Oh," Sinclair says from behind me. "You heard already."

"Enoch told us," Marnie says, rushing up to her. I step out of the way. If she's going to shiv her, I figure it's a family affair. Leave 'em to it. She pulls her into a hug instead.

The brother, Drew, stands back, but he looks pissed as hell—at *me*. "You didn't catch the guy?" he asks as he stares a hole through me.

"No," I agree, feeling the burn of it again. I hate that I let that little shit get away, but I can't outrun a bike, and I didn't want to leave Clay without any cover, in case the guy wasn't acting alone. "I was too busy catching tomatoes for your sister."

"What?"

"Catching—"

"No one cares about the tomatoes," Nicole says. "What we should focus on is that something is *finally* happening." She makes a flourish with her hands. "Let the fairy-godmothering begin."

"You're happy about this?" Drew says, taking a step toward Nicole and Damien. Interesting. This guy is either brave or stupid, because he doesn't seem to notice or care that both Damien and I could make mincemeat of him. He's not a weakling, but I'm pretty sure I could still bench-press him like that asshole at the gym bench-pressed Shauna.

"I'm happy we have some fresh leads, yes," Nicole says. "We're getting closer to nailing this guy so your sister can go back to making ugly clay things without worrying someone's going to lob a clay dildo at her."

"Yeah," I say, lifting a hand. "I'm the person that happened to. *She* did that to me."

A few people laugh, but Clay's not one of them. Neither am I.

"I'd like to go home," Clay says in a small voice. Something inside of me is rattled by it. Maybe I'm not too far removed from a caveman—a failing I've been accused of before—because I'm tempted to sweep her up off her feet and take her there.

"We haven't figured out a plan yet," Enoch says pointedly. "You need protection until this situation is resolved."

"Rafe can't live with me," Clay says at the same times as I say, "I can't live with her."

"At least you agree on something," he tells us. "Don't you live pretty close to Sinclair, Rafe?"

"Ten minutes, maybe. If there's parking available in the visitor spaces outside the building."

"I'm sure we can arrange for you to long-term borrow one, given the situation. How about this?" Enoch asks. "Sinclair can call you whenever she needs to leave the house. We'll play it like that for now, but if this guy tries anything else, we're going to revisit this conversation. We already know he's managed to get into the building more than once."

Both of us agree.

"But I want you to come home with us tonight," Marnie says. The brother nods, but he still looks like he's got a stick wedged up his ass.

"You really want to leave? Griffin's here," Clay says, pointing behind the bar like Marnie might have missed her boyfriend.

"And I'll be here all night," he says with a grin. "Try the veal." He laughs at himself before the rest of us can do it for him. "I'm reading *Hitchhiker's Guide to the Galaxy*. I couldn't help myself."

"We're reading it together," Marnie says, beaming at him.

"Maybe you and Edgar James can read *The Minerals Encyclopedia* together," I say to Clay, hoping it'll get me a laugh.

She scowls instead, proving just how good I am at pleasing women outside of the bedroom. Oh well. At least I tried.

"So what do you say?" Marnie says, tugging on her sister's hands. "Sleepover. We can watch rom-coms and wear face masks and eat cake." She gives her brother a pointed look. "*All* of us."

"Does *Scott Pilgrim vs. the World* count as a rom-com?" he asks hopefully.

"Nope."

"Okay," Clay says. "But I need to go home to check on Rue."

She named her cat after her character on *Sisters of Sin*. It's not even a female cat.

Enoch twists his mouth. "I think you should bring Sinclair to the loft, Rafe. Just in case someone followed you from the restaurant."

Well, shit.

He shifts his intense focus to her. "I know it doesn't feel like it right now, but this was a good night for you. You came off as a hero, throwing that rock when you did. Exactly the kind of badass woman who could helm an action franchise. You may not be ready to hear it, but the press is going to go wild. There'll be interview requests, offers, you name it."

Sinclair's mouth lifts a fraction, then she says, "I don't think I care."

———

"This is stupid," Sinclair tells me from the back seat. "You don't have to keep driving me around."

"You're paying me to," I say, grinning at her in the rearview mirror. "You're a regular Miss Daisy."

I catch her reaction the second before I glance away. She's amused but trying not to look it. "That's a really old movie, Rafe."

I could point out that she instantly recognized it too, but then she'll think I'm making some sort of comment about her age. She's as touchy about that as if she were sixty-four instead of thirty-two. So instead, I say, "My father's crashing on my couch. You can blame him and his taste in Turner Classic Movies."

"Reggie watches old movies?" she asks with delight.

"He has the TV on whenever he's not at the bar."

"Back to the driving-me-around thing," she pipes up. "Maybe I'm wasting my money."

"That's your prerogative," I say, turning into the garage of her loft. "You did spend seven hundred bucks on candy-making supplies last month. You don't even eat hard candy." There's a key-card reader that lets us in, and the same key can be used to activate the elevator. The precautions are intended to keep the residents safe, but Clay's stalking friend stole one or has found a workaround. More evidence that he's highly motivated. I swipe the card and park in her allotted space. My for-shit car, once blue and now rust colored, is parked outside in one of those visitor's spots.

"Do you really think it's someone I know?" she asks.

I watch in the rearview mirror as she lifts her fingers to her lips. Damn, she's beautiful. Sometimes it catches me off guard, her beauty. It's the kind that could kill a man, or at least lead him to some serious mistakes.

I get out and open her door. She gets out too, and although she's tall for a woman, she's so slender, so breakable, I feel another surge of protectiveness and a weird, primal need to feed her. I've been tasked to take care of someone who's physically weaker than me, so it's only natural that I want to make her stronger, but it still catches me off guard.

"Could be," I say, looking down at her. "It's not my job to figure that out, though."

"No," she says wryly, "Nutsack's on the case."

"And Nicole and Damien," I interject. "I'd put my money on them before Nutsack."

"Yeah, me too."

"I'm going to see you to your door." I can tell she's working on an argument—she's given me enough of them that I can tell—but nothing comes out. Despite herself, she's scared, and that makes me want to find the asshole that's been doing this and make *him* scared.

We walk toward the elevator in silence. To my surprise, I'm the one who breaks it.

"Your brother looked like he wanted to challenge me."

She laughs. "He did, huh? I'm not sure why. He's never liked me much."

She sounds so sad when she says it, so breakable. "Why would you say a dumb thing like that?" I ask as I use the card to summon the elevator.

Smooth, Rafe.

"Because it's true. He thinks I abandoned our family when I moved to LA." She stares at the doors as if they're going to be her salvation. "He's right."

"Bullshit. From what I've heard, you were a kid when your mom took you away."

"I was a teenager."

"A kid," I repeat.

She glances at me, giving me a flash of those honey-colored eyes. "I was an asshole kid."

"Probably," I agree. "Most kids are assholes. The majority of adults are too."

Her lips lift slightly, then she says, "He got into a few fights at school because of the way other kids talked about me."

"Good. That's what a brother should do."

Her eyebrows lift incredulously. "Seriously? You think violence is the answer?"

"Nothing wrong with a good fight," I say as the elevator comes to a stop and the doors open. We step inside, and I press the button for the penthouse. "So long as lessons were learned."

"If someone messed with a woman in your family, would you fight for her honor?" she asks.

"I'd do that and more," I say, feeling a familiar ache.

"Is that how you got shot?" she blurts.

I'm surprised she brought it up, finally. I showed her—and her entourage—my scar last month, in the job interview. Not very appropriate behavior for an interview, I guess, but I'm not much of an appropriate person. Better for them to know that upfront.

"I took a bullet trying to protect someone. But in all the ways that really matter, I failed," I say. Cryptic as hell, sure, but she doesn't need to know my private business. "But I did catch the bullet, Clay. There's that. I'd catch one for you too."

She risks those frown lines again for me, then opens her mouth to speak.

Saved by the elevator doors.

They open, and we both swear at once.

There's a gift bag with a large red ribbon sitting at the foot of her front door.

SINCLAIR

"ARE you sure we should open this?" I ask.

"You think Nutsack's going to come look at a present someone left for you if we don't even know for sure that it's from Bieber?"

He makes a good point. Besides, I want to know what's in there. I *need* to know.

Rafe snaps on the gloves from under the sink, left by a previous occupant whose hands are more Rafe-sized than me-sized, and reaches into the bag.

I suck in a breath, then let it out when he removes a to-go box from the restaurant that Edgar and I ate at earlier. There's a perfect chocolate *fleur de sel* tart inside, with a typewritten note taped to the lid.

You never did get dessert. When you're mine, you'll always have dessert.

"Well, we know my mother's not behind this," I say with a laugh. It's not funny, but I'm relieved. My little orange kitten, Rue, wasn't harmed and is even now weaving through my legs, and the package didn't contain anything gross, dead, or potentially danger-ous. Unless the tart's poisoned, but anyone who would eat a delicacy

44

left at their door by a stranger, stalker or not, probably deserves to get poisoned.

I reach down to pet Rue, who arches his back to get more of my palm before sauntering off like Rafe and I don't exist or matter. That's what I love about cats, I've realized—there's not a sycophantic bone in their bodies. Rue only acts like he cares about me because he does, and when I'm displeasing to him, he lets me know.

"What do you mean by that?" Rafe asks with a frown. He reaches back into the bag, feeling for anything else, and comes out empty handed.

"She'd never willingly feed me chocolate." I shrug. "She was always a fan of strict dieting. Either that or she's figured out a good way to eliminate herself as a suspect."

"Who's she to tell you what to eat?" he asks, as annoyed as if someone had given him a dos and don'ts list for *his* diet.

"Don't you tell people what to eat?" I ask pointedly. "You're a personal trainer."

"*Was* a personal trainer," he corrects. "And I only tell people what to eat if they want to bulk up. That's different."

He's right, and I say so.

"I could get used to hearing that," he tells me with a smirk.

"Don't," I say, but I can't summon much heat behind it. I'm glad he's here with me. I'm grateful he's been around all night, actually. There's something comforting about Rafe, something that goes beyond his obvious physical prowess. He's not like most of the men I know, who'll say all the right words but do none of the right things. He doesn't come off as someone who...over-promises. If he says he's going to do something, he does it.

"What about the guy with the literary porn-star name?" Rafe asks, watching me. "Did he believe in giving you dessert?"

I think back to the few weeks I spent dating Penn. "Yeah, I think we had dessert once or twice." It's a half lie. We did have dessert, twice. I remember because I have a very particular memory of every delicious cheat I've allowed myself. Every bite of cheesy pizza, every chocolate-glazed doughnut, and in Penn Reed's case, every last bite of the lavender crème brûlée and chocolate–peanut butter lava cake.

I certainly remember it more than anything we did in bed.

I shrug in a pantomime of someone who doesn't give a shit about dessert. "Could be him."

"Let's make that call to Nutsack," he says, settling into one of the chairs at the kitchen counter. It gives an ominous creak that makes me laugh. I'm guessing there's a lot of furniture that takes it personally when Rafe chooses to sit down.

"I'm going to take photos and send them to Nicole and Damien," I tell him.

"Good thought," he says. "We'll check with security to see if there's footage, but I'm guessing that he slipped in while the desk attendant was in the bathroom and didn't lose his mask."

He lifts his phone to dial the police. While he's speaking, I take the photos and send them to Nicole, who responds instantly with, *Fairy-godmothering!*

When I set my phone aside, Rafe's frowning, which suggests he's talking to Nutman.

"We'll be here," he says, then hangs up. Sighing, he tells me, "He's coming, but he doesn't seem to be in a hurry."

"I'll have to tell Marnie and Drew," I say. "This is going to disrupt movie night."

"You'd have to tell them anyway," he responds. "Otherwise, they'd probably wonder why I've moved in with you."

My eyebrows shoot as far north as my last—really last—round of Botox will allow. "*Excuse* me?"

"You heard Enoch," he says flatly, his dark eyes challenging me, that hint of his tattoo drawing my gaze. "He said we'd have to revisit the situation if anything else happened. This is *anything else*."

"But the guy didn't get inside," I say, the objection weak to my own ears. While I don't like the thought of Rafe living here—in my sanctuary, among my things—I can't deny I'd feel safer.

"He didn't get inside *this time*," Rafe says roughly. "That may change. Something tells me Rue there isn't going to suddenly transform into a panther to defend you."

He's right.

"Maybe I should have gotten a guard dog," I say, eyeing my kitten, who has somehow ended up on top of the kitchen cabinets and is looking down at us as if he's our overlord.

"You don't need a guard dog," Rafe says, wrapping his insane arms over his chest, which only makes them look more muscle stacked. "You have me."

I roll my eyes, feeling the need to deflate his ego, but here's the thing...

I believe him. When he's not wearing sunglasses indoors, I might even consider him acceptable company. Sometimes.

"Okay," I say. "Roomie."

———

I wouldn't be shocked if Nutman ends up eating that tart the second he steps out the door. He's mentioned at least twice that chocolate tarts are his favorite. Before he leaves with the gift bag, he asks if I can get Edgar James to sign something for his kid, who was a big fan of *Extreme Camping*.

"Anything," he says. "A handkerchief, a map, a box. A bra, a—"

"*Excuse* me?"

"I'm just saying it could be anything," Nutman tells me, scowling as if I'm being unreasonable.

"She's not going to have him sign one of her bras for you," Rafe says gruffly. A corner of his mouth tips up. "Maybe a pair of used boxers."

"Please," Nutman says with a scoff. "Everyone who watches that show knows Edgar James wears boxer briefs." His gaze shoots to mine. "If you go that route, white or light gray, please. I want the signature to show up."

Rue jumps down from the cupboards and yowls at him, making him flinch. "Fine," he says as if Rue were driving a hard bargain. "I'd accept powder blue."

My kitten stares at him for a full second before walking away and jumping onto the sofa.

"You're a cat person, huh?" Nutman says, making it clear it's an accusation. Then he turns and leaves, the tart bag slung over his arm, scratching his ass on his way out for good measure.

After the door closes behind him, Rafe and I exchange a look, and he says, "Do you think he even has a kid?"

"Maybe," I say, biting the inside of my mouth to keep from laughing. "But he definitely wants the signed clothing for himself."

He tilts his head, studying me, and I get another half an inch of his chest tattoo—swirling lines of ink that come together at a nexus. Is it an octopus? A woman with bad hair? An upside-down mop?

"Have you talked to him tonight?" Rafe asks, and it takes me a good ten seconds to figure out who he means.

"You saw us talking earlier," I say. But he's right, I suppose. There have been *developments*. Edgar will want to hear about them, probably, because in some ways we're in this together. I'm supposed to make guest appearances on his show, and those articles Enoch mentioned earlier will feature both of us. I sigh. "Why is being in a fake relationship nearly as much work as being in a real one?"

"Doesn't help that you've chosen a guy who's got the exact opposite interests," he says with a small, knowing smile.

"Maybe," I say.

"You doubt it?"

"I'd have to know what my interests are to know whether they're the opposite of his, wouldn't I?" I didn't mean for it to sound adversarial—I'm mad at myself, not him—but it kind of does.

"You mean, you haven't decided to leave it all behind and become an artist?" he asks, nodding to one of the paintings hung on the sage-colored wall across from the couch. My painting stage only lasted a week.

"You know I haven't," I say.

He rubs his jaw. "Can I ask you something?"

"I have a feeling you're going to whether I want you to or not."

A slow smile spreads across his face. "Did you ditch all those hobbies because you didn't like them or because you weren't any good at them?"

"Excuse you," I say, pissed again. "Not everyone's Matisse right out of the gate."

"Exactly," he says, reaching out and touching my arm. It's unexpected, and it jolts through me, like I'm being doused in a shower of sparks. "That's why you can't give up if you don't get it perfect the first time, Clay. Most people aren't good at things the first time. It takes practice. I'll bet you were one of those kids who couldn't act their way out of a paper bag."

I laugh, because it's sort of funny, but then I feel like I'm choking on the laughter. "I wouldn't know. I was in a spinach baby-food commercial years before my first memories kick in."

"Trust me, you sucked in it." There's humor in his voice—and something else. Sympathy but not pity. His eyes are like black holes, sucking me in.

"Yeah, I ruined spinach for generations of babies," I say, my voice distant, like someone else is saying the words.

Our eyes meet, and for a moment it feels like there's *something there*, but that's ludicrous. Rafe works for me, and besides, he's found dozens of different ways to tell me that he thinks I'm vain and vapid, a dumb celebrity. And *I* think he's what Nicole called him—a beefcake. Big and strong. Sexy. But not much going on upstairs.

Except that assessment doesn't seem fair. He's plenty smart *and* funny. He—

You should be thinking about Edgar, not Rafe.

"You're right about Edgar," I say, grabbing my phone off the coffee table. "I'll call him."

I do, but the phone rings until it reaches his messaging service. *Hello, you've reached Edgar James. I'm probably sleeping on a rock somewhere.*

Okay, it doesn't say that, but maybe it should. I leave a message asking him to call me back, telling him there's been another incident with Justin Bieber. I like it more than I should when Rafe laughs.

I've already talked to Marnie and Drew, who've insisted the house plan is off and they're coming over to my loft instead. I didn't fight them very hard. Truthfully, I don't like going to their house. It was our childhood home, where the three of us grew up together, and some of the memories embedded in its walls and the creaks of its floors are painful to me, especially now that our father is gone.

He died about a year ago, of a sudden heart attack. We'd never been close, and when I heard the news, my first thought was that the things that had broken between us would never be fixed. I could never tell him that I wished he'd stood up for me more with my mother. He could never explain to me why he hadn't. And I would have to carry that knowledge with me, a little ache in the back of my heart, forever.

It's a dark thought, so I'm grateful when it's interrupted by a call from Nicole. I pick it up and put it on speaker. She says she actually spoke with someone at the restaurant. They gave to-go chocolate *fleur de sel* tarts to twelve people tonight, which doesn't narrow things down much, especially since they wouldn't give her names. Nutman could probably get the information out of them, but I doubt he'll follow up.

"Don't worry," Nicole says. "We're on it. We've already scheduled an interview with the literary porn star. We're talking to him this weekend. Sunday at eleven."

"I'm coming," Rafe says, leaving no room for objection.

I roll my eyes at him. "How are you going to be my bodyguard if you're not with me?"

"We'll figure something out."

"Yes, Rafe should definitely come," Nicole agrees. "This guy seems like he's easily intimidated. Damien doesn't need help on that count, but if there were two of you…" I can practically see her shrugging. "It'll be fun to watch is all I'm saying."

"Maybe *I* want to watch it," I say, not sure why I'm being stubborn, except that I don't like handing my problem over to other people. I did that for a long time, letting my mother make all of my major decisions, and it didn't turn out so great for me. Isn't this new life all about doing things differently?

"What if we hide you in the bathroom and then prance you out after we talk to him?" Nicole asks thoughtfully. "If he spontaneously shits his pants, then we'll know we have our guy."

I don't like the way she said that—like I'm some trophy to be displayed, not a person. I open my mouth to say so, but Rafe gets there first.

"She's not a mannequin we can stow in the bathroom, Nicole," he says, his voice deep and forceful, a rumble through my bones. "And I'm pretty sure Clay's not going to sit on a public toilet for half an hour just so we can get him to react. But maybe we can arrange to meet him somewhere that has a connected room she can hide in."

I smile at him, a silent thank-you. He ignores me. I tell myself it's for the best.

The call with Nicole ends, and Rafe insists on scoping out the apartment to make sure all of my windows are still locked. He's already checked the front door to see if my visitor tried to jimmy it. According to him, there are no signs of attempted entry.

I trail him, feeling like a visitor in my own home, although I have to admit to myself that I've felt this way for a long time, both here and in Los Angeles. Like I'm trying to borrow someone else's life.

He smiles when he reaches the new macrame plant hanger in

the corner of the living room, next to a window that only Superman or a window washer could hope to reach. "How'd the macrame class go? I've been wondering."

He has? He's the one who brought me there. I'd spoken about the class in one of my Instagram Lives, and Enoch had worried someone might show up looking for me. Plenty of people *did* show up, actually—the instructor said it was the busiest class she'd ever taught. Actually, she kept saying it, like she was stressed out about it, but none of the other students spoke to me. They just snuck glances and photos on their phones. Someone posted and tagged a photo that made me look like I had a double chin, but Enoch told me not to untag myself—he claimed it would only make me look more real and relatable.

Sometimes I dislike Enoch.

"It was okay," I tell Rafe. I nod at the hanging plant. "It hasn't fallen down yet, and Petunia is the only living plant left from my gardening phase. I'm glad she has a bed."

"Petunia? I don't know what amuses me more—that you named your plant or that you named it after a different plant." His lips hike up higher, and I'm pleased to have made him smile. I can't help but think of what he said earlier. That I have to let myself get good at something. That I can't abandon it at the first sign that I'm not a master.

Shit, is that really what I've been doing? Have I—

There's a knock on the door, and Drew calls out, "We're here. Open the door quickly, or I'm going to call the cops."

Rue hisses and darts into the bedroom. I let him go.

"And we brought dessert!" Marnie calls out.

"Good," Rafe says as I make my way to the door. "I know I'm not the only one who got hungry looking at that tart. I heard the sound your stomach made, Clay."

As usual, I can't tell whether I'm annoyed with him or amused.

seven

RAFE

CLAY'S BROTHER spends ten minutes double-checking all of the windows and eyeballing the door, the little cat following him around as if he's backup. From what she's told me, Drew's a computer-game designer and is about as likely to spot evidence of tampering as she is, but I don't try to stop him. I like that he's being protective of her. All the better that he's doing it front of her. Maybe it'll banish her fool idea that he doesn't give a shit.

"Okay, we're good," he says after checking the last window. Rue, having been let off the hook, wanders off to places unknown.

I swallow a laugh. Clay and her sister are sitting on the couch with takeout boxes from a bakery. Chocolate cake, it looks like. I'm glad she's getting to eat something good again. The sounds she made when she tried those fries at the restaurant are going to be rolling through my head while I beat it in the shower later.

It's mesmerizing, watching Clay slowly mow her way through the cake. There's a certain decadent awareness about the way she slides the fork in, as if she intends to enjoy every last crumb and wants to make it last as long as possible. It's the kind of thing that gives a man ideas about how she might approach life's other pleasures.

Of course, such ideas are far above my pay grade. They're reserved for the likes of Edgar James, who certainly doesn't deserve the undivided attention of a woman like her.

Shit, where did that thought come from?

Clay's gorgeous, obviously. I've known that from the beginning, but before tonight I've never felt drawn to her. I've felt annoyed, amused, and occasionally intrigued, but not *interested.*

Well, damn, this isn't good.

"If you're all good," I say, nodding to Drew, "then I'm going to go."

"What?" Clay squawks, dropping her fork. She pushes the box with the rest of her cake in it onto the coffee table. "What do you mean you're leaving? You said—"

"You don't want me to use your toothbrush, do you?" I ask. "I need to pick up some stuff from my apartment."

"He's going to be staying in your guest room?" Drew asks. "Because I was going to suggest that you come stay with us."

"I'll be sleeping on the couch," I correct him. "Until this situation has been resolved."

Clay's mouth drops open. "But it's not big enough."

I'm glad she noticed.

"I'm going to put myself between you and any possible threat."

Drew nods, seemingly appeased. "That would work too. So you could stay at the house with us or here with Rafe."

I'm not on board with her staying at their house, with God knows how many points of entry, but I don't need to say so.

Sinclair's already shaking her head. "I won't put you or Marnie in danger."

Her brother waves a hand at me. "But you'll put Rafe in danger?"

A lesser woman might have blushed. "Obviously not," Clay says. "I don't want to put anyone in danger, but..."

"It's my job," I finish, not wanting to leave her hanging. "And the important thing to remember is that you're not putting anyone in danger. The only person who's doing that is the asshole who has a thing for bricks."

She holds my gaze and nods after a second. "Okay. But I'm glad you're coming back."

Me too. Which is more dangerous than a brick to the 'nads, so I say, "You know, it could be argued that *Hitchhiker's Guide to the Galaxy* is technically a rom-com."

"There's a movie version?" Drew asks hopefully.

I wave, sweeping my gaze over all of them and ending with her. She looks more confident with her family around. I wonder if she knows that. I wonder if they realize how important they are to her.

I leave without looking back, but one of Clay's slapdash paintings catches my eye. I'm smiling as I shut the door behind me.

———

"It's not what it looks like," my father says.

"So you're not smoking pot while watching Turner Classic Movies naked on my couch?" I glance at the coffee table and add, "And eating the last of my roast chicken?"

Okay, fine, Nicole had a point about the roast chicken, but if you can find a better source of lean protein, I'm all ears. It occurs to me that I'm going to have to eat around Clay. Go shopping with her too. I can't imagine her cooking. I'm guessing she usually subsists on a diet of birdseed and lettuce. There's no other reason a person would practically orgasm from eating french fries, steak, and chocolate cake. The memory would be more enjoyable if my father weren't still sprawled out naked on the couch with a pipe in his hand, the only thing over him a *Star Wars* blanket with a design of C-3PO and R2-D2 that he brought to the apartment with him.

Dear God, what's going to happen to this place while I'm gone?

He sits up, adjusting the blanket, and asks, "Sorry—did you have plans for it?"

"Yes, to eat it. Is this why your old roommate kicked you out?"

He sighs and sets the pipe down next to the plate of chicken. "No, Rafe, she kicked me out because I lost her cat."

I was expecting him to say he'd boned her best friend or something. It would be in character. "How the hell did *that* happen?"

He makes a face. "The little shit escaped through the door when I opened it to let someone in."

"Someone you were fucking?"

He shrugs, but his mouth tips up slightly. This is his *oh, I've been caught, but what can you do? I'm a scoundrel* look. I hope for his sake that women find it more charming than I do.

But he surprises me. "No, someone *she* was fucking. He came over to tell me."

"And you got heat for losing the cat?" I ask in disbelief.

"Life's not always fair, bud," he says, giving his white beard a tug. "Sometimes you come out ahead, and sometimes your old man pops back into your life and starts eating your chicken and watching Turner Classic Movies naked on your couch." He grins. "But hey, at least I got you a gig watching that TV starlet."

I shake my head while I laugh, because if this isn't Reggie O'Dooley in a nutshell... He's many things—a liar for fun and for sport, an asshole without really meaning to be, a Santa lookalike, and occasionally sharp and funny.

"Well, you'll get to do unspeakable things to this couch," I say. "In fact, go all out. I'm going to get a slipcover when I get back."

"Going somewhere?" he asks, lifting his bushy brows.

"Yeah," I say, "I'm going to be living with *that TV starlet.*"

He sits up straighter, the blanket slipping a distressing amount and revealing patches of white chest hair. Then he reaches for the remote and mutes the TV. Which is when I realize *Titanic* is playing. Shit. When did *Titanic* become a classic? I remember taking a girl to see it when I was a teenager, hoping it would get me laid. It did.

A second glance shows me it's on AMC, not TCM, but a classic's a classic, I guess.

I don't have time to deal with that dose of *I'm getting old* reality, though, because my father is grinning at me. "I knew you had it in you. Chip off the old block. You know, I mowed my way through half the cast of the *Young and the Restless* when I was in my prime."

"Yeah, *Dad*," I say wryly. "I've heard all about your wild oats."

He makes a face. "Well, 'half the cast' is an exaggeration. Half of them were men, and I've never swung that way."

"Good talk," I say, clapping him on the shoulder. "I'm not sleeping with her."

"Why the hell not?" he asks as if affronted.

"Because she's my boss," I say, ticking off one finger. "Because she's addicted to her own reflection." Another. "Because she's a TV star who has better things to do than mess around with an out-of-work personal trainer." Another.

"You're not just a personal trainer."

"You're right. Not every personal trainer wasted their prime personal-training years. I could have been a really good personal trainer if I'd started before I got shot."

"Nah," he says. "You have too much of an attitude."

"Some people like being yelled at."

"Not unless it's about toning up their chicken wings."

I give the plate of chicken a pointed glance.

He grins and picks up a wing, bites into it.

"You've made your point. I think," I say. "I'm staying with Sinclair because her stalker's active again. Very active, suddenly. It's not safe for her to be alone."

"Chicks dig heroes," he says without a trace of self-consciousness. Then he angles his head, studying me, and adds, "And artists." He waggles his brows and gestures to the TV. "Painting a rich lady worked for this guy."

"Until she let him freeze to death because she didn't want to share a door. I'm going to go pack."

"I borrowed a few of your shirts," he tells me. Why he'd want them is a mystery to me—I'm at least six inches taller than him and several inches broader—but I decide against asking.

"Fine."

"Make sure you tell your friend Shauna what you're up to," he adds. "She stopped by earlier, looking for you."

Laughter spills out of me. "She saw you out here with your *Star Wars* blanket, and she left with her pants on? What's happened to your animal magnetism?"

"Very funny," he says, shaking the chicken wing at me. "I'll have you know, women have always been hot for me. I was a set photographer for the original *Star Wars* movies."

"Yes, you've told me roughly half a million times." And I'm still not entirely sure I believe him.

"Your friend stopped by before I got comfortable. Said she needed to talk to you about something." He lifts his eyebrows. "Seemed upset, if you want to know the truth."

"You sure you had your pants on?"

"Very funny, kid."

I make a mental note to give Shauna a call while I'm packing up. She's not the dramatic type. If she's upset, there's probably a good reason for it.

"Good talk," I say. "Can I lend you a pair of pants to go with those shirts you're not wearing?"

He laughs but makes no move to get up. I'll take that as a no. Definitely getting new slipcovers for the couch.

I head into my bedroom and start packing, making that call to Shauna while I gather up all of my collared shirts—Enoch says I should pay at least that much homage to the part I'm playing.

Shauna answers on the second ring.

"Thank God," she says. "I was getting worried."

"About me?"

"Who else? I saw that thing about Sinclair Jones's stalker on *C+ Celeb News*."

Well, shit, they sure hadn't bothered double- and triple-checking their sources. Then again, with a name like that, I guess they wouldn't.

"We're fine," I say. "The guy threw some tomatoes. Clay clocked him with a rock. End of story." Far from it, but I don't need Shauna worrying about me. She's got enough of her own shit on her plate. "What's up with you? Was the stalker on your mind when you stopped by earlier? My dad seemed to think you needed counseling. You're lucky he didn't try to give you a hug."

"No." She laughs. "Just a shit day. My mugs didn't set right, and Rollins keeps hitting on me. Five times today. I counted."

"You should be counting. You should be on the phone with HR," I tell her, pissed all over again.

"What are you, high?" she asks, sounding just as pissed. "You know there's no one I can tell. It's not like I work for the YMCA. Plus, I need this job to cover the rent on my studio. Hell, even with this job, I'm close to not being able to pay."

"So get a new job," I grumble, throwing a couple of belts into the bag, followed by some boxers and a T-shirt. I'm not a fan of wearing clothes to bed, but unlike my father, I'm not going to wander around someone else's apartment in my birthday suit. "*I* got a new job."

"Not everyone can get a gig as a bodyguard for a celebrity. Talk about failing upward."

"Tell Rollins you're with me," I say.

"What?" she says, laughing. "You're practically my brother. No one will believe it."

"Tell him," I repeat. "He's afraid of me."

"He is," she agrees. She pauses for a minute, considering it. "No, I don't think so, Rafe. I don't like lying."

"I'm going to be staying at Sinclair's apartment for the next few days, but if you need anything, tell me. I'm not going to let that guy mess with you."

Rollins is a little shit, a kid with a power trip, who opened a gym not because he believes in fitness but because his daddy threw him a few bucks and he wanted to play.

"I will," she promises. Then, her tone speculative, she says, "How many mirrors does Sinclair have in her apartment? Are they everywhere? Is the dining room table reflective glass?"

I laugh, but it occurs to me that I didn't notice Clay checking her reflection at all after dinner. It's like…it's something she does when other people are around but not when she's by herself or just around me or her family.

"It looks like the inside of a diamond," I joke, then feel like an asshole for doing it. "I'm just messing with you," I say, rubbing my jaw. "She's not so bad."

"Oh, *real-ly*?" she asks, her voice full of insinuation.

A snort escapes me. "Leave it to you to take that to mean I'm madly in love with her."

"Would it be so bad?" she asks. "It's been years since you and Kay broke up."

"Would it be so bad to be in love with a celebrity? Absolutely. To be in love with anyone? Also absolutely."

"*Rafe.*"

"Shauna."

I throw my workout clothes and a pair of sneakers into the suitcase. There's a gym in the building. Surely I can leave her upstairs by herself for long enough to work out.

My mind is a traitor, because I find myself thinking of working out with her, watching the sweat bead on her skin. She'd probably look beautiful like that too.

"What?" Shauna says. "Can't I want the best for you? You want the best for me."

"I'm not dating my boss."

"You may complain about her, but you also seem *mighty* interested in her. I'm going to go ahead and say those are famous last words."

"Says the woman who's being hit on by Rollins."

There's a little hum of laughter over the line. "Fair point. I'll leave you alone."

"Wait," I say, already sure I'm going to regret this...but...maybe I won't regret it.

"You free this Sunday?"

She doesn't give me too much shit about it, so maybe she still has images of Rollins dancing through her head. Because she's Shauna, the best friend I've ever lucked into having, she agrees to my request. I've been mulling it over since this afternoon, when I talked to Clay about her hobbies. We hang up. I finish packing.

When I go downstairs, Rose is clinging to that door while she watches her guy freeze in the water. Feels like a bad portent, or at least a sign that I'm right about falling in love being for chumps.

So imagine my shock when I see tears in my dad's eyes. "Shit. You okay, Dad?" I ask, setting the suitcase down with a thump.

He waves me off. "Let your old man be sentimental. You know...I was in love like that once."

"With the kind of woman who'd watch you die instead of nudging over a few inches?"

He gives me an impatient look, and even though it's been months since Christmas, he really is a ringer for a pissed-off Santa. The Salvation Army should hire him to intimidate people into donating. "No, jackass. With a woman I'd die for."

"My mother?" I ask, lifting my eyebrows.

"No," he says, and a laugh tears out of me. "Sorry, but no."

"No need to apologize for that. She obviously doesn't like me much."

He gives me a look that sees deeply. "She was a beautiful

woman, but beauty and sense don't come together as often as one might hope."

That's my mother he's talking about, and I'm pissed even though we both know he's right. Even though...

"Don't go there, *Reggie*."

He lifts both hands, which unfortunately releases his hold on the *Star Wars* blanket. I sigh, my gaze dipping to the plate of chicken and then the grease stains on the couch.

"This place is going to be a mess when I get back, isn't it?"

"You won't even notice I've been here," he says.

I have the unfortunate habit of knowing when someone's lying to me. "Sure, champ."

"Rafe," he says, something serious in his voice. "Her name was Natalie. She had beauty *and* sense, and I was too young and stupid to realize what I was losing. You find a woman like that, you hang on."

"I sure wish you had," I say gruffly. "Then you'd be leaving chicken stains on *her* couch. Then again, I guess I wouldn't have been born."

"There is that," he says, sighing as he watches a frozen Leonardo DiCaprio sink into the water. "Be careful, kid. I don't want to get another phone call like that ever again."

I don't have to ask; we both know what he's talking about.

"People know better than to mess with me."

"Sure," he says, glancing at me. "It's what's driven you to get..." He holds his hands out beside either of his arms. "But guns don't care about muscle."

I know that too.

I say goodbye, my gaze skating off the paintings hanging on the wall, and head to my temporary apartment.

I stop to pick up some chocolate doughnuts on the way, because we need breakfast, don't we? If part of it is that I'd like to watch as

Sinclair Jones's teeth sink into the soft cake and listen to the little hum of pleasure that escapes her, then it's between me and my dick.

63

eight

SINCLAIR

RAFE DOESN'T SAY MUCH when he comes back. Just smiles when he sees the movie playing on the screen, then sets a box down on the kitchen island and parks his suitcase in the spare bedroom. He settles down in the empty armchair next to where I'm sitting on the couch.

Something lifts inside of me, so I guess I was afraid he'd run. But he didn't, and he sits and watches the rest of the movie with us. Rue, who's surly most of the time, shocks me by leaping into his lap and curling up; Rafe shocks me by petting him.

It's not until the closing credits roll that I realize Rafe didn't have much of a choice other than to join us. I turn to him. "We're in your bedroom, aren't we?"

His lips tip up. "Last I checked, it's still your living room, Clay." He says it so coolly he might as well be wearing his sunglasses.

We all get up, Rue running back to my bedroom once he's been displaced, and Marnie and Drew leave. Before they go, Drew insists we join them and Aunt Helen for dinner on Saturday night to give them an update on the stalker front. I don't put up a fight.

"Our social calendar's getting pretty full, Clay," Rafe comments after the door closes behind them.

"Is that a complaint?" I asked, eyeing the box of doughnuts on the counter.

"Nope, I like keeping busy. Your Aunt Helen the one who's a swinger?"

"That's her," I say with a smile, amused that he remembered. "We better not tell Edgar, huh?"

He snorts. "You worried he'll get the shits again? He *was* in the bathroom for a long time." My gaze returns to the doughnut box like I'm a magnet searching out metal. "You want a doughnut? I got them for breakfast, but if anyone deserves two desserts tonight, it's you."

"Breakfast sounds good," I say. Then, before I can swallow it back, "Thank you. For coming. For the tomato. For everything. I feel better now that you're here."

He gazes back at me with those dark eyes, inscrutable, and I feel a powerful punch of attraction.

It's as welcome as an actual punch. I've always known Rafe is attractive, obviously. It's not the kind of thing you can miss. He's big and brutish and...

Sexy. Sexy *is the word you're looking for.*

And now he's in my loft, sucking up the space like a Viking-shaped black hole.

"I'm not going to leave you until you're safe," he tells me, and I believe him. Because I've realized something surprising tonight.

Over this past month, I've come to trust Rafe. To rely on him, even.

My mother calls me at six on Tuesday morning.

I don't want to answer. I throw my phone a dirty look as if it's personally to blame for my patchy sleep. The real culprit, of course, is that brick. I keep imagining what would have happened if it had hit Rafe or me. Then there's the knowledge that Rafe is sleeping in my living room, *on my couch*. In some ways that comforts me—he's lying in between me and danger—but it unnerves me too. I mean, there's a big, muscular hunk asleep on my couch. Does he sleep with his shirt off? Is he wearing gray sweatpants?

At 3:00 a.m., when I was feeling a little punch-drunk, I thought about sneaking over to the door, like a kid on Christmas Eve, and cracking it open to take a peek. But then it occurred to me that my stalker probably feels the same way, and the fun was sucked out of the idea.

Not even the warm, soft presence of Rue, curled up on top of me, helped me rest.

The phone stops ringing and starts again.

Nicole told me to talk to my mother—to get information, in case she's behind all of this—so I pick up the phone and press Accept. I'm not happy about it, though.

"Hello, Mother," I say. "It's six o'clock."

"Sinclair, you can't imagine my worry, reading about your stalker on the news like everybody else. Why didn't you call me? I've been a mess of nerves all night."

I didn't call her because she'd spread horrible lies about me after I fired her, trying to make me unemployable in the very industry she'd pushed me into before I could walk without tripping. What she did to Marnie was even worse.

I could tell my mother all of that, but she's good at thinking on her feet. She'd lay out an argument for why it's my fault, or maybe she'd take a different tack and say she only raked me over the coals because she was setting me up for the kind of comeback story that would be guaranteed to get asses in the seats. She'd make a hell of an argument too—the kind of argument that I might have believed before I found out what she did to Marnie.

I'll *never* forgive her for that. Even if she'd acted contrite, I wouldn't have forgiven her. But she hadn't. She'd doubled down on being an asshole, saying everything had worked out to Marnie's benefit and mine. Acting like she'd played savior to the whole family.

"I didn't want to worry you unnecessarily," I say through my teeth. I'm proud of myself for saying it so evenly, as if I mean it.

I'm disappointed in myself too.

Rue shoots me a look of annoyance, probably for interrupting his rest by shifting in bed, then hops down and pads into the connected bathroom to use his litter box.

"That's why it's a bad idea for you to spend time in that place," my mother says, as if she herself isn't from Asheville. As if we didn't all live here together once upon a time. "It's not safe."

"It's plenty safe," I say, letting a little heat slip into my words. "Despite what you said to the press, Griffin's not some drug-peddling underlord and Marnie's not his pusher. You have *quite* the imagination. Besides, I have a bodyguard, Mother."

She pauses for a second, then says, "Yes, I saw that in the article. How'd you find this man? Craigslist?"

"I'd rather not go into it. Did you want something?"

"I was worried about you," she says, pouring on the honey. "I want to see you. I'd *love* to meet Edgar. He's such a handsome man."

She doesn't know the relationship is as fake as she is, although maybe she's guessed. She was always good at this sort of thing—finding me a boyfriend who'd get me press.

"Oh?"

"Of course. I'm going to be passing through town this weekend, Sinclair. Can we get lunch on Saturday?"

The timing is suspect. My stalker has upped his game, and suddenly my mother has mysterious business in Asheville. Shit. Maybe she really *is* behind this.

The last thing I want is to sit down and have a meal with her, but this will give me a chance to question her, and Nicole seems to think that's important.

"Fine."

"Can Edgar come, sweetie?"

"You don't want to see your other children?" I ask tightly. They wouldn't come, of course, but it pisses me off that she hasn't asked.

Marnie used to go to auditions with me, when we were little girls. Back then, my mother was sweet to both of us. We were her little stars. When Marnie said she didn't want to do it anymore, my mother turned on her. Drew...he was always grouped with my dad. They were "the boys," and she didn't care what they did as long as they didn't get in the way of my auditions.

"Of course," my mother says tightly. "But they've made it very clear they won't see me."

"I'll ask Edgar."

He won't be coming, of course. Maybe Nicole will want to come. The only problem is that my mother has met Nicole and would definitely recognize her as the person who helped Marnie and me figure out what a shit parent she is (Drew already knew). Still, Nicole's nothing if not resourceful.

"I'll send you the details," she says, and it strikes me that she probably already made reservations at a restaurant of her choosing, on a day and time of her choosing. She's probably already picked out what she wants me to order.

Screw that.

"No," I say, "I'll send *you* the details."

Then I hang up. I want to turn off my phone, but I already have several messages from Enoch, who apparently doesn't sleep, and Edgar, who'd like to get lunch with me today and then make a joint remote appearance on one of the talk shows that's reached out to us.

Honestly, the whole thing makes me feel worn out. I don't want to talk about my stalker or the just-a-rock on TV. I don't want to pretend I'm a hero because I did something stupid on reflex. I want to be left alone.

That makes me a hypocrite, I guess, since I've spent all these years trying to be noticed, and I want to get a job other than my guest appearances on Edgar's show. Or at least I think I do. So be it. I'll own my hypocrisy. Right now, I can't think of one single good thing my fame has brought my family.

I get up and take several steps toward the door before I realize what I'm doing. *No one* sees me like this, without a full face of makeup and a carefully chosen outfit. I consider it for half a second, and then swivel around and head to my bathroom. Half an hour later, I leave my room and nearly trip over my feet.

Rafe's doing push-ups shirtless in the living room, his back slick with sweat, the movement of his muscles hypnotic.

When he sees me, he gets to his feet. He's wearing nothing but a pair of gym shorts, and I can finally identify those whorls of black ink on his chest. It's a tree with gnarled roots, its branches lifting up toward the sky as if in supplication. It's unusual; it's beautiful. His chest is a sculpted slab of muscle, his arms hulking and huge.

"So that's what it is," I murmur.

"You've been checking out my tattoo," he says with a small, pleased smile that instantly annoys me.

"Not checking it out, no. You're always flashing it. I have eyes, and I'm not going to blind myself just so I don't have to look." Those eyes find the scar on his chest too—the one he showed us the evening of his interview. I want to know how he came by it; I don't want to ask.

He's laughing as he picks up the shirt he'd slung over a chair and pulls it on. "You do have eyes. And apparently you really *do* wake up looking like that."

His tone is wry, though, and it's obvious he's teasing me again.

I cross my arms over my chest. "There are things people expect of me, you know. And if I don't meet those expectations, I have to see my photo splashed all over the internet. *Sinclair Jones gained one pound. Newsflash: Sinclair Jones is thirty years old and actually looks like it.*"

"I thought you were thirty-two."

"You're insufferable," I say, trying to really harness that feeling because the sight of him like this—his shirt clinging to his sweaty body, the memory of his tattoo so fresh—is doing something to me. I go over to the kitchen counter and put some water in the electric kettle for tea, taking out first one cup, then two, because it would be rude not to offer him any. Then I take out a couple of small plates and pull the box of doughnuts over to me.

I can feel him watching me, but it's not the unpleasant feeling of knowing the stalker has been trailing me. I bite into a doughnut, and the rush of simple joy is so strong it almost washes away the bad taste from talking to my mother. Almost.

"It wasn't just the french fries. You make a sound whenever you eat something good," he says, his eyes deep and dark.

"I know," I say, forcing an eye roll. "You made sure to say something about it last night."

"I like it," he says. "You should eat whatever you want. Screw the paps if they want to comment on it and take pictures. Who cares? I thought they said all press is good press."

"All press is *not* good press," I say. "Only someone like Enoch thinks that way. Ask my sister if you don't believe me."

"What do you mean by that?" he says, taking a seat at the kitchen island like he owns it. I push a plate and the doughnut box over to him.

"Nah, I got those for you," he says.

"What?" I squawk and set down my half-eaten doughnut. "You'd give me one, but you wouldn't eat it yourself?"

"I already fixed some eggs. I eat protein in the morning."

"Fair is fair," I say, pushing the box closer to him.

He gives me a *you're a pain in the ass* look but takes one. I watch *him* bite into it, smiling when the smartass makes a sound of pleasure. He's teasing, but it still shivers through me.

I pour water into the teacups, then add a couple of bags. "Do you want stevia in yours?"

His brow furrows. "What the fuck is stevia?"

"It's sugar, but it has no calories."

"So it's not sugar."

"It tastes like sugar," I say tightly.

"Still, I'd like to err on the side of no fake sugar."

I mix the stevia into mine a little too aggressively, sloshing tea over the side of the cup, then hand him his mug and take a seat on the stool next to his.

"So what's the story with your sister?" he asks through a mouth of doughnut.

"Didn't your mother teach you not to chew with your mouth full?"

"No."

I don't know why I want to tell him, but I do. Maybe it's this forced intimacy between us. Maybe it's that call from my mother that's hanging over me.

"She was supposed to get married last winter," I say, looking at the counter because I can't meet his eyes while I say this. "The guy she was engaged to is Brock Tilton—the one Nicole and Damien already talked to. He was... I thought he was nice, but he was just putting on a front. People do that with me sometimes. Anyway. My brother caught on that Marnie didn't want to go through with the wedding, but I guess she felt like she had to because I was paying for it... I didn't mean to back her into anything, Rafe, I swear to God. I thought she *wanted* to marry him. I'll be honest, though, my mother had convinced me it would be good metrics if I helped him with his proposal and paid for the wedding."

"I'm guessing it didn't work out," Rafe says with a trace of amusement. "Since she's dating that bartender." He grimaces and lifts a shoulder. "Plus, I saw the video. Can't say I didn't."

"A lot of people did," I say, looking at him now. The video of

Marnie running from the wedding had gone viral. It had been turned into GIFs and memes. "It went viral because she's my sister. And it turns out our mother was the one who released it."

He whistles. "So that's why you fired her as your manager."

"That's part of it," I say, suddenly feeling like I'm being choked. "I also realized there were a lot of other things—not normal things—that she'd pushed me into doing."

"Like those spinach commercials," he says.

I smile, surprised I'm still capable of it. "Like those spinach commercials. No one wants to suck while selling spinach. Then she went on national TV a little over a month ago and lied to everyone about me. She said I got fired from my show...oh, and that I'm a drug addict. I'm guessing you saw that."

"Sure. After the fact."

"I lost my agent over it, but Enoch's helped me rehab my image. A few agents have reached out to me through Enoch, but I haven't gotten in touch with any of them yet. It's hard for me to trust people after..."

He reaches out and touches my arm. "Go figure. My mother sucks too. And somehow you and I are both mostly functional human beings."

"Speak for yourself," I say with a laugh, but it's high pitched and tinny.

I feel the points where his fingers are touching my arm, and I feel emotions, swirling and big and beneath the surface. And they're not emotions someone else told me to feel. It's...alarming.

"I said I'd go to lunch with her on Saturday. I'm guessing Nicole or Damien will come."

"And me," he says. "I'll be there." A corner of his mouth lifts up. "And not just because you're paying me." He's quiet for a moment, then he adds, "I've heard you and Enoch talking about your career. Maybe it's time to call some of those agents. You deserve to have someone on your side, Clay. Someone besides me. What's holding you back?"

No one's asked me in those terms. Enoch's said it's time to get working again now that the Edgar James plan is in motion. While he can get me good press and help me recreate my brand, he can't actually land movies or TV spots for me. An agent can. It's just...

"I guess I'm not sure I deserve it," I say in a rush. It's more complicated than that, but that's part of it.

His smile is a little sad this time. "What makes you think that?"

"My sister... I was a real bitch to Griffin when I first found out about him. I thought Marnie was..."

He laughs, though it's not an amused sound. "You thought she was slumming it?"

"I wouldn't put it like that," I say, wincing. "I thought he might be taking advantage of her. The whole thing seemed off to me in the beginning. I wasn't wrong, I guess, because it turns out he was just pretending to be her boyfriend at first. Then they fell in love. Sounds like something from a movie, right?"

He lifts his eyebrows. "Or a shitty TV show."

"Very funny. Anyway. I got a weird vibe, and it made me think of... She doesn't know this, but one of her ex-boyfriends tried to blackmail me for money. He found some embarrassing photos of me in her old albums from when we were kids and said he'd post them online."

"Did you pay him off?" he asks.

"I paid him to leave her alone," I say, feeling an old lump rise into my throat. "But I didn't pay off her shitty fiancé. My brother's the one who did that. He saw straight through him."

"Imagine that," he says wryly. "She's had two people paid to not date her. Being her boyfriend is a pretty lucrative gig."

"Griffin doesn't care about any of that," I say. "He's a good guy."

"Seems to be," Rafe says. "My dad likes him so much he practically lives at that bar." His mouth quirks up. "'Course that might also be because he has a drinking problem."

"Does he?" I ask. "I see him at the bar all the time, but he always seems to be drinking the same beer. I figured maybe he just comes in for the company."

"Probably," he says, running a hand over his stubble. "He's a talker like you are."

I give him a look, then run two fingers over my lips, zipping them, and extend my middle finger to him. He laughs.

We finish our doughnuts together, and for a while, we don't talk about anything. We just sit there, eating together, and it's comfortable. I don't feel the need to make him talk or to talk myself in order to fill the silence.

Later, I tell him about lunch with Edgar and the publicity appearance. Something seems to crack between us, and I feel a dip of disappointment for having caused it.

RAFE

SHE'S DIFFERENT ON CAMERA.

It's like she's slipped on a mask that's the same size and shape as her face but lacks her Clay spark.

I don't like it. I didn't like sitting next to her and Edgar at lunch either, watching her act for him. Because that's what she's been doing all along, trying to pick the persona that will crack him—the version of herself that will earn his approval. I wanted to tell her that wasn't likely to happen unless she could transform herself into an outcropping of rock or a rare lizard, but I figured I was being unfair.

She and Edgar are in her loft now, all nestled up on the couch I slept on last night, the little kitten positioned between them, looking like someone asked him to suck on a lemon. The cameramen from the network are positioned around them, and the anchor's being broadcast on the flat-screen TV across from them.

Enoch's here too, overseeing the filming, along with a few other people from Edgar's team.

That's another thing I don't like about this situation—Sinclair has only me and Enoch, and this guy has a team.

The anchor says something slickly sympathetic, then asks how they're handling the stress of the situation.

75

Something dark unfurls in my gut when Edgar takes Sinclair's hand. "It's not easy, Jill. Obviously I don't like that some guy is running around town in a Justin Bieber mask, terrorizing my girlfriend. In fact, I'm hoping to convince her to spend more time on set with me. I won't feel comfortable unless she's with me."

I share a glance with Enoch, whose mouth is in a hard line. I'm guessing he's thinking what I am—the rock-enthusiast shouldn't have mentioned the Bieber thing. Sure, Nutman's probably not combing the city for anyone who owns a Bieber mask, but if someone were investigating, that's probably the kind of thing they'd keep quiet.

"What do you say to that?" Jill asks Sinclair in an aggressively peppy voice. "Will you be going on set with Edgar next week? It's my understanding that he'll be leaving for set by the end of the week."

"I will," Edgar says with a nod. "Tomorrow, in fact."

"I can tell you don't want to leave her. While I'm sure you'll have a satellite phone, no distance is good distance in this situation."

For a second, Clay looks almost pissed off, then she gives both of them a smile so sweet it would give stevia a run for its money and says, "Well, Jill, I'm the one who threw that rock, so maybe *I* should lend Edgar *my* bodyguard."

I'm probably an idiot—scratch that, I'm certainly an idiot—because I want to celebrate when she pulls her hand away from his to adjust her perfect hair.

"Yes, your bodyguard," Jill says eagerly. "I want to hear about your bodyguard."

If Edgar's upset by this turn of events, he doesn't let on. "Yes, Jill, we're so glad he was there last night. Ra—"

My pulse thunders in my ears. I don't want him to say my name. I don't want to become part of their press cycle, which is why it was a shit idea to take this job in the first place. But I wasn't thinking of that at the time, I was thinking of—

"We won't be releasing his name," Clay says, taking his hand. "He's entitled to his privacy."

"Of course," Edgar says. He smiles at her like she's a rare igneous rock. "You're something else, Sinclair Jones."

"Thank you," she says with that too-sweet smile. "So are you, EJ."

He goes to pet the cat, and Rue nips his hand, which is almost enough to tease a smile from me.

"You guys are *too* cute," Jill squeals, ignoring Rue, and my almost-smile goes away as a headache crawls to the front of my head and settles in. "Your bodyguard slid in front of you, though?"

"He did," Clay says, glancing at me for a fraction of a second. I slip my sunglasses out of my pocket and put them on. Just for her. She smirks.

The interview stretches on for an impossibly long time, and even Enoch takes out his device and starts texting. Finally, it's over, and the cameramen pack up to leave, Rue darting for Clay's room as soon as he can, as if he's allergic to the cameras.

Enoch and Edgar's cheerleaders tell Clay and Edgar what a good job they did, as if they're kindergartners who pulled off some impressive macaroni art. I roll my eyes behind my glasses, and the throb of my headache deepens. Finally, after what feels like an hour spent on the rack, they all leave. Well, all except for Edgar and Clay.

"Will you give us a minute?" Edgar asks me.

"Uh, sure," I say, although that throb deepens and grows teeth. "I'll head down to the gym." Then I turn to Clay. "Come get me before he leaves."

She nods, her expression thoughtful. "I will."

I don't want to leave him with her—I won't examine my reasons —but I don't have a good excuse for saying no, and I didn't get in a proper workout this morning, so I bring my gym bag downstairs and change in the locker room.

I train hard, but I have a deep consciousness of the clock on the wall. Ten minutes. Twenty. Half an hour. What do they have to talk about that could possibly take half an hour? I've been on multiple "dates" with them, and they've barely had enough conversation to fill three minutes.

Forty minutes. I add more weight to the machine I'm using, then more. The burn isn't enough to banish my interest in the clock.

I shift to the treadmill and run until my shirt's dripping with sweat. An hour.

Finally, I see her behind the glass door of the gym, and I slow to a walk, not wanting to strain my muscles. She watches me for a moment, her expression inscrutable, and my mind fills with images of Edgar touching her, of him wrapping her hair around his fist, of him kissing those plump pink lips, of—

I grab the bar of the treadmill, and my knuckles go white.

Shit. I'm jealous, aren't I?

It's these last twenty-four hours. They've messed with my head. It's being around her, constantly. It's not possible to be around someone this beautiful for this long without being burned by it.

It's not just that, but I won't accept any other explanations.

She opens the door, her eyes on my shirt. She's probably disgusted by the sweat. I know she's not a fan of dirt. I saw the look on her face when she was out hiking with Edgar James the other week, as if she were wading through shit and not mud.

She licks her lips, and blood pulses to my dick.

"You're sweaty," she says, her voice low and throaty, thrumming through me like I've turned into a tuning fork.

"You're good at making factual observations," I reply. It's a dick thing to say, probably, but I don't like the awareness I have of her right now. I don't like the raw, cutting edge of my nerves.

"Thank you," she says.

"Why isn't he with you?" I ask. "You shouldn't have been wandering around the building alone."

"It's four p.m.," she says as if there weren't a clock mounted directly across from me.

"And you think bad shit only happens after dark?" I ask. "Unless Biebs is a vampire, I don't think sunlight's going to save you."

"You're right," she says, putting a hand on her hip. I find myself wondering what it would feel like under my hand, the curve of it, the heat. *Get your head in the game, Rafe.*

"Is that what you wanted to hear?" Clay continues. "Edgar left a while ago, actually. I should have asked him to walk me down here, but I needed some time to think."

I shouldn't be relieved.

I'm fucking relieved.

"You can't think while I'm around?"

"Not always, no."

More blood pumps to places it has no business. I swallow and think deflating thoughts. "Thank you," I force myself to say. "I'm glad you didn't share my name. I'd prefer for my personal life not to get dragged into this."

Again, kind of a shit way to put it, but I'm still wrapped up in my head.

She scowls and studies her nails, then her scowl deepens because apparently she finds something that gives her displeasure. "He shouldn't have done that," she says. "Sometimes he lacks common sense."

I snort.

She lifts her scowl to me. "He did a good job in that interview. He was nice. I guess he's leaving for the set of his show tomorrow."

"Does this mean there's a camping trip in our near future?"

"You know what I said about not knowing what I like?" she says. "I guess a good first step is knowing what I don't like."

"Camping?" I ask, laughing as I stop the treadmill. I step off and start to stretch.

"Yes, but I did sign a contract." She sighs, watching me. So maybe. Then she sighs again and asks, "Do you need to do that right now?" as if my stretching is hampering her style.

"Yes, absolutely. What are we doing this afternoon?"

She smiles at me, and there's something a little cat-like about it, like she knows I'm not going to like what she says and it amuses her. That probably shouldn't turn me on, but it does. "I thought maybe I'd get a manicure."

"Good," I say, switching to the other side. "My friend Shauna always tells me I should get a pedicure. Sounds fun."

Something glimmers in her eyes. "Shauna, huh?" she asks, lifting her eyebrows. "A girlfriend?"

"Don't women find it infantilizing to be called girls? She's a friend who's a woman, so I think it would be more appropriate to call her a woman friend."

"You're right," she says, her tone bored. "It's none of my business."

"She's no more my girlfriend than Edgar Jones is your boyfriend," I say, hoping it's true. Even though that's *definitely* none of my business.

"Oh." She pauses, watching me, her gaze beating into me, my body soaking it in as if it's hot pavement pattered by rain.

It's just an attraction, I tell myself. *Everyone* is attracted to her.

"Are we really going to get manicures and pedicures?" she asks with a slow smile that reveals her white, perfect teeth.

"You're paying me," I say. "I go where you tell me to go."

But I regret saying it as soon as I see the look of disappointment on her face.

"I get to pick my own nail polish," I tell her. "And you're going to get something other than purple."

I send Shauna photos of my pedicured feet. I chose silver, and Clay chose blue. The beautician laughed the whole time she applied mine.

Shauna responds to my text,

> Are you sleeping with Sinclair yet? Because you're already [whip emoji].

> I'm being friendly. I'm capable of being friendly.

> [Whip emoji]

> You're obnoxious.

> [Whip emoji]

> See you Sunday, champ. Can't wait to meet her.

Suddenly, Sunday no longer seems like such a good idea... except...I think Clay will like my idea, and she'll want to do something fun and relaxing after meeting with her mom and the literary porn star.

The beautician asks for my number before we go. I feel Clay watching me while I let her down easy.

Afterward, we have dinner at a salad shop. A bunch of tourists in *I Love Asheville* shirts screech when they see her. They spend five minutes quoting her show to her, as if she's never seen it before and didn't speak those lines herself. Or at least I think that's what they're doing. I've never seen it myself, and for the first time I wonder if I should change that.

She bears it in good spirits.

I warn her that she has spinach in her teeth, then take a few photos of her and the tourists before we head back to the apartment. I take a look before she goes in, making sure nothing's amiss, and find Rue fast asleep on the middle of her pillow, a dusting of orange hair around him.

"We're safe from everything except cat hair," I declare, returning to the main room.

"Do you want to watch something?" she asks as she settles onto the couch, toeing her shoes off before she draws them up and tucks them under her. "I mean...I don't want you to think you have to because this is where you're sleeping. I can watch something in my room. I have a TV in there."

"That depends," I say, lowering down next to her. "Are you going to want to watch some cheesy-ass rom-com?"

She tilts her head and studies me, those multihued eyes boring down deep. "Are you a Turner Classics Movies enthusiast like your father?"

"Maybe. What about your show?" I ask. "I've never seen it."

"You don't want to watch that," she says, looking down and picking at an invisible and possibly nonexistent thread in her sweater. There's something self-conscious about her, and if I didn't know better, I'd say she seems shy.

"Wouldn't have asked if I didn't," I say. "Although I'd settle for some of those spinach commercials."

"What about my old demo reel?" she asks, the corners of her mouth tipping up. "That'll give you a real journey through my acting career."

"Is the spinach in it?"

"Yes," she says, laughing. "And a tampon ad."

"Is that a promise?"

"It's one you'll wish I didn't keep."

We watch it, and we both nearly piss ourselves laughing. We started out with a good distance between us on the couch, but we crowded closer to watch the footage on her laptop, and our legs are touching. I don't pull away. Neither does she.

I assure her she really did suck in the spinach ad—one out of five, would not buy—but she should have gotten an Oscar, or the commercial-world equivalent, for the tampon ad.

"Well, I can always fall back on commercials for feminine products."

"Time to watch your show?" I ask, giving her arm a nudge.

She studies me for a second, her expression shifting, then says, "I'd rather we didn't. I don't want you to look at me differently."

"Why would I look at you differently?" I ask, baffled.

"Everyone else does."

I'm not sure what she means by that. The look on her face suggests she might not know either, so I don't press her on it. There are things I'd rather she didn't know either. "You're going to put on a chick flick, aren't you?" I ask, lifting my hands in pretended horror.

"I am, and you're going to like it."

She puts on *When Harry Met Sally*.

I haven't lived under a piles of rocks—I've seen it before, but I like watching her watch it, getting into the story even though she's clearly watched it dozens of times. "The dialogue is the best part," she says, leaning forward on the couch. "I used to love practicing Sally's lines when I was a kid, imagining I was Meg Ryan. Sometimes Marnie would do Harry's lines."

"Even the scene where she—"

Fakes an orgasm is the way that sentence finishes, but I'm worried I'll get an instant hard-on if I say that. Sitting here with her, our legs slightly touching, her now-familiar scent hanging around me. Shit...it's enough to make a man forget himself.

The corners of her mouth lift. "I might not have understood what I was doing, but sure."

I can't help but imagine her doing it *now*.

She's exhausted, and she falls asleep toward the end, her head lolling onto my shoulder, the heat of her plastered to my side. A rush of protectiveness washes through me. I pick her up, cradling her in my arms. She rouses but only snuggles closer to my chest as I carry her into her bedroom and lay her on the bed. Something cracks inside of me, and more warmth gushes out because she trusts me.

This woman, who has been given plenty of reasons not to trust anyone, trusts *me*.

"Good night, Clay," I say, and I turn around and leave.

As moments go, it's a good one, and I don't know what the hell that means—what it even *can* mean.

SINCLAIR

"THERE'S something different between you two," Marnie says in an undertone, glancing at Rafe. He's sitting by himself at a small table across from the booth where I'm having drinks with my sister and her best friends, Andy and Grace. Grace is engaged to Enoch, which is how I met him. Most of the time I'm grateful for that.

We're in Summer Nights, Griffin's bar. It's a little busy, but no one's stopped by our table yet to ask me if I'm me or to request an autographed shirt, hat, or napkin. Or, on one memorable occasion, a cod piece. (The guy claimed he was an actor at a local Shakespearean theater. I couldn't conceive of any other reason he'd be carrying around a codpiece, so I believed him.)

Rafe is wearing those damn glasses just to mess with me, and I have to admit it's kind of funny.

It's Friday night. Tomorrow is my lunch meeting with my mother, Nicole, and Rafe.

Rafe and I have mostly stayed indoors for the last three days, marathoning TV shows. We got so bored yesterday we played board games, but very few of them work well with just two people. We only tried a couple before switching to several rounds of Would You Rather. He'd prefer to walk through an infestation of snakes than spiders, the psychopath. We've also talked for much longer than I would have expected before this week...and we looked up Penn's Twitter account and laughed at his series of haikus about his work on *Sisters of Sin*, including "The Seven Sins of Sinclair Jones." His last tweet wasn't a haiku, and it wasn't all that laugh-worthy. He said: *You can't hide from me, Sinclair. I know your sins. And soon everyone will see them.*

Rafe's lips firmed when he saw that. He insisted on sending it to Nicole and Damien and Officer Nutman, even though he agreed that the police probably wouldn't be willing or able to follow up on anything that's not a direct threat.

I told Rafe that I'd made the power move of telling my mother that I'd choose the restaurant for our lunch but couldn't think of anywhere good, and he asked what my favorite food would be if calories weren't a consideration. The answer came quickly: my aunt Helen used to make fried chicken and mac and cheese for us. My mother had refused to go on those visits because she didn't *like* Aunt Helen, so no one except for me had watched what I ate while I was there.

"So that's what you need to get for lunch," he said with a grin. "Cluck-Clucks has great fried chicken."

"She'll hate it," I said, a smile starting on my face too.

"That's the point, isn't it?"

So I'd texted her with the plans. She'd agreed, but probably only because she had no choice. I'd decided not to warn her about Nicole, who *does* plan on coming. I just said I'd have a guest, and my mother probably presumes Edgar James will be there with a bow around his neck. Unfortunately for her, he's on the set of his show, presumably climbing mountains and sleeping on cliff faces, not that I would have asked him if he were here.

I shouldn't be at the bar tonight, especially since it's open to the public, but my sister asked me to join her and her friends, and I really needed a pick-me-up going into the weekend. So I asked Rafe if it was smart, he agreed it wasn't, and then he helped me pick out one of the wigs Nicole had lent me to use as a disguise. Red. I'm also wearing casual clothes—a hooded sweatshirt, a jean skirt, and low-heeled boots. They're not the kind of clothes I wear for the cameras, so hopefully that'll help too.

"So," Marnie prods, her eyes sparkling. It feels good to see her this happy after that douchebag left her at the altar. Her next words banish that thought. "What's been going on between you two?"

"Nothing," I say, but it doesn't exactly *feel* like nothing. "He's my bodyguard."

"And just how closely has he been guarding your body?" she asks with a suggestive smile.

"He's my employee," I say. "That would be sexual harassment. Anyway, you know he's not my type."

Only, I'm not so sure that's true.

I'm starting to wonder whether any of the other people I've dated have been my type. Maybe I'm just as clueless about who I like as what I like. At least half of my exes had been chosen for their star appeal or for how we'd look together or for what parts they could help me get rather than because I liked them. While I didn't date Penn for mercenary reasons, our short-lived relationship hadn't gone much better. It hadn't taken me long to figure out that he "borrowed" all his best jokes from other people and badmouthed everyone behind their backs. Not to mention he was selling photos of me to the press.

Andy makes a grunt of disapproval. She's been Marnie's friend since grade school, and I'm guessing she's disliked me for just as long. I don't blame her. Rafe is right—most teenagers are dicks, and I was no exception, especially after I got my first real break. I wasn't there for Marnie when she needed me.

"If that man's not your type, you need to get your eyes checked," Andy says, giving him a look that makes me bristle. "He defies type."

"So maybe *you* should go for him," I say through my teeth. Even as the words come out, I want to snap them back in and swallow them. I don't want Andy to flirt with him. I don't want anyone to flirt with him. He's my...

He's your bodyguard.

"Maybe I will," she retorts, lifting her eyebrows. She's gorgeous, with lush, curly black hair, dark eyes, and the kind of curvy figure you don't see much in Hollywood.

I'll bet she's Rafe's type. I'll bet he wouldn't carry *her* into her bedroom like a princess, only to lay her down and...leave. I might have been asleep before that, but I was awake for hours afterward, listening for any sounds from the adjoining room. Thinking about what it felt like to be in his arms. Wondering if he'd hear if I took out my vibrator.

Wondering if he'd join me.

The last two nights had been like that too.

I swallow. "Okay."

Marnie darts a hand out and grabs Andy's arm. "You'll do no such thing."

Andy rolls her eyes. "I wasn't going to. I was just testing her degree of self-denial. It goes as far down as the Challenger Deep."

"What's that?" I ask, annoyed.

"I'm so glad you asked." She raises her eyebrows and leans toward me. "It's the deepest part of the ocean."

Grace, who's been soaking everything in, says, "I've sensed it since you first hired him. There's always been this...*electric* energy between you two. Maybe you should do something about that."

She's a romance novelist and has the romantic notions to go with it. I say so, ignoring the urge to look at Rafe. They're wrong about us, obviously. This urge to look at him isn't because I want to see him—I just want to know if he's still wearing those dumb glasses.

Grace smiles knowingly, tucking her short blond hair behind her ear. "I didn't accept how I felt about Enoch at first either. I thought I hated him, and look how that worked out."

"Yes, he's busy ruining my life now," I say. "Thank you for that."

"Ruining your life?" Her lips twitch with a barely held-back smile. "What'd he do this time?"

"Okay, that's an overstatement," I admit. "But Edgar wants me to visit him on set next week. I wasn't planning on going out there so soon or staying for more than a day, but Enoch agrees that it's a good idea. He thinks I'll be safe there, and also that it'll help get people invested in our fake relationship."

"*You're* not invested in the fake relationship," Marnie points out.

"Ole EJ doesn't row your boat?" Andy teases.

"He's very attractive," I say, because that's factual. "But no. I was sort of interested in the beginning, but there aren't any sparks. Besides, I'd prefer not to go on an extended extreme camping trip."

"I don't blame you," Andy says. "Your brother is always going on about those camping trips he takes with his friends. Maybe *he* should go with EJ."

I laugh, but then something catches in my chest. I've been looking for a way to bond with my brother, and Andy's right, Drew *does* love camping. Always has. "Wait. Do you think he'd want to come?"

"Are you kidding?" Marnie asks.

"He'd bust a nut to get on that show," Andy adds.

"Gross," Marnie says, nudging her shoulder. "That's our brother you're talking about. I'd prefer to believe he doesn't have nuts."

She snorts. "You *know* he'd bust a nut. Maybe literally. Remember how much he fangirled when you told him you were doing freelance work for Edgar James?"

"He hasn't said anything about that to me," I say, feeling a hollow ache in my chest. "Why hasn't he asked me to introduce them?"

"I already have," Marnie says, with a grin. "Edgar forgot Drew's name, but Drew answered to Draco. Needless to say, he now has a new nickname whenever he gets annoying. I've got Griffin calling him that too."

I'm...well, I guess I'm hurt that Drew he hasn't mentioned any of this to me. I mean, I could get him signed merch from the show. I could introduce him to the producers. I'd be proud to be able to do those things for him. It hurts that he hasn't asked, and it seems to validate my fear that he'd prefer it if he and Marnie could get rid of me in addition to our mother. Like we're the poisoned branch on the family tree that should be snipped off so the rest can thrive.

My mind skips to Rafe, to the lines of black ink on his chest forming that tree. I've seen his tattoo again, these past two mornings, and in my mind, I've traced it.

"Would it be better if Drew went?" Grace asks, bringing me back to the present. "I'll bet you could craft a whole narrative around that."

"*Camping to the Max* with my brother and boo," Andy says, lifting her glass to lead us in a cheers.

"Actually," Marnie says. "I know you're joking, but it has a certain ring to it."

"Yeah," I say distantly. "It would take some of the pressure off, actually. And I'd still be fulfilling my contractual obligation to appear on the show. I'll talk to him at dinner tomorrow night."

"Speaking of which," Marnie says with a sigh, "do *not* eat any of Aunt Helen's cookies. She threatened to bring some over, and I'm pretty sure they're the same ones she, Griff, and I made just after Christmas. You'll either lose a tooth or get food poisoning. Either way, you'd be encouraging her bad habits."

"She's still hoarding old food, huh?" Our aunt is a fantastic cook, but she cooks more than she can eat and is constantly saving things that should have been tossed into the trash. I know this mostly from Marnie, because my aunt is someone else I've failed.

Over the years, my visits to Asheville have become less and less frequent. My mother was the one who didn't want to come back at first, but I can't deny that I agreed with her. I didn't fit anymore, like I was the foot of one of the ugly stepsisters in Cinderella, getting jammed repeatedly into a pinching glass slipper. Because *I* was the one who'd become ugly inside, not this place.

"If anything, it's gotten worse," Marnie says with a sigh. She lifts her drink for a sip and darts a glance at Rafe. "Maybe you should prepare him for her. She's almost certainly going to hit on him."

"Wouldn't it be funnier if she doesn't prepare him?" Andy says, laughing so hard she almost spills the drink she'd lifted for a sip. "Can I score an invite to this dinner?"

"Sure," Marnie says. "Bring fresh cookies, and you're a shoo-in."

"I'm tempted to crash too, but we have a thing for Enoch's nephew tomorrow night," Grace says.

I can't help but be relieved. I like Grace and Enoch, but he reminds me of work—of the Sinclair who always needs to be on—and tomorrow night I'd like to relax with my family. I'm going to need it after lunch with my mother.

As if Marnie can sense what I'm thinking, she skewers me with a look. "Do not, under any circumstances, invite our mother to this family dinner."

"Should you really call her your mother at this point?" Andy muses. "Doesn't seem like she deserves that title. What about...birth basket?"

Surprised laughter bursts out of me. "You know, it's going to be easier to see her if I get to think of her as my birth basket."

"You're welcome," she says with a grin, miming a bow.

"I wish you didn't have to see her," Marnie tells me, suddenly serious. "This sucks."

"Agreed." I swallow against a sudden blockage in my throat. "But Nicole and Damien think she could be responsible for this. I need to see her."

"She's definitely capable of it," Marnie says, her face stony. "That woman is capable of *anything*. She's like one of those boyfriends who keeps showing up at your door after you've broken up with him five hundred times."

More misgivings roll through me, gathering in my stomach, as if I'm a true of nerves made human. I don't like this situation I'm in, not any part of it.

"There's something else I've been meaning to talk to you all about," Marnie says with a small, secretive smile.

"Holy shit, you're not pregnant, are you?" Andy says, and if I'd been holding something I would have dropped it. It's hard to think of my little sister having a family. Maybe that's one of the downsides of pretending to be younger than you are for years...you start to believe it. Marnie is a perfectly reasonable age to be starting a family, but I still see her as my kid sister. Running around in pony-tails and braids, riding to auditions with me as if we were my mother's potential prize ponies.

"Would I be sitting here, casually drinking grain alcohol if I were?" Marnie asks, and relief escapes me on an exhale. "No...it's... Griffin and I want to move in together. Our own place, not his apartment or the house. It probably won't happen for a couple of months, but I'm trying to figure out how to broach the topic with Drew."

"He's not good with change," I say, rubbing a finger on the table-top. It's true. He's had the same four friends since he was a toddler. He goes camping every year for the same two weeks, in the same place. He's lived in our family home his entire life, same as Marnie.

"Yeah, I predict he will shit a brick," Andy adds. "Maybe wait until Sinclair gives him an Edgar James carrot."

"You think he'll freak out less if he's got Edgar James's carrot in his mouth?" Grace sputters.

We're all laughing at my brother's expense when my phone buzzes in my pocket. I take it out and glance at the screen, not sure what to expect.

It's Nicole, and a feeling of foreboding zaps through me.

Nicole: *I know you're at the bar, but you need to get out. Pronto. Do not pass Go, do not collect $200.*

"What is it?" Marnie asks, her face pale. "You—"

But Rafe's already at the booth, his stupid glasses stowed in his pocket, his eyes drilling into me and his big, sturdy arm extended. I take it, and he practically lifts me off the bench seat.

"Did you get a message from Nicole too?" I ask, but then I see them. A huge group of people has just entered the bar, and they're all wearing Justin Bieber masks. There must be a dozen of them, maybe *two* dozen, filtering in and filling all the empty spaces.

Panic replaces the blood in my veins.

"Oh my God," I say, just as I hear Andy say, "What the fu—"

"It's okay, Clay," Rafe tells me, his voice steady, as he steers me from the table toward the back door. Griffin's gone over all of the exits with him, multiple times, to prepare for any possible problems. "Probably just a stupid joke some college kids thought would be funny."

He's ushering me out quickly, but the Bieber-masked strangers are crowding in around us, and there are *so many of them*. My breath comes in gasps, and my mind flashes to other times, other crowds. Once, after the paparazzi swarmed me after a coffee date with another actor, someone grabbed my ass and squeezed it so hard there were bruises in the shape of fingerprints on it. Come to find out, my mother had called them.

"I...can't...breathe," I say as the masked figures move around us.

Then Rafe picks me up as if I weigh no more than a baby duck, cradling me to his chest the way he did the other night, and pushes his way toward the back. "Coming through," he shouts. "Out of the way, or you'll wish you'd moved."

We make it out into the night air amid some grumbling, but there are more of them outside, wearing those masks, *laughing*. Taking photographs of me in Rafe's arms.

Is my stalker one of them? Is he watching? Lurking?

I can't breathe. *I can't breathe.* "Can't...breathe," I repeat.

"You *can* breathe," Rafe tells me, saying the words slowly. "Slowly, Clay, in and out. We're all born knowing how to breathe. You didn't forget because of Justin Bieber."

He's right, and yet it feels like I *have* forgotten. He turns his back on the Biebers and walks steadily and firmly in the other direction. They must be following us, *they must be.* But he rubs my back and says soft things to me, and I try to let him be my whole world.

It's not as hard as it should be.

A rusty old Subaru suddenly pulls into the alley, moving too fast to be responsible with all the Biebers about.

Panic tightens its grip, but the driver's window rolls down and I see Damien, with Nicole beside him in the passenger seat. The car rolls to a stop, and Rafe stuffs me in through the rear door and then pushes in after me.

I'm still gasping for air, but I try to breathe slowly as Rafe leans in close, his presence steadying me even though he's crowding me, and cinches my belt shut. There's a protectiveness in the gesture that washes warmth through me.

"Thank you," I gasp.

"It's my job to keep you safe, Clay," he says, cupping my cheek and peering into my eyes. "I'm *going* to keep you safe."

But I feel something against my back, a crinkling, and I reach back and pull off a Post-it.

Gotcha. You can't hide from me, Sinclair, and soon you won't have to.

eleven

RAFE

MAYBE I'M OVERSTEPPING. All of this has been overstepping, actually, but I place my hand on Clay's leg, just below where her skirt cuts out. Part of it is to help ground her, part of it is to reassure myself that she's here, she's okay, and I'll still have the chance to lop the balls off whoever's doing this to her. Her skin is smooth and warm, and my hand instantly feels glued to her thigh, like I couldn't move it if I tried.

I'm protective of her, is all. I'm paid to be.

I tell Nicole and Damien about the note and its similarity to Penn Reed's tweet, and Nicole says, "Don't worry—we're going to a safe place. We can discuss everything there."

But I don't want to sit idly—my blood's running too hot—so I call Nutman's phone and get a busy signal. Damn it. I try again, and it's even more obnoxious the second time.

"Nutsack's not answering," I mutter.

"Why are you calling *him*?" Nicole scoffs, glancing back at us. "Damien's friend on the force says they've been trying to get rid of that guy for a decade. They have this joke that he got fired years ago but keeps showing up."

"Hilarious," I growl, annoyed at them, at Nutman, and especially

95

at those idiots in the Bieber masks. The look of fear on Clay's face made me want to grind every last one of them into dust. They were lucky I had to see to her.

Clay's phone buzzes, probably with a call from her sister. Marnie looked terrified when I pulled Sinclair away from her.

"You don't have to answer right now," I say, because Clay's air is still coming in gasps and that note is gripped in her hand, crinkled between her fingers. She's as pale as marble, like she's become a sculpture of herself, and I let my fingers glide in circles on her leg. Maybe it'll wake her up. "You don't have to answer," I repeat.

She sucks in a long breath, then shakes her head and lifts the phone to her ear. I go to move my hand, but she puts hers over it—just for an instant, but it's enough to send fire flashing through my veins.

It's just an attraction. Everyone's attracted to her.

She sits up a little straighter, greets her sister, then says, "I'm okay. Nicole and Damien picked us up." A pause. "He did? And what'd the guy say?"

I listen, shameless, and she says, "Oh, okay. Thanks, Marnie."

With that, she hangs up and tucks her phone away.

"Well? Don't leave us hanging," Nicole says, her whole body turned toward us in her seat. Her gaze zeroes in on my hand on Sinclair's leg. I move it, but not soon enough. A crafty look enters Nicole's eyes, and I have a feeling I'm going to be paying for that little display one way or another.

Fair enough—you *should* have to pay when you do something stupid.

Damien hits the blinker and turns into a parking lot, picking the first available space.

"You said you were bringing us somewhere safe," Clay says in an accusatory tone as she eyes the Golden Arches. It's not even the *good* McDonald's. This is the rundown, shit place you bring your friends at two in the morning when you're the designated driver and you need to pump everyone full of Big Macs.

"We did," Nicole says. "No one's going to believe you're at McDonald's. They'll recognize you and then tell themselves they're full of shit, because no way would Sinclair Jones grace the Golden Arches with her presence unless they were part of a TV or movie set and McDonald's went *all in* with the advertising."

"Ditch the wig though," Damien says, glancing back. "Better for you to look like a woman who resembles Sinclair Jones than to look like Sinclair Jones hiding in a wig."

She takes it off slowly, then pulls off the pins and holds the wig like it's a dead bird. "I don't know what to do with this," she says blandly, as if her emotions have gone numb.

I grab it from her and fling it back into the open trunk area. "There. Nicole's wig, Nicole's problem."

Nicole cocks her head. I half expect her or her husband to rip me a new one, but he chuckles under his breath and she says, "I respect that. Now, before we get distracted by McFlurries, what did Marnie have to say?"

Clay sighs and swipes a hand through her hair. It's tousled, like she just got fucked, which means I'm continuing my trend of having in stupid thoughts.

"Griffin saw the guy who put the note on my back. I guess he pulled him aside and asked him some questions."

Just how many people are doing Officer Nutman's work for him? I grip the handle above my head because I need something to bruise other than Nutman's nutsack. "What'd he say?"

"Sounds like some guy gave him a fifty to put the Post-it on my back."

"Let me guess," Damien deadpans. "The guy who paid him had on a Bieber mask."

She nods.

"Well, that doesn't help very much, does it?" Nicole asks with a sigh. "I'm guessing Griffin checked the guy's ID."

"Yeah," she says. "He says the person who offered him the money sounded male, though, so it's semi-confirmed we're dealing with a guy."

"Huh," I say. "Are we going to send Nutsack after the kid with the note? Put the fear of a sedentary lifestyle into him?"

Damien shrugs. "Can't hurt, but if that's all Griff got out of him, I'm guessing that's all there was to be gotten."

"Yes," Nicole says, "Griffin does have that perfect blend of charm and *I'm gonna kick your ass*. Ready for some shitty ice cream, Sin?"

Sinclair lifts her manicured fingers to her lips. "I don't want any."

"Correction: you don't *think* you want any."

"No, I *don't* want any," she says more resolutely. "I'm not going to have any."

"Your loss," Nicole says with a shrug as she pops her door open. She doesn't seem put out by it, though. If anything, she's pleased. "But you still have to watch me gorge myself."

I get out of the car with them. After Nicole and Damien place their order at the counter—ice cream for her and black coffee for him—we collect their things and slide into a booth, Sinclair on the inside, facing the door, me beside her.

If any little Bieber-masked shit-for-brains show up, I'll be punching first and asking questions later.

"How'd you know what was going on?" Sinclair asks Nicole, who's eating her ice cream with as much enthusiasm as if it were good.

"I found a thread on Reddit," Damien says. He pulls something up on his phone and starts stabbing at it with his finger. "Some dumb kid saw Edgar James talking about the Bieber masks and thought it would be hilarious to set up a group meetup for people wearing them. Other dumb adults agreed with him."

"Was it him?" I ask, already knowing the answer. It wouldn't be that easy. Unless you live a charmed life, and I don't, the things you want are never that easy.

Damien laughs and takes a sip of his coffee. "No, unless he's twelve, but someone should probably get the kid talking. See if he came up with the idea on his own. My guess is that he did, and our guy decided to hijack it. The better question is how they knew you'd be at the bar." He plants his elbow on the table. "Someone posted a tip on the thread at eight."

I swear under my breath. "Just after we showed."

"So either he was following you or he was already there. Could definitely be Penn. The wording's generic, but it's a close copy of what he said in that tweet you sent us the other day. Definitely worth poking him about on Sunday."

I glance at Sinclair. This news has rattled her, although she's not letting it show. Damn it. One of her last fortresses, the bar, has been compromised. Someone was probably in the bar, watching her, and none of us knew. It's bad enough that the front desk staff at her building have been completely inefficient at keeping her stalker out. The stalker has a key pass, obviously, and slips in through the garage, but they don't number their passes, so they have no way of tracking him down.

Clay wanted to be safe, to be normal, but she's not either of those things, and here's the proof.

"And the user who posted the tip?" I ask.

Damien gives me a dark look. "Probably our stalker. Looks like a burner account, no real info. No identifying features."

Of course.

"I'm going to pass all of this on to Nutsack," I say. "Penn's tweets too."

"Please," Nicole says. "We'll enjoy watching him continue to screw things up." Turning to Clay, she grins and says, "You ready for tomorrow?"

"No," she says, rubbing her throat as if she's worried she'll start gasping for air again. "What story are we going to tell my mother about why you're with me? She's not going to be that pleased to see you after Marnie's cocktail party."

"Oh, I've got that covered," Nicole says with a grin. "But you should know that I'm not going with you."

"But you said—"

She lifts her hand in a silencing gesture. "*She's* showing up with *me*. You should pretend you don't know me, though."

"Wait, what?" Clay says.

I won't lie, I'm pretty interested in her response too.

"Why do you think she's conveniently going to be in town?" Nicole asks, then presses a finger to her lips.

"You've watched too much *Gossip Girl*," Clay mutters.

"Better than *Sisters of Sin*, am I right?"

"Allow Nicole her dramatic reveal," Damien says with amusement. He wraps an arm around her shoulders, and she leans into him but keeps eating the McFlurry. "This is the kind of shit she lives for."

"You didn't just sign up for our help as detectives, Sin, my sweet," Nicole says with a smirk, straightening up. "We're your fairy godmothers, and your mother might as well be a wicked stepmother. Damien and I played rock, paper, scissors. I get your mother. He gets the literary porn star."

"But aren't you worried my mom recognize you?"

"Don't disparage my costuming skills," Nicole says, pausing for a heaping bite of ice cream. "Damien and I used to work at a theater. We have friends in low places."

I grunt. "So why are you letting Clay run around in wigs without any real disguise?"

"Would *you* disguise that face?" Nicole asks pointedly. "Besides, if and when we need to disguise her, we will. That's a hand of cards you don't want to overplay." She taps her temple. "You always need to stay one step ahead."

I hope it's not overconfidence.

"What are we doing about the possibility that the stalker is a random person?" I say. "Someone she crossed paths with."

"Not much we can do about that, bud," Damien says. "But it would help if you two could go through everyone Sinclair noticed from her crafting classes. That's where she's most likely to have come across someone since coming to town."

"Enoch thinks I should go on set with Edgar on Monday," Sinclair says. "Is that a bad idea?"

"Not at all," Nicole says, her eyes lighting up. "Your stalker might follow you, and we'll follow your stalker."

twelve

RAFE

"WHAT'D NUTMAN SAY?" Sinclair asks, padding out of her room.

For a second, I can only gape. She's not wearing any makeup, as far as I can tell, and she's wearing flannel pants and a long sleeve waffle-knit shirt. If that doesn't sound like the sexiest thing you've ever heard of, then you have a limited imagination.

"He reamed me out for making him miss the second half of his laser-tag tournament," I say with a sigh. "But he says he's going to follow up with the kid from the bar." I pause, taking her in. The green of her shirt brings out flecks of gold and green in her hazel eyes, making them look even larger, like she's one of those L.O.L. dolls Shauna's niece likes to collect. "I doubt he'll find anything. Doesn't hurt to have the police follow up, though. The more people looking for this jackass, the better."

"Thank you."

"Just doing my job," I say. She flinches, and I wish I'd kept my damn mouth shut. I'm not just doing my job. For one thing, this is nothing like being a bouncer or a personal trainer. For another, I'm starting to *like* her. That wouldn't be dangerous on its own, but combine it with the fact that I'm attracted to her and it's napalm.

I'm even more attracted to her when she's like this—her hair down, her face bare. It's like she's handing me a piece of herself that no one else gets to see. And if that's not a dangerous thought, I don't know what is.

I clear my throat, then nod to the couch. "We told Nicole and Damien we'd try to figure out if Biebs is someone you've met in Asheville. Let's go over the crafting classes you've taken," I say, "see if anyone stands out."

She sits on the couch and tugs her legs up to her chest. I want to pull them across my lap when I sit beside her, but I keep my hands to myself.

"What about the Play with Clay class?" I ask. "We both know how you took to that."

She scowls. "I thought the teacher was really nice the first time I went. She kept telling me I had natural talent. After everything else I'd sucked at, it was nice to hear. I was thinking, this is it. Maybe I've found something that I can do. Then I brought Marnie and her friends to the studio, and the woman laid it on a bit too thick. She thought my tomato was an apple, so...yeah, I suck at that too."

Her hair, still a little mussed from being under the wig, springs out from behind her ear, and I don't think—I just reach forward and tuck it back. "Did you like it, though?" I ask, my voice husky to my ears. "Before you started making clay cocks."

She smiles softly, her eyes sparkling. "Maybe I liked making clay cocks best of all. You don't know."

God, she's something else.

"You claimed it was a banana."

"It was," she says. "And it was Marnie's banana I was trying to throw away, for the record."

"You threw away your sister's work of art?" I ask, mock offended. "Well, shit. You're even more heartless than I thought. Let me guess, did your bananas look even more like cocks than Marnie's?"

Her eyes sparkle. "Dead ringers."

"Did you like it?" I repeat.

"Yeah," she says, her smile turning sad. "Yeah, I did. It felt good to make something out of nothing, or at least it did when I thought I was succeeding."

I give her a pointed look. "Remember those spinach commercials."

She laughs and pushes back into the couch cushions, getting more comfortable. "I reluctantly admit you might have a point."

"I accept your reluctant admission. You notice anyone strange in those classes, anyone who gave you more attention than they should have?"

"No," she says, lifting her fingertips to her mouth.

My gaze lands on it and lingers, because her lips are luscious and pink and perfect for kissing. I've noticed that before, obviously—I've noticed it always—but tonight they're especially tempting. It's because she came out of her room like this, without her armor on. She's here with me as a woman, and what a woman...

"There was one guy who was staring at me that first Play with Clay lesson, but he didn't talk to me or anything. And I wouldn't say that kind of attention is unusual."

I can't help but laugh. "No, Clay, I wouldn't imagine that's unusual at all."

She leans toward me. For a split second, I think she's going to kiss me. If she does, I'm going to pull her into my lap and consume her, the way I've been dying to do for days, maybe longer. But she doesn't lean any closer. She just watches me with eyes that are tired but no less beautiful for it, and says, "I don't like this, Rafe. I don't like any of it. Maybe I shouldn't have come back here. Maybe this is just one more thing I've done wrong."

I reach out and touch her knee. "You're where you need to be. You're making things right with your family. That's important." Or at least it's important for her and her siblings. With her mother, there's nothing that can be done. Sometimes the only way to make things right is to surgically excise a person from your life.

"Maybe." She worries her lips with her fingers again, and I have an urge to set them aside and claim her lips. But something tells me this moment, this conversation is more important than my need.

"What else, Clay? What about Petunia?" I gesture across the room to the plant, still mostly upright in the macrame plant holder.

"You remembered her name."

"It's a terrible name. Kind of hard to forget."

She gives me a small, self-deprecating smile. "The teacher was a stodgy old British guy, and I mean old. He didn't give off any weird vibes. If anything, he was exasperated with me. I was horrified by the fertilizer. No one ever told me it was...you know."

"Shit?" I say, laughing. I can't imagine how a person could go through thirty-two years without being informed of the source for fertilizer, but she's full of surprises. "That had to be a shock."

She gives a shudder. "It got into my gloves."

I nudge her arm. "Did you scream like a girl?"

She throws a fake punch into my arm. "I screamed like a woman, I'll have you know."

"I'm sure it was very womanly," I say, capturing her hand and holding it. I'm skirting a line, but I struggle to give a shit when her hand is wrapped up in mine. She doesn't pull away. Instead, she turns her palm so it's facing mine.

"And the painting?" I choke out. "Who was your teacher for those?"

She's breathing heavier. *I'm* breathing heavier.

"Spencer Ford. He's another one who claimed I had untapped talent. He was a little too...admiring. It was awkward."

"No," I say, putting my free hand over my heart and groaning. "Spence is the biggest douchebag in this town, and that's saying something."

"Wait," she says, shifting so she's facing me on the couch. Her hand is still enfolded in mine. We haven't acknowledged it, but I'm not going to be the one who calls chicken and lets go. "You *know* him?"

I laugh. "I am in that unfortunate position, yes."

"*How* do you know him?"

I lift my eyebrows. "What? You can't imagine me running in the same circles as a yuppy artist?"

"Don't put words into my mouth," she says, and there's that same stubborn glint in her that I saw earlier, when Nicole tried to bully her into getting shitty ice cream. It makes me smile.

"Okay, I used to have a studio in the same building as him. We can probably rule him out. He's wobbly on a bike. Learned to ride late and tells everyone about it within five minutes as part of his *woe is me* story."

"You were a painter?" she asks in shock.

"You don't need to sound so surprised," I say, a little annoyed, maybe because people always react this way when they find out.

Painting never brought me money, or at least never *enough* money, but I used to love it. It made me feel alive. Working out does that too, sometimes—it makes me feel anchored to my body, strong. But painting made something inside of me sing.

She captures her bottom lip in her teeth. "It's just...you don't *look* like a painter."

"Well, I'm not anymore," I say, my tone harsh. "Haven't been for years. But how can someone *look* like a painter?"

"I don't know," she says. "I guess I'm thinking of, you know, the actors they choose to portray painters in movies."

"Well, God save us from Hollywood producers. They cast *you* as a teenager."

She tugs her hand away from me. I feel like a prize asshole, but maybe it's for the best. I shouldn't be thinking of her as anything but my hot boss. Still, I don't like the way that came out.

"Yes," she says coldly. "I can understand why you'd find that hard to believe."

"That's not what I meant, Clay."

She gets up. "It's not my place to pry anyway," she says. "You're my employee. You don't have to share personal information with me if you don't want to." Her lips firm and then relax, like she's trying not to cry, and I feel like an even bigger prize asshole, the kind that would win a blue ribbon at a 4-H fair. "But we've been talking about my job...and my hobbies...for days, so I'm surprised you didn't feel like you could mention it."

Before I can tell her to pry with a pickaxe if she pleases, she disappears into her bedroom.

That didn't go well.

Rue, whom I hadn't even noticed, hisses at me in agreement and then slips into the bedroom just before the door slams.

———

I'm awoken by a cry, and I'm off the couch and on my feet before I can process what's going on. The door to Clay's room is still shut tight.

Blood pounding in my ears, I make for the door. I throw it open, and Clay shrieks, clutching the blankets to her chest as if I'm a pervert who busted in to peep at her.

Rue darts into the living room.

"What the hell? Are you okay?" I ask. There aren't any intruders in the room with Clay, or any sign of them, just a cavernous room that could swallow my for-shit apartment hole, lined with evidence of her abandoned hobbies. "You scared the shit out of me."

She lets the blankets fall. "I'm sorry. I...it was a bad dream."

Oh. I understand that well enough. I take a couple of steps toward the bed, then realize she probably doesn't want a big man hulking next to her bed right now if she was dreaming about the stalker. "Do you need anything? Water?"

"No," she says, her voice hesitant. Her golden-brown hair is down around her face, mussed, and one of her cheeks has impressions from her pillow. She's so gorgeous it physically harms me to look at her.

"Okay," I say. "You're safe here. He couldn't get through the window unless he's Spider-Man, and they say someone made him up."

Her smile is tepid. "You're right. I know. It was...silly."

"If he came in through the door, I'd clock him a good one, Clay."

"What if he has a gun?"

"It's like I told you. I took several classes about disarming people after I got shot. Even taught a couple of classes at the gym before they sacked me."

"Who shot you?" she asks softly, her eyes holding mine.

My heart rate picks up a notch. "I don't want to talk about that right now."

"Oh," she says softly, and I know I've hurt her feelings again. Maybe I *should* tell her. Maybe it would help her to know. But it's too raw. It'll always be too raw. Even though the wound closed over, scabbed, and healed, it'll never be just another patch of flesh.

"If I were going to tell anyone, it would be you," I say, swallowing. I'm surprised to realize that I mean that. "Good night."

I make it two steps to the door before she calls my name again, her voice soft in a way that slips under my skin.

I turn to look at her.

"Can you stay with me?" she asks, lifting the blanket. It's embroidered with gold as if she's an honest-to-god princess.

The look in her eyes...

She's silently begging me not to say no with every tool in her actress arsenal, and it's working...but how the fuck am I supposed to sleep in a queen-sized bed with this woman and keep my hands to myself?

"I don't think that's such a good idea, Clay."

"You don't have to touch me," she says, "if it's disagreeable to you."

A huff of sound escapes me, maybe laughter, but I'm not sure. "It's not *disagreeable* to me. But you were right—earlier. I'm your employee. I shouldn't be touching you."

And if I do, I might not be able to stop.

She's vulnerable tonight, and I'd be more than prize asshole—I'd be King Asshole—if I took advantage of that.

"I'm afraid to be alone," she says in a small voice.

With her talking like that, looking like that, I can't deny her. I could no sooner deny her than I could deny myself air.

I go to her but flip the blanket back into place, tucking it around her. I can't be under it with her. It would be constant torture, all night long.

"Won't you get cold?" she asks as I climb onto the bed.

I have the absurd urge to laugh, because she's nestling closer to me, her body pressed to my side as if she wants to prove to herself I'm really here, and there's no way any hot-blooded person with a taste for women would feel cold next to *her*. She's every temptation I've ever had wrapped up into one person. Hell, I'm already fighting a hard-on, and I've been in bed with her for ten seconds. "No," I say, my voice throaty and low. "I'm not going to get cold, Clay. Sleep."

At least one of us should.

I'm not going to sleep, but caffeine is a beautiful thing. Adrenaline too.

Still, I let myself wrap an arm around her. When she burrows into me, I smell the scent of her hair, citrus and spice—a perfect match for this woman who's capable of being so many things. Sour and sweet, spicy and demure.

She lets outs a little sound of contentment that shoots straight for my cock, and I prepare myself for a night of sweet torture.

thirteen

SINCLAIR

I WAKE UP FEELING GOOD, which is a shock in itself because it's been a long, long time since I've felt good—or at least good in a way that doesn't end in *but*.

I feel good, but I think I'm starting to hate my job. I was never a normal teenager, and now I might have to pretend to be one until my hair's white and I use a cane.

I feel good, but I've wanted to fire my mother for years and don't know how to tell her because she talks about herself as my best friend.

I feel good, but I have a pit of emptiness inside of me that I carry around everywhere and don't know how to fill.

Today, there's no *but*. Not yet. For half a second, I have no idea why, and then I feel him behind me. I've woken up on my side, and Rafe is pressed to my back—a hot unassailable wall of a man, protecting me in my sleep.

I was terrified when I woke up last night. In my dream, one of the Biebers caught me by the wrist. He pulled me into a car and drove away, and I knew I'd never be able to make things right with Marnie or Drew or...

Or Rafe.

I knew the stalker was going to kill me or make me wish he'd kill

111

me, and I woke up with a scream trapped in my throat. Or at least I'd thought it was trapped. Some of it must have escaped, because Rafe was with me before I even had time to work through what I'd seen in my head.

He stayed, and I slept. Because of him.

Yesterday, when we sat on the couch together, hand in hand, his toenail polish winking up at me from the pedicure he got for me, I realized something.

I'm not just attracted to him, I *like* him.

I like him in a doodling-in-my-notebook kind of way. I like him in a way that I'm very unaccustomed to liking men.

Usually, when I decide to date someone, there's an air of strategy to it. But this...it's out of my control in a way that baffles me. Rafe annoys the hell out of me half the time, and the other half...

He gets me in a way I'm not used to people getting me. And he cares in a way that feels real. If someone kidnapped me, I really believe he'd go full Liam Neeson to get me back.

If Liam Neeson were trying to save his woman and not his daughter, obviously.

That's a seductive thought. I've never had a man care so much about my safety. Actually, thinking back, I don't know that any other man has ever cared about my safety. Not even my father tried to protect me.

Rafe shifts slightly in his sleep, or at least I assume he's sleeping, and then I feel his very sizeable—and very hard—dick pressing into my back. Heat flashes through me, settling between my thighs. It's been such a long time since I've slept with anyone. The last person was Penn, in fact, and it was *far* from satisfying.

I'll bet Rafe knows how to satisfy a woman. He has the swagger of a man who's gotten lots of compliments and deserved at least some of them.

My mind flashes to watching him in the gym the other day, his shirt wet with sweat and clinging to his chest as if it liked it as much as I do. I immediately got wet as I watched his muscles bunch, his body move, so powerful and primal. I wanted to know if he'd work that hard in bed, and what it would feel like while he did. Now he's here, in *my* bed.

I'm not afraid anymore. I'm not worried about my mother or the stalker. I'm just very, very turned on.

I roll over to face him, and he instantly wakes up. My breath catches, because he's such a man. So big and imposing, yet there's gentleness in his eyes as he watches me.

It's probably a stupid thought, a selfish thought, but I want to believe it's just for me.

"Thank you for staying," I tell him. Then I pointedly look down at his very obvious erection in his shorts, visible because he's lying over the blankets. Is he wearing underwear? God, I hope not.

He swears under his breath, then starts to get up.

I reach out and touch his arm. It's hard and hot under my fingertips, and it makes me wonder what other parts of him would feel like. I'd like to run my hands over him from head to toe, making plenty of stops in between.

"It's just morning wood," he says. "It's a biological reaction. It doesn't mean anything."

Disappointment winds through me, but I pull my hand away. I'm not going to try to keep him in my bed if he doesn't want to stay.

Self-consciousness pricks at me. Is this because I'm not wearing my makeup? Does he think I look old without it? He *did* make that comment last night. "Are you saying you're not attracted to me? You think I..." My voice hitches. "You think I look old without my makeup?"

He snorts. "Of course I'm attracted to you. I have a pulse, don't I? If anything, you look better without your makeup. You look more like yourself."

"I want you," I say, emboldened by his perplexing compliment. Perplexing, because no one else has ever acted like this Sinclair, the one without makeup and in her pajamas, is the real one. Certainly no one has ever treated this version of me as the desirable one. A voice in my head reminds me that I haven't shown myself like this to many people—usually, I'd run into the bathroom in the morning after staying over at a man's place. I'd pretty myself with the makeup in my purse before making a reappearance. This morning, I didn't even consider the possibility.

I touch his arm again, letting my fingers run over his hard muscles. "I want you," I repeat. "I think maybe I have for a while now."

He swears again, wipes his mouth. "This is a bad idea."

"Do I have morning breath?" I ask, horrified as my eyes track his gesture. Is he silently miming the truth to me?

He laughs, but it's a jagged sound. "You think I give a fuck about whether you have morning breath? You just said you want me."

"Do *you* want *me*?" I ask.

His response is to growl—something I've seen in scripts but never really heard in person, not like this. "Yes, I want you. Is that what you want to hear? I've lain here awake all night thinking about nothing else but fucking you. In this bed, against the window. In the shower. On the kitchen counter. On every damn surface in this apartment. But I'm not going to."

My mouth drops open, and I sit up, affronted. "Why the hell not?"

"Because I'm here to protect you. I won't take advantage of you when you're vulnerable." He gets to his feet, that huge dick of his protruding in front of him like a flag.

"So it's not just morning wood?"

"You're impossible," he says with a groan.

"I am *not* vulnerable," I insist. "I'm a woman who knows what I want. You don't have to *infantilize* me."

"That's not what I'm doing," he says, fisting his hands at his sides. "I'm trying to be a damn gentleman."

"It's a struggle, isn't it?" I say, not really sure why except that he's not giving me what I want, and this is something else I've come to crave. Verbally sparring with Rafe is more fun than having a pleasant conversation with anyone else. I get up off the bed, and his eyes follow me, taking in every inch of my ugly flannel pants as if I were wearing red silk lingerie.

The thought only makes me wetter.

A voice inside my head tells me that he also has a point. I don't know what I want from a man, from my career, from my life, so what business do I have messing around with anyone right now?

The answer comes to me with a light-bulb burst of clarity.

"It doesn't need to mean anything," I say, the picture of reason. "We can just have sex. Once. It'll help release some of the tension from last night. No one will ever know. It'll be our little secret."

He shakes his head, lifting his hands to his temples. His arms flex in a way that makes my mouth water. "What the hell is even happening? Did I fall asleep? Is this a dream?"

"You did," I tell him, "and you were wrapped all over me. What were you doing to me in your dreams? Was it *dirty*?"

His eyes are as black as coal. He fidgets, probably because that hard-on is jutting out there with nothing to do. "I don't think I should tell you that."

"You know what they say—why tell when you can show?"

"You're killing me. You're actually killing me."

He looks like he might mean it, so even though my whole body is humming in anticipation, and I want—desperately—for his clothes to spontaneously disintegrate, I'm not going to push him. If he's saying no, the answer's no...no matter why he's saying it.

"I'm going to go make coffee," I say with a sigh and take a step toward the door. "We need lots of coffee."

He reaches out and grabs my arm, the tips of his fingers burning heat into me. "Not so fast. What's this all about, Clay?"

"It's not about anything," I say honestly, realizing only then how remarkable that is. "I just want you, and I'm sick to death of analyzing everything, trying to make sure my ideas are the right ones and whether they'll bite me in the ass. I—"

"You'd prefer it if *I* bit your ass?" he asks.

I can't quite tell whether he's joking. I go with serious. "Yes."

He reaches out and tucks my hair behind my ear, and I have a sudden prick of self-consciousness. Here I am, throwing myself at this man, and I have no idea how I look. My hair is probably a bird's nest, and I'll bet there are circles under my eyes, and—

He hooks his fingers around to cup my jaw and lifts it to him, his fingers caressing it.

"Why are we still talking about it?" I say, my blood pulsing hot as I issue the challenge. "Let me go make the coffee, and we'll pretend this never happened."

"I don't like pretending." He takes two steps forward, his body suddenly crowding my space, his proximity washing over me like a promise. "This is a bad idea," he repeats, but his voice is low and husky, and the sound settles in my belly. Then, his eyes shining like onyx, he lifts my chin up to him and kisses me, the hard press of his lips leaving no doubt that he wants me. His hand moves from my chin to my hair, spearing and gripping it—almost too hard but not, the nerve endings dancing with delight. Using his grip, he changes the angle of our kiss, deepening it, and I press my body into him, making sure to capture every last inch of his very impressive morning wood between us.

While he kisses me, I let my hands wander over his arms and then dip to the hem of his shirt, needing to feel the heat of his chest, to see his tattoo and trace it. To touch it with my tongue. *His* hand slips into the waistline of my ugly pants and then my panties, and he makes a sound in his throat when he feels how wet I am for him, how much I want this, whatever this is. I swallow the sound. His fingers stroke me lightly, tracing my opening in a tease before finding the bundle of nerves and circling it. Gentle yet rough at the same time. His mouth leaves mine, his head descending to my neck like he's a vampire. He kisses where my neck joins my shoulder, a spot that's always driven me mad, as he presses the heel of his palm against my clit. His fingers curl into me, finding the spot inside that sends pleasure sizzling through my veins. For a moment, all I can do is cling to his chest as he works me with his hand. For a moment, all I can do is *feel*.

Then my eyes catch on his cock, still jutting out proudly, and I decide to test my theory about whether he's wearing underwear. He's not. When I slide my hand into his shorts and wrap my hand around him, he hisses against my neck. "Fuck, Clay."

A laugh escapes me. "You're calling me that now?"

"It's your name, isn't it?" he asks, then nips his teeth into my neck like that vampire I was envisioning as he pulses his fingers, his palm still pressing delicious pressure into my clit. Turnabout is fair play, so I start stroking his cock. He's so hard, so big and wide, and the excitement of knowing that he's going to be inside of me soon, paired with what he's doing with his hand...

I'm already on the verge.

He moves my hand aside with the hand that's not currently inside of me, and I scowl at him, even as what he's doing with his other hand is sending sparklers of pleasure through me.

"I get to touch you too."

"I don't want to come in your hand," he says. "I have other plans for you."

Heat flashes through me. "Like what? I'd love to hear them in great detail."

"I want to make you come so hard you lose consciousness."

"Jesus—can that happen?" It sounds horrible...and wonderful.

He gives me an annoying and sexy-as-hell smirk. "Why don't we find out?"

I make a squawk of protest when he removes his hand from my

pants, but then he slowly and deliberately licks his fingers, which makes me feel like I'm going to spontaneously combust.

"Not enough," he says. "Not nearly enough."

He pulls down my pants and backs me toward the bed after I step out of them. When I'm sitting on the edge, he lowers to his knees and spreads my legs wide.

"Did this happen in your dreams?" I ask, my voice almost unrecognizable to me.

"Me burying my head between your legs?" he asks.

"Yes."

He gives me a wicked look. "I thought you wanted me to show, not tell. I'm only following orders."

Maybe I'm more twisted than I realized, because the reminder that he technically works for me and is in charge of protecting my person only makes me hotter.

"Take your shirt off," I say.

His lips tip up. "You first."

I do, conscious that my chest isn't quite as perky as it used to be. What if he's expecting something different? On the show, they made us all look better than we do in real life. Any blemishes were brushed away, any perceived imperfections banished by the super power of editing...and, in the last season, an insulting chest double who was ten years younger than me. They said it was to protect my modesty, but they certainly hadn't given a shit for my modesty until then. In real life, there's no editing away your imperfections.

But Rafe utters another swear, then leans in, his big body between my legs, and lavishes my breasts with kisses, his mouth circling one and sucking while his hand pays attention to the other. He switches, and I let my head tip back as the pleasure of his touch spirals through me.

"You're beautiful," he says, pulling back but pushing my legs wider. I'm splayed open for him, his for the taking. "You've heard that from everyone, but now you're going to hear it from me."

"You're beautiful too," I say. "Now take off your shirt. I don't like waiting."

I watch as he pulls it off, his muscles bunching, and a sigh escapes me when his chest comes into view. I've seen a lot of good-looking men. I've slept with some of them, I've acted with others, and with some I've done both. But there's something different about him. Something that makes me feel untamed and wild and needy. His tattoo is beautiful, the ink whirling around his chest to make up that tree. There's no time to study it like I want to, because he buries his head between my legs like he'd promised and lays an open-mouthed kiss there before he licks around my clit and the sucks it into his mouth. I grab his short hair, wishing it were longer for a better handhold, and press him closer. I need more of him, and I don't care if he knows it.

I can feel him laughing, just a little, but he doesn't stop. He sucks harder and then runs his tongue across my opening, tasting me, and my hand falls back, because the pleasure is pounding through me now, my near orgasm from earlier on the cusp of overwhelming me if not rendering me unconscious. Then he joins his hand with his mouth, fucking me with his fingers while he sucks my clit, and I'm a goner. I flex my hand in his hair while the first waves of pleasure wash through me. "Oh my God, Rafe, yes. Just like that."

He keeps pulling pleasure from me like it's one of those trick scarves. It feels like there's no beginning and no end, and this moment will stretch on forever. I definitely want it to.

Then the buzzer rings, indicating there's a visitor at the front desk.

I don't know who they are, but I hate them.

"Let's ignore it," I say as he lifts his head and looks at me, those eyes so dark and full of promise.

"Let's not," he says. "What if it's Nutsack with news?"

"Do you really think that's likely?" I ask, reaching down to touch him through his shorts.

He grits his teeth. "We said no one would know," he tells me. "That means we act normal."

His words are like a cold bucket of water upended over my head. He's right, but I was so lost in the moment that I'd honestly forgotten.

"Oh," I say. "Okay."

Then I look down at myself, naked, my hair a mess around my shoulders. What does my face look like?

"I can't answer the door like this."

He grunts. "I will." Then he pulls on his T-shirt, hiding away his sculpted chest and tattoos.

"What about that?" I glance at his very impressive erection through those maddening shorts, and my mouth goes dry.

"I'll take care of it," he says. "Otherwise it's not going to go away. Go into the bathroom."

"I want to watch."

I expect him to tell me no, but the buzzer rings again, and he pulls down his shorts and fists his dick. He watches me as he strokes himself, still on his knees by the bed, and I reach down to touch myself, thinking he'll come faster if I give him a little show. Thinking I'm already turned on again, by that ringing bell and the sight of him pleasuring himself while he stares at me.

He swears and his fist pumps faster. "Are you touching yourself because you want my cock?" he asks as he moves his hand, his eyes feasting on me.

"Yes," I say. "*Yes.*"

"I'm hard for you," he admits. "It wasn't just morning wood. It's been like that all night."

I slide a finger into myself, and he makes a guttural noise as his hand moves faster around his cock. The pumping sound fills the air between us, and it's so decadent, so dirty, I'm on the verge of coming again. So is he, I'm guessing.

I do it without thinking. I get down onto the floor next to him and shove his hand aside. "That's mine." Then I lower down and take the head of his cock into my mouth.

"Clay," he says, but it doesn't sound like an objection. It sounds like he very much approves. I stroke down, taking him in deeper, although he's big and if I went any deeper than this, I'd choke. It only takes a few passes of my mouth before his body stiffens. "Stop," he says, "I'm going to come."

But I don't stop. He shudders and comes into my throat, and I swallow it down. I'm not sure why, but I wanted to.

The buzzer rings again, and I pull away. "You can go out now," I say. He surprises me by kissing me once, hard. Then he gets up and leaves the room without looking back.

I'm shaken. I'm satisfied...and yet I'm not. I told him we'd do this once and never look back, but we didn't do it thoroughly, did we?

Will he agree to finish later? I won't be satisfied until I have his cock inside of me. Then maybe it'll feel like we finished what we started.

My mind is a million miles away as I quickly go through my morning routine.

Okay, it's not quick. It takes twenty minutes, even sped up, but by the time I leave the room, I'm put together. I'm the Sinclair Jones who can take on the world, not the Sinclair who woke up in the night, terrified. Not the Sinclair who just lost control.

I hear voices out in the living area when I leave my bathroom, and I step out of my room to see Rafe. He's with Edgar James.

Oh, shit. Rafe's face is glistening slightly, as if my arousal is still on him, and as he watches me he licks his lips, causing molten heat to instantly well in my core.

"Sinclair," Edgar says, "are you okay?" He hurries up to me and touches my arm, and it feels all wrong. In that moment, I'm smacked with the realization that it's always felt wrong when he's touched me or flirted with me for the cameras. "You look a little flushed. I heard about last night. You weren't answering your phone, and I had to see if you were okay. I was worried."

There's a note of chiding in his voice, as if he's my real boyfriend and I did him dirty by not filling him in on the night of the many Biebers. I'm instantly annoyed by it, especially since he seemed less interested in me than a cup of layered dirt before the incident with the just-a-rock. It's like I've become interesting to him just because someone else finds me interesting.

The stalker, I mean. Not Rafe.

It's possible he senses something has changed between Rafe and me, of course, but I don't think Edgar has the emotional range—or the interest in me—to detect such a thing.

Rafe nods to the dining room table, where a large arrangement sits, Rue perched beside it with great interest. "He brought you flowers." There's an edge to his voice, like maybe he'd prefer to throw the flowers into the compost bin.

"Oh, how nice, EJ," I say, because he's giving me an expectant look and that's probably what I should say.

Rafe heads over to the shoe rack and grabs his sneakers.

"Where are you going?" I blurt, horrified by the thought of him leaving.

"I'm going down to the gym," he says. "I'll leave you *lovebirds* alone to talk." But his eyes skewer into me before he goes. "Text me before he leaves. You shouldn't be alone right now."

So why do I feel exactly that way—alone, *bereft*—the moment he walks out the door?

RAFE

I CAN STILL TASTE HER. I can still feel her soft lips wrapped around my dick.

Shit, this wasn't just a bad idea, this was the worst idea in the history of people having shitty ideas. Lifting weights isn't helping. I can't stop thinking of her upstairs with Edgar James, who seems to have picked the worst time to form an interest outside of rocks.

I'm pissed at myself for leaving them together, but didn't she tell me it was just going to happen this once? I can't get hung up on it happening again. Or the memory of her swallowing my cum. But I'd be a liar if I didn't say I liked it that I had her taste in my mouth when I answered the door for him...when he asked me to tell it to him straight, what had happened with "his girl"?

It's ludicrous, but the words that ran through my head were *She's mine, rock fucker.*

I don't have a problem with Edgar James, or at least I didn't until recently, but he's no match for her. She's complicated and funny and deeper than the beautiful puddle I thought she was when we met over a month ago. She's too good for him.

Sweat drips down my back, collecting in my shirt, as I keep lifting. As I watch the clock again. Minutes drip by, my mind a storm of shitty and shittier thoughts.

What are they talking about?

What will she do if he tries to kiss her?

A week ago, the answer would have been obvious. She was always as sweet as that stevia crap when he was around, as if she were silently begging him to like her. Nothing like the firecracker who always had a snide comment for me. But now...

I'm in over my head. This is why I didn't want anything to happen between us. I haven't even fucked her properly, and already she's become an obsession. One I probably won't get to indulge in again.

Like it would be possible to forget about this. It's chipped into my mind like a message into stone.

My phone buzzes with a text. It's only been fifteen minutes, and I normally work out for much longer, but I'm off the bench and on my feet in an instant when I see it's her.

He's about to leave, Rafe, but Marnie just showed up. She says she's skipping work and wants to spend the morning with me for emotional support before lunch with my birth basket.

Birth basket?

Marnie's friend Andy suggested it. She says she doesn't deserve to be called our mother.

Birth basket it is.

I'm relieved. I'm disappointed. Edgar James is leaving, but we're obviously not going to pick up where we left off. I had about a dozen different fantasies to make my way through before the morning ended, and we only brought one of them to life.

Still.

I'm coming up.

Finish your workout, Rafe. We're fine.

Does Marnie know how to disarm a six-foot-tall man?

The stalker didn't look six feet tall. We saw him on that bike.

Maybe he'll be wearing stilts. Answer the question.

No, but maybe you should teach us.

Her words hit me like a sledgehammer, because shit, she's right. Why hadn't I thought about that before now?

To be fair, up until this week, the stalker was very much background noise. A potential threat, but a distant one. It had even seemed possible the guy had given up on the stalking business and decided to go into, I don't know, arranging some of those dead flowers and selling them at Halloween. But still, Sinclair and Marnie should know how to protect themselves.

Even though I don't plan on leaving Sinclair alone, or at least alone without someone who can help defend her, I can't be there every second. And a second's all it would take.

My teeth clench at the idea, and I text her back even as I wipe off the machine and leave the gym.

You're right. I'm coming.

I like to hear you say so. ;-)

Damn, she really is going to kill me.

———

While I lead them through some basic self-defense moves in the open space between the back of the couch and the open kitchen, the cat sitting and watching us from the top of the cabinets, Clay and Marnie and I go over the rest of Clay's craft teachers. Other than Spencer, none of them ring any alarm bells.

After the lesson, Clay goes into her en suite bathroom to change back into her armor. Marnie stays. She looks at me, propping a hand on her hip. "So…"

"If you're expecting me to fill in the blank, you'll be waiting for a long time. I have no idea what you're about to say."

She gives me a look of exasperation, looking so much like Clay, I nearly laugh. "You like my sister."

Is it that obvious?

"What's not to like?" I say, leaning on the back of the couch. I don't put my weight on it, because the last thing I need is for it to give out, making me look like a real dumbass.

"You know what I mean," she says in exasperation. "You *like* her."

"You just said the exact same thing twice."

She keeps her gaze on me.

I sigh and grip the back of the couch with both hands. "She's growing on me. Blame Stockholm Syndrome."

A corner of her mouth lifts up. "Don't give all the credit to Stockholm Syndrome. There's more to her than she lets most people see. She's let *you* see. It's another sign of how much she's changing. Six months ago, she wouldn't have…" She trails off, obviously recognizing that the rest of her sentence might be objectionable to me.

I laugh. "What? Would she have kicked dirt at me? Pushed me off a moving train?"

"Let's not exaggerate," she says with an eye roll that also reminds me of her sister. "She was just going through a slightly cunty phase. It happens to the best of us."

"A slightly cunty phase, huh?" I ask, rubbing my scruff. I wonder what Clay was like back then. Proud. Beautiful. The kind of woman who'd live inside of a diamond, like I joked about with Shauna, just to make sure that her appearance was flawless in every surface. I think again of the way she was this morning, rumpled with those pillow lines on her cheek, slight circles under her eyes. She looked more beautiful than any diamond, and yes, I'm ashamed of my own sentimentality.

"Slightly. Anyway, who could blame her? My mother is toxic enough to make everything she touches toxic, and they spent, like, all of their time together. Not the kind of thing someone can walk out of unscathed."

Ah, I see what this is.

"You're telling me to watch out for her today."

"I think it could fall within the purview of your bodyguard duties, yes," she says. "A person's mind can get even more messed up than their body."

"You're telling me." I nod. "If your mother causes trouble, I'm not above bodily removing her from the restaurant and shoving her onto the closest bus headed out of town."

She grins. "I think I like you, Rafe."

"I think I like you too."

"And you *definitely* like my sister."

It's a leading remark if ever I've heard one, but I'm not the sort who likes getting led. "Like I said, what's not to like?"

Clay emerges from her bedroom then, even more shellacked than earlier, in a different dress than earlier. It's that same shade of purple she told me she hates. It brings out the gold in her hair and hugs her tits as if it likes them as much as I do, but I'm sorry to see it nonetheless. She should be wearing something she likes, for one thing, and the woman I woke up with earlier, hot for me and not at all ashamed of it, is nowhere in sight. Every bit of her is perfectly groomed. She's still beautiful enough to stop traffic and cause a pileup, but I don't like seeing her like this. Like she's performing even though she's not on any kind of job.

"Are you wearing that?" she asks me.

Well, maybe she's still in there after all.

"They're clothes," I say. "Didn't see the point in dressing up for a chicken shack."

"Wait," Marnie says, her eyes wide. "You're bringing our birth basket to a chicken shack?"

"Clay likes fried chicken," I say, hoping she'll soften.

"They have salads," she says.

Marnie gives me a look, and her words echo through my head. *My mother is toxic enough to make everything she touches toxic.*

"What do you want me to wear, Clay? A suit?" I smile at her, trying to silently communicate that we're in this together, even if that's not completely true. When it comes to family drama, you're always in it alone, to a degree, because it hits everyone differently. Take these two, for example. Marnie's over it. There's nothing left in her that sees her mother as her mother, but Clay's not. There's a part of her that still longs for the kind of approval she's never going to get. "You want me to dress up like a banana? I'll do it if you ask nicely. I'd even put on a purple shirt."

She touches her hem self-consciously. "It's... She says it's my best color."

All the more reason not to wear it for her, but I can't tell her how to approach this meeting.

"No, it's fine," she says. Her gaze slowly skates over me, taking in the collared shirt I'm wearing, my jeans. "It's good."

The way she says it is a little husky, and it stirs my blood.

Her gaze lifts to the clock across from the couch, which is one of those abstract pieces that, at best, allows someone to broadly esti-mate the time. "We've got to go."

Marnie smiles. "You guys have fun. I can't wait to hear about it tonight!"

Clay flinches a little, like she forgot about her family dinner. Maybe she did. A shit ton has happened since those arrangements were made, not to mention her focus seems to be on this lunch. Her hair is arranged in perfect waves, and I have an impulse to muss it up.

"What do you want us to bring?" she asks.

"Wine," Marnie says. "Maybe two bottles. Or three. Three could be good. Aunt Helen is driving me nuts. She met this lady at a tea shop downtown who did a crystal reading for her, and now that's all she can talk about."

"We can do that," Clay says. Then she surprises me, and apparently Marnie, by stepping forward and drawing her into a tight hug.

Marnie draws away and gives her shoulders a squeeze before letting her hands drop. "Tell Mom to go screw herself for me, will you?"

"I will," she says with a small smile. "But I'm not going to lead with it. I want to see what Nicole has planned first."

Marnie grins. "Yeah, so do I. Take video footage of the whole thing if at all possible."

"It's better if there's no evidence to be used against us," I say.

I'm joking. I think.

But I meant what I said to Marnie—I'm not going to let anyone mess with Clay, not her body or her mind. Maybe she's not mine, maybe she'll never be, but I'm going to watch out for her as if she were.

fifteen

SINCLAIR

I HATE MY MOTHER.

I want my mother to think I'm successful, stunning, and above reproach. I want her to look at me and think, *Well, shit, she's doing better without me.*

What this means is that I want the approval of someone I hate… and I hate myself for that. I also hate myself for having spent so long in the bathroom mirror, applying makeup and fixing my hair with the styling tool my mother chose for me, because *you're a star, Sinclair—no one wants to see a star with hair that looks like it was snaked out of someone's drain.*

Rafe and I go downstairs with Marnie, which is good, because I don't think I can be alone with him right now. My skin is too thin, as if it's been turned into plastic wrap, and he's always known just where to poke it. I also don't know what to make out of what happened between us. This morning…it was the hottest experience of my life, but when I looked in the mirror afterward, getting ready for whichever hated visitor had interrupted us, I didn't recognize myself. I looked like a stranger, mussed and undone, completely out of control.

I looked *happy.*

Then there's Edgar. He seems genuinely concerned about me, and after Rafe left the apartment, granting me one final look at his magnificent ass, Edgar urged me again to come out to location with him next week.

"Jill was right earlier. I want you where I can take care of you," he said, as if he somehow missed the part where we're not actually interested in each other. "Come on Monday. That'll give everything time to come together."

I asked him about inviting my brother, and he said he'd love to get to know him better. Then he said something else that caught me completely off guard. "You know, I've become quite fond of you, Sinclair. I—"

Which was when the buzzer rang again—this interruption more welcome than the last, because it was Marnie, and also because I figured it would cut him short.

But let it never be said that a ticking clock could come between Edgar James and the rare occasions when he had something to say, because he took one of my hands and said, "I think we should spend more time together. Just the two of us. We can take some hikes away from the cameras. The sunrise is beautiful above the mountains. We can go on a sunrise hike, maybe bring some breakfast."

"But the stalker," I said, feeling a powerful compulsion to drop his hand, as if it were a spider that had descended onto me from the ceiling and not the tanned, masculine hand of a very good-looking man. "What if he follows us?"

"We'll take your bodyguard," he said as if it were obvious, and then Marnie knocked on the door and I *did* drop his hand and back up.

"That's an interesting idea," I told him.

It wasn't. The thought of going on a "romantic" outing with Edgar with Rafe tagging along...it does things to my brain and body. In a bad way, to be clear. And not just because I have no desire to go hiking at the crack of dawn, or any time at all.

EJ didn't try to continue the conversation after Marnie showed up, but now I'm back to thinking it would be a bad idea to join him on set, even if it would be good for both of our careers. I might have been interested in Edgar in the beginning, when I first agreed to the arrangement, but that ship has sailed. Or, more accurately, that just-a-rock has been thrown.

I don't want him anymore, so of course, he has started wanting me.

At the same time, I *did* sign a contract to make a few appearances on the show, and if I go for a few days next week, I won't have to go back.

"So," Rafe says as Marnie drives away in her car, ripping me from my thoughts, "I should probably show you this."

My heart starts thumping. Is he going to pull out his dick? What will I do if he does?

My logical mind kicks in the next second, telling me we're in a parking garage and Rafe's not a flasher. This is about something else. "What is it?"

He lifts his phone screen to me, and my face slips into a scowl when I see Penn's Twitter handle at the top, @ThePennisPowerful. Yup. He gets a lot of direct messages from porn stars and never understood why.

Who else thinks Sinclair is lying about this "stalker" to make herself look relevant?

"He's an asshole," I say heatedly.

"Definitely. He might also be saying that to take the heat off himself. I texted it to Nicole and Damien, and she was offended that I thought she might not have seen it yet."

"Sounds like Nicole."

"What'd EJ say earlier anyway?" He gives me a sidelong glance that I feel down to my toes. "Did he invite you to be a founding member of an igneous rock club?"

I give him a pointed look. "There's nothing wrong with rocks. One saved you the other night, if I remember correctly."

We walk over to my car, and he opens the back door for me. He shuts it behind me, and moments later, he's in the front seat, peering at me in the rearview mirror. "So it *was* a rock club," he says, but there's no amusement in his voice. If anything, he sounds...

"Are you jealous?" I blurt.

"Why would you think that?" he asks tightly, pulling out of the parking spot. "Nothing happened, remember?"

Oh, I remember all right. I can still feel his mouth between my legs. I'd like to feel other parts of him there too. But it's ridiculous to be lusting after my bodyguard at a time like this, when I'm being stalked and am about to have a dreaded reunion with my mother.

Maybe he's just a distraction, suggests a voice in my head.

It sounds perfectly reasonable, so I'm not sure why I say, "Less happened than I would have liked, that's for sure."

God, what happened to my filter? Then again, it's never worked quite right around him.

I look up as he scans my key card at the gate, and he's smirking. He's put on his sunglasses, because of course he has.

"You sure have a mouth on you," he says with plenty of insinuation.

"You didn't seem to mind earlier."

A grunt-slash-laugh escapes him, and he says, "No, Sinclair, I didn't mind at all."

The huskiness of his voice vibrates through me, but I just wiggle in my seat slightly and say, "That's Clay to you."

His lips lift. "Yes, *ma'am.*"

His phone rings, and he ignores it. It stops, then starts ringing again. He looks like he still plans on ignoring it, but I say, "You have a thing about bells. You should probably answer that."

"I don't want to talk while I'm driving you," he says, his tone grave. "It's my father. I'll call him back later. He's probably calling to tell me he burned my place down."

"Wouldn't that make you more inclined to answer him?" I glance out the window as we pass through downtown on the way to the highway. There are people everywhere. A chill runs down my spine at the thought that any one of them could be my stalker.

"No," Rafe says. "If the apartment burned down, it'll still be a pile of ash by the time I get back to him."

"What if he fell down and can't get up, like in one of those commercials?"

"Do you know any of the people who starred in those commercials?" he asks. "I'd like their autograph."

"Very funny, and no, unfortunately."

"If my dad fell down and can't get up, he can use the Life Alert I bought him."

"Seriously?" I ask, surprised.

"Maybe," he says with a small smile.

We're quiet for a few minutes, both of us wrapped in our own thoughts, but it's not an uncomfortable silence. It's just a thick one. Because at least a third of my thoughts are about *him*. Finally, he pulls into the lot attached to the restaurant, a nondescript brick building with a tin roof and a sign with a chicken breathing fire, and parks. Before he gets out, he unfastens his belt and turns to look at me in his seat. "Remember, Clay, we were all born knowing to breathe. That woman certainly didn't teach you. You'll be fine. And if you're not, I'll kick her ass."

A laugh breaks free from my lips. "No, you wouldn't."

He grins back at me. "No, I wouldn't. But I *will* give her a very severe look. I'm known for my severe looks."

"You'd have to lose the sunglasses."

"I'll do it if the situation calls for it. That's when you'll know I'm getting down to business."

I want to kiss him. I want to make him a medal.

No, let's be honest, I'd buy it.

I want to...

But we're here, out in the open, where we could be seen by the stalker or any passersby, and I'm in a fake relationship with Edgar James. If I were seen kissing my bodyguard, it would be a mess for everyone—for me, for EJ, for Enoch, *and* for Rafe.

He clearly doesn't give two shits what other people think of him, but he also doesn't seem like a person who bathes in the spotlight. All the more reason we should forget what happened earlier.

So I keep my lips to myself and unfasten my belt. "Thank you."

"Just doing my job," he says, and even though it sounds like an offhanded remark, one he doesn't particularly mean, I still feel it as a jab.

He gets out and comes around to open my door.

I get out too, and then we're walking toward the restaurant. It amuses me to think of my mother regarding the chicken sign with horror, but even so, fried chicken has never felt so much like doom. At least I'll have Rafe and Nicole there, I tell myself. At least I won't be dealing with my mother alone.

Before we get to the door, Rafe turns to me, his tattoo peeking out of his shirt as if to wave. "Order whatever you like," he says, his voice intense, "and eat it in front of her. If she says anything, I'll bribe the chef to spit in her dry salad."

"You just want to hear my french-fries sound," I tell him, but I'm pleased by this evidence he's on my side, if there are sides to be chosen.

"I always want to hear your french-fries sound," he says, his eyes smoldering behind those glasses. "You can be one tough bitch when you want to be, Clay. Be one now."

I feel a pulse of need between my legs, but I ignore it, and when he opens the door, I suck in a deep breath, let it out, and walk in.

Here goes nothing.

SINCLAIR

WE CALLED EARLIER and made arrangements with the staff—two tables next to each other, in the far corner of the small restaurant. This way Rafe can sit next to us, angled so he can see both the front entrance and back exit.

The whole place smells of fried chicken. It smells delicious, in other words, and my mother will hate it. She'll be complaining of the oil in her pores for days to come.

Nicole and my mother are already there when we arrive, and my mother gets to her feet, beaming at me, and opens her arms. I can tell she's had work done, and I can almost feel the prick of the Botox needle from the last time she convinced me it would be fun to get mother/daughter Botox. It's as if she thinks I've forgotten she went on national television a month and a half ago and told America that I got fired from my TV show because I'm a drug addict and all around mess of a human being.

I feel myself physically recoiling, but Rafe brushes his fingers against the small of my back, a silent encouragement no one can see, and I remember what he said outside.

You can be one tough bitch.

Yes, I can.

I ignore the would-be hug *and* the open seat next to my mother and settle into the chair beside Nicole, who's wearing a blond wig and a nose prosthesis that really *does* make her look like a different person. I never would have known it was her if not for the look of delighted mischief in her eyes. This seat has the added benefit of giving me a view of Rafe, who lowers into a chair at his table with those glasses still covering his eyes. He lifts one finger to the bridge to remind me of his promise that if the glasses come off, things are getting real.

"Darling," my mother says, sitting down and pretending the missed hug never happened. The only sign she's displeased is the slight press of her lips when she closes her mouth. She's dressed in a dark blue skirt suit. "You're wearing your best color. You look lovely."

"Mother," I say, hating that I wore this for her.

"Will EJ be joining us?"

"I didn't ask him," I say. "And who's your guest?"

Her mouth gives another small press of displeasure, then she beams at Nicole. "This is Molly O'Shea. We've been corresponding for weeks. She's interested in turning our story into a book."

My mouth falls open. I could swear I hear Rafe's swallowed snort at the other table, and if he took those sunglasses off, I'm sure there'd be a look of amusement in his eyes.

I take a breath, then say, "Oh? And what are her qualifications?"

"Sinclair," my mother snaps. "That's rude."

"Oh, I don't mind one bit, Judy," Nicole says. "I'm a big fan, Sinclair. Huge. Writing this book is my *dream*. I used to work for a dating blog," she says, lifting a hand, "but don't let that put you off. I've also written a couple of novels and biographies, and your story is a *dream*. Why, you're the Justin Bieber of your generation—a mother, lifting a child to fame. A child, rising to the occasion." Then her face twists into a pantomime of horror. "Oh, I'm *so* sorry to bring up bad memories. I'd forgotten..."

She trails off, and I struggle to contain a laugh. She's a good actress.

"Yes, I've been so frightened for you, dear," my mother says. She sounds like she means it, but she's a good actress too. She's told me so since before I could remember. If she hadn't gotten pregnant with my brother at a young age, the story goes, she would have moved to Hollywood, and she'd be the one with her hands in cement on the Walk of Fame, a hurdle I passed a few years ago.

"Yes," I say. "It's been frightening, but Rafe's good at getting me out of dangerous situations."

"Rafe?" my mother says.

"My bodyguard," I tell her, nodding to him. He salutes.

"I've been meaning to talk to you about him," my mother says, acting as if we have daily catch-up chats and this isn't the first time we've seen each other in months.

"Oh?"

"Shouldn't you be working with a professional? Someone from an agency?" She turns to give him a dirty look, as if he's an appliance that has misfired rather than a person, and a raw feeling of hate wells within me. "You should get someone with an earpiece. Someone who blends in more with the scenery."

"I can hear every word you're saying," Rafe says flatly from the other table. "Can you try to get me fired when I'm not within hearing distance?"

My mother gives me a look as if to say, *This is what I'm talking about.* She doesn't acknowledge him, though, or even look at him again.

"I like him," I say. "Enoch says it's better that he doesn't blend into the background. It'll give the stalker second thoughts."

Except maybe she doesn't want the stalker to have second thoughts. Maybe she wants him to have easy access to me, because the more terrified I am, the more I'll need her.

She's always tried to convince me that I need her.

"I also wanted to talk to you about Enoch," my mother says, her mouth in a thin line again. "Are you sure he has your best interest in mind, dear? I've heard he was fired from Parker Brand Management, an ugly business, and John Parker has made it clear that only a fool would work with him."

"So I guess I'm a fool," I tell her. I could also say that John Parker, Grace's father, is a shitty, manipulative person who deserves to get a hard push off a high place, but then again, he and my mother would probably get along.

"Well," my mother says thinly, "I wanted to introduce you to Molly. I was hoping we could get this project off the ground. She'll need our full cooperation, of course. I've already provided her with photos."

A feeling of violation wraps around me, an old and unwelcome shroud. I have no doubt Nicole drummed up some fake credentials to back up her story, but my mother still sent her private photos of me without my permission. Without even telling me.

"How interesting," I say.

Nicole taps her chin. "Can I record our conversation, gang? I don't want to miss a minute of this lunch. I think we're about to create some real memories."

"I don't mind if you don't, Mother," I say.

"Of course not," she says, patting Nicole on the arm. "You do what you think is best."

Nicole gets her phone set up and lays it on the tabletop next to a little statue of a rooster with bug eyes.

Just then, the waiter walks up with menus. She has long dark pigtails and blue eyes and is wearing a T-shirt with the same fire-breathing chicken from the sign on it. "Welcome to Cluck-Clucks," she says brightly, then hands out laminated menus. "I'm Amber, and I'll be your server. Have you been here before?"

"No," my mother says tightly. "I can't say I have."

"Oh, you're in for a treat," the woman says excitedly, playing with the end of one pigtail. "We're famous for our fried chicken and waffles. They have a special spicy syrup we serve with them." She kisses her fingers and then lifts them to the air. "It's a Cluck-Clucks special, and let me tell you, it's practically an orgasmic experience." She gives my mother a bawdy wink, and the knowledge of how much it must horrify her is an elixir.

"Sold," I say, eyeing Rafe at the other table as I hand back the menu. "One of those for me."

"Sinclair," my mother chides.

"I'll have the same," Nicole says.

My mother glances at the menu, then gives it back to the server with a disdainful look. "It's sticky."

"Oh, sorry about that," the server says. "It's that spicy syrup. Gets onto everything. Would you like to get the special too?"

"No. I'll have a salad, dressing on the side."

"Would you like the Cluck-Clucks fried chicken salad or the taco salad? The bowl is one hundred percent edible." She scrunches her nose. "Although I wouldn't recommend eating it. It gets a little moist, and not in a good way."

"Is there ever a good use for the word *moist*?" I say.

"Plain lettuce," my mother insists through her teeth.

"You really want a plate of plain lettuce?" the server asks in disbelief. "It's going to cost you the same. I'd strongly suggest you get the chicken."

"I'll eat your extra chicken," I tell my mother. "I *love* fried chicken. Maybe I'll even take it home in a doggy bag."

My mother gives me a pointed look, and I grin at her.

"Well, all right," the server says excitedly, as if the thought of that bare plate of lettuce was going to give her nightmares, "now we're talking."

She leaves the table, and my mother's still looking at me. "You're angry," she says.

No shit, although leave it to her to think I'm eating only to piss her off.

"I want to hear more about the book, Molly," I say turning to Nicole. I don't know how we're supposed to get back to the subject of the stalker, but I trust that she has some sort of plan. "What are you thinking?"

She grins at me. "I'm so glad you asked. I figured we'd start at the very beginning. What got you in to acting? What started your passion? I've seen those spinach commercials, of course. The raw talent is...inspiring. After that, you didn't book a big role for several years, just some background work. But then there was the tampon commercial, and let me tell you, I really believed you'd bled through your pants at school."

My gaze skips to Rafe, who tips down his sunglasses slightly, a reminder that he's ready with that scathing look whenever I need it. My mother's not facing him, but I have every confidence he'd make it work.

"Well," I say tightly, my gaze returning to Nicole, "that's a funny story." I glance at my mother, who looks a little unsure, as if I've suddenly become someone she can't predict and she doesn't much like it.

Good.

"I was tall for my age, but I was only ten. I'd never had my period before. She said all of the best actors practiced—"

Here, my gaze finds Rafe again, but he's not smiling like I thought he might be. He looks pissed. It sets my blood ablaze.

I've been going through my memories these last months, looking through my past without romanticizing it, and I haven't liked what I've seen.

Part of the reason I was such a bad sister to Marnie was because I was *jealous* of her. She'd quit; I hadn't. She'd made a life for herself based on interests she'd cultivated over several years of self-exploration. I'd fallen into the only thing I'd known, and fallen hard. The truth is there's a reason why I've hesitated to get in touch with the agents Enoch has recommended to me.

I don't know if I love acting or if I just don't know how to do or enjoy anything else.

I clear my throat and continue, "She colored the seat of my white jeans with red food coloring and sent me to the mall. So I guess you can say I'm a method actor."

"You got the part, didn't you?" my mother says tightly. "And it started a lot of wheels turning for you."

"Method acting," Nicole says. "How *interesting*. Did you practice for any of your other roles? Tell me everything." She sounds as peppy as our server.

"My mother always joked about how ironic it was that I booked that spinach commercial. I hated spinach, but she told me to eat it and I did. I kept making mistakes while they were shooting, so I had to eat four jars. Funny, huh? You know, she always used to tell that story in front of my dad. *He* didn't seem to find it funny, but he didn't stop her either. He didn't tell her no."

"You don't even remember that," my mother says dismissively. "I knew you wouldn't remember. Besides, I think Molly would prefer to hear about your successes. What about *Little Miss Star*?"

Little Miss Star was the competition I entered as a teenager, the competition I *won*—a combination of acting, singing, and dancing. That's what led to us moving to Hollywood. From there, I acted in supporting roles in several movies, most made for TV but some theatrical releases, most notably *Single-Dad Santa*. Then I landed the lead in *Sisters of Sin* in my mid-twenties, already too old to convincingly play the lead. I've been with the show ever since, up until I quit this winter.

I loved working for the show in the beginning. It almost felt like having a real family again, because I worked with the same people every day. But nothing ever changed. The characters didn't age with us, and the plot kept following the same tired formula that everyone liked too much for them to take risks or make changes. But *I* grew. *I* changed. I wanted...something, but I didn't know what it was. I still don't. I guess what I wanted most of all was to feel that I was someone beyond the roles I played and costumes I wore.

"My mother likes to talk about how I made my own costume for *Little Miss Star*," I say, looking at Nicole but *feeling* Rafe. He's watching me. Listening. In a weird way, that's what makes me bold enough to go on. He's the only man I've ever known who's made me feel this strong. "But I don't know how to sew. My aunt Helen made it for me. My mother said it was much too long, though, so she brought it up seven inches to show off my legs. They were always long, and she said it was my best feature. I needed to show them off. And you know what?" I look at her, her eyes chips of ice. "You were right, Mom. That judge—you know the one, he had dyed black hair —told me I was going to be a star. He said it while he had his hand on my ass. You'll remember. You were there."

"Interesting," Nicole says, "*very* interesting. These little personal details are exactly what I was hoping to include in the book." She waves her hand through the air. "A behind-the-scenes look at what success really requires. This will do very nicely. People will be talking about it everywhere."

"My daughter's joking," my mother says flatly. "Molly will want to hear about what it was like to win, Sinclair. That's the kind of thing people want to read. The thrill of success after working so hard."

"Oh, no," Nicole says. "They'll want the ass grabbing. You'll be surprised by how many books a good ass grabbing will sell. Did anyone else grab your ass?" she asks, planting her elbow on the table and her chin in her palm. Her gaze is on me, as if my mother has ceased to exist, and the frozen smile on my mother's face says she knows it. "This is getting good. If you have a list, go ahead and share it. Don't keep us in suspense, though. Start with the most objectionable."

"The guy who played my dad in that big Christmas movie I was in took my virginity just after I turned eighteen. I told my mother he'd been hitting on me, and she said that he had connections and it wouldn't be a bad idea to give him what he wanted." My lips lift at the corners. "I wasn't really ready, and he was thirty-five, but he got me a role in my next movie, so again, I guess it was good advice. Go, Mom."

"Fascinating," Nicole says. "This is real gold, right here. I can already see the headlines. '*Single-Dad Santa* is a pervert, and her mother knew.' Why, that right there will sell books. Hello, *New York Times* bestseller list." Her eyes are shining, and it strikes me that this is somehow what she wanted.

My mother grabs Nicole's phone and stops the recording. Then she throws the phone at Nicole, who easily catches it.

"Why, Judy," Nicole says with a feigned gasp. "I'm shocked. *Shocked*, I say. You told me you wanted this to be a warts-and-all autobiography. Why, just last week, you sent me that long email about your efforts to save Sinclair after she was fired from *Sisters of Sin*. Surely you want it to be a well-rounded book. That means we should include *everything*."

"You're an ungrateful little bitch," my mother says to me in a seething voice, ignoring her. "I *made* you who you are. I did everything to help you succeed."

"Yes," I say, and even though I'm angry too, even though there's still fire pumping through my veins, I sound sad to my own ears as I add, "Yes, you did." I remember what Rafe said about breathing, and I suck in a deep one and then let it out. I'm very conscious of him at the table next to us, watching all of this go down. Rooting for me. "And now it's time for me to recreate myself," I add. "If you're the one who's been encouraging this asshole who's stalking me, then you need to stop. If you don't, I'll *make* you stop. And if you say my name to the press one more time, Mother, or Marnie's or Drew's, there's plenty that I have to say too. I'm sure *Molly* here will help me."

"Oh, I'd be *delighted!*" Nicole says, slipping her phone into her pocket, but not before she presses Record again. "There's nothing I like better than a really *juicy* story. Former starlet quits her job and moves to an idyllic mountain town to take up needle art or whatever...sure." She dips her head toward her shoulder, her wig moving like real hair. Whoever does her makeup is good. "It'd sell. But it's nothing on the stories *you* seem to have."

My mother gets to her feet. "Why, you..."

"Did you do it, Mother?" I ask, getting to my feet too. I won't let her tower over me. I'm not a child anymore. I'm not that desperate little girl who'd do anything for her approval and love. Everyone is watching us, soaking this in, but I can't bring myself to care right now. "Did you pay someone to follow me around? I need to know."

It doesn't make a difference, really. She's already done enough. But I still need to know.

"No," she says, spit spraying out of her mouth in a way that would normally horrify her. "But if he hurts you, it'll be no more than you deserve, you little slut."

That's when Rafe gets up, his sunglasses off.

My heart does a little backflip in my chest, because it's obvious he really does mean business.

seventeen

RAFE

"I'LL BE SEEING YOU OUT," I tell Clay's mother. "Sorry you won't get to try your lettuce."

"You won't touch me," she says, her voice shrill. When we came in here, she was cool and collected, probably because she's the person who taught Clay whatever it is that keeps her in the bathroom for ages before she comes out with her shellacked look, but not anymore. She looks like one of the guys who came into the gym for an easy fix and leaves sweaty and defeated after a single personal-training session.

Good.

"No," I say pleasantly, "I imagine you'll want to leave all on your own when you take a second to realize everyone in this restaurant is staring at you and listening in. The picture you're presenting isn't a good look for you. But I *will* make you leave if you insist. You can put up a fuss, of course. You can call the police and try to get me arrested for unnecessary use of force, but people don't get arrested for nonviolently carrying other people. You'll be wasting department resources, and as we both know, they're supposed to be looking for your daughter's stalker." I'm pretty sure Nutman would have me arrested for less, but she doesn't need to know that—or that he

146

could give a shit that we're dealing with a Justin Bieber–impersonating stalker who's smart and motivated enough to use the internet to rally strangers to help him.

"Don't let the door hit you in the ass on the way out," Nicole says, pulling out pins from the blond wing she's wearing.

A gasp escapes Clay's mother. "You're not a real biographer."

"And you're not much of a mother," Nicole says as she tugs the wig off with a flourish. "Let's not quibble over titles. You were going to leave, and Sinclair and I are going to enjoy our lunch."

"You're *her*," Clay's mother says, pointing now. Her voice is accusatory. "You're the woman from that horrible dinner with Marnie..."

"Yes, I've helped both of your daughters. I guess that makes me the family fairy godmother." She winks and then lifts a finger, waving it back and forth in a chiding gesture. "Now, don't get to thinking I'm going to pull fairy godmother duty for *you*, Judy. I *do* have a thing for helping women, but not everyone deserves a second chance. You know, maybe I'll make an exception to my only-women rule and do a solid for Drew. I'm guessing you've fucked him up too."

"Just let her leave," Clay says. She sounds exhausted, like she's been through three rounds of a fight and wants to head home and take the frozen peas out of the refrigerator.

I make a mental note to buy her something chocolate on the way back home.

It barely registers that I've mentally referred to Clay's apartment as home in my head because Judy Jones actually tries to lunge at Nicole, who doesn't so much as fidget in her seat or show any outward sign of fear.

A sound escapes Sinclair, but I've already grabbed Judy around the shoulders and am holding her back. "What's it going to be, Judy?" I ask. "Am I going to have to carry you out the door?"

The fight goes out of her, but I can see enough of her eyes to know they're full of hate.

She's a pretty woman, Judy. Once upon a time, she might have been beautiful. But she's as hollow inside as an empty piñata.

I wonder if breaking her open has brought Clay any closure. From the look of her, it certainly hasn't brought her joy. Only Nicole seems to be having a good time.

"I'll go," Judy says, her eyes darting to Clay. Her voice is shrill and loud, her words coated in cutting ice. "But you're going to regret this, Sinclair. You're—"

Her voice cuts off as I lift her off her feet and start carrying her toward the door like a toddler mid-tantrum. "Put me down," she says, swatting at my hands.

"Goodbye, Mother," Sinclair calls. "We won't be seeing you for the holidays this or any year. You understand."

I keep lugging Judy toward the door, undaunted by the dozens of people watching and snapping pictures. Yes, those photographs might make their way to Nutman, but at this particular moment I don't give a shit. I'm not going to let this woman give Clay a single additional moment of pain. Because even though the tumor has been cut out, Clay will still be feeling the ache of it for years, maybe for the rest of her life. That thought pisses me off so much, I might as well be made of fire.

"Put me down!" Judy yells again, trying to swat at my hands. Her feet kick at my shins, the spiky heels of her shoes digging in. The server from earlier passes us with a broad grin on her face and a platter full of chicken—and lettuce—seemingly the only person in the entire restaurant who isn't watching our every move.

"I will," I tell Judy. "So long as you continue walking in the correct direction. If you try to course-correct back to that table, I *will* forcibly remove you."

I set her down. She makes for the door, but I follow her out.

"Why are you following me, you...you...brute?" she asks. Her color is high now, and it's obvious she's started to realize she's landed herself in some pretty deep shit. There're lots of tilted heads and murmuring. A few people are covertly taking photos, and others aren't even bothering with the pretense.

"Because I want to make sure you leave, Judy," I say. "And because we're going to have some words."

She doesn't look afraid of me, which I'm glad for. I don't want any woman to physically fear harm from me, but I do want her to heed my words—and Nicole's.

When we finally reach the door, I open it for her. She gives an aggravated sniff but steps outside. The door shuts with a click behind us, leaving us alone on the small porch of the restaurant. I'll bet if I turned, I'd see faces pressed to the window glass.

"Let me see you to your car."

"I don't want you to know what I'm driving," she sneers.

"I'm not going to follow you," I say. "I have zero interest in where you've been and where you're going, so long as your path won't cross with hers."

"You think you matter to my daughter?" she asks, spearing me with a cold look. "You think she gives a shit about some hired hand?" Her gaze moves slowly up and down my body, taking me in and finding me wanting. "Sure, you're good looking enough, but they all are. She'll throw you out on your ass in the cold, just like she did to me, her own mother. You just wait, *boy*."

"Where's your car, Judy?" I repeat. I'm not about to respond to her bullshit, even if it does strike home.

"I can tell you have feelings for her," she says. "They all do. You're not special."

"Neither are you," I say bluntly, lifting my eyebrows. "Now let's end this interaction, which I'm guessing isn't particularly pleasant for either of us, and get you off so you can ruin someone else's day."

She gives another sniff and then walks off toward a sleek but nondescript dark blue Lexus. I trail her there and let her open the driver's side door before I say anything else.

"I don't want to see you near her again, Judy. Don't contact her, and don't talk about her to the press. Don't you do *anything* related to Sinclair ever again."

"Or else what?" she asks, turning back to me. Her gaze is shrewd and crafty, and even though her eyes are the same shape as Sinclair's, they couldn't look less like them.

"Or else *Molly* back there isn't the only one who's going to mess up your life." I lift a hand. "I would never physically harm you or arrange for anyone else to, and I hope to God that you're not behind the shitbag who's out for your daughter..."

"I'm not," she says flatly and without any obvious tells.

I'm pretty sure I believe her. Not because doing something like that would be against her moral code, but because she's savvy enough to know she'd probably get caught. For similar reasons, I suspect she'll behave. Clay has dirt on her, and if she ever decides to build a castle with it, people will show up to ooh and ahh and gorge themselves. Nicole figured out a pretty effective way to point that out.

"Good. Like I said, I wouldn't ever hurt you, but I *would* figure out a way to make you regret it for the rest of your days. If you were a better person, you'd regret what you've done anyway—to all of your kids."

It feels good to tell her so, partly because I never spoke my mind to my own mother and partly because I hate this woman for all the things she's done to Clay. The thought makes me bristle and want to punch bricks, even though I'd be walking away with a broken fist. I didn't know Clay back then, even though I saw that damn Christmas movie, but I feel like a failure for not having protected her.

Judy's gaze turns hawkish. "Fuck off," she says, giving me the bird with a manicured finger.

I grin in response, retrieve my sunglasses from my pocket, and stick them back on my face. "Happily, *Judy*, so long as you fuck off too. If I ever see you again, it'll be too soon."

I watch the car leave the lot before I head back into the restaurant.

To my complete lack of surprise, people watch me all the way back to the table, but none of the servers intercept me or try to make me leave. I guess there's some benefit to being associated with famous people. They know I'm here with Sinclair Jones, and they're apparently more invested in making her happy than her manager mother.

My mouth hitches up at the corners when I get within view of Nicole and Clay. They're eating their fried chicken and waffles as if nothing has happened. There's a plate of lettuce in front of the third chair, along with a plate of fried chicken on the side. A blond wig sits on the chair, but Nicole clears it away when she catches sight of me.

"Join us," Nicole says, waving a chicken wing as I reach them and come to a stop next to Clay. "Feast on the bones of our enemies."

Clay twists her mouth in distaste. "I don't want to eat my mother, thank you very much." Her gaze catches on me. "You're welcome to eat her lunch, though. *Thank you.* I don't know what you said to her, but I guess I have some idea." She reaches out and touches my arm, giving me a burst of sensation even though her fingers are pressing so softly through my shirt. "*Thank you.*"

"I gave her one of those looks we talked about," I say, leaning into her touch a little.

"I know you were going to," she says. "You took your sunglasses off, so you obviously meant business." Then she gives me a mischievous look, and her hand darts up to snatch them off my face.

I take them from her, giving my head a small shake, but I'm not mad. Her fixation on my sunglasses amuses me. "Well, she's gone. Between that look and our reporter friend over here, I don't think you need to worry about her darkening your door again."

"Why are you thanking *him*?" Nicole asks with another shake of the chicken wing as I sit in front of the lettuce plate. "This was my plan, start to finish."

"And it was expertly pulled off," Clay says with a small smile, like she's indulging a naughty kid by handing over some candy. "Happy now?"

"Happier," Nicole says through a bite of chicken.

The lettuce looks listless and old. I push it aside and go for the side plate of chicken, taking a big bite.

"I knew you were one of those roast-chicken guys," Nicole says.

"Guilty."

"Seriously, though," Nicole adds after setting her wing down. "Did that not kick ass? I mean, we owned this lunch. *Owned it.*"

I feel a rush of protectiveness, because I can tell from the flash of pain in Clay's eyes that it didn't particularly kick-ass for her. She might be grateful for finally having the closure she needed, and Nicole was kind of a genius for giving it to her, but none of this was *enjoyable* for her.

You don't enjoy being let down by people, even if you know that's all they're capable of. It still hurts.

"Maybe don't be so gleeful that her mother's a piece of shit," I suggest.

"My father's a piece of shit," Nicole says conversationally as she cuts a piece of waffle. She pauses for a bite, gives a hum of pleasure, and then continues, "He walked out on us when I was seven, and I never heard from him again."

"Sometimes it's better if someone leaves than if they stay," I offer.

Clay snaps her head to the side to look at me. I can tell from the look in her eyes that she wants to ask questions, and right now, in this moment, maybe I'd answer them.

"Fair point," Nicole says, nodding as she cuts off a piece of her waffle. "You'd know."

There's insinuation threaded through her words, a sense of knowing.

"*Excuse me?*"

From the look in her eyes, she knows everything about me, probably down to the birthmark on my left ass cheek. Definitely how I came by my bullet wound. There's no pity in her eyes, just the hard look of someone who's a survivor and appreciates it in other people, maybe expects it of them.

She shrugs. "You underestimate how much time your father spends at the bar. We drink together. It's a thing."

Fantastic. Reggie's got a mouth on him. I knew that, obviously, but I didn't think he'd talk about *this.*

He must trust Nicole more than I thought. Either that or he has a more serious drinking problem than I realized.

Nicole gives me a contemplative look. "You know, it's kind of insulting that you think Damien and I wouldn't have found out anyway. We're private investigators. Finding out people's private shit is kind of our thing. Doesn't matter that you changed your name."

"I feel like I'm in the dark here," Clay says, her eyes fixed on me.

"And you'll stay that way." I feel like a shit after saying it, but I don't want to sit here in this restaurant discussing my private business.

Except the voice in my head, which occasionally enjoys calling me out for being an asshole, says, *Isn't that what just happened with her?*

"I'm not hungry," she says, pushing her plate away.

"Are you sure?" Nicole asks as she takes another bite of her food. "Our server wasn't kidding about the spicy syrup. This is really good. Actually, if you're not eating yours, I'm taking it home."

"Go for it," Clay says.

"Let's leave," I tell her.

Glancing away from me, she picks at something on the table before realizing what she's doing and giving her fingernails a horrified look. Spicy syrup, I'm guessing. "All right. Let's."

"Are you leaving me with the bill?" Nicole asks. "Because it sounds like you're leaving me with the bill. I'm good with paying for your chicken and waffles, but I absolutely refuse to pay for that travesty of a salad. My conscience won't allow it."

Before Clay can reach for her wallet, I take out mine and slap some bills onto the table.

"You'll tell us where to meet you tomorrow," I say to Nicole.

"Damien's working out the details with the literary porn star as we speak," she tells me with a grin. "We'll be in touch tonight. Buckle up, my friends, because we're going for another ride. Penn's going to regret those tweets before we're through with him."

Can't wait.

I hope to hell that that spineless little asshole is our stalker, because if not, we're left with the random-stranger theory, which would automatically make everything harder.

Unless it's Spence, and he's gotten a lot better at bike riding.

Or Marnie's ex, I guess.

Sinclair's still not looking at me. Turning to Nicole, she says, "Who's Molly O'Shea?"

Nicole makes a dismissive gesture. "A friend of mine who's a writer. She was cool with the stolen-identity thing."

I'm not totally sure I believe her, but I suppose it doesn't matter.

"Well, thank you," Sinclair says, gathering up her bag and holding it to her chest like it's a bulletproof vest. "I guess I needed that." She pauses before getting up. "Did you really think my mother had hired the stalker? Before we set this up, I mean."

Nicole taps her temple. "I was mostly sure she hadn't, but it's not a certain thing. Won't be until we find out who's really behind it. But that's not why we had this lunch. Fairy-godmothering is a multipronged approach."

I'd figured as much, and Sinclair's nod says she'd cottoned to it too. "*Thank you.*"

"You're welcome, Sin," Nicole says, her expression turning serious—or serious for her. "And believe me when I say we're going to stop this whoever's harassing you too. You've got us on your side, and we're not going to stop until this thing is done."

Sinclair gives another nod, says thank you again, and then starts to leave. I follow her.

We're quiet on the way out to the car, but I know she's just as aware of the looks as I am. The photographs. The gossip.

It's probably not a bad thing for Clay. At least a few people will have overheard part of our conversation, and Nicole's right—they'll be much more interested in the real story than they will in the one her mother is peddling.

She's quiet when we get outside. Quiet when I open the back passenger door of the car and she slides inside. Quiet when I slip behind the wheel. She's never this quiet. This is the woman who started talking about her swinger aunt in her desperation to get Edgar James to engage in chitchat.

"What...are you pissed at me?" I ask, which was objectively the wrong thing to say.

"Why would I be pissed at you?" she snaps back. "*Nothing happened.*"

And then she starts crying.

Well, shit.

eighteen

RAFE

I TURN IN MY SEAT. Tears are running down her cheeks, and sobs are wrenching from her chest. Damn it. I don't like seeing her in pain.

People might still be watching, but I couldn't care less. I slide my seat back as far as it will go and then scoop her up, pulling her onto my lap. She wraps her arms around my neck and sobs into my shirt, her tears soaking it, and all I can do is rub her back like a moron and murmur things to her. I want to fix this. I feel an aching need to, but there's only one person who can piece together the parts of her that were broken by her mother: Clay herself.

"You want to hear something really fucked up?" she says to me in a muffled voice.

"I love hearing fucked-up things," I tell her, rubbing soothing circles into her back. "Hit me with it."

"I hate her more than I've ever hated anyone, but I still love her too. I—" She sobs, her voice breaking, and I squeeze her closer, needing to show her in the only way I can that I'm here, that I get it, and that I care about what she's going through and want to help. "I don't want to ever see her again, but it hurts so bad."

"You feel whatever it is you need to feel," I tell her, running my hands through her silky hair. "You were brave to face her. You're strong. Don't let anyone make you feel otherwise."

She sobs harder, pressing into me, and the feeling of protectiveness that cracks open inside of me is surprising for its intensity. I don't know where it came from. I don't know what to do with it. I just know that I have to help her.

"What do you need, Clay?" I murmur, rubbing her silky hair. "Tell me what would make you feel better. Even a little. Tell me so I can give it to you."

She pulls away slightly, then gasps in horror. I laugh when I see why. Her makeup's all over my white shirt, splotches of black and beige and pink.

"I'm sorry, Rafe. Shit." She lifts a hand to her cheek. "My face must be a mess."

It is, and I know she'll flip a shit the second she sees a mirror, but I'm strangely relieved to see her mussed. It's one more thing to distinguish her from that horror show of a woman.

"You're beautiful," I say. "No one with half a brain would give a shit about your makeup running down your face."

"It's running down my face?" she asks with wide eyes.

I laugh, just a little, then grab a tissue from the center console and start wiping her cheeks. The smears come off easily enough, probably because her face is so wet. I take another tissue and then another and finish. More tears fall down her cheeks, wetting my hand and the final tissue.

"Clay," I say, tracing them with my fingers. "What is it this time?"

"No one's ever done something like that for me before," she says.

I lean in to kiss the place my fingers just traced, and a sigh escapes her. It's a *yes, more of that* sigh, not unlike her french fries sound. My dick twitches, which makes me feel like a tool, because I want to comfort her right now, not fuck her.

Okay, I want to fuck her too. I'd be lying if I said otherwise. I've wanted plenty of women, but never quite in this way.

"I don't want you to feel sorry for me," she says, pulling away slightly. "You don't have any reason to feel sorry for me."

"Who said I do?" I run a hand over her soft, silky hair. "But I *am* sorry you had to go through that shit, and if I could murder Single-Dad Santa and get away with it, I would. Last year would have been his last Christmas rodeo."

She shifts on my lap, which isn't helping my growing problem, then says, "I think you mean that."

"I do, but I'm usually shit at getting away with things. I'd probably get caught, and Nutsack would arrest me and throw away the key."

A smile lifts her lips, and I feel like a god made human for having put it there. I'm greedy, so I instantly want another smile from her, bigger.

"You asked what I want," she says, her gaze flitting out of the window. It's a reminder that we're out here in the open, near a restaurant full of people who watched us and our conversation with her mother. "What could make me feel better..."

"Anything—tell me," I say, even though it's a stupid thing for a person to offer, when "anything" might be unobtainable for them. Just like she shouldn't be obtainable for me.

Taking the fact that she hasn't flinched and sworn a blue streak to mean we're not currently being watched, I trace the side of her face again.

"Take me home, Rafe," she says. "I need a distraction. I need *you*. We got interrupted this morning, so I figure it didn't fully count." Her lips wobble a little. "But I don't want a pity fuck. Don't do it if it's out of pity."

"I don't think you've ever had one of those in your life," I say, my heart thumping faster, my dick very much liking this plan. "What about a victory fuck? Because however hard that was, you came out ahead. You faced your shit, and you owned it."

"I think I'd like that very much."

It would take a stronger man to tell her no, so I tell myself it's not a mistake, or at least not the kind of mistake I can avoid making. I shift her into the passenger seat and fasten the belt for her. Not because she needs me to, obviously, but because it's a small thing I can do to ensure her safety, and I need that for some reason. I need it as much as I need to get inside of her.

We're quiet on the drive back, but she puts her hand on my leg, and that small touch has me as hard as that just-a-rock from Monday.

When we park in the garage, I have the impulse to carry her upstairs, but my logical mind knows I can't. She's supposed to be with Edgar James, not her discount bodyguard. If people see us, there'll be questions. So I just adjust myself and then walk beside her, our hands glancing off each other. There's another couple waiting for the elevator, and we exchange pleasantries so empty I can actually feel them killing my brain cells before we board it with them. They get off on the first floor. I'm tempted to ask if they know about the stairs, but we have five floors to go before we get to the penthouse, and Sinclair Jones is staring at me as if I'm the chocolate cake.

"Looks like you've got a problem over there," she says, giving me a significant look and then dipping her eyes over my body.

"Do you have radar for my hard-ons?"

"Yes," she says and takes a step closer and rubs her palm over it, making me hiss. "You talk a lot about the sounds I make, but what about the sounds *you* make?"

"Do you like them, Clay?" I ask, grabbing her hand and tugging it away. I lift it and pin it to the elevator wall, and she gives me seductive smile that instantly makes me harder.

"Oh, I like them," she says.

I lean in and kiss her, and she tastes like that spicy syrup, so delicious I don't want to stop. Even when the elevator dings to let us know we've reached the penthouse. So after glancing out the open doors to make sure we're alone and there are no more unpleasant surprises waiting for us, I pick her up. She laughs into my mouth, wrapping her legs around my waist, her body pressed to my hard dick. I carry her to the door still kissing her, pausing only to use the key she produces from her pocket.

When we get inside, I lock the door behind us, my mouth still on hers, and then press her back to the door.

She finally breaks away, her eyes hooded and her breath coming in pants. "Are you going to take me here, against the door?"

"Why don't you tell me where you want me and how?" I say, cupping her ass. "This is *your* victory fuck."

She pulls my shirt free of my pants so she can slide her palm beneath it. "Do you mean it?" she asks as she grazes her fingers over my chest, pausing to trace the ridges of muscle.

"I do. The weirder the fantasy, the more shit I'm going to give you about it later, but I'll do it, Clay. Whatever you want."

Her eyes shining, she says, "I have a table in my bedroom that's from the original *90210* set. I've always had this fantasy about—"

I laugh and set her down, her hand still under my shirt. "I'm going to stop you at *you bought a table from the original 90210 set.*" She shoves my chest, which feels pretty damn nice, actually.

"Let me guess, you're Kelly and I'm Brandon—"

"Well, obviously you're not Brandon," she scoffs. "Dylan all the way."

"You're not shitting me? You actually bought that table because you love *90210*?"

She gives a small smile. "I did. I watched a lot of episodes preparing for *Sisters of Sin*. The original *90210* is still royalty in the teenagers-sleeping-around genre."

"That's a genre?" I ask, reaching down for the hem of that purple dress. I want it off of her for many reasons. The primary one is to see her bare for me, of course, but I also don't like that it's a sign of her mother's influence on her. The material is silky, but it's a sheath dress, so I have no trouble pulling it up and over her head. She's wearing a black bra and a thong and gold heels, and I've lost any interest in ever leaving this apartment again. "Is Dylan the kind of guy who'd throw her over his shoulder, or would he carry her like a princess?"

"Definitely the shoulder," she says. "Brandon's the princess-hold type."

"Won't argue with your fantasy, Clay."

I step out of my shoes and then reach for her, slinging her over my shoulder and smacking her ass.

She gives a happy squeal, and as I carry her into the bedroom, I feel like I'm doing something right, even if it's just giving her one of her fantasies. When we get into the bedroom, Rue takes one look at us, leaps off the bed, and scampers into the living room.

Smart cat.

I set Clay down carefully on her heels, and she instantly gets started on my belt. My dick strains for more of her, because the slow sexiness with which she's removing the belt is killing me, and she *knows* it's killing me, which is irrationally even more of a turn-on.

"So which table is it, *Kelly*?"

"Shouldn't you know?" she asks, lifting her eyebrows. "It was from your grandmother's house. If you can't tell, how will I know you're really Dylan and not a Brandon in disguise?"

So that's the way we're playing it, huh?

I look around. There are only a couple of end tables in the room, and one of them has a cup of water sitting out on it, no coaster. No way would she put a cup of water on her precious *90210* table.

"I know where we're going," I tell her, leaning in to kiss the swell of her tits as she finishes with the belt. The bra is sexy as hell, but it'll be even sexier off, so I unclasp it and pull it off, letting it fall to the floor. Yes, much better. I soak in the sight of her in a thong and those high heels, her hair a hot mess tumbling over her shoulders and down her back.

"You're wearing all of your clothes, and all I have on is a thong and shoes," she says, her tone sulky.

"Total Dylan move," I say, then lower my mouth to her tits, sucking one of her nipples into my mouth as she finally finishes with the belt. I reach down, slipping the thong aside, and find her wet for me. I'd wonder if I was dreaming again, but my dreams have never had a *90210* theme. Pulling my head back, I look at her. "What happens next, Kelly?"

"I don't know. Dylan's a man of action," she says her voice low and husky. "I figure he wouldn't ask."

She slowly draws the belt free of its loops and drops it to the ground. She starts unbuttoning my shirt, and I back her toward the *90210* table, my arm around her because she's wearing those heels, and no way in hell am I going to let her fall. When my shirt's open, I shrug it off. Clay's already tugging at the bottom of my tank. I let her pull that off too, then say, "Turn around."

She's practically bouncing in place as she does.

"Put your hands on the table, Kelly. I'm going to fuck you from behind against my grandmother's table."

She swears under her breath as she does, lifting her gorgeous ass to me. I run my free palm over it, then dip my fingers down to move the thong aside. Feeling how wet she is for me makes my dick even harder. I run my fingers forward to her clit, circling it, and she hikes those hips higher for me.

"Do you want my cock, Kelly?"

"Yes, Dylan, I've been dreaming about it. Don't tell Brandon."

I know it's just role-play, I know she's indulging in her fantasy, but my mind flickers to Edgar James for half a second. I remind myself their relationship is fake and this thing between Clay and me is just supposed to be a one-time thing, or a one-and-a-half-time thing, and I'd be a fool to ruin it by overthinking. Then I take off my pants and underwear.

It's only then, with my cock jutting out, that it occurs to me that I don't have a single condom. Why this has only occurred to me now, I don't know, but it's devastating.

I swear, then say, "Kelly, for the love of God, tell me you have condoms."

"I hid them in the table drawer," she says. "I'd get them for you, but I was told to put my hands on this table, and I'm a good girl."

Damn. This woman really does mean to kill me. I get the condom out so quickly that I probably deserve some kind of speed record and open the package and roll it on. She watches me, her eyes focused on what she wants.

I lean in and kiss the side of her neck as I shove the thong to the side again, running my fingers over her opening and then circling her clit before I curl my fingers up inside of her and pulse them. "You like that spot," I say, kissing her neck again, my dick pressed to her ass as I move my fingers. "I could feel your body quaking earlier when I touched you there."

"I do," she says. "You know just how to touch me. Now, show me you know how to fuck me too."

She doesn't need to tell me twice. I line myself up and thrust in slowly, so she can get used to me—and also so I don't end this party prematurely, because I can't remember ever being this worked up. Sinclair has unleashed a side of me that I didn't know existed.

I don't feel like less of a man for admitting it scares me.

"Give me all of you," she demands. Something snaps in me, and I do, thrusting in deep while she pushes back against me, my hand starting in on her clit again, because I don't know how long I can last and I want to make damn sure she comes. At the same time, it feels so incredible to be inside of her that I don't want to leave.

I draw out and thrust back in, hard, and she makes that little throaty sound that drives me wild. My blood is burning, but she wanted to do this role-play thing, and I'm invested in it, for her.

"Shh," I say, covering her mouth with my other hand, "we don't want anyone *upstairs* to hear." There's no one above us but the sky, but that's not the game we're playing.

From the way she pushes her ass up, taking me even deeper, and kisses my hand, she likes that. I release my hand and run it down her neck, catching it in her hair, which I pull back so I can kiss her neck as I thrust in and out. She hums in her throat and leans her head back to give me better access, and when I graze her skin with my teeth, she reaches one hand back and grabs my ass to push me in even deeper. I release her hair, and it waterfalls down over her shoulders and her perfect tits. I brush it aside so I can watch them, touch them as they bob from our movement. "You're beautiful," I say, thrusting. "You're strong." Another thrust. "You're aggravating as hell."

She laughs a little, her body shaking, but then another of those sounds escapes her. I give her ass a light slap since she liked it last time, and she pushes up onto my dick.

"You're right, Dylan, I don't want anyone to know."

She's playing our little game, but the words seep in anyway. I shut down the momentary unease as I keep moving into her, my hand settling on her hip. I want them to be everywhere, my hands—on her clit, on her ass, on her tits. I want to feel her everywhere, especially if this might only happen once. I want the memory to be seared into her brain as much as it's carved into mine. I don't want her to look at this table again without thinking of me fucking her against it.

I—

I feel her tightening around me. "You're going to come for me, aren't you?" I ask, leaning in closer to kiss her neck again, using my hand on her hip to guide my thrusts and deepen them. "I can feel it."

"Give me everything, Rafe," she says, panting. "I want everything. I want you to come with me."

And it's her saying my name that pushes me over the edge. I pump into her hard as she rises to meet me, my hand on her clit, and she squeezes around me so tightly, the sound my name still ringing in my ears, that I have no choice but to give her what she asked for. I come so hard I nearly black out, like I said I wanted her to earlier, but I move my arm to encircle her chest, because I can feel her leaning harder into the table, and she won't be falling on my watch. I hug her body to me.

"You know, maybe I should give that show more consideration," I say.

She laughs, looking back at me with a radiant smile that's graced millions of TVs. "No time like the present."

We clean up and watch an episode of the show in bed—the one where Kelly and Dylan finally give in to their feelings for each other.

When it's over, I turn to Clay. "Felt a lot hotter than that."

"Sex against tables was probably discouraged on set." She switches off the TV and snuggles close. We're both still naked.

"Do you like acting, Clay?" I ask, because it's something I've become intensely curious about. In the beginning, I figured there was no doubt. She was an actress because she loved those bright lights, but I've gotten to know her over the past month, especially over this past week, and it's more complicated than that.

"I don't know anymore," she says with a sigh, her breath warm against my chest. "I thought I did, but now I can't help but wondering if it's just the only thing I know how to do. I don't like that I was cornered into it. It feels...tainted." She moves slightly, so her head is facing me, our eyes meeting. "You want to hear something messed up?"

"Always."

"I think I love and hate it, kind of like how I feel about my mother. But the things I love...maybe it's wrong to love them."

"Why?" I ask, running my fingers over her hair.

"Because I love slipping into someone else's skin."

"Yeah, I wouldn't put it that way if someone asks you about it in a press conference," I joke. "They might get the wrong idea."

She gives me a shove that doesn't move me at all. "Very funny, wise guy. You know what I mean." I nod that I do. "I'm guessing it's wrong to feel that way, to want to be someone else. A therapist would probably have a field day with me."

"Maybe you should talk to one," I say. "See if you can unwind those feelings. Figure out a way to enjoy it for what it is."

She flinches. "You think I'm crazy?"

"I saw a therapist after I got shot," I say with a shrug. "Does that make me crazy?"

"You did?" she asks, so surprised I almost laugh. Almost. She shakes her head. "Sorry. You just don't seem like the kind of person who'd go to one."

"What, because I have muscles?"

"Because you have a *lot* of muscles," she says.

That does make me laugh. She's still nestled against my chest, so she quakes with it.

"Nicole knows what happened," she says, and the laughter dries up. She said it as a statement of fact, but I know it's also a question.

"I'll tell you," I say, "but not yet. It's not easy for me to talk about it."

I expect her to push me, to tell me that I know all of her shit so it's only fair if I give her some of mine, but she surprises me. Instead, she starts tracing the tree on my chest. It tickles, but I'm not about to say so. I'm guessing she'd double down. "What'd you say when you went to the tattoo artist?" she asks. "Did you just ask for a tree, and they drew this one? What if they gave you, like, a really sickly looking tree, or a stupid one?"

I laugh, grabbing up her hand and weaving it with mine. "I drew it, so I knew what it would look like."

"*You* drew it?"

"I like trees," I say, laughing again, this time at the look of shock on her face. "You know...a tree can lose twenty percent of its root system without showing any damage." I squeeze her hand. " Don't look so surprised. I told you I used to paint."

"I guess I figured your paintings might be paint splotches like that Spencer guy was into."

"No, I didn't paint like that. Maybe I should've, though. His stuff sells." I rub my jaw, thinking again about Spence and his bike-riding skills, or lack thereof. That's the kind of thing a person could improve upon, probably. Maybe I'll give him a call this weekend. Or show up at his studio space and scare the shit out of him.

Of course, Clay's going to be with me, so she'd have to be the Bonnie to my Clyde.

Clay releases my hand and abruptly sits up, her eyes glowing with excitement. "Will you paint with me?"

My mind shifts to my dad. To his suggestion that painting worked well enough for Joe or Jack or whatever the hell his name is in *Titanic*.

Then I flash to that phone call from earlier, the one I didn't answer. Maybe I should have picked up, but we were heading into the breach, and nine times out of ten, his calls are requests for me to pick up Cheez Whiz or other heavily processed foods for the refrigerator.

Clay's still looking at me, expectant, and my heart thumps hard in my chest. I'm surprised by how much I want this.

For the first time in ten years, I want to paint again.

With her.

I don't stop to question why, or whether it's intelligent to lean into the feeling. I just ask, "Do you still have materials from your painting phase?"

"Acrylics and some canvases and brushes." She tilts her head slightly. "And an easel and a drop cloth."

I sit up next to her. "Did you go all in like this with all of your hobbies?"

"You know I did," she says, her eyes sparkling.

"Why don't you go get them?" I ask, tucking her hair behind her ear. "And put on some clothes you don't mind ruining. I'll do the same. I need to call my dad back, and then we'll get painting."

"You won't regret it," she says, all excitement.

But in some senses I already do. I'm giving her too much of myself, taking too much of her. It's not going to be easy to remember that this—whatever the hell it is—can't last.

nineteen

SINCLAIR

MY BLOOD FEELS effervescent in my veins. There's a feeling of *anything can happen* that lifts me up. Because I faced my mother today and told her how I really feel. Because I told Rafe what I wanted from him without any games or artifice, and, let's be honest, because I just had the hottest sex of my life.

And now he and I are going to paint together.

When I went to Spencer's classes, he was complimentary, but I only saw what I wasn't doing right. I saw the flower that looked more like a spaceship, the banana that looked like a dick. I'll probably never be much of a painter, but Rafe's right. I can learn to be better at any of these undertakings if I devote myself to them the way I devoted myself to acting. And it will be my decision that gets me there.

Maybe I'll quit acting. Maybe I'll decide to knit hats for the rest of my life in this loft apartment in Asheville or paint bad paintings people will only buy because they were made by that dotty woman who used to be on *Sisters of Sin*.

Or maybe I'll be able to reclaim this thing I've loved and hated, this thing that has so defined my life.

I bet Nicole would tell me to make acting my bitch.

Tomorrow, I'm going to call those agents Enoch referred me to. It's time. And even though it makes my heart race to think of it, maybe Rafe's suggestion about seeing a therapist was on point too. I have friends who've been to therapy, but my mother always acted like it was a dirty word.

I get all of the supplies set up, but when Rafe comes out in a T-shirt and a worn pair of jeans, he's not smiling. There's a heavy look on his face that tells me something's wrong.

"What is it?" I ask, dropping the cup of paint brushes I was holding. "Did he really need the Life Alert?"

He laughs, then scrubs a hand over his short hair, his muscles bunching pleasingly. "No, but he sounds lonely. I'm a little worried about him. And not just because I'm guessing the entire apartment is covered in grease and smells like a corn chip."

"Why don't you invite him to dinner?" I blurt. "I mean, it'll probably be dysfunctional and terrible, but he's more than welcome. He already knows Marnie. Griffin's going to be there too." Marnie told me so earlier, when she stopped by to check on me.

"You want me to invite my father to dinner with your family?" he asks.

Shit. It occurs to me that this might seem needy from his point of view. Does he think it's presumptive of me? Like I'm going to become his stalker because he gave me some good dick and promised to teach me to paint?

It takes me aback, because I realize I've gotten a little worked up over Rafe. He's no longer just the annoying bodyguard who gets my blood boiling. I feel a strange connection to him that I'm not sure I've ever felt with anyone. I feel understood by him, although I'm not so sure I understand *him*. I just know that he's more than he appears to be, the kind of water that you step into thinking it's shallow, but then it engulfs you and threatens you with drowning.

"I didn't mean it like that," I say quickly.

"Too bad," he says, checking out my setup. "Because he would love it. Just be prepared for him to make at least a dozen inappropriate comments."

"Don't forget my swinger aunt," I say.

"Oh, I haven't," he says, taking up one of the palettes I set on the dining room table and starting to fill it with different colors of paint. "And neither has EJ. I'll bet he has dreams about her."

———

We don't talk about what it means.

We don't talk about whether it'll happen again.

Maybe we're both afraid to. Maybe *I'm* afraid to. All I know is that my apartment has come to feel like my safe haven, and it's because of him.

With guidance from Rafe, I paint a sunrise that would probably have people running for their lives if it ever appeared in the sky over their heads. I say as much, and he tells me that's why he likes it. I respond that he can have it, and he says he's going to hang it in his living room.

I want to hang *his* painting in my living room, although that would probably be awkward, because it's of *me*—and more so, of me naked, peering over my shoulder.

Somehow he managed to create that on a canvas propped on a drop cloth on the table. I only have one easel, since I didn't think I was going to have any painting parties, and he insisted that I use it.

I don't look perfect in Rafe's portrait. My hair is a mess of waves, and my coloring isn't even, but I love it. Looking at it fills me with a warmth that I already crave more of. In fact, even though I was looking forward to this dinner with my family, I can't deny that I'd prefer never to leave the loft. I want to stay here with Rafe in this stolen moment and pretend the rest of the world can't touch us.

I'm not naïve, though. The world *does* exist, and it *can* touch us. It will.

Staring at his finished painting again, I press my fingers to my throat. This is how he sees me, and I would like to see myself like this too. "You're so talented," I say.

"You're just saying that because it's of you," he says with a smirk, adding a dab of paint before returning the paintbrush to a jar of water.

I put my hand on my hip. "I'd shove you if I could."

"You've tried," he says. "You can't."

I try again, and when that doesn't get me anywhere, I shove a paintbrush covered in red paint at him. He reciprocates, and soon we're both covered with paint and laughing. To further the chaos, Rue steps into the paint spatters and spreads more red around the floor in his tiny kitten footprints. It's like a murder scene, a thought that shouldn't strike me funny but does.

I laugh harder, until I'm almost dizzy from it, and Rafe holds me up. I'm sure he's going to kiss me, but he doesn't. He just swipes back my hair, which is almost certainly covered in paint, and says, "Almost time to go, Clay. Something tells me you're going to insist on taking an unreasonable amount of time in the bathroom."

I want to invite him to take a shower with me, but I don't.

I've shown him so much of myself that's raw. So many of my barriers have been broken down, but his are still erected. Maybe that's the fate of anyone whose life is in the public eye, but at this particular moment I can't help but resent it.

"You're right," I say glibly. "Give me two hours."

"I choose to assume you're joking."

I am. But not by as much as he thinks, because I have to clean and feed Rue, plus it takes me at least an hour to get clean and dressed and free of paint. By the time I come out, Rafe's dressed in fresh clothes and the mess has been taken care of.

He looks at me with an expression that puts a knot in my throat. I'm wearing nothing special, just a casual blue dress with a floral design, but he makes me *feel* beautiful. I'm also uncomfortable, though, raw and vulnerable, and I find myself saying, "You're doing double duty as my maid?"

He flinches half a second before he gives me one of his patented smirks. "That's me," he says, "the gigolo-bodyguard-maid—three for the price of one."

"It's not like that," I say, reaching for his hand.

He gives it to me. "It's okay. I'm good with being used for my body. Feel free to use me for it again."

I like that promise, but not the rest of it. "I'm not using you just for your body. I'm also becoming quite partial to your mind and your painting skills."

That gets me a smile. "Come on, Clay, the old man is waiting for us."

We're going to pick up his father on the way to my family's house. I'm glad, because I want to get a look at Rafe's apartment. I'm curious about him, I guess. I'd like to snoop around and ask his father questions. I want to know if Rafe used to make macaroni paintings or his you-only-get-better-if-you-practice schtick is the kind of bullshit spewed by someone who's always been naturally talented.

We head down to my car, both of us quiet. Rafe goes to open the back door for me, but I close it and circle around to the front passenger seat.

When he gets in next to me, he gives me a flat look. "What if I wanted the front row to myself?"

"Then you must be pretty pissed that you have company," I say, lifting my eyebrows. "Sucks to be you."

"No," he says, looking over his shoulder and pulling out of the spot, "I have to say it doesn't suck being me at the present moment. But that may very easily change once we get to the apartment."

He uses the key card to leave the garage and then turns onto the street.

"What do you think he could have possibly done in four days?" I ask.

"That's the kind of thinking that could get a person in trouble," he says, his lips tipping up. "*What couldn't he have done?* is probably a better question."

I give him a sidelong glance, taking in his strong jaw, those coal-dark eyes. "You didn't grow up with Reggie, did you?"

"No," he says, taking a turn. "He lived in LA for a long time, actually. Used to visit, but he only moved here permanently a couple of years ago."

"Did he get sick of the nice weather?"

"Weather's nicer here."

He doesn't want to talk about it, obviously, so I let the conversation lapse into silence. But I can tell he's getting broody as he keeps driving toward his place, so I give in to my impulse to break the silence and pull up the *90210* theme song on my phone and play it on the car's Bluetooth system.

He shakes his head slightly, a smile on his face, and reaches out and puts his big hand on my leg. "You're impossible."

But it's shaken him out of his mood, and he seems lighter as he pulls into an apartment-complex parking lot and chooses a spot. The buildings have large windows and neutral paint, somewhere between brown and gray. They remind me a bit of the complex my mother and I lived in when we first moved to Los Angeles.

"It's nice," I say encouragingly.

He gives me a dubious look, eyebrows raised. "No need for condescension, Clay. It's not a hovel, but no one would call it nice."

So much for trying to be supportive. It feels like he read me the wrong way intentionally.

I reach for the door handle in a huff, and he says, "No need to get out. I'll let him know we're here to pick him up."

"You don't want me to see your place?"

He crosses his arms, his seat belt still on, and watches me for a moment. "It's probably been wrecked."

"And you're a gigolo-bodyguard-maid who's apparently type A about such things," I agree. "I still want to see it. You've been in my apartment for days."

"I work for you, Clay," he says, not unkindly. "That means you get a hall pass. You don't have to slum it in my apartment."

Something sinks inside of me, because not so long ago, I'd accused my sister of slumming it with Griffin, although I didn't use those exact words. What a horrible thing to think or say. I can appreciate that more now, in this moment. "I don't look at it that way," I tell him, choosing my words carefully. "I just...we're sort of friends, aren't we? I wanted to see where you live, is all."

He takes my hand and squeezes it. "Yeah, we're sort of friends... but I don't let just anyone suck my dick." He's smirking as he says it, and his smirk widens when I give his shoulder a feeble shove.

Then he gets out of the car and leads the way to one of the nondescript doors on the first floor. I don't say anything, because I don't want him to change his mind. He knocks and says loudly, "I'm coming in, Dad. Make sure you have clothes on."

"Is there a possibility he won't?" I ask, suddenly having second thoughts.

"Probability," he corrects, lifting his eyebrows. "You did want to come in, didn't you?"

He gets out his key, but Reggie throws the door open before he can get it in the lock. If Reggie was feeling down earlier, there's no sign of it. He looks as jolly as Old Saint Nick, with his long white beard and hair, an effect that's accentuated by his red sweater but underplayed by the bottles of wine he's holding.

"Are we ready to go?" he asks exuberantly.

"I'm glad you're dressed, at any rate," Rafe says. "But Clay here was hoping to get a tour."

Some of his father's joie de vivre slips away, and he uses one of the wine bottles to scratch his ass. Note to self: do not drink the Chianti. "Are you sure you want to do that?"

"What happened?" Rafe grumbles. "Other than the obvious ruination of the couch."

"Just a little spill. Nothing to be worried about. I was going to clean it up when I got home."

Rafe nods for me to go in, and I do, then gasp and glance back at Reggie, even as Rafe follows me inside.

"Is that—"

"It'll probably come out eventually," Reggie says, scratching the back of his neck. "It's white in the middle because I tried baking soda and vinegar, but that didn't work."

No, it just made the whole apartment smell like a salad, but that's not what's concerning—there's a red stain on the carpet next to the couch. It looks like the murder scene of a small animal.

"Christ, Dad," Rafe says. "What happened? Why didn't you mention this earlier?"

Reggie sighs and sets the wine bottles down on the counter in the kitchen. "I figured I could handle it myself, and then you mentioned the dinner, and I really wanted to get out of the house." He hikes up the arm of his shirt, revealing a makeshift bandage that used to be a kitchen towel with a slogan about meat, attached with what looks like masking tape. Blood is seeping through.

"I don't think it should look like that," I say, horrified.

"Oh, it's nothing. Little love scratch," Reggie says. "I was just cutting up a charcuterie board while I was sitting on the couch. An ad for a Slanket come on, and I got distracted and cut myself. Kind of thing that could happen to anyone. I'll clean the rug later."

"You need to go to the emergency room," I say firmly, looking from the "meat" towel to the soaked rug.

"No," Reggie says in distress. "I don't want to miss the party. Besides, I don't like doctors much. I don't want to go in there for a scratch and come out with half a kidney."

"I don't think that would happen," I tell him. I feel like retching, but I'm aware that this situation isn't just distressing for me—it must be much worse for Rafe.

"He doesn't have insurance," Rafe says gruffly. "Wait here."

I do, smiling awkwardly at Reggie, who seems disappointed that we're not en route to my family house. It takes me a second, but what Rafe said settles on me. Does *Rafe* have insurance? He hasn't been getting it from me.

"It would have been okay," Reggie says sulkily. "There's no need for all this trouble."

"Oh, I think there is," I say, eyeing the red spot on his towel bandage, which seems to be getting bigger. "Besides, we're not missing much if we're late. It's just a family dinner."

I let my gaze stray from the bloody towel and take in the room around us. It's not in a state of tidiness, but it has all the marks of a place that's used to being tidy. There's an old flat screen mounted on the wall across from the beige sofa, and there are several paintings on the wall.

I can tell from the brushstrokes that at least a few of them are Rafe's. He may not be famous, but he's good. Really good. That rattles my understanding of the world a little, because I was raised to believe that if you try hard enough, if you give it your all, you'll get what you want.

I'd been hoping for some family photos, but there's only one that I can see—a framed picture of Reggie and Rafe sitting on a bookcase in the corner. Truthfully, I'd like to go through the place with a fine-toothed comb and gather a body of evidence about what makes Rafe O'Dooley tick. But I don't want to become the stalker of the man who's trying to save me from one. Besides. I'm only interested in him as a friend.

I think.

"He was good, huh?" Reggie says, and I start a little, realizing my gaze has been fixed on a painting of the sky that it so superior in artistry to the one I made earlier that a kid with crayons might as well have made mine. "Hasn't picked up a brush in ten years."

I suck in a breath, because that's not true anymore. He painted with me, at his suggestion. I hadn't realized it had been so long. I'm not sure what that means, but I suspect it means something. Then I realize Reggie's still watching me for an answer, and I manage to say, "Really good."

It comes out breathier than I meant for it to, and Reggie gives me an interested look.

"He really would protect you with his life, you know," he says, watching me.

"Yeah," I say, suddenly uncomfortable. "I think you're right."

Rafe storms back into the room with a first aid kit. "What'd you do with all the alcohol wipes, Dad?" he asks. "I had to find the bottle."

"I used them all to clean my Happy Meal toy collection," he says without any self-consciousness.

It's hard to place this bumbling but sweet man as Rafe's father. Then again, I'd like to believe we're not fated to be our parents. My father was a sweet man, a quiet man—even when he should have spoken up—and my mother...

From what Rafe's told me, his mother's a peach too.

I look away while Rafe removes the "meat" bandage, and he whistles. "You're going to need a couple of stitches, Dad."

"We can use my car to go to the ER," I say.

"Those aren't headlines you need," Rafe tells me as he guides his father to the couch, steering clear from the splotch. He sets the things out on the coffee table. "We don't need to go to the ER. I know how to do stitches. They'd make us wait ten hours to do what I can do in less than ten minutes."

"Are you kidding me?" I say, putting a hand on my hip. "We're going to take your father to the ER, and I don't give a quarter of a shit what people think about it. I'm paying for this."

Rafe drops a roll of gauze onto the table and stands. Anger radiates from him, but he keeps his distance, as if he knows just how large he is and is careful about it. "We're not a charity, *Sinclair*."

"No, you work for me, and this happened while you were on the job. If you weren't with me, you would have been at home to help him."

"I'm fine," Reggie says with unwarranted confidence. "Really. I think we should just patch it back up, grab those wine bottles, and go."

Why's he this excited to have dinner with my family?

"You're not paying for this," Rafe tells me, the set of his jaw stubborn.

"Consider it a bonus."

"For services rendered?" he asks. He sounds so pissed that I almost take a step back. *Almost* being the important word. This stubborn asshole is going to let me do something for him. He's going to let me in whether he wants to or not. And I refuse to feel bad for that.

"No. For going above and beyond to keep me safe this week. Maybe I want to go above and beyond for you too."

"Remember what I said to you the other night, boy," Reggie tells him.

I have no idea what it was, but maybe it had something to do with listening to highly intelligent women, because Rafe swears under his breath, then nods. "Fine. But my stitches would have been better."

So that's how we end up going to the emergency room.

twenty

RAFE

TURNS out it's a different experience when you go to the ER with a celebrity.

Of course, the only other time I've been to one was when I was wheeled in on a stretcher with a bullet wound. Those, they tend to take seriously.

The memories this has shaken up aren't great. I would have preferred not to take a bath in them. Then again, I also would have preferred it if my father hadn't stabbed himself with a meat cleaver and waited hours to say anything.

Shit. Maybe he *does* need a Life Alert. I'll have to ask Shauna about it. She lives with the two elderly grandparents who raised her, and they have his-and-hers Life Alerts.

When we got to the front desk at the ER, Sinclair talked to the woman for half a minute, most of which the lady spent quoting her show to her, and the next thing I knew, we were being steered into a private room. That's where we are now, nice and private.

My father immediately starts fidgeting with the TV remote.

"She seemed sweet enough, but she'll probably say something to the press," I tell Sinclair, because I'm still butt hurt about having to

180

come here. I'm also very aware of the fact that she just saw my apartment.

I'm not embarrassed of who I am, but there's a vast divide between Clay's penthouse and the dump I rent, with its carpeted floors and the faint scent of smoke that never went away after I moved in—and the little puddle of vinegar-scented blood in front of the couch. I didn't want her in there, but she went in, and now she knows.

"I don't care," she says, her mouth a stubborn line.

"Say," my father says, pulling at his beard, "can you get me one of those coffees from the vending machine? I've always had a thing for vending-machine coffee."

"No one has a thing for vending-machine coffee," I say. "Those machines are only there to prey on desperate people."

"Of course we'll get you one," Clay says, sweet as sugar, as if she didn't agree with me. As if she's ever, in her thirty-two years of life, willingly drunk vending-machine coffee. Then I pick up on the reason for that.

She wants to talk.

I don't feel inclined to play along. Then again, I did just walk into my apartment to find a pool of vinegar-blood next to my couch and my father with a bleeding *Heat Your Meat*–towel bandage. I'm ready to cut myself plenty of slack for being in a shit mood.

"Manage your expectations," I say to my dad, then I pop my sunglasses on as we leave the room to find the coffee machine. The sunglasses thing may have started as a in-joke, but they feel like armor tonight.

"Does that mean you're not going to talk to me?" Clay asks. I can feel her eyeing me. She'll have her lips slightly pushed out, something she does when she's thinking.

I don't like the fact that I've noticed that. It suggests she's slid under my skin in a way that's dangerous.

"Not even if you start in about your swinger aunt. I don't feel like talking."

"I can see that," she says softly, but she's...her, so I'm not all that surprised when she tugs me into a room and closes the door. Then locks it.

I look around, amused. It's dimly lit and my sunglasses make everything dark, but I know a bathroom when I see it. "Clay, I don't know how to break it to you, but this is a single-occupancy bathroom. I get that the coffee is shit, but I still don't think they keep the machine in here."

She scrunches her nose slightly, probably because it smells like the sink gargled an industrial-sized tub of disinfectant. Better than the alternative, I guess.

"You didn't want to come to the ER because of what happened after you got shot," she says, her hand still on my arm.

My first thought: *She's right.* My second thought: *I like having her hand there.*

"No one would like to think about getting shot," I say, forcing myself to pull away. "But it's bullshit to pretend that not having insurance isn't a good reason for avoiding hospitalization. Do you know what hospitals charge for this sort of thing?"

She makes a face that's just this side of guilty.

"Yeah, I didn't think so." It's not fair of me to be pissed at her, and I'm not, exactly. I just feel...wound up.

"I want to know what happened," she says. Then pauses, frowning. She doesn't glance in the mirror to make sure her face isn't creasing, something she used to do regularly when I first came to work for her. She's changing, like a caterpillar in a chrysalis, and I have the inane thought that I'd like to be the first one to see her when she comes out. "Nicole knows."

"She doesn't know because *I* told her," I say. "Not to critique your detecting skills, but you should be working my dad for information. You'd have a better success rate."

"You're being kind of a dick," she says. "You've been kind of a dick ever since I made that comment about you pulling double duty as my maid. You know I was just kidding."

Sure I do. But it served as a reminder that I shouldn't be messing around with my boss. I definitely shouldn't be doing that *and* enjoying her company.

"You've always thought I was a dick. Today you decided you like my dick."

"You're so frustrating," she says, giving her foot a stomp. It should be ridiculous, but it's kind of hot.

"Can we go?" I ask as I take the sunglasses off and shove them into my shirt pocket. It's one of the collared ones I bought especially for this gig.

"It's hard to see with those on in a dim room, isn't it?" she says, her gaze pointed.

The corners of my lips twitch up without my permission. "Yeah," I admit. "It takes real dedication. See what I'm willing to do for you?"

She surprises me by taking a step closer and grabbing the lapels of my white shirt. My dick twitches in a Pavlovian response. "I know what you'll do for me," she says. "You've told me you'd take a bullet for me, and I believe you. I don't understand why. I'd like to know."

I think of the way she looked in the restaurant earlier. Lost. Scared. Broken. I think of the little girl she was, shoved into things she had no hope of properly understanding. Shoved at men like she was a pretty party favor.

I want to *kill* Judy Jones.

I'm going to talk to Nicole about that—not actual murder, of course, but maybe the kind of killing that would hurt a woman like her worse than death. I want to stomp her public image into the ground and then torch whatever's left and fuck Clay in the ashes. Clay, who's still looking at me.

I could tell her I'm just doing it for the money, but that would be a lie.

"I don't like it when men take advantage of women or scare them," I say, "but that's not why I want to protect you. Why wouldn't someone want to help you for your sake?"

"You don't even like me most of the time," she says, and then she shocks me by blushing, the first time I've seen that happen. I don't even think. I reach up to touch her soft cheek.

"Oh, I'd say I like you. I like you a lot more than I want to or should." As if they're working of their own volition, my fingers weave into her hair and grab on, bringing her close. She makes that little sound that drives me crazy an instant before my mouth descends on hers. I kiss her hard, and she kisses me back the same way, sucking at my lips and tongue as she puts her arms around my neck, her fingers clawing into my hair too. Our teeth clash in our urgency to take the kiss deeper.

I pull back, my cock throbbing, and the sight of her mussed hair nearly makes me crazy. "Let's get you out of here," I say. "I'm surprised you've survived in a public bathroom for this long. It must be some kind of record. Besides, we promised my dad some of that shitty coffee."

There's a slight tremble to her fingers when she lifts them to her lips. "Okay." But she pauses. "You painted with me today, Rafe. Your father said it had been ten years. Why?"

I don't have an answer for why I broke my painting fast for her, but I feel the need to tell her something. I take her hand from her mouth and squeeze it. "Something shitty happened to me when I was in my early twenties. It changed everything." It's obvious she wants to know more, but she doesn't press me. Maybe that's why I tell her. "My mother's the one who shot me. That's why I don't like talking about it."

Her mouth drops open, and I can see in her eyes that she wants to feel bad for me.

"I met your mother earlier," I say, still holding her hand. "Would you want me to feel sorry for you?"

"No," she says, her gaze lasering into mine. "I have questions."

I raise my eyebrows. "Naturally."

"Why?"

I laugh, even though it's not particularly funny. "You think I gave her a good reason?"

"No, that's not what I meant." Her look of horror is enough to make me stop teasing her.

I rub my brow, feeling a phantom ache in my side where the bullet went through. It was a miracle, they said. I should have died. Didn't feel like much of a miracle, though.

I brace a hand against the cold tile wall. "She called me up, said her boyfriend was acting like he was on something. We weren't close, but when you get a call like that, you check on someone. She didn't come to the door, but it wasn't locked, so I saw myself in." I swallow, seeing it again, as if this bathroom has been transfigured into her butter-yellow kitchen, splashes of blood on the white tile floor. My heart beats faster in my chest, sweat rising in my pores. "She'd fallen, but the asshole was still beating her. Kicking her with his feet. Her arm was broken. So I started in on him."

Clay's watching me seriously, her hand still in mine. I look away, focusing on the metal hand drier mounted to the wall. One of the screws is coming out. The antiseptic smell makes my nostrils twitch.

"He fought back, but I was bigger. Didn't take me long to get the upper hand." I could still feel him under my fists. "She started crying, telling me to leave him alone. I'm not going to lie to you...I didn't want to stop. I wanted to hurt him. Then she took a gun out of his bag, and she said if I didn't leave him alone she was going to shoot me."

"Rafe," she says softly. I still don't look at her.

"It happened so quickly. I didn't let go of him right away, and she pulled the trigger. I don't know if she actually meant to do it or it happened on reflex." I swallow. "They didn't press charges against me. Or *him*. But my mother went away for two years. She blames me because he didn't wait for her. She was always like that with men—choosing the wrong ones. Putting them above everything else." I snort. "The funny thing is that my dad turned out to be a mostly decent guy. He wasn't around when I was a kid. He was the kind of father who'd take me to Disneyland for a week and then disappear for two years. But he moved back to Asheville from Los Angeles to take care of me for a whole year. That was before he came back for good. Back then, he did it just for me."

"*Rafe.*"

This time I do look at her. I don't know what I expected I'd see on her face. Pity, maybe, even though I didn't ask for it and certainly do not want it. Disgust, possibly. But there's none of that, thank God. Instead, there's something fiercely protective about her expression. And a glassiness in her eyes that tells me she's fighting tears. I hope she keeps up the good fight. I can't handle seeing her cry for me.

"Thank you for telling me," she says, swallowing. "Thank you for *trusting* me."

"You trusted me first." I release her hand to trace the line of her cheek again. "But you should know this isn't just about me wanting to protect you because I did such a shit job of it back then. I won't let this asshole hurt you because I won't let *anyone* hurt you. Seems to me you've had plenty of that."

"Don't forget who threw that rock at the stalker," she says, lifting up and kissing my cheek. "I want to protect you too."

"God save the man who messes with you, Sinclair Jones," I say—and mean it.

"Nicole says you changed your name…"

"To my dad's last name," I say. "You can understand why."

She studies me, the harsh lighting doing nothing to dim her sparkle. "You don't want anyone to know about this, but working with me, being in the public eye…your privacy is in danger."

"It's not a secret, exactly," I say, swallowing. "If it comes out, fine. But I'd rather keep it under wraps if I can. There are a lot of people in my life who don't know."

"But you told me."

"But I told you."

She edges closer, our hands still locked together, and a strange feeling unfolds within me. It's warm and protective; it's *happy*. It's for her.

"One time wasn't enough," she says in a near whisper, and my dick stirs because this is the best news it's heard. My brain's less sure of what to make of it.

"No," I say. "Not even a little. *Kelly*."

She gives me a look that heats my blood, sexy and sweet, those eyes like sunbursts as she leans toward me, her tits pressing against the front of her dress like they want to say hello. "I'm going to be honest," she says, leaning in more, "after you told me that, I really want you inside of me. *Now*."

"Hearing about my messed-up family life made you want to fuck me?" I ask incredulously.

She squeezes my hand. "I'm not sure what that means about me, but yes. I think I need it. I think maybe you do too."

I'm all about this plan. There's one obvious problem: "You want to have sex in a *bathroom*?"

"It smells very clean." She releases my hand and then trails hers down the front of my shirt in a zigzag motion that makes me feel every zig and zag—and also the fact that I still don't have any condoms when I need them. I'm going to have to start carrying them around by the handful.

"I don't have any protection," I say, my voice strangled.

"I put some condoms in my purse," she says, practically glowing.

"You were planning to seduce me in a bathroom?" I ask in disbelief as she continues to run her fingers over me like she owns me. Maybe I should mind, but I can't say I do.

"No," she says, starting to unfasten my belt. "We were supposed to go to my family's house, remember? I was kind of hoping I could lead you off and have my way with you in my childhood bedroom."

"That's messed up," I say as she keeps at it with the belt. "It's too bad we won't get the chance." I like that she thought of it. I *really* like that she prepared for it. I flip up her skirt and slide my hand underneath, smoothing it up her thigh to her center. A breath hisses out of me when I feel how wet she is. "So what'll it be this time, Clay? Up against the wall, your legs wrapped around me, my cock buried inside you?"

"Please," she says, unfastening my pants and pulling them down. Maybe she sees or feels the flash of heat in my eyes because she smirks a little and adds, "*Please* fuck me against the wall, Doctor. I've been a bad, bad girl."

"Don't mind if I do."

twenty-one

SINCLAIR

"YOU KNOW the nurses aren't allowed to masturbate inside of empty rooms," Rafe says, his hand playing with me under my skirt. My back is pressed to the wall, but I'm not even thinking about where we are. All I'm thinking about is him. Getting him inside of me. Showing him that I want him. Showing myself that he still wants me...

"I couldn't help myself," I say, palming his hard dick, remembering the way it felt inside of me earlier. I want him from another angle, from *every* angle. I don't know why I have this need for him, but I don't care to analyze it. I just want to feel. I just want to enjoy myself. "I was thinking about *you*."

"You'll need to be more disciplined," he says, his gaze wicked.

I love how he takes my games and builds upon them. How he humors me and seems to enjoy doing it.

He thrusts two fingers inside of me, the heel of his hand rubbing against my clit. "Did it feel like this when you were touching yourself?"

"No, Doctor."

"I think you'd better show me," he says, his eyes on fire.

He pulls his hand back and sucks on his fingers, watching while I lower my underwear and then start to rub myself and slip a finger inside. "It's not enough," I complain. "I need a thick dick to make me come. I've tried everything else."

"You've got a mouth on you," he says. "I like it." He reaches into my bag and finds the condoms, takes one out and, while I'm still touching myself, lowers his boxer briefs and runs a fist over his cock once, twice before rolling on the condom. I'm not sure why, but the sight of him touching himself drives me wild.

He reaches for me, my fingers still seeing to my needs, and smacks my ass lightly with his hand. "That's for touching yourself in an empty room." He smacks the other side, his hand curling around to touch where I'm wet for him. "That's for not coming to get me first."

I'm laughing and moaning as he grips my hand and pulls it out and up to him, sucking on my fingers like he did his. "You're delicious. A fucking feast."

My knees feel like they might buckle, because I like the way he talks too. I like the way he touches me and tastes me.

He kisses me hard and grips me by the hips, lifting me up even as he backs me into the wall. I wrap my legs around his butt as he presses into me, lowering his head to kiss the tops of my breasts before reaching down and, in one stroke that's quick and rough and enough to take my breath away, thrusts into me.

"Is that better?" he asks, then leans in to kiss me, his mouth claiming mine. I squeeze my legs harder around him as I kiss back, bucking against him to prompt him to start moving, and he laughs deep in his throat and does as I'm silently requesting, thrusting in and out, pushing my back into the wall. I'm so confident he has my weight, that he can handle me, that I push into him too, taking him deeper each time.

"Yes, Doctor. *Much* better. You can give me this treatment anytime."

He laughs, then his laughter fades as he shoves my dress and bra down with one hand. Using his other hand to steady my hip, he sees to my nipple with his lips and tongue as he continues to move inside of me. Then he shifts to the other breast. He's a man who sees the value in fucking a woman thoroughly, which is another thing to like about him.

Hot, dirty pleasure pulses through me. I wanted him again—I wanted this—but if I'm being honest, that's not why I seduced him in a bathroom, of all places. It was because I needed to give him something as comfort. No, I wanted to give him myself as comfort. To show that his story didn't make me want him any less.

Pleasure spikes within me as his strokes hit a spot that makes me see colors that don't exist. "There," I say. "Definitely there."

He listens, his hand pressing my hip to the wall, pinning me easily in place for him while he takes what he wants—giving me what I want. And the pleasure of what we're doing, dialed up by the wrongness of where we're doing it, starts to spiral through me.

"I'm going to come, Doctor," I announce.

He weaves the hand that was on my breasts into my hair and pulls my head back so I'm looking at him while I tumble over the edge, pleasure spiraling through me and making forget where we are and why, that I have a stalker, and maybe even that my name is Sinclair Jones. Right now, right here, there's only this moment, the two of us, and the way he's making me feel. The way I'm making him feel too, because he swears loudly and then pulses into me, his hands flexing in my hair and around my hip.

I don't for a second worry he'll drop me, because he's not the kind of man who ever would. He releases my hair and nuzzles his face into my neck, then lifts it and smiles at me, still buried inside of me. There's a burst of something bright in my chest. "Well, hell, remind me to drag you into more bathrooms."

Then he pulls out, the lack of him giving me a slight ping of sadness, because seconds ago this—*us*—was all that mattered.

He lowers me to my feet, kisses me again, slow and leisurely and not at all like we've been hogging this bathroom for fifteen minutes, and then takes off the condom and disposes of it. He's completely unselfconscious, totally comfortable in his skin.

"Turn around," I hiss, righting my clothes so it looks less like I just had sex in a bathroom.

"What?" he says with a laugh as he pulls up his pants and secures the belt. "What haven't I already seen?"

"I need to pee," I say, giving him a pointed look.

"So?" he says with a smirk. "Go ahead and pee. I know that women pee."

"Turn around and put your hands over your ears," I insist, giving him a look that could kill. The last thing I want is for him—or anyone—to see me on the toilet.

Laughing, he turns his back to me, puts his hands over his ears, and, because he's him, starts singing, "Rain, rain, go away."

"Very funny," I mutter as I see to my business and then flush the toilet.

"Can I turn back around now?" he asks, his hands dropping from his ears.

"No, wait like that until I wash my hands."

"Seriously?" he gripes as I start the water and apply the soap. "Why don't you want me to see your germ-riddled hands?"

"It's not that," I tell him as I finish and turn off the tap. "You have a nice butt, and I like looking back at it. You're an artist—you'll understand."

"Well, in that case." He turns, and I squeal as he lifts me up over his shoulder the way he did in his apartment earlier, my upper half slung over his back, giving me what I have to admit is a very good view of his butt.

"Put me down," I complain after enjoying the view for a second. "I need to wipe my hands, and then we have to get some of that terrible coffee for your father."

"So you're admitting it's terrible?" he says, setting me on my feet.

I glance in the mirror in horrified fascination. My hair is a mess, my cheeks pink, and I look...I look kind of nice. I look happy. I fix the makeup around my eyes slightly, since I'm only human, and then wipe my hands. If we end up going to my sister's and she sees me like this, so be it. Maybe it's not such a bad thing to show people that I'm human—that I bleed and my makeup smears and my hair gets messed up. Maybe that's as it should be.

"Obviously the coffee's terrible," I mutter, tucking my hair behind my ears and turning to him. "But I had to get you to talk to me, didn't I?"

He shakes his head a little, a smile playing on his lips. "You're surprising, Sinclair Jones."

"A good surprise or a bad one?"

"A surprising one," he says.

I cast a dirty look at him, but I can't deny I'm pleased.

He opens the door and holds it for me. "My lady?"

I step out and nearly swear. There's an elderly woman with lilac hair waiting outside. God only knows how long she's been there. She smiles knowingly when Rafe follows me out.

"Well done," she says.

"Uh, I'm sorry we made you wait," I say. "My friend was..."

Making me come?

Trying to live up to his promise to make me black out from pleasure?

Bodyguarding my pussy?

I clear my throat. "Helping me get a contact lens out of my eye."

"Oh, is *that* what I heard?" she asks.

Even though I should be mortified, I'm much too satisfied to feel that way. So I settle for laughing.

She beams at me. "You keep enjoying yourself and your young man, my dear. It's a beautiful thing to be young and in love."

"We're not—"

She touches my arm as if we're old friends and not two strangers who met a matter of seconds ago. "Oh, I know what it looks like when two people are becoming each other's worlds. I've been there once or twice myself. Why, I'm here because my partner's son is having a baby."

"He's having a baby?" I ask in confusion.

"His wife, of course," she says with a tittering laugh.

"But why are you on this floor, then? It's not the maternity floor."

"I like to go around and leave crystals in the waiting rooms and bathrooms. They're a lovely surprise, don't you think? And they help balance the energy."

My aunt would probably love that, but I think it's a pretty bad idea to go around leaving crystals places, especially in a hospital where they might be mistaken for something else. I mean, I doubt anyone's going to think they're bombs, but even so. I'm not about to say that to a stranger, though, so I just smile.

Rafe nods to her and leads me off down the harshly lit hallway toward the coffee vending machine. He doesn't touch me, but he shoots me a look that settles between my legs and reminds me of what we just did together. I've never been like this with anyone else —so daring, so dirty.

"That lady was right about one thing," he says with a smirk. "I *did* rock your world."

"Oh, for God's sake." I try to sound annoyed, but it doesn't take.

We get a crappy coffee for his father, plus another two for us, because I suggested that we shouldn't let Reggie suffer alone. "You're gonna regret that, Clay," Rafe says, but it sounds like he's amused and maybe even a little pleased by the suggestion.

When I get back, I brace myself for Reggie to make some sort of insinuation about what we were doing, but he barely seems to have noticed we were gone for longer than five minutes. He has found Turner Classic Movies and is deep into *The Shop Around the Corner*.

We do a cheers with our coffees. I immediately regret my decision to sip some, and Rafe must notice it because he takes both of our cups without comment and trashes them.

Meanwhile, Reggie sips away at his with as much enthusiasm as if it were one of those honey oat-milk lattes I used to sneak from the coffee shop close to the set for *Sisters of Sin*.

A doctor shows up a few minutes later to stitch up the cut, which he makes quick work of. While we wait for the discharge paperwork, we watch the movie together, Rafe and me sitting side by side in the two visitor's chairs, close enough for our arms to touch.

The three of us make comments back and forth as the movie wraps up, and it's surprisingly enjoyable considering we're in the hospital, almost like a family movie night.

That thought burns a little, because I'm supposed to be bonding with my family, and instead I'm missing their dinner to be here with Rafe. Is this another mistake? It doesn't *feel* like a mistake, but my mother seemed reasonable right up until she didn't. Can I trust my own instincts?

When Reggie is finally discharged, after a mostly inedible dinner Rafe grabbed for us from the cafeteria, he glances mournfully at the clock. "It's probably too late for us to pop in for dessert, and I think I forgot the wine at the apartment."

"It's never too late for dessert," I say warmly. It's nine o'clock and dinner was at six, but Marnie's been texting me all night, and she's worried enough that she'll pull a pumpkin pie out of the back of the freezer just to get me to come over. Worst-case scenario: Reggie survived a stabbing; he can probably make it through one of my aunt's Christmas cookies.

twenty-two

SINCLAIR

"COME IN," Marnie says, Griffin standing just behind her. "Come in, *please*, for the love of God. Aunt Helen is doing a tarot reading for Andy, and Drew's up next. We need some fresh energy in here."

Suddenly, I don't want to come in. The house smells like lasagna, with a hint of something sweet, and there's a cozy murmuring of voices against a backdrop of low-volume music. This house isn't mine anymore, though, and in truth, it's been a long, long time since it felt like home. Besides, maybe it's stupid—scratch that, it's definitely stupid—but I don't want to know what the future holds right now. Of course, my aunt can no more read the tarot than I can, but still...

"Oh, it's fine," Marnie says with a wave of her hand as she ushers us inside and closes the door. "I can see what you're thinking, and you have nothing to worry about. Aunt Helen just told me that I'm going to marry royalty, so you're in no danger of an accurate reading."

"You don't know," Griffin says with a grin. "I might be the illegitimate son of someone important."

"Uh-huh, sure."

196

Turning to Reggie, Griffin says, "How you doing, man? I heard there was a mishap."

Reggie, of course, instantly pulls up his sleeve and lifts the bandage, something he was told not to do, to show off his stitches.

At least they already ate?

"Dad," Rafe says, rolling his eyes.

"Very even," Griffin pronounces, a smile pulling at the corners of his mouth. "Let's get you some dessert. I'd say you earned it."

"Don't worry," Marnie hastens to add, "Aunt Helen didn't make the strawberry shortcake, so you don't have to worry about the berries being from last strawberry season. Andy brought it."

She leads us through the living room, past the mantel, where my father's ashes sit in a large wooden urn, and into the open dining room. Andy's frowning at my snowy-haired aunt. They're sitting opposite each other, the tarot cards laid out on the surface between them. The strawberry shortcake sits on a cake stand, half-eaten. They've gotten started with dessert, not that I blame them. That's what happens when you show up to dinner several hours too late.

"Didn't you know you're supposed to make up good news for people who've just received shitty news?" Andy says. "It's a whole thing."

"What happened?" I ask.

Marnie waves to the empty seats, each of which has a place setting with a wine glass in front of it, and we sit. Rafe and Reggie are across the table from me, next to Aunt Helen and my brother, and I'm directly opposite them, next to Griffin, Marnie, and Andy, who's across from my brother. I recognize the delicate rose pattern on the dessert dishes from my childhood. My mother used to film me eating so we could watch the footage later and dissect whether it was elegant enough for meals with agents or actors.

My heart starts beating faster. My aunt beams at me and blows a kiss. I pour myself a large glass of wine and then push the bottle toward Rafe, who immediately pushes it back.

"I'm on duty, Clay," he says, and before those words can prick me like needles, he adds, "Can't dull my reflexes if I'm going to protect you."

"Andy got fired," Drew says, popping a strawberry from his plate into his mouth. "The director of the daycare she worked at found out about her OnlyFans account."

Andy throws a strawberry at him, which leaves a red smear on his nose. "It's not funny, you dumbass."

He starts to choke a little, then swallows his mouthful of dessert down with a swig of wine.

"So you don't have an OnlyFans account?" I ask.

She throws her long, curly hair over her shoulder as if it offended her. "I do, but he doesn't have to make it sound salacious. I mean, sure, some of the people on there put up porn and that's how they make their big bank, but I don't do anything like that."

Drew gives her a dubious look, and she frowns at him. "*Seriously*. People have some very weird kinks. I just make videos of my feet holding different things. I mean, the income is way higher than what I make—made—at the daycare. A woman's gotta make money." She scowls. "Look at it this way, the fact that my boss was on there in the first place suggests *he* has an OnlyFans account, and it's a little suspicious that he identified me solely on the basis of my feet and hair. Yes, I do have a toe ring, and yes, it is unusual, but is it *that* unusual?" She pulls her mouth to one side and lifts a shoulder. "I think the two of us would have had a very different conversation if I'd offered to rub my feet over his—"

"My ears are bleeding," Drew complains. "They're actually bleeding."

"I know a lot of actresses who have accounts on there," I interject. "It's not a big deal, or at least it shouldn't be. Plenty of people just put up photographs." I give a supportive nod in Andy's direction. "Like of Andy's feet."

"People don't want their children to be corrupted by Andy's big feet," Drew says, which earns him another strawberry to the face. He lets it fall and then picks it up and pops it into his mouth. "Keep them coming. I like strawberries."

Her response is to throw a piece of the shortcake at him. If I hadn't known better, I'd have thought they were flirting, but they've known each other since Marnie and Andy were six, and I've seen Andy's previous boyfriends. They're all jacked alpha types.

In other words, they're nothing like my brother.

"Would you two quit it?" Marnie says with a scowl. "I cleaned the floor, like, three days ago. I don't want to have to revisit that for at least two weeks."

"Yes, and I don't condone violence." Aunt Helen sounds genuinely distressed. "Even with dessert items. It creates bad energy to use something sweet for something sour."

"Oh, we're not sour, are we, Andrew?" Andy says to him with a smirk. "He's practically one of my brothers, Aunt H."

The look he gives her is pretty sour.

It's a homey scene, a family scene, and *I don't belong*.

I feel Rafe watching me from across the table, and when I meet his gaze, he winks at me. It's incredibly sexy, but the warmth I feel unfurling inside of me, like a fire was just lit at my center, isn't because of that. It's because...

He knew I needed something, a sign that I wasn't alone, and he gave it to me. He's a giving man, Rafe. He helped me breathe when I needed air, he held me at night when I needed sleep, and he also gave me his cock very generously.

"Who are you, handsome man?" Aunt Helen says, and I internally groan. She fawns over beautiful men—always has and always will. According to my sister, she has an even bigger roster of sexual partners now than she did during her (very open) marriage to my uncle. It was inevitable she'd hit on Rafe. The vast majority of people who are attracted to men would want to hit on him.

But when I glance at her, she's making speculative eyes at *Reggie.*

Fair enough, I guess. She and Reggie are close in age, and he must have been attractive back in the day. There are signs of it on his face, whispers of Rafe in his dark eyes and strong jaw, but I've never gone for the Santa Claus look.

He introduces himself, and within twenty seconds has shown his stitches to the rest of the table. There's a fond annoyance in the way Rafe handles this exhibitionism.

"So we're all in the mood to eat dessert now, I'm guessing?" he says with a smirk at his dad. I find it endearing.

"You haven't finished my tarot reading," Andy tells my aunt, eyeing the cards on the table with distrust.

"You didn't care for the way it was going, dear," Aunt Helen says as she reaches across the table to pat Andy's hand. "Maybe it would be best to let the future surprise you."

"Sounds like a surprise that's going to bite me in the ass," Andy gripes. "You know, my former boss said he was going to make sure that I can't find work at any other daycares in the city because of my —and I quote—perversions."

"What a douche," Marnie says as my aunt heaps more dessert onto Andy's plate. It looks fantastic. Staring at it is making my mouth water. I flinch in surprise as Rafe silently slides my plate across the table to him and doles out a large serving before sliding it back. My sister's watching, and the small smile on her face says that she approves. Turning back to Andy, she says, "Enoch would tell you to sue him. Maybe he'd be right."

Andy frowns and rolls her curls into a knot at the nape of her neck. Drew is watching her, but he snaps his gaze back to his plate the instant he sees me noticing. Interesting.

"Sure," Andy says, "but I don't want my grandmother to find out about the OnlyFans thing. She's already in hospice care. I don't want to be the one to push her over the edge. I'd also prefer not to be homeless on top of being jobless. One *-less* is enough."

Drew lifts his eyebrows. "They weren't having you teach those kids vocabulary, were they?"

This time she just makes a death glare at him. "I'm not wasting any more of my dessert on you."

"What bad news did Aunt Helen tell you before we got here?" I ask Andy. The cards are still spread across the table, but I never learned how to read them.

"She said I was going to fall in love."

Marnie laughs and nudges Griffin, who puts an arm around her. He's looking at her the way the people who know every single quote from every single episode of *Sisters of Sin* look at me. Only he's doing it because she's herself, not because she can convincingly pretend to be someone else. I find myself glancing at Rafe. He meets my eyes, and the unease I was starting to feel dissipates. He has a way of doing that, like the night I had a panic attack.

"Falling in love is truly the worst of fates," Marnie says to Andy. "Poor you."

"Yes," Andy says loudly, lifting her wine glass. "Poor me. I like the sound of that."

"Would you like me to do a reading for you, dear?" my aunt asks, looking to me.

"No thanks," I say. "I'm not feeling very lucky."

"I have something for that," she says, brightening. She picks something out of her pocket, which probably contains everything from old ketchup packets to pictures she's sketched on napkins, and slides it across the table. It's a blue crystal on a simple chain. My mother would have turned her nose up at it, but it's actually quite pretty. "It's kyanite, for protection."

I slip it around my neck and fasten the clasp.

"At least she didn't tell you to sleep on one," Marnie says. "You should be thankful for that. Last time she was here, she hid four crystals under my pillow. I didn't even notice, but Griff found them the second he laid down on my pillow."

"The princess with the pea you are not," he comments.

"Would you want me to be?"

"Hell no," he says as he wraps an arm around her. "My mattress feels like it has an industrial-sized bag of frozen peas inside it. If that kind of thing bothered you, you'd never want to stay over."

"Oh, it bothers me," she says, leaning into him. "But I've gotten kind of fond of you. I think I'll keep you."

God, they're perfect for each other. I feel another stab of regret for having been such a jerk about Griffin in the beginning. Worse, for being jealous.

Not of Griffin, but of Marnie. Of her freedom to be herself. Of her ability to date whoever she wants. Of the way she's always known what she likes.

"Thank you, Aunt Helen," I say, wrapping my hand around the crystal pendant and squeezing it.

"Did you know crystals can also be aphrodisiacs?" Aunt Helen asks, eyeing Reggie. "There's no end to their usefulness."

"You're some woman," he says with appreciation.

Well, that's moving along like an off-the-rails freight train. I hope he remembers that Aunt Helen isn't exactly a one-man woman. Then again, that might be part of her allure.

"How was lunch with the bread basket?" Andy asks in an obvious bid to change the subject.

"Is there bread?" Reggie asks with interest, glancing around the table top. He's been quietly stuffing his face with the strawberry shortcake.

"I love a man with a good appetite," Aunt Helen says, eyeing him up. She heads into the kitchen and comes back with a mostly empty basket of garlic bread. At least it's not something she pulled out of her endless bag of horrors. I'm pretty sure she has breath mints in there that date back to my childhood.

I'd prefer not to tell them the whole story about lunch. My sister and brother and aunt don't know about my aversion to spinach, let alone Single-Dad Santa. They don't know what it was like for me to wander around that mall, knowing my pants were red and people were laughing at me, talking in loud voices about that idiot girl who didn't even realize she was bleeding. About that gross girl who should just kill herself.

But then I think about what Rafe told me earlier. I know how hard that was for him. I know what it cost him, but it made me understand him better. It removed a barrier between us, and I'm sick of the walls that separate me from my sister and especially my brother, making it hard for us to truly know each other. Maybe it's time to give them a push.

"Why didn't we know all of this?" my brother asks when I finish. He's been swearing under his breath ever since my story got rolling, but he let me finish, even though he looks like he'd like to punch the table or maybe our mother.

"Yeah," Marnie says, turning toward me on her chair. "Why not?"

For a second, I don't know how to answer, then the truth punches me in the solar plexus. The pain is excruciating, as if every last thing she did to me were happening *now*. "I was protecting her. I thought she was trying to look out for me, and I was protecting her, because I knew what other people would think."

"Do you think we could bribe Nicole to actually write that book?" Andy says, lifting her eyebrows. "Because, fuuuuck, I want that book to be a bestseller. I will personally buy fifty copies." She tugs her bun, and the knot falls out, spilling her curls out around her face. "Or I would if I weren't unemployed."

"There's always your feet," Drew tells her.

"Seriously, Drew?"

He inclines his head, a silent admission that he went too far. "Sorry. Just trying to inject some levity into things."

"Speaking of levity," Griffin says, "I once saw a grocery list Nicole wrote. You don't want her writing any books."

"So, not her," Rafe says. His words roll through me and settle down deep. "Someone else. Someone will want to write about it, and they should."

"I don't want all of my secrets spilled to the world," I tell him, our eyes locking. He should understand that, if no one else. He holds my gaze and then gives a slight nod. I can practically hear him saying, *Your move, Clay.*

"Don't you think this Single-Dad guy has tried his schtick on other young girls?" Andy says, snapping my attention to her. "If people know he's a perv, then they're forewarned. I dunno. I'm not saying it's your duty, or whatever, because you didn't ask to get exploited, but I'd want to call him out if it were me. And then kick him the balls—repeatedly."

"I was young and inexperienced, but it was consensual," I say, lifting a hand to my throat. It's tightening, as if my airway were shrinking to the size of a pea.

"Barely," Rafe says, his voice a growl. I remember what he said to me earlier, that he'd kill Single-Dad Santa if he could get away with it. I half believe him, especially after what he told me at the hospital. Maybe that should scare me, but it doesn't. It makes me grateful that he's the man who's responsible for protecting me.

"We don't need Sinclair to say anything she's not comfortable saying," my sister says supportively. Then she grins and adds, "Nicole and Damien can absolutely make him pay without involving our names. Mom too."

Reggie doesn't say anything. Then again, he's been mowing through that garlic bread slowly but steadily while my aunt compliments his eating prowess. Maybe they're an ideal pairing. He's clearly looking for someone to feed him, and she's constantly looking for someone to feed.

"They're not gods, Marnie," Drew says, rolling his eyes. "Yes, they've done some pretty awesome shit, I'll grant you that. But they're not going to be able to tank some celeb's career. And the best punishment for Mom—and gift to ourselves—is to never see her again."

"Agreed," I say, relieved. Because I don't want to have to recount my story on national television. Nor do I want to get in some endless *she said, they said* battle with my mom and Single-Dad Santa. "But if Nicole and Damien could get word out that Single-Dad Santa is a perv, I'm all for it. I didn't...I didn't totally get how awful I felt about the whole thing until earlier."

It feels like I've been choking for years but didn't realize there was a massive bone lodged in my throat.

Okay, that came out wrong.

"There's still the ball-kicking plan," Andy says. She brightens. "Hey, I can wear a Bieber mask and run in and kick this guy in the balls repeatedly before darting away. If they blame anyone, it'll be Sinclair's guy."

"Please do *not* call him my guy," I say with a shudder.

"No, that's supposed to be Edgar James," Drew says, and I remember my plan to bring him camping. I especially want his company now, after the way Edgar was acting the other day, talking about "romantic" hikes at sunrise. It'll be harder for him to try to romance me if my clueless big brother is trailing around after us.

"Speaking of which," I say to him, "looks like I'm going to see Edgar on set for a few days next week. I was wondering if you'd want to come with me. I know you're into all the"—I wave a hand around, truly at a loss—"camping shit."

Yeah, that probably wasn't the right thing to say.

"What, really?" Drew says, his light brown eyes lighting up. I'm reminded of when we were kids. He'd look like that when he eyed up the presents under the Christmas tree or when our father announced they were going hiking. Dad had brought Marnie some-times, but he'd never once asked if I wanted to come. I wish I'd been asked. Maybe I would have felt like I'd had options and didn't belong to my mother just because I was the child she'd chosen.

But it feels like I'm being given a second chance.

"Yes, really!" I say with a grin. "I'd love it if you came. You can help me pick out what to pack. Maybe we can go to the outdoors store before we leave on Monday. I bet Nicole would help me disguise myself."

One of Edgar's assistants has already texted me a list of recommended purchases.

I hear a chair shove back, loudly, and Rafe gets up to leave the room. He looks as pissed as if someone had snapped his sunglasses in half—a move I've considered half a dozen times.

My heart starts racing in my chest. Is he mad at me?

"Are you—"

"Do I need permission to use the restroom, *boss*?" he asks pointedly, looking over his shoulder. He's already halfway out of the room.

My cheeks heat, because I'm thinking of a different restroom. But also because now I *know* he's pissed. I just don't understand why.

twenty-three

RAFE

"YEAH, I CAN DO THAT," Damien says. From the sound of his voice, he's eating something. I wonder if it's that fried chicken from earlier. "Actually, I think we'll have fun with this one, but it'll have to wait until after the stalker situation has been resolved."

"You and your wife have some strange ideas about what's fun."

"Keeps life interesting, brother. Looking forward to tomorrow. We're meeting Penn in Hendersonville. There's this little tea shop that has a rentable space upstairs with a private conference room attached. We rented it out so Sinclair can listen in and pop out when Nicole gives the signal."

"What's the plan?" I ask. Because presumably we should know something going in.

"He thinks we're meeting him to talk about a screenplay he's been shopping around. A screenplay about a writer dating a celebrity." He gives a hearty laugh. "This guy's not breaking any creativity molds, huh?"

"Does he think we're producers?"

"You and Nicole are the producers. I'm just the actor who wants to play the part."

"You sure he'll buy it?"

"He's so desperate to believe he's got something good, he'd believe anyone who says so." He pauses. "You know, I'm looking forward to this. I used to act in community theater. I kind of miss it sometimes."

My mind shifts to Sinclair, to her love-hate relationship with acting.

"Anyway," he continues. "I gotta go talk to Nicole. See you tomorrow, man."

"See you," I say, but he's already hung up.

I splash water on my face, but it doesn't do anything to snuff the fire beneath my skin. I knew Clay was going out there next week. I'd been told that was the plan. But I can't digest the thought of spending a week trailing after her and her fake boyfriend. Especially since he's obviously started to realize what I know—that Clay is maddening and annoying and asks too many questions...and is also devastatingly funny and beautiful and smart, and that her pussy feels and tastes like the promised land.

Well, he better not have figured that last part out. The thought of him even attempting it has my hands rolling into fists, but I know, I goddamn know, she can't be mine. I've let myself pretend today, but the facts are stacked against me. She's a celebrity, and I'm a failed artist–slash–failed personal trainer. I might have gotten a D in high school algebra, but I can do the math.

I have no right to ask her not to go, especially if she'll be safer there than she is here.

I have no right to tell her she should publicly break up with the fake boyfriend who's supposed to boost her career. Her acting career, which might bring her back to LA or Rome or Timbuktu.

But I want to. And I want to tell Edgar James he can go fuck a rock because he won't be touching my woman. Yes, my woman.

I feel a need for Clay that I don't like one single bit, a need that's pressing a little harder with every minute I spend in her presence, next to her, in her bed.

My mother made stupid decisions about men, and it ruined her life and mine. My father is constantly making stupid decisions about women, my mother being one of a long line.

I'm supposed to be smarter. To avoid the traps of my shitty genetic code, but that woman does something to me that makes me stupid. Worse, she makes me *want* to be stupid.

I text Shauna.

> I think I'm an idiot. Any cure for that?

> Alcohol. It'll make it worse, actually, but we'll have fun.

> After it's over.

A prickle spreads across me skin after I send the message, because I know what that'll mean. After the stalker is found, Clay and I will be over too.

Shauna texts again.

> Still coming to the studio tomorrow?

I pause before responding, because I'm not sure what to say. If I keep this up...talking to Clay, painting with her, fucking her against various surfaces, it's going to be harder when I have to say good-bye. But I think she'll enjoy going to the studio, and worse, I want Shauna to meet her. It feels wrong that they don't know each other.

> Yeah, we'll be there. Rollins still bothering you?

> Nah, I've gotten really good at avoiding him. The new guy helps me out by blasting Tick Tick Boom every time Rollins leaves his office.

> You shouldn't have to do that. Keep documentation of his shit.

To give to whom? My fairy godmother?

Thinking about Nicole and Damien, I type back,

Stranger things have happened. Hey. You seen Spence around?

Unfortunately.

Does he come to his studio on Sundays? I have to talk to him.

Well, that IS unfortunate for you. But yes, he should be there. You gonna leave me alone with your girlfriend?

No. Not for long anyway. I was thinking I'd invite him over for a chat.

Maybe we should rethink this whole arrangement.

Just kidding. Looking forward to it. (The you and Sinclair part, not the Spencer thing.)

When I leave the bathroom, Clay is waiting for me outside the door. She looks...nervous.

"Don't worry," I say, "I won't get lost on the way back to the dining room."

She glances back that way, then grabs my arm and pulls me in the opposite direction, into what looks like a bedroom. It takes me about thirty seconds to figure out it's *her* old bedroom. I smirk at her when I notice the *90210* posters on the wall. There's a carriage-style bed with a canopy covered in flowers.

"What did your childhood bedroom look like?" she says pointedly.

"Just like this."

A smile lifts her lips before it fades, her gaze moving over the bed, which looks like it got puked out of a preteen girl's imagination.

"I haven't slept in that bed since I was a teenager, but my dad kept it this way all this time."

"He must have wanted you to come back."

"He never said so. He didn't object to my mother taking me away. To...any of it."

I shouldn't be touching her, but the *shoulda-woulda-couldas* can go screw themselves. I span the space between us and touch her arm. "You don't know that, Clay. You only know what you saw."

"I wanted him to fight for me," she says, her voice hitching a little. "I wanted him to protect me."

"So he wasn't strong. That doesn't mean he didn't love you. It doesn't mean he was a bad man."

Truthfully, if he were alive, I'd want to tear him a new one, but he's not, and I can tell she needs to hear this. There's a decent chance it's true. From what Clay's told me, Marnie and Drew were close to their father, and they both seem like mostly decent judges of character. But there's no question the guy failed Clay. That's as obvious as the *90210* poster staring me in the face.

It's harder to resent a dead man. Harder, mind you, not impossible.

She turns in my arms and looks up at me, her eyes full of...something. "You're strong."

"Glad you noticed," I say, but her words don't fail to make their mark. I have to be strong for her. I have to make sure she's safe.

"You're mad at me," she says softly. "I could tell from the way you got up."

"It's not you I'm mad at, Clay," I say, tucking some of her honeyed hair behind her ear.

"Who, then? Edgar?"

"I can't keep doing this...whatever we're doing. I can't watch you with him."

Panic flickers in her gaze, the same way it did the other night. "You're leaving me?"

I smooth my hands up and then down her arms. "I'm not leaving you. I *won't* leave you. Not until we find this asshole and give Nutman the chance to do his job for what may be the first time ever. I'm going to keep you safe, Clay. I'm going to be there every step of the way.

"But I'm not the kind of guy who can fuck you in private and watch you play footsie with someone else for the cameras. Edgar James hasn't done anything to me, or you, and I still want to rip him a new one for the way he looks at you. It's only going to get worse if we keep playing this game." My hands reach hers, and I grip them. "We both know this is no fairytale. You're going to go on with your life when this is over, like you should. I'll still be here."

"I live here too," she says. "I'm not leaving Asheville, Rafe. That's what all of this is about. I want a normal life."

I smile and lift a hand to her cheek. "Yeah, but you're not normal. And before you tear into me, let me say I mean it as a compliment. Just this once. You shine brighter, Clay. You can't help it. And whatever it is you decide to do, whether it's acting or making clay dildos, you're going to keep on shining."

"I...I liked today. I *loved* it," she says, tipping her face up to me. "Even after lunch with my mother, I can't think of a better day. I don't want to give up on this before we even know what this is."

Neither do I, if I'm being honest with myself.

I trace her cheek and then lower my hand. "Unless Enoch pushes you down the aisle, you're not going to marry Edgar James. So maybe, after it's done—"

"I'll send him a rock with a break-up note painted on it. He'll like that," she says, grabbing my hand and bringing it back up to her cheek. "You can help me paint it."

"Enoch seemed to think this thing with Edgar was important for you. You can't mess up your career for me, especially since we don't even know if this means anything. For all we know, we both got hit hard with Stockholm Syndrome."

"I don't even know if I want to be an actor anymore," she says in a small voice.

"There are things you love about it," I say, smiling at her, soaking her in while she stands in this space that used to be hers. I force myself to lower my hand before it can weave into her hair and pull her to me. "I've noticed the way you watch the movies you love. It's the same way you look at chocolate cake."

She nods slowly. "You're right. I'm going to call those agents tomorrow. I'd already decided."

"Good. Except tomorrow's Sunday."

"Oh," she says with a slight smile.

"Could be a power move to call them in the morning on the weekend." I nudge her arm.

"I won't do that. I'll let them enjoy their families."

"Mighty big of you, Clay."

She watches me for a long moment, her lips pursing, like she's struggling to hold in words but isn't up for the fight. "Why did you stop painting, Rafe? You're talented. I'm hardly an art connoisseur, but I know a little."

My smile is bitter this time. I probably look a little bit like Dylan on the poster, actually. "I wasn't doing that hot with it." I pause, knowing I shouldn't tell her this next bit, but fuck it. "I hadn't painted for years before today. I... After my mother shot me, I was physically incapable of it for a while, and then I didn't want to anymore. I didn't have any passion for it. I started working out a lot after physical therapy, trying to get strong again, and it became a kind of obsession. So I took a job as a bouncer and then started personal training, and I just didn't paint anymore."

Her eyes look shiny with emotion. "But you did it with me?"

I run a thumb across her cheek. "Yeah," I say wryly. "I'd do anything to shut you up."

"Uh-huh. Thank you, Rafe. That's a beautiful gift. But..." She bites her lip. "Don't you want to try again? I mean, you're so, so *good.*"

"I'm glad you think so." I wink at her, trying for levity. I don't feel any levity, though. Emotion's stirring inside of me, uncomfortable as hell. "But maybe it's best to leave the past in the past. Like I said, I wasn't selling much before all of that went down. You know, being good at something is no guarantee, Clay. Most things in life are decided by luck, and luck's never been on my side."

"You're not going to take a chance for yourself, but you want me to count on myself?" She raises her eyebrows, and it strikes me again that she's becoming more expressive. When I first met her, the night of the clay dildo, she was plenty expressive—and she used most of that expressiveness to tell me I was a dick—but after that, there was a coolness to her, a detachment, like if she lifted her eyebrows too high or moved her mouth too much, it might damage her appearance permanently. It had reminded me of that old saying of mothers everywhere, even mine—*if you keep making that expression, your face will stay that way.*

One corner of my mouth lifts in a lopsided smile. "I never said I wasn't a hypocrite."

"You shouldn't give up on your dream," she insists. "Can't you at least take it up as a hobby again?"

"Maybe," I say, because when I think about it, the idea doesn't leave me cold anymore. There's a spark in the ashes, and I'm self-aware enough to know she put it there. "But if you try selling the paintings I have left to your rich friends, we're going to have a problem."

She lifts her hands toward me, palms out. "I wouldn't do that. I know you'd hate that." She pauses, her eyes fixed on mine, and there's a feeling of electricity in the air that'll either short the light bulbs or my sanity. "I'm not interested in Edgar," she says intently before letting her hands fall. "You know, I don't even know if I like him. He's perfectly nice, but he's kind of...dull."

"I know that," I say, feeling my lips lift a little. "I knew before you did."

"Doesn't that matter?" she asks sadly.

"Not right now." I shift on my feet. "I wish it did, but he was starting to bug me before he left last week, and now I understand why. If I have to watch him put his hands on you—"

"I'm going to talk to Enoch about this. See if we can't figure out a breakup solution that somehow makes Edgar and me insanely popular."

I grin at her. "I like that idea, but hey, wait until your brother goes up there with you. I know you've been wanting to spend more time with him."

"Look at you being sensitive," she says with an appropriate amount of shock.

"Don't get used to it." I squeeze her hand and release it before I'm tempted to do anything else, like pin her to the wall that's displaying that poster. "Let's get back to the dining room before my dad and your aunt start going at it against the dining room table."

"Oh, you noticed too?" she asks, sounding delighted.

I laugh. "Are you trying to get them laid?"

"Maybe. I'm starting to think everyone would benefit from getting laid."

My whole body throbs with her words. "You're not going to make this easy for me, are you?"

"Most things in life are decided by luck, Rafe," she says, her eyes twinkling, "and you've just told me luck isn't on your side."

Of course she's quoting me back to myself disparagingly, and for some reason, it makes me like her more.

REGGIE STAYED LATE LAST NIGHT, after Rafe and I left, and then went home with Aunt Helen. I know this because Marnie texted me well past midnight. I saw it immediately, because I was still awake.

I was exhausted when we got back to the loft, but I couldn't fall asleep, my mind working on dozens of things, from that note the stalker had left on my back to Rafe telling me that the sand in our hourglass had run out—for now, at least. To my mother calling me a slut.

Then Rafe came in at two in the morning. I didn't ask him to come, so he must have heard me tossing and turning. He must have known. He didn't say anything; he just lay beside me and put an arm around me. Surrounded by his warmth, his safety, I fell asleep within five minutes.

When I woke up just now, he was gone. The bed feels cold and empty, other than the small spot where Rue is curled up by my head. There's a feeling of profound loss and abandonment, and then I hear Rafe grunting in the other room. Exercising, I'm sure.

I avoid coming out, because if I see him shirtless and glistening with sweat from exertion, there's no guarantee I'll remember that we've agreed to put things on hold. So I spend a long time getting ready for our meeting with Penn, thinking about how it'll go down. Wondering whether it's him.

If Penn's not my stalker, who could it be? I struggle to believe my Play in Clay teacher or the sweet old man who taught my gardening class could be behind all of this. Reginald from gardening was horrified when he learned I'd accidentally killed a plant because I'd poured my leftover coffee into it every morning, thinking it was a smooth move because someone had told me that coffee grounds were basically free fertilizer...but I don't think he'd *stalk* me over it.

I get dressed, still turning everything around in my mind.

Once I'm ready, I listen at the door like a kid who's afraid to walk in on her parents boning, then suck in a breath, tell myself I'm being stupid and it's my apartment for God's sake, and leave the room.

Rafe's in the kitchen, a T-shirt slung over his muscular shoulder, drinking a glass of orange juice. It's like he belongs here. It's like he's been here always, and there's a funny feeling in my chest.

I obviously don't want to continue to get stalked, but...

I don't want him to leave.

Rue comes running out of the bedroom and does curlicues around Rafe's legs, acting like he wants to climb him like a tree too. Fair. Probably everyone wants to climb him like a tree.

So I'm not sure that why the first thing I say to him is, "You'll have to wear a shirt to the meeting, you know. A shirt will be expected, and probably not a sweaty one."

But I'd be happy to take it off his hands and hoard it under my mattress like Christmas candy, a thought that horrifies me but is undeniably mine.

"Good morning to you too," he says with a slight smile. "I made you your tea."

"You did?" I ask in shock. "Did you add the fake sweetener?"

"It was an assault to my integrity, but I did it. I know what you like."

There's a swell of warmth in me as I pick up the mug from the counter, smiling when I see he's chosen the one kitschy mug in my possession, a *Yes, I'm THAT Sinclair Jones* mug Marnie made for me for Christmas one year.

"You *would* choose that one." I pause, taking a sip of the tea. It's perfect, and I feel a little choked up that he's taking care of me like this, not just protecting me. "Thank you. For the tea. For last night. I didn't sleep at all before you came in."

He grins at me, and it's like a slap to my senses. "And I didn't sleep at all afterward."

I set the mug down with a clack. "Crap, I'm sorry."

"Don't be," he says. "It's not your fault that you're an eleven. We're meeting Nicole and Damien at ten thirty. It takes about forty-five minutes to get to Hendersonville, so we've got about an hour before we have to be there."

"You should shower," I say, then inanely add, "Alone, obviously. Not with me."

"Only takes me five minutes to shower...when I'm alone," he says. "I was thinking we could watch your show before we head out. If you're okay with that."

"I told you," I say, clutching the handle of the mug. "I don't want—"

"I'm not going to look at you differently. I want *you* to see that. And I want to see you acting in something other than that tampon commercial and *Single-Dad Santa*, because if I ever see that movie again, I'm going to break something, and I presume you don't want me to break your shit."

I want to hug him. I mean, I want other things too, because he looks sinful without a shirt on, his gorgeous tattoo a testament to his artistic talent and his muscles a testament to the hard work he puts into everything, but right now I just want a hug.

I don't, though, because everything feels so tenuous between us right now.

"Okay," I stammer out. "I'll get it cued up."

I do, listening as the shower spits out water in the bathroom, imagining it pouring down on Rafe. Imagining him smoothing soap over his muscles, over that scar. Imagining him putting shampoo in his hair.

I almost knock on the door. There's only so much torment one woman can take, but instead I sit on the couch, staring blankly at the TV screen with my face on it until the buzzer rings.

I go to the door and turn on the intercom. "What is it?" I ask, nervous.

"Flowers for you," the attendant says, but he sounds as nervous as I am.

"What's wrong?"

"I know I shouldn't have looked at the card, but I looked at the card. It says they're from Justin Bieber." Fear slides down my spine. The front desk staff knows about the stalker, of course. They've been told to watch out for him. He's eluded them. According to Rafe, it's because they're not very good at their jobs and don't keep an eye on the garage, but maybe he's just that good at stalking.

"Oh. You can bring them up," I say. I should read the note, after all. And take a photo of it for Nicole and Damien before we call Nutman.

A couple of minutes later, the door buzzer rings, and I look through the peephole to see the very nervous boy from the desk carrying an enormous arrangement of red-and-purple flowers. Or maybe not a boy. He has a mop of curly red-gold hair and one of those round baby faces that could be fifteen or thirty. I've met him several times, but I've never asked for his age because it's a rude question, or at least it would be considered one in Hollywood.

Rafe would probably be pissed, but this guy's no threat to me and I know he works for the building. I open the door.

"I'm sorry," he blurts, pushing the heavy vase toward me. He does it so quickly, I nearly topple, but I manage to get a grip on the crystal. In the background, I can hear the shower stopping, mainly because my ears were as attuned to it as a dog to its food bowl.

"You don't have anything to be sorry for, John," I say, trying to sound sympathetic and understanding. Then I catch sight of his name tag. *Joffrey*. Well, shit.

"You know my name?" he asks excitedly, perking up. I can hear footfalls behind me, but I don't turn around. I didn't see Rafe carry any clothes into the bathroom, so it's possible he's in a towel right now. I don't want to draw attention to him, because he wouldn't want Joffrey to see him like that.

I don't want Joffrey to see him like that either, and not just because I'm supposed to be dating Edgar James. I feel protective of Rafe—and of anything like vulnerability on his part. I shift in the doorway, trying to take up more space.

"Well, it looks like I got your name wrong, actually." I can feel Rafe behind me, a prickle of awareness. A pulsing. He's close. It's like my body planted a censor on him so it could be aware of his movements at all time. I clear my throat. "I'm the sorry one."

"No, no," Joffrey says, lifting his hands and taking a step back. "You're right. John's a better name. You know, people have been cracking jokes about my name ever since *Game of Thrones* came out. Maybe I'll change it. It's hard being a Joffrey. Maybe—"

Rafe, suddenly right behind the door, shuts it in the kid's face.

"You shouldn't have opened it while I was in the bathroom," he says, giving me a thunderous look as I turn to him. He's wearing nothing but a pair of athletic shorts, the tree flexing its branches at me. I want to bite it.

"That was really rude," I say, my mouth suddenly dry. "Joffrey and I were having a wonderful conversation about *Game of Thrones*."

"Tell me about the flowers," he says.

Suddenly my hands start shaking, the enormous bouquet shaking with them, and he reaches out to steady them, laying his big palms over mine. "Let's go put them on the table."

"The note says they're from Justin Bieber," I say thinly.

We get them to the table, and he grabs the note and reads it. "That little shit is messing with us," he says under his breath, then pushes it toward me.

The guy even went to the trouble of *sounding* like Justin Bieber. It's written as an apology.

"Let me get my phone," I say. "We should get a photo before we call Nutman."

But when I retrieve my phone, the first thing I see is a text from Enoch:

> Don't be alarmed, but Justin Bieber heard about
> what's going on. He's sending a big-ass flower
> arrangement as an apology because of the masks.
> Should be arriving soon.

Laughter rips out of me, so violent it almost hurts. Tears form in my eyes.

"Shit," Rafe says, sounding horrified. "What's wrong? Are you crying?"

He rushes over to me, and I laugh harder. I can't think of anything that's ever felt this funny before.

"It's... The flowers..." I start, but the words aren't coming out properly, so I thrust my phone at him so he can see the message from Enoch.

Then he's laughing too, and I put my arms around him so I can stay upright, because I'm laughing hard enough that it hurts. Truthfully, that's only part of it though—it feels so damn good to touch him, I don't want to stop. I want to climb him like a tree and cling on for dear life, but I settle for this, for laughing together.

It takes us a long time to quiet down.

"I can't believe the real Justin Bieber sent you flowers," Rafe finally says, looking down at my face. He runs a rough thumb over my bottom lip. There's a second when I'm sure he's going to kiss me, but he doesn't.

"He's nice enough," I sputter out. "I've met him a couple of times."

"Bite your tongue. You're going to take a picture of them for Instagram, aren't you?"

"I kind of have to, don't I?"

"For once, I agree with that," he says, and he actually helps me set up the shot.

When we're done, there's not enough time to watch a full episode of *Sisters of Sin*, and I tell him as much, hoping he'll let it go. Also hoping he won't.

"So we can watch some of it now and some of it later," he says with a grin. "Or is it going to be such a cliffhanger I won't be able to wait?"

I shove his arm, enjoying the burst of fizzy energy I get from touching him. Of course, his arm doesn't move at all. In some ways, it feels like yesterday didn't happen, and it's also the only thing I want to think about.

We sit on the couch, touching slightly, as if our bodies can't bear to not be touching, and I turn the show on.

———

"It totally changed the way you think of me," I say, trying to sound glib and not panicked. We're in the car, on the way to Henderson-ville, and Rafe has barely said two words to me since we turned the show off. Okay, three. He said *Ready to go?*

Is he purposefully tormenting me, or does it just come naturally?

"Yes," he says seriously, his gaze out the windshield, his sunglasses on. I'm sitting next to him again, like I did yesterday. "I'm now convinced you're a college girl named Rue. I can never look at you the same way again."

"You're a jerk."

"You're a great actress," he says, glancing at me quickly. "If there are things you love about it, you really should give it another shot. On your own terms."

I feel like a glowworm, lit from within.

"The show totally sucks, though. It's like what the baby would be if *90210* got it on with *The Young and the Restless*."

I scowl at him. "I wish I were eating a snack so I could throw some at you. And also because I'm hungry. And also, you've just admitted to watching *The Young and the Restless*."

"My dad made me." He grins back at me, shameless. "I'll get you a snack before I tuck you into your time-out room, how about that?"

"You just got another invisible chocolate-covered pretzel thrown at you."

"Seems like a waste."

I'll bet his eyes are sparkling behind his glasses. His mouth is tipped up on one side, and his strong jaw seems to be begging for my touch. *This* seems like a waste. Ignoring this connection between us. I've never felt this kind of spark with anyone else. Of course, the brighter it burns, the quicker it might snuff out, or so my mother always told me before bemoaning the fate that had landed her pregnant and married to my father, but...

I like Rafe, is all. I'm glad he's here.

We spend the rest of the drive talking, Rafe honoring my need to fill the space with chatter to calm my nerves. He tells me what little he knows of Damien's plan, and I have to admit it sounds like the right strategy. Penn believes in the power of positive thinking—most people might be skeptical of a stranger contacting them out of the blue with *fantastic news*, but he probably thinks his intentions are coming back to him a thousandfold.

When we get to the teahouse, a little brick building with a red stucco roof, we park outside and head in. The interior looks like the set of a Bohemian movie, with thick Persian rugs, copper teapots, and various floor pillows and low tables. There aren't many people here, just a group of twentysomething men and women sitting on pillows around a small round table with a copper pot of tea and a platter of small cakes.

It doesn't seem like the kind of place you'd question a potential stalker. Then again, it *does* look like the kind of place Penn would come to pretend to write screenplays. Maybe they wanted to give him a false sense of comfort.

A peppy brunette woman in a crisp red apron approaches us. "Would you like to sit on the floor or on a poof?" she asks.

Rafe shoots me a *get me out of here* look, then says, "We're meeting some friends. They've rented the meeting space and the private room upstairs." Glancing at me, he adds, "Clay here would like some snacks delivered to the room."

If the woman recognizes me, there's no sign, and I'm grateful for it. Right now, I feel like a hedgehog with its prickles out. I don't want eyes on me; I want snacks.

"What kind of snacks?"

"Get her a party platter," he says, folding his glasses and tucking them away. "And some chamomile." He shoots me a look. "With stevia."

"We don't carry stevia," the woman says with obvious disgust. "It's not that kind of establishment, sir."

"She'll settle for sugar."

Then Damien climbs down the circular staircase at the back and beckons us up. He's wearing a suit without a tie, the first three buttons undone. It takes me a half a second to recognize Nicole as the woman who's standing two stairs above him in a prim skirt suit with rectangular spectacles and a brunette wig. She's altered her nose to make it more prominent. She has the expression of someone who's spent a long time smelling shit and doesn't remember what roses smell like.

I turn to Rafe as we walk toward them and then start up the

stairs. "What if it's not Penn?" I say in an undertone. I don't like how scared I sound.

He reaches for my hand and squeezes it, sending warmth unfurling through me as if he's a space heater made human. "Then we'll keep talking to people. We're not going to stop until we find this guy and make him pay. I've already made plans to talk to Spencer later today, and if we need to, we can circle back to that guy Marnie used to see. Then the other people from your craft classes. We're going to figure out who's behind this, Clay. I won't rest until we do."

I believe him. And in that moment, even if the feeling doesn't last, even if it *can't*, I feel like everything's going to be okay.

I WANT to strangle Penn Reed.

I want to drown him in an industrial-sized kettle of tea so he dies with the taste of chamomile in this mouth.

These murder wishes started within fifty seconds of the literary porn star sitting down on a gold-embroidered red poof, and they have nothing to do with his tweed coat, glasses that are probably made of clear glass rather than prescription lenses, and the pretentious little goatee that he probably spends twenty minutes tending to each morning. No, my loathing really kicked in when he took out a folder of printed personal photos of Sinclair and offered to show us—complete strangers to him—before he'd even ordered his tea, specifying to the server that it had to be not too hot, not too cold, like he was Goldilocks of the woods.

I'm seeing red.

Nicole and Damien are much better at hiding their judgment, if they feel any. They pore over the photos with interest, and Nicole asks him, without any judgement in her voice, if he took a few of them while she was sleeping.

"Oh, you know," he answers. "It's what lovers do. I didn't sell any of those to the press, though. Just the ones she knew about."

Maybe the tea is too good for him. I'll drown him in diet soda instead. Or nonalcoholic beer.

"You know, I like to really live the role," Damien says, a convincing smile on his face. "What's it like dating a movie star? Here you were, this writer, and Sinclair Jones asked you out." He scrunches his face. "Is that how it went? Did *she* ask you out? In the script, Poe was approached by Claire."

Yeah, Penn's real creative with the names.

"Well...I might have changed things a bit." He looks like a grinning rat. "But she said yes, huh? Only took her forty-eight hours and three bouquets to answer me."

"So you weren't afraid to come on a little strong," Damien says, writing that down in a little moleskin notebook he'd set out in front of him. "I like that. Everyone loves a confident man."

"Sometimes women need to be told what they want," he says with a self-satisfied grin. "It was like that with her. I might not be her usual type, but I knew she'd give me a shot."

"Or maybe she said no and you chose not to listen," I say, my tone not quite as easy-going as I was trying for. Thinking about Clay in the next room, listening to this crap, and Clay of however many months ago, trying to let this shitbag down easy but getting bothered by him until she gave in, I pick up my teacup. The delicate handle instantly cracks off. I throw it down, and it lands with a clink next to Penn, who edges his chair away from mine.

"It wasn't like that, man," he says, his skin taking on a pallor. Good.

"Of course it wasn't," Nicole says soothingly. "My friend here is a bit...mercurial. It's what makes his movies so charged with emotion. You're right, of course. Most of us women like a big, strong man to tell us what to do. You get me?"

"Uh, sure," he says, giving me a sidelong look.

"So how'd you handle it when she left you in the cold, bud?" she says. "Did you try to do some more talking? Since talking her around worked so well the first time, I mean."

He nudges the professionally bound manuscript on the table. "It's in the script," he says. "You read it, right?"

"Yeah," Damien slides in, his tone smooth as good whiskey. "But it's like I said—I need to really embody your experience to get the role right. Igor and Dana say they'll only do the movie if I'm attached as the star, and I'm interested, but only if I can do it the right way. That's why I insisted on meeting you with them."

"Uh, what movies were you in, man? You didn't say."

And Shitbird was too dumb to ask.

"Me?" Damien says, pressing a hand to his chest. "My background is in theater."

"Ah," Penn says knowingly. "So that's why you like to method act."

I'm not sure what one has to do with the other, but I don't say so. I just drink some of the tea. It needs sugar or even stevia, but I wouldn't tell Clay that. Don't want her to take too much satisfaction in it.

"Well," Penn says, rubbing his hands together, "I guess I got a little...poetic at the end. Perils of being a writer." He gives Damien a *you'd understand* look and pushes his chair farther away from me, correctly deducing that I will not understand. "I brought some dead flowers to her trailer. Three different bouquets so it would—"

"Match up with the ones you sent her at the beginning," Damien says, snapping his fingers as if it were a genius thing to do and not creepy as hell. "Nice touch. That'll work well in the movie. A lovelorn man giving dead flowers to his lover to signify the demise of their love. Poetic, like you said." His grin spreads wider. "Everyone loves to root for the underdog, the loser. You know, pathetic characters are my favorite, because they require some real acting chops."

"It's true," Nicole offers. "It's hard for him to play characters like that, because he's so confident and sexy, but he can pull it off if he pushes hard."

"I'm not pathetic," Penn snaps. "I was making a point. I wasn't lovelorn. I was telling her that she did me dirty and I knew it. That I wasn't going to let her get away with it."

"Yeah, nothing makes a point like a bunch of dead flowers someone's going to stuff in the trash," Damien says, winking at Penn as if they're in on a joke together. "It's okay, brother. You can be vulnerable with us. The best movies in cinema are the ones where the man really lets himself be crushed. Speaking of which, let's take a look at the ending of your script. They end up getting back together, which Igor and Dana here were over the moon about. They just love a happy ending to a romance." He grimaces. "I gotta tell you, though. I just didn't buy it."

"Why's that?" Penn asks thickly, like he's realized this isn't going the way he thought it would or wanted it to. Like he's not sure where it's going next, but he doesn't want to put a halt to things because this might still be his dream—or as close as a man like him is likely to get to it.

Damien takes a slow sip of tea, knowing full well he's got Shitbird on the hook, and some of the tension in me drains. They know what they're doing here. The real question is whether Penn's our guy. He could be. He has the same build as the stalker, or close enough, and even if he didn't do those things personally, he could have paid someone to do them. He's not nearly as smart as he thinks he is, but I have to admit he's probably smart enough to outwit Nutman. Plus, anyone with a TV and access to old episodes of *Law & Order* knows to wear gloves or wipe their prints.

Finally, Damien sets the cup down. "Here's the thing: it's not believable. Sure, people might believe a starlet would have a fling with an average joe, but will they really buy it that she'd end up with one?"

Well, damn. It feels like Damien reached into my head and

pulled out the snarl of thoughts that kept me up last night. Not that I want a happily ever after with Clay, necessarily, but I have to admit I'd like to have something.

"People love fairytales," Penn objects, his lower lip jutting out. "It's a fairytale."

"Oh, for sure," Damien says. "Maybe the reason I'm having trouble with it is because things didn't work out so well between you two in real life, did they? I think that's what's messing with my mojo. What are the chances you can work it out with her? I feel like that would help me channel the ending more. Right now, I'm coming up with a blank, because I can't see it happening."

Penn looks like someone slapped him in the face. Before he can say anything, Damien snaps his fingers again. "Hey, why don't you send her some more flowers? Living, dead, whatever floats your boat, kemosabe. I bet that'd be the ticket. She'd return your calls anyway. Maybe even send you a text."

"As it happens, I did send her some flowers recently," Penn says sullenly. "She didn't have the decency to respond, so what can I say? Some things work out better in fiction. That's why people need fairytales like this one."

"Were they dead like the other ones?" Nicole asks. "Speaking as a woman here, I don't think anyone would be happy to receive dead flowers, even if they're meant as some sort of message. I mean, send something shitty like baby's breath if you want to tell her you're sad. Dead flowers?" She juts her fist out, thumb down, and makes a raspberry noise as she quickly lowers it.

"I thought she was the kind of woman who appreciated poetry," he says bitterly. "She told me she was. And she didn't respond when I sent her the fresh bouquet."

"Did you include your name when you sent either bouquet?" Nicole asks.

"Why would I?" he asks as if offended by the suggestion. "Who else would they have been from?"

A prickle travels up my back.

He's admitted to sending Clay two bouquets of anonymous flowers, alive and dead. Still, I've learned some self-control over the years. I'm no longer the man who beat that asshole in my mother's kitchen while she held a gun on me. The man who might have killed him if she hadn't almost killed me.

I didn't even hurt him that badly, but I would have, if given the chance, and I think she knew it.

I ball my hands into fists and give a derisive laugh. "Yeah, man, who else would send the most beautiful woman in the country flowers? Could only be you. Then again, you're probably the only one who's sent her *dead* flowers."

"Huh," Damien says, scratching the back of his neck. "You should be more careful. I heard that Sinclair has a stalker. If the police find out about the dead flowers, you could be in some shit."

Nicole nudges his arm. "Don't say that, James. For all we know, he's the one who's been stalking her, and if so, that's his own business." She turns to Penn, who's staring at her with an open-mouthed look of shock. "You should know we're nonjudgmental. We like to have a happy set, the kind where people can be free to be themselves without any of that Me Too shit. So sexually harass and stalk away, since that seems to be your thing."

"That's not... I'm not the person who's been stalking her. I wouldn't do that."

"Huh, I figured you were," Damien says. "Did you think he was?" he asks me.

"Yes," I growl.

Nicole nods several times. "Yup, me three. It was all those tweets that cinched it for me. But like I said, we're not judgmental. We understand the kind of love that'll turn a man into a creeper."

"I'm trying to, at least," Damien says. "But I've only gotten dumped once, and it was kind of a relief, to be honest, so I don't know what it feels like." He taps the end of his pen on the table. "Can you tell me in great detail?"

"What's going on here?" Penn asks, pushing back from the table. "Are you really interested in the script, or is this—" He gasps. "Are you paparazzi?"

I give him a dubious look. "If we were, would we be following *you*?"

"Police?" he asks, his face getting paler.

"Huh, we don't get accused of that often," Nicole says. "Do we, James?"

"Friend, we're here to make a movie," Damien says. "The kind of movie that will earn awards and accolades for all of us. You can't do that without getting a little uncomfortable. That's what this is about —we want to delve deep, really get a sense of what you've been through. Maybe it drove you a bit crazy when she left...you wouldn't be the only one." He grins at Penn, a *we're just a couple of guys talking about crazy women* grin, and it seems to work because the guy stays in his seat.

"Sorry," he says, scrubbing a hand over his face. "It's just...it *did* drive me a little crazy, I guess. First she dumped me, and then she got me fired from the show. Who does that?"

"Are you sure it was her?" Damien asks sympathetically.

"Who else would it have been?" Penn says in the same tone that he used to ask who else would have sent Clay flowers. Then he takes a long, contemplative sip of his tea.

"You sure it wasn't because you sucked at your job?" Nicole says. "Because if that's why they fired you, we should really know going into this."

He sputters out chamomile. "Excuse me?"

"We need to make sure you have a solid reputation in the biz," she says. "You understand. Sexual harassment on set is one thing, but if you suck a ding-dong at rewrites, that's salient information, you know? So what was it? What clued you off that you got fired because of Sinclair?"

His expression stormy, he says, "I was told one of the stars had filed a complaint about me. Who else would it have been?"

"Seems to me you're taking a lot on faith," I say. "Did her mother like you?"

He looks like he just swallowed the tea ball. "Are you implying...?"

"That she's the one who ratted you out?" I ask. "Maybe. Seems to me you wouldn't be her first choice for her daughter. You're a little..."

"He's being nice," Nicole says. "You're a *lot* unimpressive as a match for a TV star. But hey, that's okay as long as you didn't get fired for being a shit writer. I mean, James here is going to play you in the movie, and he's *very* impressive." She winks bawdily. "Leveling up, aren't you, buddy?"

He stiffens as if someone shoved a poker up his ass, and I decide that for all their bullshit, I like Nicole and Damien. "I'm not sure I appreciate the tenor of this conversation."

She gives several micronods, then says, "Growing a backbone, huh? Good for you. Does it hurt? It totally hurts, doesn't it?"

He pushes his chair back again, but before he can stand, Damien says, "Stay seated," in a tone of voice that brooks no argument. Sure enough, his ass stays glued to the chair. Damien pulls up a photo on his phone and shows it to him. "Are these the dead flowers you sent to Sinclair Jones?"

Penn looks around, as if one of the servers might save him. "Yes," he finally answers. "It was supposed to be a poetic gesture, man. I didn't do her any harm. I'm not stalking her. I wouldn't *do* that."

"Not going to ask us who we really are?" Damien says, tilting his head. "That seems suspicious to me. It comes off as a guilty conscience at work."

"No," Penn says, coming off jittery. "No, that's not it. I just...I know how it looks, man. But—" He pans his gaze from Damien to Nicole to me and pushes his chair away a little more because apparently I'm still staring at him like he's a bug I'd like to squash. A gasp escapes him. "It's you. You're that bodyguard from the pictures. You..."

"Seen me before?" I say, cracking my knuckles. "Maybe from behind a Justin Bieber mask?"

His laughter is slightly hysterical. "You really think I'd mess with you? No, thank you. No. I wouldn't take that risk. I like my face the way it is."

Nicole snorts.

"I don't think you'd challenge me to a fight, no," I say. "But you seem like exactly the sort of person who'd run around making threats. I'd say that's exactly who you come off as."

His color is even chalkier than before, and he looks like he wishes he didn't drink all that subpar tea. "I'm not," he says. "I'm not! And I can prove it. I heard some guy messed with her at a bar on Friday night. I was here in Hendersonville, working at my part-time job." He takes a deep breath as if he needs to steel himself. "I was at Chuck E. Cheese."

"Maybe you should have tried being a literary porn star," Nicole says, not even bothering to whisper it.

"Excuse me?" he says.

"You could have hired someone to make the arrangements," Damien suggests, lifting his eyebrows.

"But I didn't. I didn't!" he insists. "I'm...I'm broke. I've spent all the money from the show and selling those photographs. Do you really think I have the resources to hire people to harass Sinclair? I don't. She took that from me."

"Sounds like you want revenge," Damien comments mildly.

Penn pushes back from his chair. "I just want her to know what she took from me," he says. "I'd like her to look me in the face and apologize."

I really want to kick him in the ass, but I don't want to take away Sinclair's opportunity to do it. So I satisfy myself by saying, "Seems to me she gave you inspiration for this screenplay and several photos you've sold to the press. Who needs to apologize to who?"

"Whom," he says in a small voice. "It would be *who needs to apologize to whom.*"

"This is why no one likes you," Nicole offers. Then she calls out to Clay, and the door to the private meeting room opens.

Clay stands in the opening like a goddess, her honeyed hair in waves, her eyes full of fire, her hand on the curves of her hips.

"Oh, shit," Penn says, staggering back. I choose that moment to stretch out my leg.

He falls down, and Sinclair storms into the room.

"I didn't get you fired, you jerk," she says. He tries to crabwalk away from her. "You're shopping a screenplay about me?"

"Loosely inspired," he says, finally getting to his feet.

"No," Nicole says in a bored tone as she removes her prosthetic nose.

Penn gasps in horror.

"I'm sorry to say I had the misfortune of reading the entire thing. It's pretty by the book," Nicole continues. "Until they get back together, that is."

"You sent those flower arrangements to my apartment," Sinclair says, staring him down. "How'd you get my address?"

"I saw something on a blog about your sister's boyfriend's bar. I..." He gulps and looks at me. I wave at him and smile threateningly. "I followed you. But just once. The flowers were a message I wanted to send, but I wouldn't have done any of that other shit. I don't care that you're with Edgar James. I *love* Edgar James. Actually, I was hoping you might agree to—"

"I'm not getting you his autograph," she fumes. "Did you throw that brick at us?"

"No," he says adamantly.

I'm not sure whether I believe him. Evidence suggests he's our guy, but he's right about one thing—he's a coward, and some of the stunts the stalker has pulled have been ballsy. Risky. I'm not sure I believe this guy would have put himself in the line of fire. Even so, he followed her. He trailed her to her apartment. My mind goes back to drowning him in chamomile or nonalcoholic beer. Maybe both, at the same time.

The thought of this prick following her makes me physically ill, and from the look on Clay's face, she feels violated. Afraid. She's mad right now, but beneath it is the knowledge that someone she trusted, even if she shouldn't have, chose to sell photos of her and follow her without her knowledge.

I get up and lean over him, letting him feel the effect of my size and physique. Then I grab his collar and lift him up by it, just slightly, so he can tell that I could lift him off his feet with almost no effort at all if I so chose. "We'll be passing all of this information on to the cops, *friend*. And if you ever talk to her or about her again, we'll know, and we will not be pleased. That includes trying to shop around this absolute travesty of a screenplay or any more photos of her, asleep or not. Got it?"

"I'm not afraid of you," he says.

"Yes, you are," I refute. "And if you're not, you should be."

"That's a threat," he sputters as I set him on his feet. "You *threatened* me."

"Yes, I did. If you're smart, you'll remember that."

SINCLAIR

"I SORT OF GET WHY you'd break off a piece of that," Nicole says. "He might be a twerpy little bit of a thing, but he has a voice like a bottle of bourbon fucked a pecan pie."

"*I* don't get it," I say, glancing at Rafe, who's still glowering. I've never witnessed such a sexy takedown of someone on my behalf. It's hard to remember why we should stay away from each other. In fact, I wish Nicole and Damien would peace out of the private room, where we relocated after Penn stumbled off, so I can show him how much I appreciate him.

Then again, he's the one who said he needed some distance until the EJ thing is over, so I should respect that. I do. But I also want him in a way that I've never wanted anyone else. Especially not Penn.

It made me feel like a goose had walked over my grave, to borrow Aunt Helen's phrase, to learn he'd followed me to my apartment from the bar. That he's been watching me. I mean, he has to be the person behind all of this, right?

"Do you think Nutman will talk to him?" I ask.

"Sure, I think so," Damien says, popping one of the tiny cakes from the party platter into his mouth. He chews, turning his lips down and nodding slightly as if it's surprisingly good, swallows, then says, "Don't know how much good it'll do, but that guy seems easily spooked. Might be enough to get him to step down...if it *is* him."

"You don't think it's him?" I practically screech. Because he's been following me around and sending me flowers. Because he took photographs of me while I was asleep and is shopping a screenplay about our five-minute relationship. It has to be him, doesn't it?

Damien lifts a hand, palm out. "Didn't say that. It's definitely partly him. But he says he has an alibi for that night at the bar and claims he's too broke to pay people to harass you. We have to look into that."

"We need to keep you safe until they do," Rafe says, looking at me. "We're not taking any chances."

I'm relieved. I want this to be over, obviously, but I also don't think the loft will feel safe after Rafe leaves. It'll definitely feel lonely. It did before he came. My place isn't even that big, but it felt empty and echoing, as if I'd been put away in a box like a Christmas ornament no one wanted. That's why I adopted Rue, even though I had no faith in my ability to nurture him.

"Okay," I say, giving a small nod. Then, looking at Nicole and Damien, I add, "So you're going to stick around here, look into Penn's alibi?"

"Yeah," Nicole says, "plus there's a pretty chill spa downtown. We might check that out. I wouldn't mind a hot stone massage."

She doesn't seem like the kind of person who'd go for something like that, but I have to admit it sounds nice. I wouldn't mind having a two-hour massage, followed by a several-hour nap.

"Don't forget Chuck E. Cheese." Damien grins at her.

"We'll call Nutsack from the car," Rafe says with a sigh, because it obviously brings him no joy to talk to that man. "What are we going to do if the guy's alibi checks out?"

"We'll circle back," Nicole says. "You said you were going to talk to the painting guy?"

He gives a nod, and I remember what he said about Spencer.

"Yeah, we're heading over there right now."

"When were you going to tell me about this?" I ask, frowning at him.

"Right now seemed like a good time," he says with a simple tipping up of his lips.

"Maybe you should ask him to have tea with you," Nicole says, popping a little cake from the tray into her mouth. Still chewing, she says, "Then you can snap off the handle of another teacup. That was a baller move. Literally. That guy looked like his testicles were crawling up into his body."

"You broke a teacup?" I ask Rafe, my eyes widening.

In my head, I ask, *You broke a teacup for me?*

Before this week, he seemed amused by me, not with me. It's surprising how far we've come, how fast. Then again, he's right— we've spent practically every minute together this week. That's a sure way to end up hating someone or...

Learning to tolerate them, my logical brain insists.

"Shoddy craftsmanship," Rafe says with snort. "It practically broke itself."

"Let us know what you find out from him," Damien says with a nod. "You all go ahead. Nicole seems fond of this snack board, so we'll probably be here awhile."

"Yes, I will be bringing the leftovers with me, absolutely," she says.

"Did you eat anything?" Rafe asks me, his scrutiny intense.

"No," I say, lifting a hand to my throat. "I heard his voice and lost my appetite."

He swears under his breath, then gets up from his chair, the movement so powerful it nearly topples over. "Let's go."

So we do.

We're quiet in the car at first, even as Rafe pulls out of the parking space and gets us to the highway. Then he put his sunglasses on, and I snort-laugh.

"What?" he says, but his voice is more fond than annoyed. "It's sunny."

"You're right. I just feel a little punch drunk." And sad. And turned on. And hopeful. And scared. And so many emotions I can barely name them all. When I look at my life before this year, before the horrible thing my mother did to Marnie, I can barely remember feeling anything. The drive to succeed. The emptiness that grew inside of me because each day was the same, planned by other people and not me. The conflicting feelings I had for the mother who never seemed to be more than a few feet away from me.

"I have a surprise for you," Rafe says, giving me a quick sidelong glance before he peers forward again.

"What is it?" I ask, feeling a sense of excitement that's totally ludicrous since he hasn't confirmed it's a good surprise. "It's not a bad surprise, is it? Because I'm not in the mood for a bad surprise."

"I guess you'll have to tell me," he says in a maddening nonanswer.

"It's not going to be Spencer's dick on a platter, is it? He wasn't that bad."

He laughs and drums the wheel with his fingers. "Not this time." I get another sidelong glance. "I'm sorry, Clay. That Penn guy's a real dick. It's bullshit that he took photos of you and sold them."

I give a little lift of my shoulders as if to say it's no big deal. "It happens. It's not the first time. Sometimes I'm the one who sells them."

"Your mother, you mean," he comments.

I don't respond. We both know he's right.

My phone rings then, and I check the readout. "It's Enoch," I say as I lift it to my ear and pick up the call. "Hello?"

"So, want the bad news or the worse news?"

"I'm not going to like this conversation, then," I say with a sigh, feeling Rafe's regard. "Tell me everything in a way that flows naturally, I guess. I can take it."

"People have been talking online about the scene with your mother at the restaurant yesterday," he says. "But that's not a big deal. I say you do an Instagram Live about it, tell everyone you were trying to make nice but she was being her big old exploitive self. You're taking a break from toxicity. Huh. Too bad it's not January. It would have made a nice *New Year, New You* segment. Anyway, that's the bad news."

"And the worse?" I mutter, because it's better to know, I suppose.

"There's online chatter about you and Rafe. Someone says they saw you sitting on his lap in the car outside of the restaurant. And there were sightings of you two in the emergency room last night. What happened, anyway? I'm hoping everyone still has all of their limbs?"

"Yeah," I mutter. "Long story, but Reggie cut himself with a carving knife because he was drawn in by a Slanket commercial. Okay, now that I'm saying it, I have to admit it's not a long story so much as a weird one."

He laughs, then pauses and says, "I think your mother might be behind some of the speculation, to be honest. I recognized one of her Reddit handles in the thread."

Reddit.

"She has multiple handles on Reddit?" It's the first I've heard she has any.

"Yeah," he says. "She was using them a month and a half ago, when she was making all those baseless accusations about you, trying to fuel the fire. We talked about this."

Maybe we did, but that was before those Justin Biebers showed up at that bar, brought there by a Reddit thread. I feel a frown coming on, but I hold it back. Not because of the lines it would create, but because I know Rafe is paying close attention to me and I don't want to worry him. Not yet.

"So. What's this mean?"

"EJ's fans are up in arms, and everyone's worried you've broken up."

Maybe I should be more worried about that, but maintaining the image of my false relationship is the last thing that interests me. Still, I know this is important to Enoch. Edgar and I are both his clients, and if I bail without smoothing the situation over, it'll look bad for him. I don't want to screw him over. He helped me when I desperately needed help, and that means something to me.

"Speaking of which," I say slowly, "I'm not saying it needs to happen imminently, but if I wanted to put an end to that situation, could you come up with a strategy for me?"

He curses, and I'm certain I've pissed him off. Then I hear him addressing someone else, the words muffled. He comes back. "Sorry. I was just telling Gracie her favorite words: *you're right*. There's something between you and Rafe, isn't there?"

I let myself glance at Rafe. "I don't know. Maybe. I know I signed a contract, but I just... It doesn't feel right anymore, lying. I don't want that. Even if it helps my career. Maybe I can appear on the show as his ex or something."

"I'm not sure you need him, to be honest. The thing with the rock looked great for you, and people are rooting for you after your falling out with your mother. But give me a few days to work something out. In the meantime, I'd suggest announcing that you went to the emergency room with Rafe to help his dad and you're just friends. That'll keep people satisfied for the time being. You might want to do it now, though. Don't give things time to escalate, especially with the stalker situation unresolved."

"It might be," I say, feeling a blossoming of hope in my chest. I tell him quickly about the situation with Penn.

"Good," he says. "That's great. I hope you've got your guy."

His words wrap around me in a funny way, and I find myself thinking about Rafe and how I'll no longer need a bodyguard if I no longer have a stalker. I don't want him to go. Everything inside of me rejects the idea.

"Yeah," I say softly, peering out of the side window and watching some trees blur by. "I hope so too."

We hang up, and I see that I have two missed calls from Edgar James's sat phone. Crap. He must have seen the news reports too. I don't feel like calling him back, though, so I just shoot off a quick text saying that I've spoken with Enoch about the gossip and am going to handle the situation.

He immediately texts back:

> I'm worried about you. Do you still plan on joining us on Monday? We'd love to have you—and your brother, of course. The producers are excited about your storyline.

I feel a spurt of annoyance, then type:

> They're excited I'm being stalked?

> No, that didn't come out right. They just think we're great on camera together. So do I. I don't think we should let that go to waste.

I tap the side of my phone before responding:

> I don't think I'm coming on Monday. Maybe not at all, although I realize I'd have to work something out with the producers. We'll talk later, but this has all been a bit much. I think I need some time to myself.

> I hope you'll reconsider. I really think you'll be safer here. Plus, there's something I've been wanting to talk to you about.

We'll talk later.

I have to tell him about Penn and my mother, obviously—he deserves an update—but I can't stomach the thought of calling him right now. The last time we saw each other, he was coming on a little strong, or at least strong for him, and the reason Rafe doesn't want to explore the spark between us is because he can't watch another man touching me, flirting with me. Even if it's an act.

Even if it's an act.

I plop the phone onto my lap and turn toward Rafe.

"I'm not going to pretend I didn't hear everything you said," he says. "I can't force my ears to be nonoperational at will."

"I know," I say. I need to tell him everything, and I will, but for some reason the words that pop out of my mouth are these: "You said you don't want to see where this"—I wave between the two of us—"goes because you don't want to see me with EJ, even if it's an act...but I'm an actress. Would you feel the same way about watching me on-screen or when I'm filming?"

"No," he says, facing forward.

"So what's your issue with EJ?" I ask, baffled and a little annoyed.

"For one thing, he wants you."

I flinch. "What are you talking about? Up until a few days ago, he could barely stand to look at me. He spent half of our dinner in the bathroom last week."

"He's always wanted you." His lips twitch. "He just doesn't like listening to you."

"Ha, ha, very funny."

"I didn't say I don't like to listen to you, Clay." He gives me a quick glance. "Just that he doesn't."

"Some of my costars have wanted me too," I gripe. "Would that be a problem for you?"

"Not as such," he says. "Which brings us to my other gripe with ole EJ: the whole world thinks you're his. *That's* a problem for me."

"But why?"

Another quick glance—this one so hot, so heavy with wanting, I'm instantly wet for him. "Because if you were mine, I'd be proud of it. I wouldn't want to hide it like it's a dirty little secret. Besides, you make me want to paint. Something tells me I'd paint a whole museum of you. People would know."

That feeling of need spreads. If we were anywhere but a highway, I'd be tempted to force him to pull over so I could straddle him in the driver's seat. I'd even let him leave his sunglasses on. "Do you want me to be yours?"

"I don't break teacups for just anyone. But the problems I mentioned the other day, those are still real." He glances ruminatively out of the front windshield, then says, "They saw you at the hospital."

There's something a little self-satisfied about his tone, and I roll my eyes and say, "Oh my God. Are you seriously going to say *I told you so*? Your father had a very serious wound. He got seven stitches."

He laughs. "I'm kidding. Mostly. Anyway, what else did Enoch tell you?"

I tell him about my mother and Reddit, and a scowl forms on his face. "We need to tell Damien and Nicole."

"On it," I say, getting out my phone and texting them.

"And Nutsack," he says. "Let's call him over Bluetooth. He needs to know everything we've learned about Penn too. Especially about those flowers."

"One of these days you're going to call him Nutsack by accident."

"Nah, when I do it, it'll be on purpose."

I give him another sidelong glance. "After we talk to him, I'm going to have to do an Instagram Live to defuse the situation with my mother...and EJ. Enoch's going to come up with a strategy for us to publicly break up, but he asked me to give him a few days. I feel like I owe him that much. I do have a contractual obligation to appear on a few episodes of the show, but I think Enoch can figure out a way to work around it."

"You don't have to explain yourself to me, Clay," he says tightly. If I peeked behind his sunglasses, I bet he'd look peeved, the way he does when something falls out of his sandwich or the wrong person gets eliminated on one of the shows we've been marathon watching when we're bored at the loft.

"I know," I say softly. "But I want to. I'm not going to go to set with him tomorrow."

I hope it's not my imagination that the corners of his lips lift slightly.

I meant what I said to him. I want to see where this thing between us can lead, what it can be. Because I can't imagine what my life would look like anymore without Rafe. Wearing those sunglasses of his, smirking at me and giving me sidelong glances. Taking in everything I say and offering his advice, sought after or not.

"What about your brother? He was counting on some quality time with EJ."

"He'll live," I say. "Maybe EJ will sign a hat for him as a parting gift."

He grunts a laugh, but I can tell he's pleased.

"I'll find another way to connect with my brother. Maybe I'll ask him to invite me to his D&D games."

"You're going to play D&D?" he asks, as if amused by the thought. "I think we should do an Instagram Live about *that*."

"Very funny. Should I call Nutman?"

He gives a long, world-weary sigh. "Hell, I guess so. You ready to get pissed off?"

"We'll be pissed off together," I tell him.

He looks at me briefly, in a way I can't interpret because of those sunglasses. "Hey, that's almost romantic."

twenty-seven

RAFE

NUTMAN DIDN'T ANSWER, not that I'm surprised, but I left him a long, detailed message he'll probably skip. Now I'm struggling to listen to Sinclair's IG Live without rolling my eyes. It's a wasted effort, because no one would be able to see behind my sunglasses, but I'm fighting the good fight. Logically, I know why she's saying these things about Edgar and me. I understand the need for it. But I'm still a little pissed by the whole thing.

Maybe I'm not cut out to be involved with a celebrity. I've never cared what people think of me—the opposite, in fact. If I don't care for someone, I'd rather tell them to go get stuffed than try to butter them up.

Or maybe I'm just jealous. Maybe I don't like the way she talks about EJ, with a playful little twist of her lips because it reminds me of when they first started this farce.

I could tell she wanted him then. It was in those little looks she gave him, the way she'd try to touch his arm. Maybe that's leaked into my attitude toward the whole thing. Or maybe it's the firm way she tells her fans that she and I are just friends and she only brought my father to the emergency room because she was concerned he might lose his arm—a pretty extreme exaggeration. Then she swivels the camera to me and says, "Look, we're buddies out for a drive! I love to give him shit about his sunglasses. Say something, Rafe!"

I grunt, "Something."

Her laughter is real for a moment, and I soak it in. I'm starting to need her laughter, not just crave it.

It hasn't passed me by that this arrangement between us, this constant togetherness, is probably coming to an end sooner rather than later.

I don't like the thought of leaving her alone. I'd like to think it's just because I'm protective of her, because it's been my job to watch out for her for over a month and I'm used to it, the way you get used to a callous on your foot or a cold you can't shake, but I know that's not true. I have feelings for her, feelings that have twined around me tighter and tighter before I even realized they were there.

I don't know what to do with that. It would be one thing if my dick were the only part of me that reacts to her presence—that's happened since the beginning—but it's more than that. It's deeper. Like I don't want to just protect her body but her soul. Her happiness. Her fulfillment.

I'm definitely in trouble.

Clay ends her one-sided chat, thank God, and we keep driving for another couple of minutes before we reach our destination.

"We're going to Spencer's studio?" she asks, giving me a wide-eyed look as I park the car in the gravel lot outside the big, sprawling building.

"Not his studio," I say, "although I will be talking to Spence while we're here." I get out and start to circle around the for her door, but she's out before I can get to it.

"So whose studio are we visiting?" she asks, spanning the short distance between us.

"That's the surprise. Allow me my gesture."

She gives me a sidelong look but then nods, and I feel a swell of...

pride, maybe. Because she trusts me, and I must have done something right to have earned that trust. If I don't fail her, then maybe I won't have to feel like a failure.

We walk toward the building together. I have the urge to take her hand, something I'm not sure I've ever felt since I was a kid, reaching for my mother's hand. It puts a little stitch in my chest because I know I can't reach for her.

Not yet.

If she really breaks things off with Edgar James, if she's willing to give it a shot...

Then...what?

Once she's free from her stalker, I'll be liberated from my job. I had to put all my private training appointments on pause this past week. A few of those clients will come back to me, but I'll probably have to find another steady gig to pay the bills for that shitty apartment. Sometimes you hear about celebrities who are dating neuroscientists or CEOs or other "normal people," but you sure as hell don't hear about them dating a failed painter–slash–failed personal trainer. There's a reason for that.

It doesn't happen.

Whatever Clay might be thinking now, she'll change her mind once she has a chance to reflect. We've existed in place beyond time this last week, and once time kicks back on in the normal way, she'll realize that I'm the same man she unapologetically threw a clay dick at several weeks ago.

My mood darkens as we enter the building, the exterior a mixture of brick and rustic wood, as if the three little pigs got it in their heads to work together. Well, two of them. They obviously told the straw lover to get bent.

"You're kind of killing me here," she says, and the excitement in her voice is enough to blow away some of my bad mood. "If we're not just here to put the fear of Rafe into Spencer, then why are we here?"

"'The fear of Rafe,' huh?"

"Yeah," she says, looking around the lobby, taking in the signs that direct visitors to the various studios. "I heard what you said to Penn." She glances around again, as if making sure we're alone, then adds, "I probably shouldn't say this, given...you know, but it made me really wet. Especially when I saw the broken teacup."

"Christ."

"Yeah, I definitely don't want to tell him about it," she jokes.

I give her a look, taking in her honeyed hair and her blue dress—the shade she's chosen for herself, no one else. "You're too honest by half sometimes."

"Not with most people," she says, giving me a sidelong look. "Only with you, for some reason."

I take my sunglasses off, and her face stretches into a grin. "He's ready to get down to business."

My dick twitches. I tell it to settle the hell down. "Not that kind of business. You ready for your surprise?"

"Absolutely," she says, beaming at me. "I'm sick of waiting. These five or so minutes of not knowing have been really difficult for me."

"That's my Clay, all about the instant gratification."

Her smile wavers, and I feel like a dick.

"I can wait for things that matter," she says softly, and something inside of me buzzes to life. It takes me a second to realize what it is, then I feel like an idiot.

Hope.

"Here we go," I say, nudging her down the long hallway, a creaky old wood floor lined with windows and signs announcing the various studios along the way. There are little two-top metal tables with chairs arranged on one side, inviting people to bring their coffees there for a chat.

"Are we going to the one with the big-head paintings?" she asks in a whispers as we move along the hall, pointing at a studio down the way. Several paintings hang in the window, all of them of people with enormous heads and bodies that couldn't possibly support them.

There are a few people milling about, and I catch one of them looking at her. He pulls out his phone to take a photo, but I gave a severe shake of my head, accompanied by a glare that promises violence, and he pockets it again. Clay doesn't notice, her gaze pinging around.

"No big-head paintings," I confirm.

She looks ahead at an artist's studio that has handmade dolls in the window. I'm not ashamed to say they give me a shiver, and not the good kind. "Are we learning to make those dolls? Because I'm not so sure about that."

"No, I think we both have enough nightmares."

She gives me a sharp look. "Still?"

I don't mean to answer, but I do. "Always. They come and go."

We keep walking, but she brushes her knuckles against my hand, and I hold the back of my hand to hers for half a second, feeling it everywhere.

Shauna steps out of her studio a little down the way, grinning at me, her hair dyed neon purple, suggesting she had a bad day recently and decided on a change.

Shit. Was this a bad idea?

Yes, I decide, it was definitely a bad idea, and I knew it all along. I did it anyway. I did it for the smile I see spreading across Clay's face as we reach Shauna's studio. I did it because I wanted to share this part of myself with her, like I did with our painting session yesterday, even though I'd thought it was dead and buried.

I did this because in some essential way she's bringing me back to life.

If Clay didn't know this was our destination from Shauna waving at her as if she were one of those blow-up noodles at a car lot, she'd know from the sign over the door to my friend's studio: Shauna's Clay Creations.

"You liked getting hit with that clay banana," Clay accuses.

I bump her with my shoulder. "Behave. I figured you might actually like this. Maybe your nickname was all leading up to this moment. You know, over-the-top foreshadowing, like in that show of yours."

twenty-eight

SINCLAIR

"HI," says the woman with the bright purple hair. She's wearing a gym T-shirt, leggings, and a thick gray apron, the kind of combo my mother warned me never to wear out in public, yet she looks good. Comfortable too. It makes me wish I weren't wearing the dress I put on for the tea-shop confrontation.

Judging by the sign, I'm guessing this is Shauna, Rafe's woman friend. I'm touched that he brought me here to meet someone who's obviously important to him. I'm amused that he did it so I could play with clay.

"Hi," I say, putting out my hand for a shake. She pulls me into a hug. She's surprisingly strong, and a surprised and graceless "Oof" escapes me.

"I'm so happy to meet you."

"Be cool, Shauna," Rafe says, his tone the same slightly annoyed one that has been my soundtrack for weeks.

"I was born cool," she says as she pulls away.

"Too bad things went downhill so quickly," he rebuts with a smile as she turns and gives him a hug.

I take a look around, giving them a moment. There are display shelves in the front area, which is set up like a shop, and there appears to be a work area in back. Everywhere I look, there are beautiful, weird, and beautifully weird clay creations. There's what looks like a cereal bowl, designed to resemble a shark's gaping maw. There's a mug with a handle formed from a perfectly sculpted flower. A bowl that's formed from a tangle of snakes. A vase made to look like a dancing woman lifting her skirts.

"Wow, you're *way* better than my teacher."

She laughs, shifting her attention to me. "Thank you. If you didn't think I was better than the lady at Play with Clay, I'd have an existential crisis."

"You don't think much of them, huh?"

"No," she says bluntly. "I don't even think little of them. But I *am* looking forward to getting to know you. We're going to have so much fun. I figured we'd start with a bowl." She lifts a hand. "Now, I know what you're thinking, but it doesn't have to be a boring bowl like the one you probably made in Play with Clay."

"It was fruit," I say, eyeing Rafe. Is he worried about what Shauna will say to me—or what I'll say to her?

"She especially likes making bananas," he offers.

"Oh, I remember," Shauna tells us both. "That's not the sort of meet-cute a person forgets."

"Meet-cute?" Rafe says witheringly. "It wasn't a meet-cute."

"No," I agree. "He didn't think very much of me at first."

"I don't know about *that*," Shauna says, adjusting her apron. "He was meeting up with me that night, as it happens, and he wouldn't stop talking about the whole clay-dick thing. Which means it didn't just piss him off—it interested him."

"Behave," Rafe says, giving her a *you're embarrassing me* look. Then his gaze shifts to me. "You didn't much like me either."

"No," I admit. "But I also couldn't stop talking about how much you annoyed me. Marnie had to impose a rule on how many minutes I was allowed to talk about it every day."

"Seriously?" he says, on the hook.

"No, but I'll bet she wanted to."

Shauna laughs with obvious delight. "Oh, we're going to have fun. Go off and find that dickwad, Rafe. We're good here."

"You're leaving?" I say, alarm dripping over me like hot caramel, cloying and sticky.

"Just to find Spence," he says. "I'm going to bring him out to one of those tables in the hall." He gives me a barely there smile. "If someone bothers you before I get back out there, scream like Rue did in the show when Jessie borrowed her hair gel."

Now it feels like that caramel is being drizzled into my mouth. "So, you were watching?"

"It was right in front of me," he says, eyes twinkling. "I could hardly escape."

"Don't listen to him." Shauna gives him a shove toward the door. With the arm muscles she has, I'll bet she can actually make him move, if only by a quarter of an inch.

"I'll be right out there." He points, then waits until I give him the go-ahead. It's not the way an employee would ask a boss for permission, though, and I'm glad for it.

I give him a slight nod. "I'm good. I want to learn how to make a snake bowl."

Shauna grins at me. "Bananas, snakes...am I sensing a theme?"

"Yes. Maybe you can teach your friend over there how to see the obvious," I say, because what the hell. There's something about her that invites confidences.

"Yeah, I'm definitely leaving now. I can see which way the wind is blowing." He doesn't sound displeased by it.

"Hopefully blowing you out the door," Shauna says, giving him a shooing motion.

I watch him go, because he really *does* have a nice butt, and when I turn to Shauna, she's studying me with pursed lips and light eyes that see deep.

"C'mon back," she says, indicating the sparkly orange curtain hung across the back row of shelves. "You get to see the Great Oz's underwear."

I'm laughing a little, slightly nervous, slightly amused, as I head into the back. It's not a huge space, but there are a couple of large work tables with large storage containers beneath them. There are no windows.

"I share a kiln with a few other people," she explains.

"I didn't know you were an artist," I say. "Rafe told me you work at his old gym."

She lifts her eyebrows. "The one he got fired from because he punched that guy for bench-pressing me."

"Yeah, I guess," I say. "Is that how you met, or..."

"No, actually he got me a job at the gym because I needed to make a little more cash."

"But you're so good," I blurt out. It's a dense comment, probably. The kind that would have Rafe rolling his eyes. But she *is* good. She should be successful and yet she's not, and Rafe said the same was true of him before his injury. My former worldview—that all you have to do is try hard enough, try until you bleed—gets another puncture.

She laughs, her eyes sparkling. "Thanks, I guess. But what makes you think I'm not a good personal trainer? Maybe I'm out there changing lives."

"Sorry, yes," I say. "Plus, Rafe would tell me that being good doesn't always matter."

Her smile dims. "I'm guessing he told you that he used to paint?"

I nod, riveted.

"He had studio space here too, before..." She scratches her forehead. "He had an accident..."

"You're talking about when he got shot."

"Yeah," she says, scrutinizing me. "He doesn't like talking about that."

From the way she says it, she knows the whole story, not that

I'm surprised. They were clearly friends before it happened. "For obvious reasons," I agree.

"Do you mind if I'm blunt with you?" she asks.

"Are you capable of being anything less?"

For a second I'm worried I've offended her, but she grins. "No, probably not."

She gestures to a wooden bench next to the closest work table, and I sit. She sits next to me, straddling the bench to face me. "Rafe's my best friend."

"You're protective of him," I say. "That's good. I'm glad he has someone like you."

She's silent for a moment, but her eyes delve into me. It's enough to make me squirm after a moment, like all the snakes from that bowl have set their sights on me. "He obviously told you what happened to him. He doesn't tell many people willingly. I guess...I'm worried that because of who you are, people will start talking about it again."

"Are you telling me to stay away from him?" I ask, my heart pounding hard, because somehow—maybe because I'm selfish and I've only been thinking of my own want and need for him—this hadn't occurred to me.

She slaps the table, making me jump. "No. Absolutely not. I had a feeling he was a bit too loudly disinterested in you, if you know what I mean, and now I can see it goes deeper than he was letting on. He likes you, and he doesn't let himself like a lot of people. No offense, Sinclair, but I noticed the way you were looking at him too."

"Have you ever..." I can't bring myself to say it, although I'm not sure why. Maybe because if they were ever involved it would have meant something, and I don't like to think of Rafe being driven crazy by anyone but me.

"No," she says, scrunching her nose. "It would be like banging my brother, if I had a brother. It's never been like that with us. He's not my type—" She waves a hand toward me. "And I'm clearly not his."

"Okay," I say slowly. "Thanks."

"I'm not done," she tells me. "What I was getting to, very circuitously, is that if you put him through that shit again and *then* break his heart, I'm going to make that stalker look like a teddy bear. You get me?"

"Wow," I say. "I'm not sure there was much room for misinterpretation. So you *do* want me to stay away from him." I feel sick, because I can't deny that she's right. It absolutely will become public knowledge if he and I make a go of it. People will dig, and they'll find paydirt. They'll publish articles that are sympathetic on the surface, all the while pulling up his shirt to show everyone his wounds.

"What?" she asks, getting up and putting a hand on her hip. "Did I say that? I didn't say that. He's a grown man. He can take it. What I said is that I'll find a way to get back at you if you make him go through that shit and *then* break his heart. The *then* was a crucial word."

"I wouldn't hurt him on purpose," I say slowly, my mind whirring. I didn't mean to hurt Marnie either, but I did. And my brother. And I can only imagine I was as much of a disappointment to my father as he was to me.

"Sometimes it happens anyway," I admit. "Even if you don't mean it to. Even if it's the last thing you want to do."

She moves her lips from side to side, studying me. "Good." She nods. "You're honest. I hate bullshitters, and I was under the impression most Hollywood types fit into that category. You're right, of course. Every day I fail to get married to a sugar daddy who'll take care of me breaks my grandparents' hearts a little more. Since we've reached an understanding, I can tell you how happy I am that Rafe's met someone he likes. Now let's have some fun playing with clay, and if you tell anyone I used that phrase, I'm going to call you a liar."

"Just a second," I say, pausing. My chest feels tight as I ask, "What was he like...before?"

She's quiet for a couple of beats, and I'm certain she won't answer me. Then she asks, "Have you heard of the Japanese art of kintsugi?"

"No," I say slowly, not wanting to sound ignorant but hampered by the fact that I am ignorant. "Is that something he does? I've seen some of his paintings."

"No," she says, with a small shake of her head. "It's what he is. Before he was like a bowl, fresh out of the kiln. What happened broke him, Sinclair. But if you ask me, broken things are more beautiful than pieces that have never been chipped. Japanese artisans join the pieces together with gold."

"Expensive accident," I say through numb lips. I glance at the curtain, but it's stubbornly opaque. If Rafe has found Spence and dragged him into the hall, there's no way to tell.

"Aren't they all? More expensive if you don't learn from them, though." Her gaze turns shrewd. "I expect you know all of this from personal experience."

I take a second to survey her. "I find it very hard to believe someone tried to lift you like a dumbbell."

"Not everyone's smart," she says with smile. "I very much hope his rich daddy had to pay for a nose job."

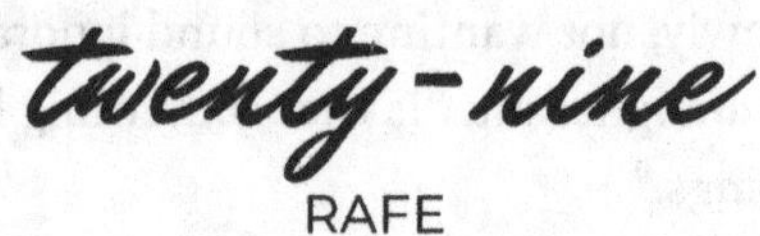

twenty-nine

RAFE

IT FEELS weird to be here, like I'm stepping back into a different life—a life I loved before I left it.

It feels weird to walk away from Clay, even for just a few minutes, although Shauna is one of the few people I'd trust to protect her. Part of it is that I'm concerned about what will be said between them. Women don't talk to each other like men do. Call me sexist for saying so, but I know how it goes. Within five minutes, they'll probably know each other's life histories.

So I'm already prickly when I step into Spence's setup. He's standing in front of a canvas, the back of the easel to the door, probably spending an hour trying to decide just how large he wants the singular dot he's painting to be. He's dressed the way an artist would be in a movie, with a red beret tipped over his forehead, red-striped pants, and a white shirt covered with very intentional splotches of paint. If they were there from actual work, they wouldn't look like that—perfectly spaced, color-coordinated. Life doesn't give you such happy accidents often.

I'd prefer not to talk to him. I'd prefer never to talk to him, but if there's even a single percentage chance he's behind what's happening to Sinclair, I need to pound fear into him. Nonliterally.

Probably. I've never liked Spence, and it's not because I don't "get" his art. There's not much to "get" about a couple of paint circles sitting on a canvas, although he always gives them names like *The Lights at Midnight after a Funeral*. Don't get me wrong, I'm not on a one-man war against modern art, but Spence isn't trying to break any molds. He's lazy. He's a hack. He's successful in spite of it, or maybe because of it.

Sour grapes, you're probably thinking, and you'd be right, but it's not just sour grapes, because he's also fake, the kind of person I thought Clay was when I took this job. He'll smile in your face and offer over-the-top platitudes, and the second your back is turned, he'll sleep with your ex-girlfriend.

Yeah. That happened. My ex did it to get a reaction out of me. My reaction was to delete her number.

"Well, well," Spence says, catching sight of me. "Haven't seen you around lately."

"Yes, there are some things in life I'm thankful for."

He snorts and sets down his brush. It's dry, no paint on it. "What do you want?"

I place a hand over my heart. "Is that any way to treat an old friend? You and I need to have a talk, out in the hall in front of Shauna's place."

He makes an affronted sound. "You're asking me for favors and telling me where and how I can deliver them? I haven't even seen you in....must be a year or two."

"Yes, that's exactly what I'm doing." I shift my weight, sending a subtle message: *I can carry you out here if I have to.*

"I'm not intimidated by you."

"Sure you are," I say, "but that's not why you're coming with me. You're coming with me because one of the women who took your sad excuse for a class is being stalked, and you're on the suspect list. Seems like you'd want to clear your name—and that you'd prefer to talk to me than the police."

His eyes widen in surprise or a convincing pantomime of it. "What? Are you...are you talking about Sinclair Jones? I heard something about that." Then those eyes narrow to raisins. "What the hell do you have to do with any of this?"

"I work for her," I say. "I'm her bodyguard." I'm surprised he hasn't seen the pictures if he's up to date on his gossip, but I'm not about to complain. The longer it takes for my name to make the rounds, the better. Of course, talking to this asshole all but ensures there'll be three articles about me before dinnertime. It'll be worth it, though, if we can eliminate him from the roster of suspects.

He scoffs. "You, a bodyguard?"

"I'm not asking *you* to hire me."

He glances around again. "So where is she?"

"Somewhere you can't leer at her. *Sorry about that,*" I say, letting the menace I feel at the thought of him staring at her leak into the words.

"I don't have anything to do with this," he says as he lifts his hands. They're clean except for a single dot of red paint on his index finger. He notices and wipes it off with a rag.

"So come with me and tell me just how innocent you are."

He thinks for a minute and then nods. "Okay, man. But you're wasting your time."

Story of my life.

———

He's right. This *is* a colossal waste of time. Spence has an alibi. He's putting together a show of his splotch paintings, and he was at a warehouse across town the night someone threw a brick at me. He also has an alibi for the night of the many Biebers. Apparently, he was at a tantric sex party, and there are five people who can attest that he was "very busy" all night. I listened with gritted teeth and eyes that felt like they were stuck in a permanent roll. Still, I tell him that Nicole and Damien might give him a call to ask for more information.

"You know, this show's gonna be a big deal," he says, beaming and scratching at the red beret. We're sitting at the little metal table across from Shauna's studio, which I now recognize as a mistake. Sitting down seems to have turned him into monologuing mode. Another scratch.

"You got lice?" I ask.

"No." He scowls as he gets in another good scratch. "The hat's itchy."

"So take it off."

"It lends to the aesthetic."

"I think we're done here," I tell him. "Maybe I'll be unlucky enough to run into you in another two years." Then, because the guy's a prick and I don't like the thought of him looking at Clay, even if he's not the one who's been stalking her, I add, "You'll stay away from Sinclair if you know what's good for you."

He lifts his hands, palms out, but then smirks at me. "You been tapping that, Rafe? I've got this bet going with my friend that her relationship with Edgar James is a front. She didn't look like a woman who was getting enough dick, if you know what I mean."

Rage wraps around me and curls its fingers in. I reach out and grab his collar, pulling it tight and pulling him in toward me across the table. "Don't talk about her, don't look at her, don't even *think* about her," I say, pouring plenty of menace into it. "You got me? You do, and I'll know."

His eyes go wide and he reaches up for his collar, clawing at me to free himself. I don't budge.

"Yeah, man. It was a joke. I won't...I'm just—"

Shauna and Clay flip back the curtain concealing the workshop. They're moving fast, and Clay looks like she did the night of the Biebers. Her color is all wrong, her pouty lips pressed into a bloodless line. They both still have aprons on, but it doesn't seem like Clay notices.

My heart immediately starts thumping, and I give Spence a little push, releasing his collar, then jump out of my chair so fast it falls. I don't bother righting it. I don't say anything to Spence; I just go to her.

"What happened?" I ask, because something clearly did.

She shocks me by wrapping her arms around me. It takes me only half a second to hug her back. I know I'm giving Spence a show, but at the moment I couldn't give a shit. She's shaking in my arms, and all I want to do is make her feel better. To make whatever happened okay.

"What is it?" I say into her ear, stroking a hand down her back.

"My apartment...it's on fire."

Well, shit. That's not an easy fix. My mind shoots to the little cat whom I've become begrudgingly fond of. "Rue?"

"He got out," she says, crying now, her tears soaking into my shirt. "He got out."

"See," Spence calls out. "I told you I didn't have anything to do with this!"

I glance back at him, furious, but he's staring at the wall fixedly as if it's one of those *Magic Eye* pictures that used to be popular when I was a kid. I guess he took my threat literally. Good. It *was* literal.

Looks like we've struck a potential suspect off our list.

"Let's go," Shauna says, scowling at the back of Spence's head.

"You're coming?" I ask, my arms still around Clay, because I don't want to let her go. Not yet.

"Obviously." For good measure, she levels a look at Spence, who's still studying the wall. "Your hat's stupid."

"It's French!"

I release Clay but keep hold of her hand because I need to touch her right now, and we hurry out of the building and to the car.

SINCLAIR

"I DON'T MEAN to alarm you, ma'am," Officer Nutman says, smacking his gum. He's sitting across the table from me, but I can still smell it. Juicy Fruit. It makes my stomach twist. "But I think you may have a stalker."

"Are you fucking kidding me?" Rafe says. He's standing behind my chair, alternately pacing and holding the two little wooden balls on top of the chair hard enough that I'm surprised they haven't snapped off.

We're in Marnie's house. By the time we got to the apartment, a news crew had shown up. Either they'd been keeping tabs on me for the last several days or the person who'd started the fire had tipped them off. Because there's no other way they would have found out so quickly, before I even arrived to see my sanctuary reduced to ash.

Well, not ash, maybe. They were able to contain the damage to my unit, and I'm told it'll be fine after some renovations, but most of my things have been destroyed—if not by the fire than by the act of putting it out. My *90210* table. Petunia the plant. Justin Bieber's epic flower arrangement. Rafe's painting of me. The only survivor is my kitten, cradled in my lap because I can't bear to let him out of my sight just now. Whoever started the fire had broken the lock so thoroughly the door wouldn't shut, and Rue had scampered out to the elevator. He was the first thing poor Joffrey saw when he went upstairs to check on my downstairs neighbor's report of smoke. If Rue had died...

A shudder courses through me, and Rafe's strong hands descend on my shoulders. Warmth radiates from them, and I relax back into the chair. I can hear murmuring voices in the adjoining room—my sister and brother and Shauna.

Nutman, of course, instantly zones in on Rafe's hands, frowning. "Hey, now. That's Edgar James's girl."

"Last I checked, she's a woman," Rafe says. "And where I put my hands is none of your business. We've been telling you for a week she has a stalker. We called you earlier to give you an update, and you didn't answer."

Nutman's mouth twists to the side. "I was at a laser tag competition," he says. "Should be there now." He gives a little grunt that says he's put out by the disintegration of my life.

"We thank you for giving so generously of your time," Rafe says.

Nutman nods and smacks his gum, clearly taking Rafe at his word. "Anything for Edgar James's girl."

Good God. Can't we get someone else assigned to my case?

"Nicole and Damien are on their way, right?" I ask Rafe in an undertone.

"Should be here any minute," he confirms tightly.

"Those the private dicks?" Nutman says disparagingly. "Because I don't want them getting in the way of the real work."

"They spent their morning following up on Penn Reed's alibi," I say. "I'd say it's important for us to talk to them."

Especially in light of the message scrawled by the door. *I know all of your sins.*

Again, it's not identical to his tweets, but it's close enough.

Either he did this or whoever's behind it really wants me to think he did.

That brings me back to my mother, whom I'd rather not think about ever again. I mean...she wouldn't burn down my apartment, would she?

But I think again about that little scar beneath Rafe's shirt. It's not impossible. In fact, it's exactly the kind of action one would expect of a desperate woman who's lost control of her human bankbook.

"Any other shifty characters?" Nutman asks me, his gaze settling on Rafe's hands again.

"He can put his hands wherever he likes," I say.

It's not until I've said it that I realize what it sounds like, but hell, it's true. There's something to be said for speaking the truth, I've realized. For living your truth. I don't know how yet—I'm still learning, but the only way to learn is to practice. I feel something like strength shore up inside of me as Rafe laughs lightly under his breath.

Nutman clucks his tongue, and the wad of gum falls out of his mouth and onto the table. He sticks it back in without more than a half second's hesitation. "Shock's a helluva thing, ma'am. You won't hear me saying anything different. I won't tattle on you."

"We've kept you up to date," Rafe says tightly. "Her mother's a suspect. Sinclair met with her the other day, and it wasn't—"

"Oh, yeah. Yup. I saw that blog post." His gaze tightens. "Saw the other one too."

The one about Rafe and me.

"Yeah, that was true," I say. "Can we move on? Edgar James isn't my boyfriend."

"Ma'am," Nutman says in a tone of affront, "I saw that man stand up for you with my own two eyes after the tomato incident. And he invited you to join him on the set of his show less than a week ago." He shoots another disgusted look at Rafe, who rubs my shoulders for good measure. It feels so good, I almost start purring like Rue on my lap. "You should go. As soon as possible. Not a good idea to hang around town when someone's following you and making violent acts."

Rafe's hands fall away, and I'd grab them back if he hadn't fisted them at his sides.

"Officer Nutman's a policeman, Rafe," I say tightly.

"You didn't seem to give a damn about her safety when I called you after the stalker arranged that little trick at the bar the other night," he tells Nutman.

"That, son, was a game. This is an attack on her person." He blows a bubble, and it pops on his face, leaving behind sticky flecks of gum that he starts collecting with his tongue. Dear God, how did this man pass the police academy? Did he bribe someone? Is this a case of nepotism?

I grab one of Rafe's fists, and it instantly flattens into his palm, which curls around mine. I squeeze it. "Rafe. Give me a minute with the detective, okay?"

He gives me a dubious look but doesn't fight me. "I'll be in the next room."

"I know."

I watch as he goes, feeling a pulse of gratitude for him.

"We *will* find who did this," Nutman says severely, drawing my attention back to him. There's something almost convincing about his tone, or at least there would be if he didn't still have flecks of Juicy Fruit all over his face. "Mark my words. Anyone else stand out to you other than this Pencil Guy?"

"Penn Reed," I correct. "And Rafe's right. My...my mother could be behind this. She was in Asheville the other day, and she was upset when she left lunch. I don't know where she is now."

Nutman nods and pulls out a little pad from his front shirt pocket, making a note in it.

I catch a sketch of a woman's boobs in the margins.

"Anyone else we should talk to?" he asks, biting the end of his pen. "Maybe a scorned lover?" He glances toward Rafe, who's standing just beyond the threshold of the other room, probably too far to hear but definitely close enough to intervene if necessary.

"Why do you keep looking at him?" I say with a scowl. "He obviously didn't do it. He was with me. He's been with me the whole time. It would have been physically impossible for him to do it."

"Keep your enemies close," Nutman says knowingly, smacking the table gum with as much vigor as if it were a slice fresh out of the pack.

"He's not my enemy," I tell him, annoyed. "He's my friend."

He makes a sound of disbelief, and Rue hisses at him. I'd like to shower him with treats for that, but his treats were probably destroyed along with most everything else in my apartment, so I settle for a pet.

"You sure about that? That man's violent, ma'am. A violent man isn't always in control of himself."

I stand from my chair, Rue still cradled in my arms. "He isn't a suspect here, do you understand? He's the man who has been protecting me, from the *beginning*. There is no one I trust more." I realize it's true as I say it. I know that he'd only resort to violence to keep me safe. I glare at Nutman, who flinches away as if I have laser eyes. "You thought I was doing all of this myself in the beginning."

"We look at all the possibilities, ma'am," he says with annoyance. "That's what an investigative officer does. Now, is there anyone else who's threatened you? Someone who might be holding a grudge?" He lifts a hand to rub his chin, probably going for a serious look, but his hand gets tripped up by some of the remaining gum, prompting a scowl. If I liked him, I'd get him a napkin.

My gaze finds an old invitation on the fridge, the eyes of the groom X-ed out, devil horns gracing his head. I set Rue down and go the fridge, grab it off and hand it over to Nutman. "Brock," I say. "Brock Tilton. He's Marnie's ex-fiancé. He... Maybe he blames all of us for the way things worked out for him."

"And he must blame Edgar too," Nutman says thoughtfully, his eyes lighting up. "Couldn't have liked it when Edgar called him out for making up that story about almost drowning. I've heard Tilton's on the verge of bankruptcy."

Huh.

Call me conceited, but it never occurred to me that someone might be giving me a hard time to get to Edgar. And if Brock *is* behind this, he'd have plenty of motive to go after both of us. Nicole and Damien don't like him for it, but maybe he paid someone to do it. Or...

What if he and my mother are working together to torment me, using Penn as a smokescreen? Again, I'd like to say she'd never do something like that. But she would. She absolutely would.

"Hey," Nutman says, his tone so poignant that I half expect him to say something profound or at least comforting, but then he tilts his head, biting his lip, and says, "You were making that up about Edgar, right? It's a real relationship, isn't it? Because I was really counting on getting his John Hancock." He pauses, chagrined, but doesn't apologize. "I know what you're thinking—I could have asked him that first night, but I'll be honest, I lost my nerve."

At least he's not pretending it's for his son anymore.

I don't have to answer, though, because I can hear the front door opening.

"The real detectives have arrived," Nicole announces.

thirty-one

RAFE

"WHAT DO you mean 'Penn's gone'?"

"Exactly what I said," Nicole tells me. When she and Damien arrived, I returned to the kitchen with them because there's no way in hell I wasn't going to be part of this conversation. I heard part of Clay's exchange with Nutman, although I'm more inclined to use his nickname just now. It's not every day you get accused of being the stalker of the woman you'd do anything to protect. Good guy, Nutsack. I wonder if Damien and Nicole can screw up his credit score. "We checked up on his alibi, but the dude got fired from Chuck E. Cheese a week and a half ago for punching an animatronic mouse. I mean, I think we can all side with Penn on that one."

In response to my scowl, Sinclair's incredulous gaze, and Nutsack's gum popping, she says, "Just me? Anyway, yeah. We checked up on him, got our massages on, and then took your call. Naturally, since we were over there anyway, we swung by his place of residence."

"Are you saying you broke into this man's house?" Nutsack asks with a glower. "If so, you're as much of a lawbreaker as that man."

"No, man," Damien says with a wry smile. "His mother was home."

"Penn was living with his mother?" Sinclair asks. She put Rue down, but he's lingering by her chair as if he's an attack dog rather than a tough-as-balls little kitten.

"Yeah, and she said he grabbed his clothes and beat it," Nicole says. "I think she was so relieved she didn't ask any questions. So it could be him. He sent the dead flowers, and there are the quotes to consider."

"If it looks like a duck and sounds like a duck, it's a duck," Nutsack says, closing his little notebook. "We'll put out an APB."

"Don't be so hasty, Nutsack," Nicole says, and laughter rises in my throat at the look on Nutman's face and his red cheeks. "Don't you think this is all a little bit too clean and tidy? What kind of idiot would be accused of stalking in the morning and spend his afternoon committing arson? Sure, maybe you think he snapped or he's ready to get caught, but even so. I'm leaning toward him being an idiot and someone using his idiocy to frame him."

"*Nutman*," he insists. "It's British."

"My mistake," she says carelessly. "I'm sure you get that all the time."

"No, I—" He starts blustering.

"Anyhoo," Nicole says, "we didn't think it was Brock. His alibi seemed to check out, and he's a spineless blubbering sort of sad sack, but you're right, Sin. It's possible he's working with someone more cunning. So that might be worth some extra poking. Maybe I'll bring Marnie with him so I can really screw with his head. And Griffin. He seemed to be afraid of Griffin."

"I—" Nutman tries again, his face a brighter red.

"But I have to say, I think Nutsack here is also right."

"Excuse me?" he says, his eyes bugging out. Then he catches the last part of her comment and says, "Of course I'm right."

"About what?" I ask tightly.

"We think she should get out of town," Damien says. "Not a bad idea for her to go on set for that camping show. It'd give *Nutman* here time to chase down some leads."

I wouldn't hold my breath, but neither would they, so I'm wondering what the hell they're up to. Are they still hoping the stalker will follow her out of Asheville?

I'm not so keen on that plan, because if it *does* happen, we'll have an arsonist and potential murderer on our tail. Not exactly the dreams vacations are made of. Not to mention I'd rather not have ole EJ around, trying to turn things around with my woman.

She's not yours.

"EJ says they've hired security for the set," Damien adds pointedly. "It's safer than staying in Asheville."

Clay glances at me, worry in her eyes, and sucks her lip between her teeth. "I don't think that's a good idea," she tells them. "I was going to end things with EJ."

"Interesting," Nicole says. "But I think waiting until this is over is probably your best bet."

"Yes," Nutsack says, clearly invested in Clay's fake relationship. "You might want to take time to think things over too. Maybe you'll realize there's only one Edgar James, but there are a lot of meat—" He looks at me and cuts himself off.

"Were you going to call Rafe a meathead?" Nicole says, her eyes dancing. "He tells me he's not fond of Beefcake, so I'm guessing Meathead would be a no for him too."

"None of this is amusing," I say, pissed that they're still taking it so lightly, that our assigned investigative officer is still Nutsack after he failed to do jack shit to prevent this from happening. "And I don't think it's a good idea for her to follow this guy out into the middle of nowhere when we know someone is following her around."

"We'll make sure she's not followed," Nicole says, as if we hadn't been trying for that all along. "You'll stay at our house tonight. We have, like, five alarm systems and several fail-safes. You don't want to be the person who manages to break into our house."

Damien nods and grins, lifting his shoulder in a slight shrug.

I'd imagine they're probably right. "Okay. We'll stay with you tonight."

"Don't I get a say?" Clay asks, swiveling to look at me.

"Yes, Clay. What's your say?"

"We'll stay with them," she says, and if I weren't so keyed up, I'd laugh.

"I'm going to put out an APB for this Penn fella," Nutsack says, which has to be the first intelligent thing he's offered since this whole mess began. "We'll want to locate your mother too, ma'am," he says to Sinclair, the word *ma'am* probably raising her stress level. "So I'll need her contact information. For that asshole there too." He points at a photo on the fridge, of Marnie next to a man who's been gifted some devil's horns and features. Brock.

"Good going. Way to make yourself useful," Nicole says encouragingly, as if speaking to a two-year-old child, but Nutsack doesn't seem to realize he's being insulted. He puffs up like a prize parakeet, then gives her a cautionary look. "Now, don't go stepping on my toes by talking to the same people."

"Wouldn't dream of it," Nicole says airily.

"So you're leaving town tomorrow?" he asks Clay.

I look at her. Hell, we're all looking at her.

She's looking at me. "What do you think, Rafe?"

I feel a sheen of sweat on my skin, because this feels so damn real now. The fire. The messages. The threat to her. If something happens to her, I wouldn't be able to live with it.

I want to keep her safe even more than I want to keep her away from EJ. Everyone seems to think it's safer for her to go, at least for now, and I can't deny that I want her to stay away from EJ for purely personal reasons.

"I guess we're going camping," I say, trying for a smile and probably ending with a grimace.

———

Clay called EJ's sat phone after Nutman left. Sounds like he's happy we'll be coming to set after all. I can't help but wonder if it's because it'll make for more interesting TV than people watching him make a fire or hunt down acorns or whatever the hell it is he does out there.

The plan is for us to head to the set early tomorrow morning. I'm guessing he'll have the whole thing filmed—the dramatic arrival of his girlfriend, whom he's whisked away from her stalker. The bitter taste of dislike fills my mouth. The insincerity of the situation grates on me, although I suppose it grates more that the way he looks at her has changed. As irresistible as Clay is, I'd prefer for him to continue to show resistance to her. I liked it better when her personality kept sending him to the bathroom for ten minute jags because he preferred to be alone and look at photos of rocks or whatever on his phone than talk to a beautiful woman.

Drew orders a few pizzas, and Shauna agrees to stay for dinner. I call my dad and ask him to join us, but he tells me with plenty of obvious satisfaction that he's with Clay's aunt at her retirement community.

"You know she's a swinger, right, Dad?" I ask, glancing at Clay, who's talking with Shauna and Marnie across the room from where I'm sitting. She doesn't look troubled, but then, she's good at pretending when she has a mind to, and I'm guessing she has a mind to. Her sister looks so worried she might spontaneously combust or start throwing Life Alert buttons around people's necks, and Clay is a better sister than she thinks. She cares about easing Marnie's and Drew's minds even though she's far from at ease herself.

"Yeah," he says, "what's the problem?"

"No problem, I guess," I say. "I just…"

Can't imagine sharing a woman.

Can't imagine standing by and watching while Edgar James touches her. While he looks at her.

Even the thought makes me grit my teeth.

Maybe part of it is my own sense of inadequacy. I know he's worth more than me in the eyes of the world, and Clay still cares about things like perception, even if she'd rather not anymore. It's like a perfume someone's sprayed on her. She doesn't like the scent, but it's not easy to get off.

There's also a nagging sense that maybe I'm too much like my mother. Maybe this overwhelming need to protect Clay, to be with her, is going to be my undoing. Maybe it's the opposite of a healthy attachment.

"I'm living the dream," my father says. "No commitment, no expectations. Plenty of se—"

"Christ, Dad. Don't tell me you're having plenty of sex. I don't want to know that."

"Those little blue pills are magic, Rafey."

"I'm hanging up now," I say, watching as Shauna says something that makes Marnie and Clay laugh. I like that they're getting along. I like it a little too much, seeing these two sides of my life seam together.

"Don't hang up," he blurts. "Rafe, for a man like me, this sort of arrangement is perfect. I never have been able to keep the old bait and tackle in my pants."

I feel a strong urge to hang up, but something tells me he plans on passing on a piece of wisdom, and since one out of every ten pearls he offers is actually useful, I stay on the line.

"No shit," I say.

"But you're different, son."

I feel a little stab of misgiving, because part of me worries that what'll come next is *You're like your mother.*

In some senses, it's true. Part of the reason I haven't gotten close to anyone for years is that I've never been able to keep that distance, hold that line. Toeing it feels dangerous. With Clay, I'm starting to realize I leapt over it without starting with an exploratory nudge. But instead he says, "You've got a big heart, kid. You know what they say—use it or lose it."

It doesn't really make sense, and yet it does. Which is probably the most accurate thing anyone could say about my father.

When I get off the phone and stow it into my pocket. Rue, who's been roaming the house with the kind of audacity that's a cat's birth right, leaps into my lap and pads around in a circle before he finds a comfortable position and lies down. Drew, who's been sitting quietly in his armchair, messing around on his phone, abandons it on the arm of his chair.

"So," he says in an undertone, "you have a thing for my sister?"

"What gives you that idea?" I ask.

"You're protective of her," he says, rubbing a hand ruminatively across his scruff. "That's good."

"I'm paid to be." I'm not sure why I'm being a dick, except I don't know how much I'm willing to let on yet—to him or myself. It feels dangerous to admit to what's growing between us.

"It's more than that."

"It's more than that," I acknowledge. A corner of my mouth twitches up. "You going to ask me about my intentions?"

"Nah." He glances at her. "She may be my little sister, but she's a grown woman. Has been for a long time. She can make her own decisions. Lately, she's been making pretty good ones. I'm proud of her."

"So you're not going to throw her at EJ like that cop?"

"No, but I wouldn't mind getting an autograph, and I'm not ashamed to admit it." He pauses, then says, "You're good for her. She's more...herself around you."

Something swells in my chest. I give a slow nod, then say, "She wants to get closer to you, but she doesn't know how."

He grins, his smile a lot like the one Clay makes when she

doesn't think anyone's watching. It makes me more kindly disposed toward him. "That makes two of us."

"Nah, three of us," I say, and we laugh together. We get to talking, and he tells me a bit about his job designing computer games. In a lot of ways, he's an artist, although not the kind who stains his hands with paint.

The pizzas show up not that long afterward, and we all sit around the table to eat. Nicole recounts our takedown of Penn Reed, and there's a gleam of excitement in her eyes when she says she's already arranged to drop in on Marnie's ex the day after tomorrow. The pretense for the meeting is that she's a reporter—Molly—who wants to talk to him about his falling out with Edgar James.

"He sounded worried," she says, "but he doesn't sound *nearly* as worried as he should." She plucks a piece of pepperoni from Damien's pizza and pops it into her mouth. "He also sounds like a man who thinks he's been done wrong, which was very amusing to me. Griffin's coming with me, of course. I already texted him at the bar."

Marnie gives Clay at least a dozen worried looks. Dinner ends, and Shauna heads home to check on her grandparents. The three of them normally eat dinner together every night at five, as if she's an octogenarian too. She left them a frozen pizza to warm up, but I can tell she's suddenly having visions of them burning down the house and half the neighborhood for good measure. I've met them, so I can attest it's a valid concern. She gives me a significant look before she goes, and I know I'll be facing an interrogation at some point. A problem for a different day.

"Well, kids," Damien says in a wry tone, glancing from me to Clay. "Shall we?"

Clay bites her lip and glances at Rue, who's curled up on the sofa, twitching slightly with kitty dreams. "Should I leave him here?"

"I'll take care of him," Marnie offers. "I'll stuff him with catnip and cookies."

"Yeah, that's not how you're supposed to take care of a cat," I say, my side brushing Clay's as we stand next to each other.

"He'll be fine," Nicole says flippantly. "He's a survivor."

"Griffin will help her take care of him while we're out of town," Drew says.

"Um, excuse me?" Marnie objects, putting a hand on her hip. "I'm perfectly capable of taking care of a little cat."

"I'm not," Nicole says. "I won't even pretend otherwise. Cactuses die under my care. He's much better off here."

"Okay," Clay says, but she heads over to the couch and leans down to press a kiss to the little cat's fuzzy head. I feel a little pulse of warmth watching her, further proof that I've vaulted over that line.

"Let's go before Marnie says something else to indicate she's incapable of taking care of a cat," I say. "We brought over a litter box earlier and some food. He'll be fine. People say cats can practically raise themselves." We picked up some other stuff at the store, too, and stopped by my house to grab a few changes of clothes for me. Her apartment is still a crime scene, and anything left undamaged reeks of smoke.

Marnie hugs Clay for practically a minute and then whispers something to her before letting her go. Then, to my surprise, she approaches me while Clay says good night to Drew.

"I know you'll keep her safe," Marnie tells me, her eyes intent and probing. "Thank you for that. Do me a favor and keep yourself safe too."

I smile. "I'm not going to intentionally trip over a rock and plummet over a cliff, if that's your concern. I've gone camping before. I'm guessing the only thing extreme about this situation is that EJ has a camera crew at his beck and call. He might talk big, but he's an actor, just like Clay."

Marnie gives me a serious look, tucking her short hair behind her ear. "Sure, in some ways. But sometimes the act and the reality get fused together." She glances at Clay, who's hugging Drew now. "It happened with my sister for a while, and she's just now seeing her way out of it."

It's the kind of statement that makes you think, and I nod as her words seep in.

"All right," Nicole says, clapping her hands as she stands by the now-open front door. "This isn't the great goodbye. You'll all see each other again. We guarantee it. So let's get moving. Scoot!"

Damien nods his agreement, and we all head out to the car. It's been decided that we'll ride with them, since they don't want anyone tailing us to their house. They're both good at losing tails, so they flip a coin to decide which of them will be our chauffeur. Damien wins, and Nicole gives him a pouty look and tells him he cheated.

"You can take it out on me later," he says with a grin.

Clay and I slide into the back seat, and I'm reminded of a few days ago, when they picked us up after that asshole terrorized her at the bar. Determination washes over me. I'm going to find this guy, and I'm going to make him leave her alone for good. Even if I have to hog-tie him, stick him in the trunk of whatever car we're riding, and bring him to Nutman with a bow on his head.

I tell her as much.

"You *would* do that for me, wouldn't you?" she asks, looking up at me with *something* glimmering in her eyes.

"Of course," I say, running a hand through her hair, because even though Nicole and Damien have gotten into the car, I don't give a shit if they know there's something between us. Maybe it's the fire fucking with my head, but it's gotten to the point where I *want* people to know. "I'd do that for you and more." Then I give her a wicked grin and say, "Is it just me, or are you also curious to see where these people live?"

"We should have insisted on blindfolds," Nicole says in the front passenger seat.

"We would've looked anyway," Clay says, and for some stupid reason, that *we* burns a hole in me.

thirty-two

SINCLAIR

ENOCH CALLS me in the car. I take the call because I need to talk to him—and also because I'm hoping he'll make the arrangements with EJ so I don't have to. He tells me that he heard about the fire from Grace, who heard about it from Marnie, and he was concerned.

After I share our plan to visit the set of the show, he pauses for a second, quiet on the other end. I'm about to ask if he's still there when he says, "Are you sure about that, Sinclair? You told me earlier that you wanted to publicly break it off with Edgar, and I've been thinking of ways to do that. Honestly, you don't need him. Most of the press you've been getting has been favorable, and even the shit that isn't...it shows people are *interested*. Hell, if you call those agents whose numbers I gave you, I'll bet they'll fight over the chance to represent you."

I glance at Rafe, who's quiet beside me, his sunglasses on, his eyes out the window. He's still listening to my end, though, I can tell.

"What about him?" I ask, glancing out the window as we whizz past little independently owned stores and supermarkets and chain restaurants. "Will it be bad for him?"

"It won't be great," he says. "To be honest, his show's not getting the kind of early buzz we were hoping for. People are still finding it hilarious to troll him for the water thing." He pauses. "And if you dump him for Rafe, a guy who's, like, twice as big as him, that won't be great for his manliness brand."

I resist the urge to roll my eyes. I feel bad for EJ, but it's not my job to pump hot air into him. "How long would you want me to wait?" I ask, thinking that maybe I can make it work if it's a couple of weeks.

"Ideally until the premiere," he says.

"But that's months from now!" I say, feeling Rafe's gaze on me.

"Which is why I said *ideally*," Enoch tells me. "But no, I wouldn't ask you to do that. I don't even think you *should* do that. Just give me a little more time to sit with this. I'm thinking it might play best if he dumps you, though."

Surprised laughter sputters out of me. "Okay."

"The three of us can talk about it while you're out there."

"Are you coming to the set?" I ask, surprised.

It's his turn to laugh. "God, no. Regular camping isn't my thing. I have no wish to take it to extremes."

"Fair. I can't say I'm looking forward to it. Hey, I'm sorry to ask, but will you make the arrangements with him for tomorrow? And remind him that my brother's coming?"

"Sure. I was going to call him anyway to talk about the show. Be careful when you're out there. I hear there are bears near the set."

Fantastic.

Nicole and Damien's house is shockingly normal on the outside. It's a bright turquoise Arts and Crafts house with a red door. Inside, the walls are painted bright colors too, and the furniture is an eclectic mix that looks like it was pieced together from a combination of

Bohemian flea markets and high-end stores. A beat-up antique red armchair with a colorful afghan draped over it sits next to a couch that I know must have set them back at least ten thousand bucks. Maybe fifteen.

"Some of this stuff belonged to Damien's grandmother," Nicole says, scrunching her nose. "Not really our taste, but we couldn't let it go."

He squeezes her to his side.

"We could give you two rooms," Nicole continues, gesturing toward a hallway off the great room, "but let's be honest, we have this bet going that you've been sleeping in the same bed." She scrunches her face. "Except it's not strictly a bet, since we agree that it's totally on and the terms are pretty favorable for us both."

"One room," I say, partly to shut her up. "One room is good." Then I look to Rafe, realizing he may not be on the same page. He said we couldn't explore this thing between us until things were done with EJ, and now we're visiting the set of the show after all.

"One room," he agrees, a note of command ringing in his voice, and I feel it everywhere in my body, comforting and an enormous turn-on all at once. "I don't want to let you out of my sight."

Good, because I don't want him to be out of my sight either. It's not just because I'm scared, although I'm very afraid. It's because he makes me feel balanced...at peace. Being with him makes me feel like I did that night when I couldn't remember to breathe and he reminded me.

"Cool, cool," Nicole says with a wide smile. "I won't say I called it, but I totally called it. I am good at this fairy-godmothering shit. I'm the fairy-godmotheringest fairy godmother."

"Sometimes I think you don't listen to the words that come out of your own mouth," Damien says, but he seems amused by it. He puts an arm around her shoulders and leads the way down the hall to a decent-sized bedroom with an en suite bathroom. It's shockingly normal, with a beige comforter and a lamp that has no defining features beyond a plain white shade and a brass base.

"Someone gave that to us," Nicole says, waving at the comforter. "All the normal shit people gives us gets put into this room. It's like our suburban suite. You're welcome."

"We'll see you in the morning," Damien says with a nod. "Hope you can get some sleep." His mouth shifts to one side. "I'll leave out a Valium in the kitchen—help yourself if you have trouble sleeping. To any food you want too. It's on the other side of the great room." He gives Nicole a fond glance. "Nicole here's not too fond of giving tours."

"Why lift the curtain?" she asks. "A certain sense of mystery is good for the soul."

He made the offer of meds like someone who knows what it's like to toss and turn. I guess he's seen some things as a private investigator, maybe been in the middle of them too.

"Thank you."

He gives me a salute and a smirk. "Just fairy-godmothering."

Then they're gone, and Rafe and I are alone together. It's as if a mask has been taken off, and all the weight of the day settles on my shoulders. His arms are around me before I know I need them.

"It's okay, Clay," he says, squeezing me to his chest. "You're not going to be alone. We'll deal with this together. All of it."

Somehow he knew just what I needed to hear.

"I seem to be making a habit of crying into your shirts," I say as I feel the tears coming.

"They're from a multipack I bought at Walmart. No one's going to mourn them."

I laugh through a sob. "No, they're not. They're nice."

His hand soothes down my back, his touch calming me.

"Don't lie to me," he says into my hair, his breath hot against my skin. "You know a bad shirt when you feel it."

I pull back slightly, my eyes still welling with tears, and run my hands down the front of his shirt, moving slowly, feeling the muscles bunch beneath the admittedly shitty fabric. "So maybe it's what's under it I like."

"That I will absolutely take credit for," he says with a smile. I have a feeling he's putting it on for me, because he knows I need that too. But I don't want him to put on a brave face for me. He lets me be real—he almost demands it—and I want that same freedom for him.

"You're scared too."

His hand runs over my back again, so firm, so self-assured. It sends comfort coursing through me, as if his touch is serotonin rushing through my veins. I have to have more of it, of him.

"Terrified," he says, meeting my eyes, his gaze dark and unflinching. His grip on my back tightens. "But I'm also stubborn. Don't underestimate how stubborn I am. And I said nothing is going to happen to you under my watch. So. Nothing. Is. Going. To. Happen. To. You. I won't let it."

I reach for the top button of his shirt, a question in my eyes. Then, because I don't want to be a coward who only asks questions with my eyes, I say, "I need you tonight. But I respect your decision if you don't want to because we're going—"

He wraps his hand around my neck, lifting my chin with his thumb and forefinger, and kisses me hard. I melt into him, my arms working those buttons, because suddenly I'm desperate to feel him against me. He doesn't fill those empty places inside of me, but he makes me feel strong enough that I can look at them and gauge their shapes and sizes. He makes me feel like I can learn how to fill them myself someday.

"I need you too," he murmurs, slipping his hands under my dress. "So bad." He grips the hem and then pulls it over my head while I'm still working on one of his buttons, making me laugh. But I don't stop what I'm doing, because I want that damn shirt off. He runs his big hands over my body, spreading comfort and desire until

I'm heady from the feeling, and my hands work a little faster at that shirt. He shrugs out of it when I finish, and I start in on his belt as he reaches around and detaches the clasp of my bra, tugging it over my hands as I work on the buckle of his belt, my fingers clumsy in their haste.

"You shouldn't wear belts," I say. "I need easier access."

His laughter is low in his throat as he cups my breasts, leaning down to suck on one of my nipples, his touch sending liquid fire through my veins. "You like taking off my belts—don't deny it."

He's right.

The buckle undone, I go for his pants, my fingers fumbling for the button, the zipper. He kicks off his shoes, and then I'm pushing his pants down, revealing what I want. He's hard and ready for me, just like he always seems to be.

"Take them all the way off," I say, my voice husky.

He does, maybe because he knows I need us both to be bared to each other tonight. He's so sexy, with his muscular chest and tattoo, with that raised scar on his abdomen. With the light in his dark, brooding eyes that says he really does need this too. We need each other.

"I don't have any protection," he says, running his hands over my breasts, down my sides. "Although I'm starting to question why I don't carry around a multipack of condoms at all times when we're together." He kisses me slowly, rubbing his palm over my underwear, a tease of a touch that I feel everywhere. I nip his lip in revenge, and he laughs into my mouth. "Don't worry, Clay. That's not going to stop me from making you come. Repeatedly."

I told Nutman that I trusted Rafe more than anyone, and I meant it. "I have an IUD," I say, giving him a stroke with my hand, savoring how hard he is for me, "and I'm clean. If you are too, then we don't need to worry about them."

"Are you sure?" he asks, peering into my eyes.

"You don't want to?" I ask. I hate it, but I feel a stab of vulnerability and the old worry that he's looking at my face and body—at the only parts of myself that have ever been treated like they're worth anything—and finding them lacking.

"I didn't say that. If it were up to me, my dick would constantly be inside of you. Everywhere."

"I kind of like that thought," I say, smiling. "And yes, I'm sure. I want to know what you feel like without anything between us."

His pupils dilate, and his dick seems to get even harder in my hand.

"Who are we tonight?" he asks.

I love that he humors my games. I love that he enjoys them too. The thing is I don't feel like playing tonight. I don't *want* to pretend to be someone else. "We're us," I say. "We're Sinclair and Rafe."

"*Clay* and Rafe," he says with a small smile.

I smile back. "I feel like you're taking that joke too far."

He slips his hand under my panties, finding me wet for him like *I* always seem to be, and makes a happy sound that pumps more serotonin into my veins as he circles my clit and then starts fucking me with one finger, two, angling his fingers to hit another place that sends sizzles of pleasure through me. He looks into my eyes as he does it. Then he pulls my panties down around my heels and lowers to his knees between my legs. "I like having a nickname for you that no one else calls you, one only we understand. That's something no one can take from us."

Pleasure curls through me as he kisses the inside of my thigh and then backs me into the mattress, spreading my legs wide for him as I lower to sitting. The need I feel is so strong it frightens me. That's when I understand for the first time—really understand—that he's more than my friend and my protector. More than someone I'm sleeping with.

I'm falling in love with him.

thirty-three

SINCLAIR

RAFE FEELS SO good inside of me, skin to skin, that I almost start crying again. Because I'm scared that I'm going to screw this up and lose him, like I've screwed up so many things in my life. Because I'm scared that the realities of dating a quasi-celebrity will drive him away. Because I'm scared that they *won't* and I'll prove no more capable of being in a real relationship than my mother was. Cold and distant. Judgmental. Resentful. *Narcissistic.*

People have called me that before. My sister, when she was mad at me. The press. Penn Reed, after I broke up with him. (It was in his poem actually.) There's a part of me that worries that they're all right. That there's something broken in me that can never be fixed. That I'm not capable of lasting happiness the way other people are —like there's some gauge in me that's broken.

Afterward, lying next to him, curled into his side because I can't stand not to be touching him, I ask in a quiet voice, "Do you think I'm a narcissist?"

"Yes," he grumbles instantly.

I try to get up, but he clasps me to him. "No, you're not a narcissist, Clay. You were just raised by one."

"Was your mother like that too?" I ask softly.

289

"No," he says, running his fingers over my back, through my hair. "Your mother's fixated on you. She sees you as her only way to be successful. My mother was barely around to screw me up. My grandmother basically raised me."

"You had a grandmother?" I ask, interested.

"Yeah," he says with an amused smirk. "We all get two of them, last I checked."

I shove the arm he has wrapped around me. It doesn't move an inch. In fact, it tightens around me.

"Yeah," he says again, leaning in to kiss the side of my face. "She was something else. She taught me how to paint."

"I'm glad you had her," I say. "Was she your mother's mother or Reggie's mother?"

"My mom's. God only knows what sort of people brought Reggie into the world." His grins at me. "You know, something's going on between him and your aunt. He was over there when I called him earlier."

"Seriously? Does he know she's a swinger?"

He gives his head a small, rueful shake. "I guess it's his kind of thing too. I know... shocking."

I lift my fingers to my lips, feeling a press of vulnerability. "Isn't that what every man wants? A carte blanche to mess around with whoever he wants?"

"No," he says, tipping my chin so I'm looking directly into his eyes. "Not me. When I'm with a woman, I want her to be mine. Only mine."

"Women aren't handbags, Rafe," I say, even though my stupid heart is beating faster.

"I like carrying you. You like carrying handbags," he says. Then he gives his head another small shake. "That's not what I meant. I wouldn't want any other men touching her, but I'd want her to feel the same way about me. It goes both ways."

"Women look at you all the time," I say, challenging him. "I notice."

"I like that you've noticed," he says with a smirk that lights his eyes up. "But are you sure they weren't just looking at you, biding their time to ask for an autograph?"

"They were looking at *you*," I say, my mouth suddenly dry. "I'm guessing they couldn't look away if they wanted to." I've never been able to, and it's always made me furious at him and myself. Because I knew where I was supposed to be looking—at Edgar—but who could look at anyone else with Rafe so close by?

"Why do you think I always wear the sunglasses inside?" he asks.

Something blooms inside of me, and I feel lighter than I should in my situation. I feel *happy*. "You never said."

He huffs a laugh. "Why would I? You made it very clear what you thought of me."

"You were rude," I say, lifting my eyebrows. "Obnoxious."

"And you weren't?"

"I didn't want to be attracted to you," I say, because I realize it's true. I might not have liked him in the beginning, or him me, but there's always been something sizzling between us, inviting us to explore it.

He's smiling at me again. "Then we have something in common. But make no mistake, Clay, I've always wanted you. Turns out I like you too. A lot. I just wish you weren't so hard on yourself."

"You think I'm hard on myself?"

He gives me a dubious look that's very familiar by now. "I know you are. You expect yourself to be perfect at everything. If you haven't found anything you like doing, I'd say that's why. You're too busy critiquing yourself to know whether you had fun."

"I had fun painting with you," I say. "And with Shauna...you know, before someone burned down my apartment."

"Good," he says. "I'm glad you like her. That means a lot to me."

"What's going on, Rafe?" I say, pulling away to sit up. He lets me, then sits beside me, the mattress dipping me toward his much bigger frame. I let it, and he slides an arm around me.

"Well, I'm glad you asked," he answers wryly. "You're being stalked."

I go to shove him again, and he captures my hand and kisses it. "I'd like to see how things can be between us."

"Even though I can't end the EJ thing yet? Enoch says he's working on it."

Rafe runs his big callused fingers over mine, sending hot and cold shivers through me. "Even then. But I reserve the right to glower at him the entire time we're there. I still don't like the situation."

"Neither do I," I admit. I'm sick of pretending in my personal life. Pretending on the job is one thing. It can be invigorating and fun, a challenge. But when it bleeds into everything, you're left with a life that feels all pretend.

"But I'm less worried about EJ than I am about getting in your way," he continues. "I don't want to ever get in your way."

"How could you get in my way?" I ask, baffled. "All you've ever done is help and support me. If anything, I'm getting in your way."

He smirks at me and cradles my hand. "Yes, I feel professionally stunted because of taking this job. If I weren't here, I could be begging for jobs at half a dozen different gyms that smell like sweaty balls."

"Stop," I say, turning my hand around and grabbing his. "Just stop. You're in a middle place too."

"Like the waiting place in that Dr. Seuss book," he says, bemused. "*Oh, the Places You'll Go!* My grandma used to read that to me."

"Never read it," I say.

"You're not going to be in the waiting place for long, Clay. You're capable of doing whatever it is you want. This is your time to find out what that is. That's a gift—a gift you deserve."

"I want *you*," I say, because I know that, at least, is true.

"That's not what I meant," he says, with a half smile, "and we both know that would never be enough." He lowers down again and pulls me on top of him, his big hands cradling my ass. "Still, there's no harm in trying."

———

Even after his breathing goes even, his eyes closed in sleep, his surprisingly long lashes against his cheek, I can't sleep.

That would never be enough.

I don't think he means it the way my brain is telling me he does, but I still can't sleep. So I move to get up, only for him to instantly wrap an arm around me. Laughing, I whisper, "Let me get up. They said the house is like Fort Knox, and I need a glass of water."

He does, but not before he presses a kiss to the side of my face.

I get dressed and then pad into the kitchen, only to find Damien there, sipping a glass of whiskey at the granite kitchen island. Without commenting, he pours me an identical glass.

"You can't sleep either?"

"We all have our demons," he says, sliding the glass across the counter to me. "They like to come out at night."

He sits down again, and I sit on the stool across from him. For half a second, I worry about my face, about what it might look like to him. Then I tell my mother's voice to shut up, because I don't need it in my head anymore.

"You were good today," I say, circling the top of the glass with my finger. "I mean with Penn. You were everything he needed you to be."

"I know," he says with characteristic self-assurance. He smiles at me—a smile that's probably devastated thousands of women, particularly after they find out he's not only married but is married to a woman who would probably wreak destruction on their lives if they so much as winked at him. It does nothing to me or my panties. "It wasn't totally a lie, you know. I used to act in a local theater company."

"Really?" I ask, surprised. I stop playing with the rim of my glass.

"Yeah, it was a low time in my life. It felt good slipping into someone else's skin."

His words are eerily similar to something I told Rafe the other day, and I feel a prickle of something down my back. Foreboding, maybe.

"Why'd you quit?"

"One time a producer came in with his girlfriend. They were passing through town for the weekend. He wanted me to audition for a role in a major film."

"And you said no?" I ask in shock. I'm not used to people turning things like that down. I'm used to them doing whatever they can to secure a part, even if it makes it hard for them to look in the mirror. Even if it makes them a stranger to themselves.

"I did," he tells me. "This was what I wanted." He waves at the house. "To live this life with Nicole. To run an agency with her. I realized I was putting that in danger by showing too many people my face."

"It's a memorable face," I say, because it's true. He's unreasonably handsome in a way that must turn heads.

"So I've been told," he says, not smug but not falsely modest either. I'm so used to people simpering, saying things they don't mean, that I appreciate that about him. He takes a sip of his drink, ruminative, and I try mine too. It's a smooth whiskey that goes down easy.

"That's not the only reason I stopped acting."

"Oh?" I ask, tilting my head.

"The reasons I liked it in the beginning, they didn't apply

anymore. I wanted to get away from my life, to be someone else, but toward the end...my life was everything I'd ever wanted it to be. I didn't need to seek out that high anymore."

I think again of what I told Rafe. About how I'd always liked slipping into someone else's skin.

"You don't miss it?" I ask.

"Sometimes," he says ruefully. "But you can enjoy something, even indulge in it, without making it your whole life."

I laugh through a sip of whiskey and nearly choke. Clutching my chest, I say, "Feels like everyone's been telling me that lately, in one way or another. I guess I don't know how to not make something my life."

He lifts his eyebrows. "Sometimes the greatest lessons we can learn are the ones we teach ourselves." Then he tips his glass back, draining it, and stands. "It'll be an early morning. Better try to get some sleep."

I'm still trying to process what he said as I watch him walk off.

When I get back to the room, Rafe's awake and watching the door, his eyes dark and searching. Something seems to settle in him the instant he sees me.

"You were worried?" I ask as I approach the bed.

"Like I said," he tells me, pulling me down to him, wrapping me up in his arms like I'm something precious. "I don't want to let you out of my sight right now."

I DON'T LIKE THIS.

Last night, I realized something.

I'm falling in love with Sinclair Jones. I didn't mean to, didn't want to, but there it is. No woman has ever affected me like this. No woman has made me want the things I want with her, which feel so out of reach, I'd have to borrow Shauna's trampoline to brush them with my fingers.

It's not a comfortable realization, particularly since we're driving out to pay a visit to her fake boyfriend.

To be honest, I feel like a toddler having a temper tantrum.

At least I have those damn glasses.

We left the house at 6:00 a.m. Nicole picked up Drew and then dropped us off at a car rental place an hour out of town, in the direction of set. Before we left, she gave us a satellite phone that can be charged in the car, because none of us have the first idea whether we'll be able to use our phones up there. Nutman has the number, although I suspect he'll only call in the hopes of talking to Edgar James.

We rented an SUV, got breakfast from a McDonald's drive-through with shockingly few complaints from Clay, and drove another couple of hours before stopping at an outdoors supply store and buying the shit Edgar had told them they'd need, which he offered to charge to the show. Half of it seems unnecessary if you ask me, but I'm guessing *Camping to the Max* is as much about style as it is substance. God forbid you squat to take a shit wearing anything other than three-hundred-dollar shoes.

Throughout it all, I was fighting a headache and a black mood that was no one's fault but my own—and maybe Enoch Laskin for coming up with the idea of Clay's fake relationship in the first place. The only thing I got was a lighter, mostly because Drew started talking about the logistics of starting a fire with a couple of sticks.

Still, there's no denying this trip has already been a bonding experience for Clay and Drew. They spent half their time at the store laughing their asses off while looking for some of the bizarre items on the list, and they've been talking in the back seat for the last few hours. She needs this, and I'm glad she's getting what was taken from her all those years ago. This relationship with Drew is important to her.

I have to use a map to navigate the last little way, because the GPS on my phone cuts out before we arrive at the address we were given. It's a good thing we rented a vehicle with four-wheel drive, because the rendezvous spot is halfway up the mountain. I steal glances in the rearview mirror every few minutes, and Clay is worrying her lips, glancing out the window at the ridges of rock and the long drop to the bottom.

"Maybe this was a bad idea," she says slowly.

Meanwhile, her brother looks like he took a handful of uppers, his energy practically jumping around the SUV. "It's gorgeous out here," he says. "I can't believe we're really doing this."

Yeah, me either.

When we get to the meeting place, there are a few other cars and a van. A kid in a *Camping to the Max* cap is waiting for us. He has on hiking boots, athletic shorts, and a band T-shirt, so I'm guessing the expensive shopping lists are reserved for the stars. He's also wearing a backpack with the *Camping to the Max* logo.

He looks a little bowled over when Clay gets out of the car, not that I'm surprised. She's a knockout, dressed in a cobalt shirt, paired with light gray hiking pants and her new boots. It's a color she's chosen for herself, not one that was hand-selected for her by her mother and pressed on her by different stylists, and it shows in the way she carries herself.

"I'm here," the kid says.

I swallow the *Yes, we can see that.*

"I'll take your bags."

This kid is vastly underestimating the amount of shit they purchased for the trip. "I'll help," I say, then pop the trunk and grab everything except a small duffel bag Drew stowed in the trunk this morning.

"I can carry my own stuff," Drew says, on the cusp of being annoyed. "I might not be a body builder, but I'm in good shape."

"No," the kid says, looking a little green. "I was told to carry everything."

He physically can't, and I can tell he knows it when he glances at the bags I'm toting.

"It's fine," I tell him. "I've got this. I work for her."

Clay presses her lips together in a flat line, and I can tell she didn't like that. I didn't either. But that's the only context I have for being here—I can't exactly tell the kid that I'm the guy who's banging her.

"Well, okay, if you're sure. I just...I don't want Mr. James to think I didn't offer."

That furrows my brow. "What? Would he be a dick to you about it?"

"The camp's a two-hour hike from here," the kid says in a chipper tone, very pointedly ignoring my question.

"Two hours?" Clay asks in obvious despair.

"I think we can make it in an hour and fifty minutes if we hurry," the kid says proudly.

"What's your name?" Drew asks him.

"Assistant Three."

"That's your actual name?" he asks, his brow furrowed.

"Oh," the kid says, blushing. "It's just...that's what people call me around here. I'm Stanley."

Maybe old EJ isn't the salt of the earth he's been pretending to be. Clay looks a little taken aback too, and I can tell her mind's stuck on that two-hour hike she'll be taking in new shoes guaranteed to give her blisters.

I take a couple of steps toward her and say in an undertone, "If you get tired, I'll carry you, and your brother can carry the bags."

"Sure," Drew says, chipper again. "Besides, look at it this way, Sinclair. No one's going to follow us up here."

He's right. Except a feeling of foreboding trickles through me.

My phone doesn't work up here. Neither do Drew's or Clay's. Only the sat phone will work.

I can't help but think that if someone did follow us, it wouldn't be very easy for help to arrive. They'd need a chopper to get to us in time. Damien is planning on heading this way and keeping an eye out for anyone who might have gotten it into their heads to follow us—if they somehow managed to track the rental through backroads—but what if he misses them?

———

There are several tents set up at the site, some of them obviously luxurious. It doesn't look like the middle of nowhere, but the hours we drove and hiked to get here say otherwise. Still, I'm guessing that the sea of tents will be shown in none of the shots of Edgar. The whole thing smacks of artifice, of the bad kind of pretending, and I can think of at least two dozen places I'd prefer to be.

The producers, a red-haired man and woman who look like they could be brother and sister, meet us with hot drinks—it's chilly up here, even at the end of April—and s'mores prepared by Assistants One and Two. We take a seat around a campfire in chairs that must have been lugged up this mountain by the assistants, unless there's another road leading directly here and we were brought the long way for dramatic purposes. I'd believe it.

I can see the war on Clay's face. She craves a s'more but worries what it might do to her face. It feels like a mild victory when she takes one. So does Drew. I'm offered a gooey snack but shake my head.

"We're so glad you're here," the woman, Dani, says, leaning toward Clay in her eagerness. Something about the way she's acting suggests she's a *Sisters of Sin* fan. "Edgar's told us all about you and, of course, your recent troubles. I don't mind telling you that you're a major reason that I wanted to move forward with this project. We really think we're making something special here. A love story set against *this* backdrop." She waves toward the view, which *is* phenomenal. "An external threat. Danger from animals and falling rocks and an inhospitable environment."

"Um, are there actual snakes on set?" Clay asks in discomfort. "I heard rumors about that, and I have to say, I'm not a big fan of—"

"Oh, don't worry about that," Dani says dismissively, tucking her fiery hair behind her ear. "We have Assistant Three clear the campsite every morning."

I glance at him. "His name's Stanley."

"It's okay, sir," Stanley says hurriedly, his expression worried. "I answer to Assistant Three. It's much more convenient for everyone."

"To call you by a longer name?"

Dani laughs as if I've said something funny. Clay's lips twitch for a different reason. "Oh, we have a different way of doing things here." It strikes me that the guy next to her hasn't said a single thing, but he's been watching us with a hint of hostility, as if he, too, would prefer to be anywhere else than on this mountain ridge. Fair enough.

"Where's Edgar?" I ask, because I'd rather pull that particular Band-Aid off.

She smiles beatifically at Clay. "He didn't expect you so soon, to be honest. He took a hike to make a call on his sat phone. He's talking to your brand manager, actually."

"Oh," Clay says around a bite of s'more.

"And this must be your brother, Drake," she says, nodding to Drew, who's made himself comfortable. "Edgar told us you'd be coming."

"His name's Drew," I say, because he's got a mouth full of marshmallow. Maybe I'll just be the asshole who goes around spouting people's names.

"And *you* must be Rafe," she says to me, her smile slipping. I'd guess she's seen those blog posts about Clay and me. Good. Her silent friend gives me a hard look too. "For the purposes of the show, it would be best if you stay in the background," Dani tells me, "but we'll need to get you to sign a release too. It'll add to dramatic tension if you're seen following Sinclair around."

"Fine," I say. "But I'm not following her around for dramatic tension. I'm doing it because she has a stalker." I'm proud of myself for not saying *fucking* in front of *stalker*. I almost sound like a professional and not a man who's worried about his woman. A man who'd take part in this absolute farce if it means keeping her safe.

We sit around the fire a little while longer, Dani making small talk that feels pointless, until Edgar James tramps back into camp, cameras in tow. He looks genuinely excited to see Sinclair, his eyes lingering over her in a way that pisses me off. She doesn't belong to him, never has. Of course, she doesn't belong to me either. No one person can belong to another. But that fire made me realize something: I don't want this to end.

I grit my teeth when Dani calls for an official greeting between

EJ and Clay. My only comfort is that while she asks for a kiss, Clay insists on a hug. Four hugs, because that's the number of takes it requires.

The first time, Clay doesn't look enthusiastic enough.

The second, Edgar trips over something and nearly takes her down with him.

The third, *neither* of them look enthusiastic enough.

By the fourth, Drew has a bit of a hangdog look. Munching on a third s'more, he shifts to the seat next to mine. "Huh," he says to me in an undertone. "This is kind of bullshit, isn't it?"

I knew I liked him.

thirty-five

RAFE

WE'VE MADE it through one day of *Camping to the Max.*

Drew is as disillusioned as a kid who pulled down Santa's beard and saw his father's face, and Clay has dozens of blisters on her feet from wearing her new boots on a hike Edgar brought us on yesterday evening. Two cameramen followed us, which took away from Drew's fun, especially since they kept calling out things for us to do. *Sinclair, why don't you give Edgar an admiring look. Drew, look at the sun...no, not directly at it—you'll go blind.* At one point, one of them even put a snake from a pet carrier in Clay's path so she could act appropriately horrified.

I massaged her feet last night in the tent that she, Drew, and I are sharing, and Drew moaned something about feet taking over his life. My best guess is that he's referring to those videos Marnie's friend was making, although I'm less sure what it has to do with him.

We've all agreed that we'd like to leave, but we're waiting on an update from Damien and Nicole. Apparently Enoch broke the news to Edgar yesterday about his impending breakup with Clay. My guess is that he'd be pleased for the stalker search to go on a little longer so he can get more footage, because we've been filmed pretty much every instant we're outside the tent. They've asked for several outfit changes too, suggesting they're going to make the "relationship" look like it has a longer duration than a day.

"We should probably go back out, shouldn't we?" Drew says with a groan, checking out his watch. It's just past lunch, and we were asked to go back to our tent for, you guessed it, another outfit change. It hasn't been easy since the tent's not huge and we're all on the tall side. Plus, neither Drew nor Clay wants to traumatize the other for life by seeing anything they shouldn't. I've had to hold up a travel mirror for her while she puts on her makeup routine, because even though she's started wearing less since moving to Asheville—and even less this last week—she refuses to go on camera looking anything other than perfect. Even if she's hiking up a mountainside.

"I thought EJ was your hero?" Clay asks, bemused.

"I don't like all the cameras." He scratches the back of his neck. "I don't know how you do it. And that snake thing was a stupid joke. Did you hear the assistants talking? The snake has a name. That was Joe you jumped over in horror."

"I'm glad it's not just me," I say.

"It's not just you," Clay says, the back of her hand glancing against mine. "The sooner we leave, the better."

It's then that the sat phone finally rings, like the golden fucking goose. A quick glance tells me it's Nicole. I put it on speaker, and we all sit around it like it's our campfire, our sleeping bags plush under our legs, Drew's gray and mine—because it made Clay laugh—patterned including various desserts. Clay sits close enough that our sides are brushing, and since Drew already knows there's something between us, I scoop her up into my lap. He groans but seems mostly okay with it.

"What's the word, Nicole?" I ask.

"It's over," she says. "Am I fabulous, or am I fabulous?"

"Tell us what you did, and then we'll decide," I respond. Clay leans her head back against me, and I can practically feel the relief coursing through her.

It's over.

But my body doesn't believe it yet. I've been in a state of constant alert for weeks, and it's like it's forgotten how to settle down.

"Bringing Griff with me was a good move. It took all of five minutes to get Brock to confess to starting the fire," she says, and Clay flinches in my lap. I wrap an arm around her, and she grips it with her hands as if she's afraid I'll take it away. "I guess he still had a key to Marnie's house. Bad move, Marnie. Anyway, it sounds like he broke in and nabbed her key card to Sinclair's apartment, and that's how he's been getting in. I have no idea how he managed to copy it, but you can bet I'm going to find out and put the person who did it on our payroll. Booyah. Now, here's where it gets interesting."

"That's not interesting enough?" Drew asks. He looks pissed, and I don't blame him. He paid the guy to not marry one of his sisters, and here he is, still hanging around and making life hell for his other sister. If Brock doesn't go to the slammer, Drew and I could go knocking on his door together.

"He claims he was paid to do that and also to make a few deliveries to your apartment. Says he needed the money because he's teetering on bankruptcy after the Edgar James deal fell through."

"Paid by whom?" Clay asks, her hands digging into me. I draw her closer.

"Someone he met on Reddit. Shocking, huh? I'm guessing it was your old buddy, old pal Penn Reed. There's still no sign of him, and consider this: He was living with his mother and working at Chuck E. Cheese. Where'd the money from the show go? I looked into it, and the writers are fairly compensated. Unless he likes to roll the dice, there's no way he could have blown through all that dough in a couple of months. I'm liking him for it. Damien does too."

"Is Officer Nutman looking for him?" I say, internally sighing.

"He just arrested Brock, and suddenly he thinks he's cock of the walk. Even though, let's be honest, I basically gift wrapped him. But yes, he's looking to make a second arrest. I'm betting Damien will find the guy first."

"So we can't leave the set yet?" Clay asks.

"Stick it out another day or two," Nicole says. There's a popping noise in the background of the call. "You know, Nutman gave me some of his gum, and it's actually pretty good."

"I'll buy you a case of gum," I tell her. "Just please, for the love of God, don't tell Nutman you like it."

She's laughing as she hangs up on us.

Clay swivels to look at me.

"They found him, Clay," I say, reaching up to touch her cheek. "He's not going to hurt you anymore."

"But Penn's still out there," she says, her lips quivering a little. She's sad, and not just because Penn's out there, trying to orchestrate some bullshit.

She's *hurt*. She tried to help that asshole Brock, and he hurt her little sister and then tried to burn her apartment down, her little cat with it.

"You really think that twerp can get up here without a team to help him?"

Her lips tip up slightly, but she still looks a little lost and sad. So even though her brother's a few feet away, I lean and give her a quick kiss. "It's gonna be okay."

"I feel like I shouldn't be here," Drew says, scratching his chin, "but I don't really want to go out there."

"You can stay," I tell him, still holding her close. "We've only got a couple of days left here, max. We can control ourselves."

Maybe.

Truthfully, it's hard as hell, because I want to comfort her...and I also want to lay claim on her. I don't like the way Edgar's been looking at her. He's finally realized what a good thing he had going on—and he wants to hang on to it.

I can understand that, but that doesn't mean I don't want to get her out of here the instant the threat is neutralized.

Clay rocks back into me, giving my dick ideas that can't go anywhere, and I hold her for a moment, savoring the hot press of her. Her soft skin. Her familiar scent.

"It's going to be okay," I tell her. Because I believe that's true, at least as far as the stalker situation is concerned. I'm not worried about Penn being on the run. Damien will be able to find him if Nutman can't. I meant what I said—I truly can't imagine him making his way up here unless Assistants One through Three have mutinied and are accepting money from him.

She nods slightly.

"Do you guys want to sneak off and go on a no-cameras hike?" Drew asks, acting like he's making the kind of offer no one sane would refuse.

"No, thanks," Clay says. "We should probably let Edgar know what's going on."

He makes a face. "Can I sneak off?"

"I don't think anyone would care," Clay says, then immediately course-corrects. "I mean, I don't think they'd be mad. Everyone wants you to enjoy yourself. I think EJ will understand. He told me he gets sick of the cameras too."

Laughing, Drew grabs for his boots and starts putting them on. "Don't lie to be nice. I prefer you when you're brutally honest."

"So do I," I say, squeezing her hip.

I'm about to suggest that we stick around in the tent for a little while once Drew leaves, when Stanley pops his head in through the opening.

His eyes widen at the sight of Clay in my lap, and he pointedly looks at the side wall of the tent. His voice shakes a little as he says,

"I know I should have knocked. Actually, there's no door, but I probably should have announced myself, and—"

It's obvious he doesn't know the relationship between Sinclair and Edgar is fake. Who has Edgar told?

"It's a fake relationship," I say as Clay eases off my lap, taking her sweet pressure with her, and starts putting on her boots with a pinched face that says it hurts.

"Yes, sir. My friends sit on my lap sometimes. My female friends, I mean, and—"

"He means my relationship with EJ is fake," Clay says, tying up the first boot. "It's just for publicity."

Some of his worry fades, but he looks confused.

"Are you sure?" he asks, pulling on the ends of his hair. "He really seems to think you're dating."

"Yes," Drew answers. "She knows who she's dating and not dating. Man, this set is really a trip." He grumbles to himself as he slides past Stanley and leaves the tent, hefting his daypack and water bottle and probably half a dozen things recommended by the crew of the show that he won't actually need.

Stanley says sorry half a dozen times, and I feel bad enough for the kid that I ask, "Are they bad to you here? Do they treat you poorly?"

"No, sir," he stammers. He looks like I just shoved an exam in front of him for a class he didn't know he was taking. "I'm lucky to have this job. So lucky. It's a *dream*."

Seems more like a nightmare, but hey, to each their own.

"What's up, Stanley?" Clay asks. She already has her boots on, so I make short work of putting on my own. I've been wearing casual clothes, like everyone else, since there are no reporters to impress or unimpress, as the case may be. "We were just going to go out to talk to EJ."

He lights up like someone shoved a light bulb up his ass. "That's good, great! He wants to talk to *you*. He feels bad about all of the outfit changes."

He should, but I don't say so. It's certainly not Stanley's fault.

"I think he wanted you to bring your packs. He was talking about showing you an outcropping where there's this really great view of—"

"Well, let's go," Clay says with a sigh. I grab my bag. Yesterday, I made the executive decision to carry both of our shit. Clay may still be learning what she likes, but she sure as hell knows camping doesn't make the list.

She's tired of this whole mess. We talked about it last night, and there are still so many arrangements for her to make. Her apartment. Those agents she needs to call. And us...

We haven't spoken about our future since leaving Nicole and Damien's house, so whatever we're going to be is up in the air too, along with whatever the hell it is I'm going to do next.

We follow Stanley past a couple of cameramen, who make sure to catch us on tape. "Smile, Sinclair," one of them shouts.

She does; I hate the bastard.

"Stop acting like the paps," I say with a glower as we pass him, and he has the grace to look embarrassed. Or maybe he's just scared of me. Either will do.

Edgar's waiting by a campfire, his pack on his back. He looks as upbeat as if he just climbed to the top of the mountain and took a ride on a waiting bald eagle. Does this man never lag? It's hard to imagine him sleeping at night. Or stopping, for anything.

"What do you say, shall we take a hike?" he asks Clay.

"Okay," she says with a sigh. "There's something we need to tell you."

"Oh," he says, his gaze shifting to me. He gives a slight nod. "You probably don't need to come if you don't want to, man. I don't think anyone's getting up here."

He's right, but I shake my head. "Job's the job," I say, just as Clay says, "I'd prefer for him to come."

"Where's your brother?" Edgar asks.

"He's going off on a solo hike."

He nods again, gesturing for her to speak.

She bites her lip and glances around, taking in Stanley, Assistants One and Two, and the producers, who are several feet from us, sitting on a couple of rocks and watching something on a laptop, powered by a solar-powered battery.

Drew didn't make it very far, because he's standing next to them, talking to Dani.

There are a few other people roaming around too, drinking coffee from *Camping to the Max* travel cups, which feels ironic at the very least.

"Maybe we should wait until we get a little ways away from camp."

Edgar gives a nod. We follow a trail away from camp and then start hiking on a path he clearly knows well. I follow them, keeping close enough that I can help Clay if she needs a boost.

Once we're a distance from camp, she tells him what she learned from Nicole, including that Penn, the primary suspect for Brock's collaborator, is at large.

He shakes his head in disgust. "Tilton's no kind of man at all. I should never have considered working with him. He calls himself an outdoorsman, but he doesn't even own a pair of hiking boots."

"Agreed. Though I find him more objectionable for what he did to my sister."

"Of course. Marnie's very professional."

It's a weird thing to say about someone he's worked with for months, although I'm guessing they don't have tea and sympathy dates. It's a long, ambling hike, with Edgar taking several detours so he can show Clay things he thinks she'll love. Each stop further convinces me he doesn't know her at all.

When we finally get to the top of a ridge, there's a somewhat flat area next to an outcropping of rock, and Edgar gestures for us to sit. There's a pretty steep drop-off on either side, with a little outcropping of trees on the slope beneath it, flattening out before dropping further.

"I'll stay standing," I say, mostly because I have a good view of every direction. If anyone tries to climb up after us, they'll deal with me.

"Sure, sure," he says, glancing at Clay. "Join me, Sinclair."

She nods, gives the dirty patch a distasteful look, and then lowers to sitting. After sitting down next to her, he claps his hands and then grabs a thermos out of his bag and gets out three plastic cups. "I brought hot toddies."

"No one should drink before climbing down from here," I say, frowning down at him. I'd thought he'd have more sense than that. This is no place for a tipsy amble. A couple of wrong steps could walk you into a lot of regret.

"Oh," he says with surprise, as if the potential for dissent had never occurred to him. "Well"—he reaches into the bag—"I have water too."

It's another strange offer, because he must see the enormous thermos strapped to my bag.

"That's okay," Clay says slowly. "I'm not thirsty. What's up?"

"Enoch told me you're ready to sever our arrangement," he says, tilting his head to study her. He throws a glance at me, maybe hoping I'll offer to give them privacy. Nope, not happening.

"Yeah," she says. "Sorry about that, but I'm sure he'll think of something that'll make both of us look good. He suggested that you could be the one who breaks up with me, and I'm totally fine with that."

"Here's the thing," Edgar says, tapping his knee. "The producers really like the storyline about your stalker. They think the show's going to blow up because of it."

A sense of foreboding slides into me.

"Dani says she has a friend who's casting a domestic drama filming in Greenville, and she thinks you'd be perfect for the part. It's a big role, Sinclair." He gives her a sheepish smile and swipes a hand over his face. "To be honest, I was hoping you'd hang in with me for a bit longer. This arrangement can be mutually beneficial. What do you say?"

A big movie role. Shit, that's why she's been doing this, isn't it? She wanted to jumpstart her career, and this would probably do it.

I watch her for a response, but it only takes her half a second to give a firm shake of her head, her eyes flitting to me.

"I'm sorry, Edgar. I can't do that. I'm sick of living an act. It hasn't been good for me."

Pride pulses through me. Not because she's turned him down, but because of why. She may not realize it, but she's grown so much since we met. I think maybe I have too. I've worked out for hours every single day since the accident, driven to be stronger, better, untouchable, but I've barely done anything the past couple of days and haven't felt that compulsion and drive itching at the back of my mind. I've been present.

And the other day, with her, I *painted*. The desire to paint more is coming back to me. It hits me when I see the different angles of her face, the vulnerability and strength playing in her eyes.

"The thing is," he says, drawing my attention back to him, "I really need this to work out. The whole mess with Tilton...the gossip about my phobia...it's been a bad year for me, Sinclair. I really need something to work out, or I'm done."

Alarm flashes through me, and I feel like a fucking idiot for not guessing. I start forward without saying anything, without even really consciously thinking anything.

"It was you," Clay blurts, her eyes wide as she gets to her feet. "You're the one who—"

She glances at me. No, her gaze is on something over my shoulder. The realization settles in the instant before someone knocks me in the head.

SINCLAIR

"RAFE!" I scream, leaping to my feet as he collapses to the ground. Penn stands behind him, having stepped out from the rocks. He has a rock in his hand. He hit Rafe's head with a *rock*. Maybe because I'd hit him with a rock.

Together. The three of them—Penn, Brock, and *Edgar*—were all working together.

My brain is racing, my blood boiling. I take a step toward them, but Edgar's hand wraps tightly around my arm like a vise.

His voice is regretful as he turns me toward him. "I didn't want it to be like this."

"Like what, you fucking psychopath?" I scream. Even in the midst of my brain's worry—Rafe could be dead, he could have a concussion, they're going to kill us both—I remember what he taught me and Marnie the other day, and I knee Edgar as hard as I can in the balls.

He cries out and releases me, just for a second, but it's long enough for me to lean down and grab the thermos he took out of his bag. His eyes bulge with shock as I hit him as hard as I can across the head. He goes down like a sack of potatoes, and I think he's unconscious. He better be unconscious, because Penn is at my back.

I'm already turning, but it's not quick enough because he shoves me *hard*, and I fall off the top of the ridge. My heart pounds as my body turns round and round on the rough ground, the short grass cutting me and my mouth filling with dust, and then I hit a tree hard, my left arm out, and I know it's broken. Still, I keep falling until my middle hits a tree. It stops me, but it takes all of the breath out of my lungs, and for a long moment—too long—I can only lie there, shocked, unable to breathe.

It's Rafe's voice that gets me out of it. *Breathe, Sinclair. We're all born knowing how to breathe.* So I do. I take slow, even breaths, even as my mind and heart race with worry. How am I going to get out of this?

It's obvious they mean to kill us—or me, because it's possible...

I can't think like that. I can't. My mind refuses to accept the possibility. My arm feels like it's on fire, and the sick, crooked look of it makes me want to vomit, but I can't. I need to find a way to get out of this. So I force myself to my feet and glance up to see Penn carefully easing his way down. He's no mountain man, so his progress is slow, but he's coming for me, and the desperation on his face tells me he thinks all of his problems are going to go away if I'm not around to tell anyone about them.

"They already know," I call up as I slip into the trees. It's risky to give away my position, but I need him to realize that his problems don't begin and end with me. That he'll be in much bigger trouble if he kills us. "Damien and Nicole from the tea shop. They're private investigators, and they're cooperating with the police on my case. They know you're involved, Penn. If you hurt us, you'll be in more trouble."

"You've ruined my life!" he shouts, his tone unhinged. I realize then that it no longer matters to him that he'll get in more trouble if he hurts me. He wants to hurt me because he wants his ten pounds of flesh. He thinks I destroyed him, and he won't be happy until there's nothing left of me. Nothing but a smear of blood and flesh at the bottom of the mountain. Pain and terror pulse through me, but I keep picking through the trees, leaving droplets of blood behind.

I don't have the pack—Rafe did—so I don't have anything that can be used as a weapon. But then I nearly trip over a thick branch.

I pick it up with my good arm, tears welling into my eyes from the pain of the other and the bruising in my gut. I step in behind a thick-trunked tree, waiting. Because I can't get away and I can't wait in this patch of trees forever. I need to check on Rafe—and on Edgar, because I know for sure that I didn't kill him. That means he's up there alone with Rafe, who's unconscious or worse, and—

Breathe, Sinclair.

I do. Slowly. Listening as Penn rustles his way down the hill, cursing. Listening as he starts a path through the trees.

"Are you *fucking* that guy?" he calls, obviously trying to get a rise out of me. "He was awfully protective of you the other day. I think he might be dead."

I bite back a sob, because he's lying—he *has* to be lying.

"You know, I'm smarter than you ever gave me credit for."

He's *definitely* lying.

"I'm the one who gave him the idea, you know? When I sent you those dead flowers. He got in touch with me, and we got to talking. *He* thinks I'm a good screenwriter. He hired me to come up with this whole plot. That other guy's just a tool, but *I'm* the real deal. We were working together, you know?"

Yeah, *now* I know. I feel like an idiot, a fool, a woman wearing blinders. He was the one person I'd never considered as a possibility, because he'd seemed like such a nice guy. Decent. He'd helped my sister. He'd even given her work. He'd offered to help me too, and even though I'd always known he was doing it partly for himself, I'd believed it was for me too.

Now Rafe is—

Breathe.

Penn's getting closer. I can feel him making his clumsy way through the trees. How hard can I hit him one-handed?

I already know I'll only have one shot. He's not a big guy the way Rafe is, but he's stronger than me, especially since I only have one working arm. My other arm pulses pain through me, but the adrenaline is pushing it back.

He takes another step through the brush, getting close now. I can hear him breathing.

"I can hear you breathing," he says, moving forward. Another step. Another. "You know, I didn't just do it for the money, Sinclair. I did it to get back at you, you cun—"

It happens in an instant. I step out and slam him with the branch as hard as I can with one arm. It's enough. For now, it's enough. He falls down, grabbing his head with both hands, and I hit him again, then again. I don't want to kill him accidentally, though. I don't want that on my head. So when he stops moving, when he seems to be unconscious—his chest rising and falling—I give him an exploratory tap to the balls, not hard enough to cause permanent damage. His body twitches, but there's no other reaction. A guy getting hit in the balls would instantly start overreacting if he were awake.

I consider tearing off his jacket to make a temporary sling for my arm, but I'd need two hands to make the sling.

So I just keep my hold on the branch, even though it's getting heavy in my hand, and head back up the incline. I need to get to Rafe, to see if he's okay. And I need the sat phone. I have no idea how to get back to camp on my own. That phone's the only thing that will save me.

My arm is excruciating now, my vision turning black around the edges, but I'm not going to pass out, I'm going to keep breathing. I'm going to get Rafe and that phone.

No is not an acceptable answer.

I'm going to hear him call me Clay again. *I'm going to.*

When I get far enough up the incline, though, I can already tell that Edgar isn't where I left him. My heart lodged firmly in my throat, I glance across to Rafe. Tears rise to my eyes because *he* hasn't moved.

If Edgar stayed—and I can't believe he left, not when news of this will ruin him—then the only place he could be is behind that outcropping of rocks where Penn hid. The last thing I should do is go to Rafe, but I need that phone and I need to know...

My mind spinning, I try to think of what to do. That's when I remember that lighter Rafe got at the sporting supplies store. There's a chance it might still be in his pocket.

I don't know how in the hell I'm going to light the dead branch I'm holding with only one arm for both the branch and the lighter, but maybe...

I try to move the hand of my broken hand just slightly, but those black edges of my vision start to close in, the pain cinching around and squeezing.

Still, it's the best I've got. I inch toward him, eyes wet, horror slowing my steps, because if he's dead...

"He's not dead," Edgar says, stepping calmly out from behind the rocks. He's holding our sat phone, and I watch in horror as he pitches it over the side of the outcropping. "Yet."

He still doesn't seem worked up like Penn. Somehow that makes him more frightening.

"Why are you doing this?" I ask, hoping that his logical side will make him easier to negotiate with. "If you kill us, you're going to get in a hell of a lot more trouble than if you admit to stalking me."

One side of his mouth lifts up. "Horrible accident, dead girlfriend. If you need goodwill, that's an even better story than having a girlfriend who's being stalked. But I meant what I said—I didn't want to play it this way. This wasn't about anyone getting hurt." He shrugs. "Well, not about you getting hurt. That little weasel was always going to have an accident." He points in the direction of the hill. "You should know that's the story I would have preferred: Edgar James saves his girlfriend from her stalker on the set of his new show." His mouth twists to the side in distaste. "It would have been perfect. Man versus man versus nature. All the better if he bested your bodyguard but not me."

If he wants an apology, he's going to spend a long time waiting. "You didn't want to hurt me? You burned down my apartment!" I shriek, my arms quivering. I still have the branch, but I know it won't do much against him. I can't catch him by surprise like I did with Penn, and he's a much bigger and fitter man.

For the first time, he looks a little put out. "Brock took things much further than he was supposed to."

"I thought you hated him," I say, stepping back. "You acted like you hated him."

"He's *beneath* my hate," Edgar says. He looks unhurried, like he knows there's no chance I'm going to make it off this ridge alive. "But not beneath being useful. It was the least he owed me for making me a laughingstock. I'm nothing if not resourceful, Sinclair."

"Lucky you," I say, taking a step back.

He moves another step toward me, and my gaze falls to his hands, bunched at his sides. To his muscular arms.

What's he going to do? Pitch me off the edge of the mountain?

Maybe I should be worried about dying, about the grief it will put my sister and brother through, but instead I'm irrationally pissed off by the thought that he wants to murder me and then publicly mourn my death. It *infuriates* me.

"You're a coward," I say.

Honestly, I should try to run, but if I do, he'd outpace me, easily. I glance in the direction he threw the sat phone. Maybe I could get to it, maybe it's not broken, but what are the odds that someone would be able to get to me quickly?

"I'm a man who knows what he wants and goes for it," he says. "I didn't want it to happen this way. You weren't supposed to figure it out." He says it as if he expects me to say, *Yes, you absolutely deserve to have a stellar reputation and a popular TV show. You know, why don't I throw myself off the cliff to save you the trouble of killing me? By the way, kudos for concocting that plan with Penn.*

My heart thumps as he takes another step forward.

Then it thumps for a different reasons, because there's a fast motion at ground level, and I watch with shock as Rafe's hand wraps around Edgar James's ankle. He tugs as hard as he can. Edgar falls like a stack of bricks and starts rolling down the outcropping, just like I did earlier.

I run to Rafe, heart pounding, pounding, pounding, my arm numb and hurting at the same time. He doesn't lift his head, but his eyes are opened to slits. "Check," he croaks out, his voice little more than a whisper. "Make sure..."

I don't want to leave him, but I also don't want Edgar James to come back up here and murder both of us, so I do as he asks. Edgar's still falling, but he's screaming and he's hit a couple of trees that are certain to injure him. I watch, emotionless, as he finally stops falling. He doesn't get up, although that's no guarantee he never will. But I'm guessing we have time to...what?

I'm not leaving Rafe, whatever he says to me. No way.

I go back to his side, gripping his hand with my one good one, and even though his eyes have shut again, he squeezes it slightly. The tears that have been welling in my eyes tumble down, because part of me thought I would never see him again. Never hear his voice or feel his touch, and—

"I love you, you asshole," I say. "If you die on me, I'm going to kill you."

A slight rumble comes from his chest, like a laugh is trying to come out.

Knowing him, he's focusing on the fact that I wouldn't be able to kill him because he'd already be dead.

"Go... Help," he says, but I'm paralyzed. I sit with him for several minutes or maybe half an hour, the pain of my arm wrapping around me even through the rush of adrenaline. His hand has gone lax in mine, but he's still breathing.

I need to get help. I need to find the strength to find that phone or stumble my way back to camp, wherever it's hidden.

I'm about to leave, tears welling in my eyes, when a familiar voice reaches my ears, swearing a blue streak. It's Drew, holding his hiking stick aloft like he's about to hit someone with it. "What the fuck happened, Sinclair?"

I look up, and hope blooms in my chest, because he's with Damien...and Officer Nutman.

SINCLAIR

IT'S TUESDAY NIGHT.

Both Edgar and Penn survived, although Edgar has two broken legs and Penn has a ruptured testicle. Oops. I feel no sympathy for them and their injuries, which will both require surgery. My arm didn't need surgery, although I'm told I'll be wearing this plaster cast for six to eight weeks.

I don't feel bad for Officer Nutman either. He offered several apologies while reading Edgar his rights, not that Edgar probably listened because of the aforementioned broken legs. I didn't see that part go down, but Drew did and he claims that Nutman also asked Edgar for his "John Hancock" after first verifying that his legs were broken, not his arms. It's anyone's guess if he got it before we were all medevacked off the mountain.

I'm in the hospital with Rafe right now, sitting at his bedside, my head buzzy from pain killers and stress. He's dipped in and out of consciousness but never fully crested the water. They say it's a mild traumatic brain injury, which doesn't sound very mild to me. It's that word.

Traumatic.

I'm staring at him, willing him to wake up for real, when I hear someone entering the room behind me. I look back and see Drew.

Tears spring to my eyes. It's that big brother look on his face.

"Come on," he says, his eyes dipping to my cast. "I'm going to buy you a shit cup of coffee in the cafeteria."

"I thought you were with Damien," I say.

"I was," he tells me. "He went back to Asheville to pick up Rafe's dad." He shrugs. "And Marnie and Griffin and Nicole. I guess he must be renting a party bus."

We're a few hours away, at the hospital closest to the camping site. It has an antiseptic smell and white tiled floors that remind me miserably of Mission Hospital, where someone stitched up Reggie and Rafe and I got busy in the bathroom.

"But they said he'll be discharged soon," I tell Drew.

"I don't think they'll kick him out before he's conscious," he says wryly, glancing at Rafe. His eyes squint as he studies him. "Did you put that around his neck?" He gestures to the crystal necklace Aunt Helen gave me.

"Yeah," I say, flushing. "I figured it couldn't hurt. I've been wearing it around the last few days. The nurse helped me because I couldn't do the clasp one-handed."

He's giving me the kind of look you'd give a kid who asks why the tooth fairy didn't pick up the tooth no one knew they'd lost.

"I didn't think it would *do* anything," I say in self-defense, and that's true. But I'm also desperate enough to try anything. In fact, before Drew came into the room, I had Aunt Helen on speakerphone and she set a spell for good fortune.

He shrugs. Then my famously skeptic brother adds, "Well, who knows, right?"

"Oh my God," I say. "Please mock me about this. If you don't, I'm going to think you fear the worst."

"I don't," he says, lifting his hands palm out. "Sorry, I shouldn't have tried to be nice. The doctors said it was a relatively minor injury. He's going to be fine. Now, what do you say to that shitty coffee?"

I bite my lip, then admit, "I don't want to leave him, and I don't think it's a good idea for me to go down there."

I know this will be a press frenzy. People will be writing about us for months to come.

I've already spoken with Enoch, and he's promised to negotiate with the press—I'll tell them whatever they want to know about Edgar James, Penn, and Brock, but only if they keep Rafe and his history out of the papers. What happened with his mother is no one else's business.

"I'm going to shoot straight with you, Sinclair," Enoch said. "This might be too big for us to contain. There's no end to the publicity this will generate."

He had the grace not to sound excited about that. If anything, he's been acting guilty and contrite, even though he had no more reason to suspect Edgar of being a monster than I did. But Enoch *is* a brand manager, and he did tell me that I need to pick an agent *now*, because offers will be coming in by the truckload.

Hearing that only made me feel more tired. I don't want the attention. The person who wanted it is Edgar, and I doubt it'll do him much good while he's making license plates in jail. To be fair, I'm guessing previous episodes of his old show *will* get popular if the network chooses to leave them on air.

Enoch thinks they won't. The profit must be enticing, he says, but an attitude of righteous indignation will do more for them in the long run.

"How 'bout this?" Drew says. "I'll bring you the shitty coffee. I'll even throw in a shitty doughnut because you've had a bad day."

I manage half a smile. "Thanks. You're a good brother."

He swipes a hand back through his messy hair. "I'm not, Clair, but I'm trying."

"You're a good brother," I repeat. "You and Damien saved our lives."

He lets out a mostly humorless laugh. "I think you mean you saved yourselves."

"Nope. I have a terrible sense of direction. If I'd left Rafe to get help, I would have ended up getting eaten by a bear."

"Well, when you put it that way," he teases. He hesitates and then walks over and gives me a careful hug, avoiding my cast. "I was so damn scared," he says into my hair.

Although he'd intended to go on a hike of his own, he'd been slow in leaving camp. I guess Dani, the producer, had found out he was a video game designer and pulled him aside to ask about a game she was interested in developing for film—a subject that he would have gladly conversed about for several hours.

Officer Nutman had gotten a search warrant for Penn's phone and traced it to the mountaintop. For some reason that probably has a lot to do with Damien's charisma and very little to do with Officer Nutman's clear-mindedness, Damien was allowed to come with him. Damien had put it together that Penn was working with Edgar, although Nutman refused to even consider the possibility until it was shoved into his face.

The sat-phone signal had brought them to our general area, but it blinked out when Edgar hurled it. My brother brought them the rest of the way by following our tracks. I'm sure Edgar didn't make any, but I'm no outdoorswoman. There were plenty of broken branches and heelprints to follow. Still, he's basically a superhero.

"I'm glad you came home," Drew continues. "Other than the whole stalking thing, it's been pretty great."

"I'm glad too," I say.

"I get it if you have to leave," he tells me, pulling away. "But I hope you don't. I hope you'll want to stay."

I watch him walk out to get the coffee, my heart in my throat. My brother never has liked change. Having me back here, in Asheville, is a big change, but he wants me to stay. Even after this hellish experience, he wants me around.

I know Enoch's right. There'll be plenty of opportunities for me now. Acting roles. Interviews. Hell, Enoch thinks publishers will approach me to write a memoir. All of that to say, I have no idea what comes next. I don't even know what I want to come next, except...

I sit down next to Rafe again, willing him to wake up. Then I remember that book he mentioned, *Oh, the Places You'll Go!*, and I buy the e-book on my phone, something that takes much longer than it should with one working arm.

I feel a bit dumb, buying a book meant for children, even more so when I clear my throat and start reading.

But tears well in my eyes as I read the words out loud.

The book is about believing in yourself, even when you're scared.

It's about correcting missteps and finding your way.

It's about finding the courage to be yourself and live life *your* way.

It's about stepping out of the waiting game and taking a chance.

I want that. More than anything, I want that. For me and for Rafe. We've been lost, but when we're together, I feel capable of finding my way.

As I finish the book, I think about what Damien said. You don't need to become everything you like, and sometimes it's enough to dabble.

Maybe acting can be a part of who I am, but not everything. Maybe it can be a single piece of the new life I build for myself.

Then I close the app and look up at Rafe, finding his eyes on me, his pupils still slightly mismatched from his concussion. I let the phone fall, the screen protector cracking, and every other thought leaves my head.

"Guess I'm a shitty bodyguard," he says in a raspy voice, his gaze lowering to my cast.

I make a one-handed fumble for the water on the side table and practically shove the straw in his mouth.

He laughs slightly, then cringes, so I'm guessing it hurt.

After he drinks a little, I put the cup back on the table.

"You're not," I say firmly. "You saved my life."

"I should have realized…" He takes a breath. "Something…off about him. Thought I was just jealous."

"Well, no one said you had to be a detective. That was Nicole and Damien's job, and they didn't know he was a psychopath either. And I hope you *were* jealous."

His hand reaches for my good hand, and I take it, relief unfurling in my veins.

He's okay. He's okay. He's okay.

"What you said on the mountain…" He pauses, swallows. "I don't know what I'm going to do next, Clay. And now…I'm guessing I won't be able to train for a while."

"That's okay," I say, squeezing his hand lightly. "I'm going to take care of you."

"With one arm?"

There's that flash of guilt again, and I won't stand for it. "Damn straight. I gave Penn a ruptured testicle with one arm. Don't underestimate me."

Amusement dancing in his eyes, he says, "Only a fool would. Still, I didn't…take you for the nursemaid type."

"Nope, I'm terrible at it. It's going to be a strong motivation to you to get better. And we're going to have to stay at your apartment until my place gets cleaned up."

He moves his head slightly to study me, pain glinting in his features. I hate that he's hurting. I hate that I can't do anything to make it better.

"You can't…"

"Good—I'm glad you're the one who said so. Your place doesn't exactly have great security features, so we're going to rent a new place. Your dad can stay with us too, if he's not still shacked up with my aunt."

"Clay—"

Fear seizes me, because I'm worried he's about to tell me that there can be no *us* outside of the context of bodyguard and guarded body. That we won't work in the real world. That he isn't willing to risk that every painful detail about his past might be pulled out into the light for strangers to gawk at.

"I think I know what I want to do, Rafe, or at least I'm starting to figure it out, and maybe we can do part of it together. So please don't tell me it's not going to work or that we're too different. I understand that you might not want to deal with the press, especially if they start talking about your mom, and if that's why you don't want to give this a try, then I'll have no choice but to respect your decision, but I think we're really great together, and—"

"Jesus Christ, Clay, will you let..." He winces. "Let me get a word in edgewise?"

I sputter to a stop, my heart practically freezing in anticipation as I wait for him to tell me no. Instead, he squeezes my hand, looking into my eyes, and says, "I love you too, you insane woman."

"You do?" I ask, my heart pumping back into life, warmth spreading from my head to my toes. I want to lavish kisses on him. I want to climb onto the hospital bed and straddle him, but I obviously don't want to cause either of us further injuries, so I settle for leaning in for a gentle kiss. His lips are warm and chapped, and I'm so relieved that he's alive, that he's *mine*, that my joy is overwhelming.

"I do," he says when I pull back. "You know, I heard you reading that book... I inspired you, didn't I?"

Laughter bubbles up inside of me. "Yes, you're truly remarkable. I never would have figured out that I need to put my left foot in front of my right if not for your suggestion."

"Good, Clay," he says softly, one side of his mouth lifting up.

"Didn't want to have to be the one to tell you that you've been walking all wrong."

Drew shows up in the doorway then, and a huge smile spreads across his face when he sees that Rafe is awake. "Hey," he says, "I brought three coffees on a whim, and he's awake! It's like all that positive-visualization shit Aunt Helen's always going on about actually means something. Or maybe it's the crystal."

I'm not going to let him pump my concussion patient full of caffeine, but I'll break the news later. Right now, I'm happy to just be with them. I'm happy to know that I've ended up exactly where I need to be.

Rafe looks down with a frown. "Why's there a crystal around my neck?"

epilogue
RAFE

IT TOOK well over a month for me to fully recover from the attack. It's embarrassing that a little twerp like Penn laid me out, and my father hasn't wasted any opportunities to point out that I've wasted years working out when I should have been practicing my swing instead.

"Sinclair got him, huh?" he said just this morning for what had to be the hundredth time. "Hell of a swing on her."

Of course, he sides with her on basically everything. He offers his opinion very freely. When he told me last week that he and Clay's aunt are getting more serious, though still open, I begged him to please, for the love of God, ask if he could move in with her. It's been two months now that he's stayed with us, upgraded from my couch to a guest suite in the very tiny apartment Clay's renting until her place is fixed up. Two months too long, if you ask me, although I *will* miss our Turner Classic Movie nights. Drew comes over for them every Thursday night. Marnie too, sometimes, although she spends a lot of her time at the bar when Griffin is working.

In the beginning, it was hard to shake the feeling that I was holding Clay back. Everyone and their uncle wanted her story. Everyone and their uncle and their third cousin's best friend wanted to hire her for something. She couldn't leave the apartment building without getting flocked by reporters and fans.

It physically pained to know I was in no shape to protect her, but it took me four weeks to get the medical all-clear, and longer for me to be on my feet for any amount of time. Clay had to hire someone Damien knew to keep her safe.

Even though she's assured me dozens of times that I'm not responsible for her broken arm, I still feel guilty. I was supposed to look out for her, to be two steps ahead, and I fell short. So when she asked me to doodle on her cast with Sharpies, I went all out, drawing the *90210* table and a strawberry shortcake and her aunt Helen's crystals. When she got it off a couple of weeks ago, she insisted she was keeping it as a token, until they actually took the thing off and she saw it was dirty as hell inside.

"Why does it look like that?" she asked me in a horrified whisper.

"Because you have remarkably bad hygiene," I answered, before laughing at her horrified expression and wrapping an arm around her. "They always look like that. It's gone six weeks without being properly cleaned inside."

Things have calmed down on the press front, thank God, and Clay doesn't need Damien's friend anymore. I'm usually with her, and I'll be damned if I'll let anyone hurt or harass her or even ask for her autograph when she's in the middle of enjoying a piece of choco-late cake. It's been humbling to realize she's just as protective of me. Although one big-mouth reporter wrote about my past, Clay refuses to let anyone ask me questions about it, and she once walked out of an interview for that very reason.

She's decided to stick to Asheville and only accept opportunities she could get to by driving, and for now, she's stayed firm on that. Her new agent found her a movie that's filming locally, at the Bilt-more Estate. Made for TV. Clay worried she was letting Enoch down by accepting, and although he admitted he'd have preferred to see her star in the next big *badass woman kicks lots of ass* movie, he's happy for her on a personal level—and more than satisfied with the amount of business he's gotten for being her brand manager.

In another interesting development, Nicole's friend Molly O'Shea is both real and a genuine writer-slash-reporter. She just had a baby a couple of months ago, but she wants to write Clay's story as soon as she gets back to work. Marnie and Drew have given her the green light, and after talking to the therapist she started to see after we were nearly murdered—yeah, I'm back on the fainting couch too—she's decided to move forward with it.

I can't say I'm sorry that Judy's going to find herself in the hot seat. Rumor has it she's found some teenage pop star to microman-age, and it would give all of us immense satisfaction to get her fired.

There's something else that will give me immense satisfaction, a gift Nicole and Damien have been working on for me—something I can give to Clay. I want to give her everything. Because she hasn't just given me the love of an infuriating, sexy-as-hell woman—she's also given me my purpose. Together with Shauna, we're working on developing the Waiting Place, a center where artists will teach classes to people who've never picked up a paintbrush or piece of clay. Because we agree that being in the Waiting Place, between two phases of your life, shouldn't be a shit thing. It should be a time of discovery. We'll sell art too, and part of the money will go to a free art program for kids.

Shauna and I obviously aren't funding any of it, other than small monthly contributions that are a drop in the theoretical bucket, and I feel like a fucking freeloader the majority of the time. Whenever I say something about it, Clay insists that I saved her life by throwing Edgar James down that embankment, and also by loving her. And while being Sinclair James's patient is no fun—once she actually swatted me on the head before remembering I had a head injury—she has thousands of ideas for the center, and working with her on our dream is a joy.

It's a Monday night, just like when all of this began, and we're gathered at Summer Nights, which is closed to the public for our private event. Right now, it's Clay, my dad, and me, plus Marnie, Griffin, and Drew, but Shauna's going to show later, plus Enoch, Grace, and Andy. Tonight's a two-fold celebration: Marnie and Griffin got engaged this past weekend, and Nicole and Damien are returning from a lengthy trip to Los Angeles.

"So, you're definitely moving out, huh?" Drew asks Marnie, then takes a big sip of his whiskey.

Griffin laughs and tops it up for him. "Yeah, man, sorry about that. But let's be real, you don't want to live with a couple."

"I don't know," says my dad from the stool next to mine. "Rafe and Sinclair and I seem to be getting along all right. Why, just this morning, she told me I never had to leave."

I look at her in horror, and both she and my dad start laughing, then reach around me to exchange fist bumps.

This is the kind of thing I deal with on a nearly daily basis. And he wonders why I'm trying to push him off on Clay's aunt.

"Yup," I say, "really funny. Hilarious stuff." I bump Clay with my shoulder. "Will you still be laughing when Drew tries to move in with us?"

"Hey," he says with a wounded look. "I'm a fine roommate."

"You're the greatest," Marnie says, leaning over on her stool to give him a hug. "A truly superlative roommate. If I weren't reasonably sure I wanted to marry this guy"—she nods to Griffin, who's stayed behind the bar so he can make everyone drinks as they show up—"I would've lived with you forever."

There's the sound of the door unlatching, and then it swings forward with so much force it probably leaves a dent in the wall. Griffin just rolls his eyes, accustomed to Nicole's theatrics.

"The cavalry has arrived," she announces as she struts into the room, Damien following her with an indulgent smile.

"How was your trip?" I ask. Although what I really want to know is whether they were successful. The hyped-up way Nicole is walking, a grin stretching across her face, suggests the answer is yes.

"Let's give the news a little look-see," she says with a grin. "Who has a phone? I need a phone. No, a tablet. A tablet would be preferable so we can really see the salt enter the wound."

Damien, who came prepared, is already pulling it out. With a few clicks of her finger, she pulls up a website and the proudly flourishes the tablet to us so we can all see the photo of Single-Dad Santa hiding his face while he walks through a grocery store fruit aisle.

"'Single-Dad Santa' Caught on Tape."

"Hopefully they did more than catch the chump buying a pair of juicy melons," my father says. *Of course* it was my father who said that.

Clay gasps, glancing from me to Nicole and Damien, then back. I can hear the others murmuring and my dad chuckling to himself over his attempted joke, but my attention is focused on her. This is about when I would've slid on my sunglasses in the past, because I know everything I'm feeling must be showing in my eyes. My admiration. My need. My *love.*

"Rafe, you knew about this, didn't you?" she asks softly.

I feel as self-satisfied as Rue after he chases an inanimate mouse toy around the room. Then again, credit where it's due.

"I didn't have much to do with it," I say, sliding an arm around her. "They're the ones who pulled it off."

"But you did give us the idea," Damien says with a nod to me as he and Nicole reach the bar. Griffin's already mixing them drinks. "Thanks, man—we had fun."

Clay grabs the tablet from Nicole and starts reading. Looking up, she says, "Several women have come forward about Dave."

"After we got him on tape trying to seduce *'Nancy'* by offering her a bigger part," Nicole says with a grin.

Clay points at the screen. "It says here that he was caught trying to solicit sexual favors from a teenager."

Her answer's a smirk. "You're not the only one who can play a teenager convincingly."

"Well, I don't know about convincingly," I say, glancing at Clay, but I'm only doing it to mess with her. Once I could stand the sound of the TV, I watched my way through the entire series. I maintain that it sucks. Royally. But she's mesmerizing. And even though it makes me feel like a chump to admit it, I liked watching episodes when she was off doing interviews or taking calls, because I miss her when she's not around. Like that week and a half we spent practically conjoined gave me an appetite for her that no amount of proximity can fulfill.

"Now, that's how to make an entrance," my father tells Nicole and Damien as Griffin slides their drinks across the bar.

"I'll buy this round because you nabbed that asshole," Drew says, but he's grinning as he says it, because we all know that none of us are going to be paying the bartender tonight. He always refuses to accept money from "family."

There's a weird feeling in my chest. I've found a sort of belonging here, with Clay and her friends, with my dad and this bar he can't seem to quit. After I got shot, I lost part of myself, and I tried to bring it back in all the wrong ways. Then my life got shoved together with Clay's, and I finally saw it for what it was: a holding pattern. I'll never be able to thank Clay properly for giving me the chance to be something more than what I was. She claims the same is true for her —that if not for me, she'd have fallen back into the trap her mother had set for her, acting because it was the only thing she thought she knew how to do.

She leans into me and nips my ear, prompting to me laugh—and also my dick to get hard.

"Thank you," she whispers. Then, louder, "Thank you. You guys are the best."

"We really are, aren't we?" Nicole says agreeably, then slips around the counter to give Griffin a hug. "Congratu-fucking-lations, man. We're having an engagement party for you at your brother's house on Saturday night."

Damien gives her a nudge with his shoulder. "I think that was supposed to be a surprise."

"Act surprised," Nicole tells them. Then, turning to Clay, she adds, "You now, this means we're officially done with you. You've been fairy-godmothered. So, now it's time—"

The door slams open a second time, even harder than Nicole managed, which is impressive in itself. It's Marnie's friend, Andy. She's got the crazy-eyed look of someone who's gotten bad news and wants to drown it in alcohol and bad decisions.

"What's wrong?" Drew blurts, getting off his stool so fast it almost falls over. He's protective of Andy. I've seen it before. Then again, she's been his little sister's best friend since the two of them were in pigtails. I've seen the pictures.

"I need a drink, Griff," she says as she approaches the bar and then steals the stool Drew vacated to check on her. It's next to Marnie, who's turned in her seat to face her friend. "A really strong one. Like, take your strongest drink and add two shots."

"What happened?" Drew asks, annoyed now. There's practically a whole row of empty seats, but you can tell he had his heart set on that one.

"That's his favorite stool," Clay confirms in a whisper. I lift her into my lap, earning me a squeal, and shove her now-empty stool toward him with my foot.

"If it's good enough for her, it's good enough for you," I say as Clay snuggles into me.

"Does that mean you're going to let him sit in your lap too?" my dad asks.

I swear to Christ, I'm going to send Helen a damn fruit basket if she lets him move in with her. She'd be here tonight if she weren't off on a date with another dude. You'd think my father would be troubled by that, but when I asked him if it had started to bother him, he slapped me on the back and said, "Not at all, son. He lends me his little blue pills. Sharing is caring."

Andy turns to look at us, and every last person stares back at her, except for Griffin, who's already got something going on with the cocktail shaker.

"They found out about OnlyFans," she says. "My grandmother. My brothers. They kicked me out of the house. I have two weeks to find somewhere else to live." Her voice shaking, she adds, "They won't even look at me."

Griffin slides the drink across the bar to her. "Only one, Andy," he says. "It's worse to be drunk and depressed than just to be depressed."

"Agree to disagree," she says, taking a sip as Marnie leans over and wraps her arms around her. Andy slaps the bar. "Damn, that's tight. You know your shit, Griffin."

She takes another sip, then looks at Marnie. "I got fired again."

"Because of the foot thing?" Drew asks, swearing under his breath. "Shit, you've got to stop doing that, Andy. Keep your feet in your socks."

"I haven't been," she snaps at him. "I stopped after I got fired from the daycare. I got fired from *this* shitty job because I took issue with having my ass grabbed."

"Someone did what?" he asks, his cheeks turning red. "We can sue them. We'll—"

"I don't have the money or the time to sue them," she says. "Besides, I slapped him in the face and threw a stapler at him. Nobody messes with my ass unless I want them too."

Drew's color deepens, and I notice the way Clay's watching him.

"Far out," Nicole says. "Anyway, like I was saying to Sinclair over here before what was a pretty A+ entrance, it's time for you to pick our next victim, Sinclair. So what'll it be? Who do we help next?"

Clay gives Andy the kind of look she usually reserves for me. "Her," she says slowly. "Obviously her."

"Excellent." Nicole claps her hands, then points at Drew. "Marnie's moving out, Andy's moving in. Problem Number One solved. Boom." She grins back at Damien. "This is almost too easy."

Everyone starts talking at once, but my attention's on the woman in my lap. She turns to look at me, a twinkle in her eye. "I have a good feeling about this. You know what happened when we moved in together..."

"You gave me a taste for shitty television and pedicures?"

"Exactly," she says, laughing. I lean forward and kiss her, because if you're lucky enough to get a woman like Clay, you kiss her every chance you get. And get pedicures with her, and help her pick out outfits for her damn cat, and even suffer through the occasional IG Live. I'll do whatever it takes to not just protect my woman but make her happy as hell—because that's what I am when I'm with her.

about the author

ANGELA CASELLA is a romcom fanatic. Writing them, reading them, watching them—she's greedy, and she does it all. In addition to her solo releases, she's lucky enough to collaborate with Denise Grover Swank on multiple series.

She lives in Asheville, NC. Her hobbies include herding her daughter toward less dangerous activities, the aforementioned romcom addiction, and dreaming of having someone else clean her house.

Visit her website at www.angelacasella.com or Angela and Denise's shared website at www.arcdgs.com.